I0686821

A Kinder, Greener Vampire

Vampire

And Other Stories

by

Martin Schiller
&
Guest Author Thomas Trujillo

PANTARI PRESS™

Pantari Press, Seattle Washington, USA

Copyright © 2017 Martin Schiller
All rights reserved.
Cover Illustration Copyright © 2017 by Martin Schiller
Photo Model: Christine Harlan
Graphic Design Consultant: Henry Hall
ISBN-13: 978-0692825587
ISBN-10: 0692825584

For the Guardian, the Singer and the Smith

A Kinder, Greener Vampire

For Natasha, and all those who are still in chains, waiting...

Like most people, Detective Joe Sheridan tended to take a lot of things in his life for granted. The sun rose in the east, set in the west, and when it did, the vampires walked the night.

They had always been part of the landscape. Something that he had grown up with. But thanks to his recent assignment as a Diurnal Liaison Officer, he'd been doing a lot of thinking about the vamps and psyching himself up for his posting. The Los Angeles Nocturnal Police Department did things a lot differently than its diurnal counterpart, and he knew that he would be facing some real challenges working alongside the undead.

Driving down Sunset Boulevard, his attention was captured by a huge billboard. It showed the Hubbard Glacier in Alaska calving off pieces of itself back when global warming had still been an issue. Underneath this was the statement, *"You were the Problem. We were the Solution. Celebrating Vampiric Ascendance Day 2045. 25 years of Progress for All Mankind."* He had seen it, and other billboards just like it, ever since he'd been a kid, but today it brought his thoughts into sharper focus.

The vamps *really* had been the solution, he reflected. His parent's generation had been well into the process of destroying the planet itself, and after centuries of watching Diurnals like them mismanage their affairs, the Nocturnals had finally stepped in. Although it had taken a short, but bloody war to bring about VA day, things had gotten onto the right track.

The economy was stable, everyone knew who the President would be for the next two hundred years, and wars between nations were a thing of the past. More importantly, the Earth was being healed through strict environmental measures and wise governmental policies. Humanity finally had a real future to look forwards to.

The fact that daytimers had been required to accept a subservient role, and paid their taxes to the Nocturnal Revenue Service in blood, was a small price to pay for such unparalleled peace and prosperity. And as a member of law enforcement, it was up to him to help foster the sense of interdepartmental cooperation that helped make all of his possible for the people of Los Angeles, whether living or undead.

He just hoped that he wouldn't screw up and make his Department look bad.

Turning onto Wilcox Avenue, he pushed his concern aside and got his first look at the Hollywood Community Police Station. He could tell the difference between it and his old precinct right away. The LANPD had done away with the black and white paint scheme for their cars. The cruisers that drove by him were *all* black with heavily tinted windows and blue light bars. No one could ever confuse them with their daytimer counterparts.

He encountered another difference when he parked his car and walked into the lobby. Every one of the police officers working at the front desk were pale, and wearing real guns.

Firearms had been one of the very first things that the vamps had taken away when they'd assumed power. They didn't trust their human 'herds' with weapons and Sheridan wholeheartedly agreed with this. Daytimers simply didn't have the self-control required to use weapons wisely. Centuries of cold blooded murder and brutal war had proven that beyond any debate. No Diurnal owned a gun anymore and even his Department had limited its officers to stun pistols and other non-lethal devices.

As he came up to the desk, a vamp Sergeant eyed him appraisingly. "You lost, *blood cow?*"

Sheridan frowned at the slight. The vamp wasn't supposed to be calling him that--not with all the effort that the Lord of Los Angeles had been expending to make vampires more culturally sensitive. The city's undead leader had dubbed his campaign *"A*

3

Kinder, Greener Vampire" and the Sergeant wasn't getting with the program.

He didn't call him out on it though. He had to get along with his new co-workers.

"I'm looking for Detective Karnstein," he answered, flashing his LADPD identity card.

"Oh, you must be the new Diurnal Liaison Officer," the Sergeant said in a much warmer tone. "Karnstein's office is through the door and just down the hall in Investigative Services. I'll buzz you in. Good luck by the way."

"Am I gonna need it?" Sheridan asked.

"Just don't get on her bad side," the vamp advised with a grin that revealed his fangs. "I once saw her make a 6-foot tall gang banger into a baseball bat. He got mouthy with her and she grabbed him up by his ankles and used him to club all his homies down. It wasn't a pretty sight. Oh yeah, and don't say anything about her disco music. She gets *really* touchy about it."

Nodding uncertainly, Sheridan thanked him for this bit of wisdom and went through the door into the station. When he finally found the IS Department and Karnstein's office, he wasn't quite prepared for the woman he encountered there.

Carmilla Karnstein didn't seem to be a day over 18, although he knew from his pre-assignment briefing that she was actually 83. She had been born in 1958 and 'turned' into a vamp in 1976 on the night of her high school graduation, right along with the rest of her cheerleading team.

And except for her shoulder holster and the enormous revolver it held, she didn't look very much like a cop. Her shoulder length blond hair was feathered in a style that would have been quite fashionable in the disco era--but apparently no one had bothered to tell her that the 70's were only a faint memory now, or she simply didn't care.

Karnstein was also uncomfortably pretty, even if her skin was as pale as a sheet of printout paper. If Sheridan had had to

4

guess, he wouldn't have placed her at any more than 100 pounds soaking wet, and every inch of that was perfectly proportioned.

She was a typical female vamp, built to seduce and ensnare males--and then lure them to their deaths. Or more accurately, she was the undead equivalent of the living cheerleaders that he had known in his teens. The only difference was how long they tended to let their prey suffer.

The minute that their eyes met, she sneezed. "Holy shit!" she complained. "You had *Italian* last night—*ahchoo*--and *sex*—*achoo*--oh gawd, that's so grossssss!

"What? How did you know that?"

"Because I can smell the fucking garlic on you, you cheese weasel", she snapped. "--*and* the sex. Jeez, are you trying to make me sick? What do you want anyhow?"

"I'm Sheridan," he said. "Your new partner."

"Oh. My. *God!*" she frowned. "A *blood cow!* I just knew the Captain had it in for me. All right, put your box on the desk." She indicated an empty workspace. It had a nameplate on it. Someone called "Johansen."

"Isn't Johansen going to mind?" he asked.

"Nah," she replied, sneezing again and wiping her pert little nose. "He's dead. He was a DA, a daytimer, just like you, and a vamp up in Laurel Canyon killed him, so he won't care."

Suddenly, she spotted something in his box. She was out of her seat, and across the room almost faster than his eye could track. Before he had even fully processed this, she had grabbed his desk lamp out of the box and thrown it in the trashcan. Vamps could move like that when they really wanted to.

"Don't they tell you daytimers *anything*?" she demanded. "You can't use that here! I don't feel like getting sunburn just so you can do your paperwork. *Fuck!*"

"Sorry, Detective," Sheridan replied abashedly. In his haste to report to his new assignment, he'd forgotten that the bulb was the old fashioned incandescent kind, not the LED's that the vamps preferred. It had something to do with the fact that they didn't give off UV light, he recalled.

It was a bad start for their partnership.

"Whatever," she said, waving it off. "Also it's Cami, not 'Detective' and definitely not *Carmilla*. Only my *mom* calls me that and she's a classics freak! Now, go take a shower. You stink! And while you're cleaning yourself up, I'm going to have a little *chat* with Captain Van Helsing."

Van Helsing? Sheridan wondered. *Is that really his name?*

Guessing his thoughts, or just reading them (which was something else that vamps could do when they were in the mood), Cami answered, "Don't ask. It's a *long* story. Now go take a shower *ferchistsakes*. The locker room is just down the hall and to the right."

Then, with the same preternatural speed that she had used to dispose of his lamp, she was gone. Sheridan put down his box with a sigh, and made his way down to the locker room.

When he entered it, he received some odd looks from the vamp Officers. Although he tried to smile and nod back at them, they just stared, or went back to what they were doing without acknowledging his presence.

"Hey Renfield," he heard one of them say, "I heard you got Air Patrol tonight."

This got Sheridan's attention. To create a greener Department, the vamps of the LANPD had replaced their old-fashioned helicopters with a natural alternative. Since their officers could turn themselves into bats at will, they were still able to provide air-patrol, and at the same time, vastly reduced their agencies' carbon footprint, and its dependency on fossil fuel. The public loved it, and it served as a model for the rest of the world's police agencies to emulate. Just as it had in so many other things, *'LA had led the way'*.

"Yeah," Renfield answered. "My arms are gonna ache like hell by the end of the shift, but at least it isn't as bad as working

K9. The last time I did that, I came home with god damned fleas. I still itch just thinkin about it."

"Yeah, I know what you mean," his partner agreed. "Those things are a bitch to get out of a coffin lining. But hey, look at the night side; you're not pulling duty with some dumbass daytimer, right?"

"True dat," Renfield replied, looking straight at Sheridan. It was becoming painfully obvious that being a Diurnal Liaison Officer was going to be an uphill battle, and then some.

***

Cami was still visibly upset when he returned to her a few minutes later.

"Well, it looks as if I'm *stuck* with you," she pouted. If anything, the expression only accentuated her good looks. "Since Captain Van Helsing can hear every-thing-I-say-or-think, I'm sorry for calling you a blood cow. Okay? You're just nocturnally-challenged. *There.* Happy now?"

She was looking back in the direction of the Captain's office as she said this, and Sheridan knew that the apology hadn't been meant for him. A moment later, she sniffed.

"Well at least the garlic isn't so bad now. So, rule *numero uno* partner: no Italian unless you want to walk behind the car for the whole shift."

Sheridan nodded sheepishly, and as he sat down at his new desk, Cami came over and perched herself on the corner of the desktop. "So, what have you got for us?" she asked.

Struggling to ignore her nearness, he opened up the first case file on his laptop. It was a Missing Persons Report. He'd handled plenty of them during his career with the LADPD, but this was the first one that would involve working with the vamps.

"Rayven Black, aka Sherryl Gaustad, Caucasian female, 22," he began. "She's been missing for two weeks. We've already checked the usual angles. No jealous boyfriend in the picture, no spouse stalking her, and she didn't owe any large amounts of money, or have any history of mental problems."

"Criminal connections?" Cami inquired.

"None," he stated. "She has no rap-sheet at all. Just a few parking tickets. All paid."

"What about the family?"

Sheridan shook his head. "Her relatives are just as out of the loop as we are. None of them have heard from her. The same goes for her friends. She's not surfing anyone's couch, and her bank account and credit card haven't been touched."

"Okay, that covers most of the bases," Cami agreed. "So, why send the case to us?"

"Because my department thinks that a Nocturnal might be involved," he replied.

Cami raised a delicate little eyebrow. "Oh, and why's that?"

"She filed for Transformation," Sheridan answered, "and when she got turned down, she contacted someone on the Internet who told her that they could get her changed. She disappeared right after that."

"What about suicide?" Cami countered. "Lots of daytimer's do that when they get rejected. Maybe she was so depressed that she just took herself out." She pantomimed a pistol and placed it against her head, firing the imaginary trigger.

"The Medical Examiner doesn't have any Jane Does matching her description, and neither do the hospitals," he told her.

"Sounds like you've done all your homework then," she conceded. "Okay, let's see her."

He turned the screen around so she could peer at the image. Their missing person was what Sheridan would have labeled a classic 'Goth'. Her black hair had been cut in a severe pageboy, and she wore heavy eye makeup and dark lipstick that was offset by a complexion almost as pale as Cami's. Naturally, every item of clothing that she wore was black.

8

"Well, I'm not surprised that she got turned down," Cami remarked. "She's a classic *'Bela'*"

"Bela?" he asked. Like any Diurnal American, Sheridan was quite familiar with the Transformation Process. Anyone who wanted to be turned into one of the undead could simply apply for it through the Department of Diurnal Affairs. A sponsor (formerly referred to as a 'master') would be matched to the candidate, and after they had changed them into a vamp, the sponsor would be accountable for them until they had acclimatized to their new way of un-life.

It was all fairly straight forwards, and a vast improvement over the ancient practice of seducing a mortal, or simply taking them by force. And although the program had been in place for over two decades, Diurnals still applied for it by the thousands. Local DDA offices were perpetually backlogged and desperate to find enough sponsors. He'd never heard the term 'Bela' though.

"Yeah," she answered. "You know, Bela Lugosi? The famous vampire guy?"

"Don't you Nocturnals like him?" Sheridan asked. He'd seen the 30's version of *'Dracula'* a couple of times and he didn't understand what the problem could be. Admittedly, Bela Lugosi had been campy, and even a little silly at times, but that was about it.

"Look," Cami explained. "We're predators, right? Or at least we were until we came out of the coffin."

Sheridan nodded tentatively.

"And you? You're--well--you're prey," she continued, glancing briefly towards the Captain's office. "Sorry, but it's true. And a good predator knows how to blend in until they're ready to strike. If they don't, their dinner will just run away.'

"Well, these 'Bela' types just don't get that. They think that being a vampire is some kind of weirdo fashion statement. You know, all that *'I vant to suck your blaaad'* bullshit?"

9

"I thought that was the point," Sheridan returned. "Sucking the blood, I mean."

"It *is*," Cami said, "but not like *that*. That's not the message that we want to send. We're trying damned hard to get Mr. and Mrs. Average-Joe-Daytimer to accept the fact that we're here and we're here to stay. That we're a normal part of life. If we let these Bela's start calling the shots, you Diurnals might freak out, or…"

Or worse, Sheridan thought. Despite the fact the vamps had employed an overwhelmingly superior pre-human technology to conquer humanity, there had still been plenty of stiff resistance to the Ascension and a lot of lives lost on both sides. No one wanted to see that happen again.

Cami nodded. "I mean, the whole point is to blend in. Think about it Sheridan--do I *look* like a predator to you?"

She didn't. Instead, she looked like a walking, talking wet dream, and not something out of a B-grade horror movie.

"Which is what makes me such a good hunter," she said. "Guys always wanna get *niiiice* and close to me, which really came in handy back when I had to hunt for my supper. Even though we all get our blood rations now, it hasn't changed what I am.'

"This little wanna-be shot herself down with her own picture. Whoever got her case probably took one look and denied her app without even reading it. I know I sure as shit would have. Real vamps don't want Bela's around. Real vamps want their herds to stay calm, happy and going with the program."

"Okay," he said. "So we know why she got rejected. Let's talk about the vamp."

Cami gestured towards the laptop. "Okay, lets."

He scrolled down to the internet address. It was linked to an elementary school in Hong Kong, remotely accessed by another account in Russia, which led to one in Nigeria, and after that, it got lost in a digital tangle that led absolutely nowhere. The

EarPhone number was just as useless. It had been assigned to a disposable, pay-as-you-go burner model.

When he told her this, Cami sighed tiredly. "Sheridan, every time anything big happens in history, there's always a bunch of rip-offs. After we took over, some vamps got the bright idea to take advantage of the Bela's. They know they're desperate, and desperate is just what a scammer wants."

"Why?" Sheridan inquired. "You said yourself that you don't need to worry about the blood. You get it in taxes now." There wasn't a public building anywhere that didn't have the *"Give Blood. It's the Law"* posters to remind everybody of their obligations.

His new partner laughed, exposing her fangs. They looked extremely sharp, and Sheridan had no trouble imagining them being used on a horny jock in some dark lover's lane.

"Well, some of the really old farts," she said, "you know, the vamps from *waaayy* back, they just don't trust the system. They're too used to getting their own meals, or they don't think that they'll get their fair share. So, sometimes they hoard humans."

Sheridan couldn't quite believe what he was hearing. "*Hoard* humans? I thought that was nothing but an urban legend."

"It's not," Cami responded. "It's the real deal, all right. There are even networks of old vamps who help each other traffic in daytimers out on the Deep Web."

He didn't know how to respond to this. A simple kidnapping was something that he could accept--even *if* a vamp was the suspect. But the idea that there were groups of vampires out there who were systematically creating their own blood farms went against everything he had ever been taught about humanity's Nocturnal masters. It was as if she had just told him that Bigfoot didn't exist, or that werewolves weren't real.

For just an instant, he even wondered if she was having him on. Her expression was serious though, and he suddenly felt like he had been transported back in time. Back to the 'bad old days' before the Ascension, when serial killers, terrorists and pedophiles had preyed on the innocent and the weak. Back before the vamps had hunted them all down and made the streets safe again.

Cami went on. "The way they do it is they grab up a bunch of Bela's like Rayven and hide them away in a safe house. It's been happening a lot lately, and being old, some of these vamps are damned smart when it comes to covering up their tracks."

Sheridan grimaced, hating what she was telling him. Vampires weren't supposed to be the enemy any longer.

If this got out, there could be panic, he thought. The notion sent a shiver down his spine, and he marveled at how well the Nocturnals had managed to keep this ugly little secret from their Diurnal 'herds'.

"Face it, Sheridan, the vamp who set this up is in the wind, right along with little Miss Bela here. He's got her stuffed away somewhere, and he's milking her for every drop of *hemo* that she's got in her. I'd bet a pint of the best Montana cowboy on that.'

"And before you say it, *I know*. We still have to *try*." A pause followed, then, "So? Do you *have* any leads for us to follow, *Detective?*"

"One," he answered, regaining his composure. "Her roommate told us that Rayven didn't get the information about the website by surfing the Net. She said that she got it from a flyer. It was one of those tear-off deals that she found at a local market. We checked, and nobody at the market remembers seeing anyone post it."

"That figures," Cami remarked dryly. "A vamp could make them forget and he wouldn't show up on surveillance cams either. Let's see it."

He reached into the file that he had brought with him and produced the plastic evidence baggie. The tear-off inside of it had been printed on bright red paper, with black ink. She took it from him and held it up to the light. "That's strange," she said at last. "It has some kind of watermark or a Photoshop layer on it."

Sheridan tried, but he couldn't see what she was talking about.

"Don't bother," Cami told him. "It's too faint for daytimers to see, but trust me, it's there. Lemee check something else." To his dismay, she unsealed the bag, took out the tab and smelled it.

"Oh it's a vamp all right," she stated. "I can still smell a tiny bit of him—and it *is* a 'him' by the way. A woman smells different."

She didn't bother to elaborate on what that was and held up the paper to the light again. "I have an occult expert that might be able to tell us something about this watermark…"

Then she put the stub in its bag and handed it back. "You got anything else for me to look at?"

He did. It was a black leather notebook, embossed with spider webs, and crescent moons. "Her journal. Her roommate turned it over to us."

Cami sneered as she took it from him. "*Classic* Bela. Anything in there worth reading?"

He shook his head. "Not that we could make out. I brought it along in case you can do something with it."

She stuffed it into the purse hanging off her chair with a dismissive expression. "I'll page through it. Right now, I think we need to hit the streets just like Starsky and Hutch and dig up some more clues. By the way, I'm Hutch. You're Starsky."

Sheridan had no idea who or what she was referring to, and he didn't try to find out. He just followed her as she walked out of the station.

"We'll go see my expert about that mark," she said over her shoulder. "I also think that on our way there, we should drop by the market where little Bela got her flyer. No offense, but I think your Department might have missed something."

Sheridan was more than willing to set aside his pride for the sake of the case. "I'm game."

Cami's department car was parked right next to the Bloodmobile. Sheridan had heard that all of the LANPD stations let the collection vehicles park in the police lot. This was partly out of courtesy, and partly because it was the same thing for the vamps that the infamous roach-coaches were for Diurnals.

It was lunch. After VA Day, the donut had gone the way of the Black Maria and call boxes. Now, the Bloodmobile was the place for vamp cops to grab themselves a quick snack.

"Did you want to get something?" Cami asked, inclining her head towards the Bloodmobile. It was open for business, and there were a few vamps buying themselves a cup of hemo to take out with them on patrol.

"Uh, no thanks," Sheridan replied politely. "I'll stick with some coffee. Later."

Cami shrugged and led him over to her car. It was a yellow 1976 Camaro in pristine shape, emblazoned with black racing stripes, and a license plate that told the whole story about its owner, "DNCNQWN"

"I didn't know that those came in electric," Sheridan commented, admiring the muscle cars sleek lines.

"They don't," she said as she opened the door. "Straight-up V-8, burning dinosaurs. Pretty far out, huh?"

Sheridan gaped at her incredulously. By law, all cars and trucks were electric now. Gas-powered vehicles were reserved for government agencies, or sat in museums, gathering dust and memories.

"Joe," she said patiently. "Being a cop's bogus, but it does have a few perks. This is one of them. So chill out, and find out what got your grandpa's rocks off. Really, you'll like it. I'll even let you drive."

Sheridan shook his head, feeling a combination of amazement, wonder and revulsion towards the machine. It was the very epitome of everything that had brought about the Vampire Advent. It was also extremely sexy. *No wonder we got ourselves in the mess we did,* he decided.

14

"Okay, whatever," she responded as she got in and took the wheel. "You're riding shotgun."

***

Rayven's entire existence had been reduced to a 5 x 5 foot chamber hidden behind a false wall in the back of a cellar. She was sealed off from the rest of the universe by a heavy wooden door reinforced by rebar and filled with concrete. At times, sitting there in the darkness, handcuffed to a pipe, she found it hard to believe that her world had ever been any larger.

Two sentences on a piece of paper had brought her to this. *"We regret to inform you that you application for Transformation has been denied. If you disagree with this decision, you have a right to a hearing."*

After a lifetime of being the outsider, and dreaming about life as a vampire, her denial by the Office of Diurnal Affairs had sent her spiraling into a deep depression. When she had gone to the market, it had been to buy enough sleeping pills to guarantee that she would never have to see the sun, or the daytimers who reveled in it, ever again.

Then she had found the tear-off, and for a brief period, hope had returned. But Athanasius had betrayed her trust, and since then, he had done everything in his power to crush her spirit and pollute all that was good and pure about the undead.

He had failed though.

Her longing for death had faded, and she had come to understand him for what he truly was; an aberration, a freak, and a monster. Not a true Nocturnal, but an outcast and a madman.

Rescue was starting to seem as ephemeral as Transformation though. Her windowless cell made time impossible to track, but she knew that eventually, her searchers would give up.

This was certainly what her captor wanted her to believe. Every time he came to her, he reminded her of how hopeless her situation was, and how her very existence depended on his generosity.

I can't let myself believe his lies, she told herself. *I'm not the first girl to be abducted, and I certainly won't be the last. But there's still hope--no matter what he says. There's someone out there, looking for me.*

I have to remember that. I have to stay strong. That's what that one girl in Austria did. She never gave up. What was her name?

Watching a roach climb up towards the ceiling, Rayven tried to recall it. It had been a long time since she'd watched the documentary, but because the young woman's story had been so compelling, it had stayed with her.

Finally, she remembered. *Natasha. Natasha Kampusch. That was her name. She survived for eight years, Rayven. She survived because she never lost hope. She kept believing in herself and when she saw her chance, she escaped.*

A moment later, the door to her cell opened and her jailer entered.

"Yes, yes!" he said, cupping her chin roughly. "You keep telling yourself all that nonsense! Keep *pretending* that you matter. But no one really cares about you anymore. You *know* that. They've forgotten all about you, and I'll *never* let you go."

Flashing her a cruel grin, he released her chin and took ahold of her arm, tapping her veins with his fingers. "I see that my little peach is still nice and juicy. Excellent."

He had an intravenous kit, and ignoring her squirming, he jabbed the needle into her flesh and let the blood flow through the tubing into the collection pouch. When he was satisfied, he withdrew the needle, carefully swabbed over the spot with a cotton ball soaked in alcohol, and bandaged the wound.

"Mustn't let my little peach get infected. No, that would not do at all. Not with your *special* blood."

As he told her this, he produced another item; a TV dinner. He set it down on the dirty concrete, and pulled off the cellophane with a flourish. "Eat! Eat up my little peach!" he urged. "I need you to stay strong for my great work."

Leering, he retreated and shut the door. When Rayven heard him throw the bolts, she leaned against her shackle, wincing as the handcuff bit into her wrist, and started stuffing the food into her mouth. It was cold and greasy, and she had to force herself to choke it down, but it was still food.

And food meant life, and as long as there was life, there was still hope.

***

After his interview with the LADPD, the Manager of the Top-Top Market had retained a copy of the digital surveillance file covering the days leading up to and after Rayven's disappearance. It showed the entrance, and just outside the glass doors, the community bulletin board that the Market had in place to serve its customers. Watching it a second time in the cramped confines of the Manager's office, Sheridan seriously doubted that they would spot anything that would add up to a lead. Cami however, felt differently, and had run through it twice. At 16x speed.

"There," she finally declared, stopping the playback and pointing at the monitor. He didn't see anything remarkable and said as much.

She directed his attention to the bulletin board. "See? Nothing there. But then we go forwards a day…and *ta-da!*"

A brochure was there now, and just from its color alone, Sheridan could tell that it was the source of their tear-off stub. And Cami didn't have to explain to him why the footage didn't show their suspect. Vamps didn't register on cameras any more than they cast a reflection in a mirror. This was common knowledge, and he felt a flush of embarrassment on behalf of his Department for missing such a basic detail.

"So, now we know when our suspect put it there," she stated. She fast forwarded, and stopped when the image of Rayven appeared. The young woman was looking at the document and then taking the tear-off with her.

"We also know when she took it—but no big deal there," she added. Which it wasn't. They already knew this part. "*Buuut*— "She advanced the file again, and stopped.

The brochure was gone, and according to the date and time, it was just a little over 24 hours after Rayven had been reported missing. "We also know when our perp came back to cover his tracks. That gives us two shots at identifying him."

She turned to the Manager. "Who was picking up carts on those nights?"

The man thought about it for a second, and then answered. "That'd be Jerry. He's on tonight. Do you want to see him?"

"Do zombies eat brains?" she quipped. "Tell ya what, just tell me where Jerry is, and we'll go talk to him."

The Manager obliged her, and following his directions, they found the cart boy out in the parking lot wrangling a group of fifty carts with a motorized caddy. Walking towards him, Cami flashed Sheridan a wicked grin, and undid the first few buttons of her blouse.

"Are you Jerry?" she asked. Sheridan sensed the pheromones that he was putting out, and although he didn't know what was hitting him, so did Jerry. It was a trick that vamps used to lure their prey and it worked beautifully on the cart-boy.

"Uh, yeah," he answered, his eyes alight with interest.

"I was wondering if you remembered seeing anything out of the ordinary on the nights of the 9th and the 15th," she said, moving much closer to him than she actually needed to. "Any unusual customers or cars? It'd make me *really* happy if you did."

Sweat had actually broken out on the poor man's forehead, and Sheridan could almost hear the gears in his mind grinding as he tried to recall anything that would please the gorgeous woman standing before him. Then it came to him.

"Yeah," he said. "Yeah, there *was* something weird. It was a car--an old one, and all black. A real classy job. My uncle used to collect old cars, and that's why it got my attention. It might have even been a gas-burner once."

"Could you identify the model if we showed you a few pictures?" Sheridan inquired. Jerry didn't even look in his direction. His gaze was riveted on Cami.

"Jerry," she purred, "Think hard. What did it look like?"

Jerry worked at it for a moment. "It was real old," he said at last, "maybe one of those classic Cadillac's. No, wait, that's not right, but it looked a lot like one. I can't place the model. I'm sorry." His features were the epitome of regret.

"No," she countered, astonishing Sheridan by reaching out and gently caressing the man's face with her hand. "You did great, Jerry. Really, really great. Thank you." For his part, Jerry looked like a dog that had just pleased its master by performing a particularly clever trick.

"Thank you *so much*, Jerry. You're wonderful." She inclined her head to Sheridan. "Let's go. I have what we need."

Leaving Jerry standing there, they walked back to the car and she fished her tablet out of her purse and set it on the trunk. After a few seconds of searching on the browser, she turned it around so that Sheridan could see the screen. It displayed an image of a black 1980 Lincoln Continental Town Car.

"Jerry *really* wanted to help me," she explained with a grin. "It popped right up in his mind as he was talking to me, even though he didn't know what it was called."

Sheridan was duly impressed. Being able to read minds was a powerful skill for any investigator to possess--although he couldn't picture himself using seduction to jog a witness's memory like she had.

Cami giggled. "There's a little side effect though. When he plays with himself this week, all he'll be able to think about will be me. God, I love daytimers."

Sheridan winced.

"Now," she said. "Let's find our perp..."

Cami went to work with her tablet again and a familiar website popped up. It was the LA Department of Transportation log-in page for law enforcement, and it allowed subscribers to access traffic camera footage. She entered the dates and times, along with the general location, and the images appeared a second later.

They were supplied by a camera mounted at a nearby intersection, and showed the Town Car pulling up and stopping for the light before moving on. More importantly, it didn't display a driver behind the wheel, and the license plate was plainly visible.

"Bingo, *bay-bee!*" she cried, pumping her fist in triumph. "Oh, I am *soo* good!"

She brought up another site. This one remotely accessed the LANPD data-base.

"A 1980 Lincoln Town Car, Black," she announced, "registered to one Athanasius Alexandrías, aka Athanásios Alexandrías, 2034 Corbin Avenue, Tarzana. Vamp registration, No wants, no warrants. Joe, I'd bet the nails in my coffin that that's our guy."

Sheridan couldn't disagree, but they were both aware that their evidence was circumstantial at best. Just because he liked to shop at a market that was way out of his neighborhood wasn't proof of a kidnaping. They needed more.

"What's next?" he asked her.

"We go see my expert," she answered "and we hit up some copy places." Sheridan grasped why immediately. Most suspects didn't want to create incriminating documents on their home computer. They tended to prefer the anonymity that came with renting time on someone else's machine. Especially since most commercial copy shops purged their computers on a daily basis, and cash was always welcome.

***

Cami's expert lived in a secluded home just off of Laurel Canyon and Sheridan was surprised to see a 1960's era Volkswagen van parked in the driveway. It was covered in wild psychedelic patterns and prominently emblazoned with the familiar logo of the Grateful Undead.

That's our 'expert'? he wondered. A 'Deadhead' hadn't been exactly what he'd pictured when Cami had suggested consulting an occult scholar.

"Chill, Sheridan," Cami assured him. "My mom may be a hippy, but she knows just about everything there is to know about vampire lore. I told you, she's a real traditionalist. She'll give us the skinny on that mark."

Another surprise. "Your—*mom?*"

"My *vampire* mom," she explained as they exited the car together. "When you get turned, you need someone to show you the ropes, to raise you like a kid—especially if your sack of shit *master* splits on you like mine did right after he turned my whole cheerleading team. Mom's been there for me for years. Just so you know, she got turned back in the 60's, so get ready for all of that peace, love and moonlight jive."

"Okay," Sheridan replied doubtfully.

They were met at the door by a pungent gust of marijuana smoke, Led Zeppelin singing about going to California and a woman who didn't look much older than Cami. Just as he had been warned, her vampire mom was the very definition of the classic 'hippie chick' with long straight hair, a flamboyant dashiki and leather sandals. The only thing that was *off* about her was her unnaturally pale skin and the fangs that were exposed when she smiled at them.

21

"Oh Carmilla!" she said, embracing her. "It's so *groovy* to see you! You look so *thin* though. Are you drinking enough blood?"

Then she realized that Sheridan was standing there. "Who's this? Are you dating daytimers now? That's *so* far out. I knew you'd loosen up. Just like the time I dated Hendrix.'

"Now Jimmy was *some* man. Not like Mick at all. You know, it's sad about Mick; he got turned but only his lips stayed young. Can you believe that? Oh, and did you hear about Michael? He still can't keep his nose on. It fell off during a concert in Paris."

"Mom," Cami interrupted. "He's not a *date*. He's my new partner."

Not quite certain what proper flower-child etiquette was, Sheridan decided to extend his hand to the woman. "Joe Sheridan."

She responded to this by gathering him up in a patchouli-scented hug. "Welcome Joe. My name is Star, Star Bright. Welcome to my home in peace and love!"

Cami rolled her eyes in exasperation. "Mom, we need to talk to you about this freaky-deaky design we found. It's part of a case we're working. A missing daytimer."

Star let Sheridan go and frowned disapprovingly. "Oh, a *cop* thing. When are you gonna stop working for the *Man*, Carmilla? You know how I feel about the *fuzz*." Clearly, Cami's choice of occupation was the source of a long standing disagreement between them.

"She's been missing for two weeks," he interjected, pulling out a picture of Rayven. "We're afraid that someone kidnapped her."

"A *vamp*, mom," Cami added. "We think a vamp's got her and he's using her for a blood cow. You know how some of the old ones get."

This time, Star's unhappy expression wasn't meant for her adopted daughter. "Oh that's bad karma. Really bad, bad karma, man." She took the picture from Sheridan and looked at it for a moment. Then she handed it back and led them into the house.

Inside, Sheridan spotted the source of the marijuana smell immediately. A half-smoked joint sat in an abalone shell ashtray, and there was an open wooden box next to it, filled with the stuff. The only thing that was odd was that the loose weed in the box was glowing faintly, and so was the joint.

"*Cosmic Charlie*," Cami explained. "Vamps need something really potent to get them high, so some Serbian Count got the bright idea of turning his spare crypt into a grow operation. He spent a few centuries working on the stuff and it's ten times more powerful than that rag weed you daytimers use. If you smoked it, you'd be knocked on your ass with the first toke."

Sheridan was about to inform her that he didn't smoke anything--and especially not marijuana--when Star spoke up. "You know, you could use a little Cosmic Charlie yourself, Carmilla. You wouldn't be so uptight all the time."

This earned her another eye roll from her vamp daughter. "The design, mom. What is it?"

"First, I want you to meet my new old man," Star insisted. "Eddie? This is my daughter Carmilla and her friend, Joe. He's a *daytimer*."

A rather haggard looking vamp looked up at them from a wicker chair across the room. He had unkempt hair and dark, haunted eyes that were made even duskier by his undead pallor. He also had a bottle of liquor sitting next to him, along with a small army of empties, and a full glass in his hand. He set it down, rose, and came over to them on slightly unsteady legs. "Edgar Poe" he said, his voice slightly slurred, "at your service, sir."

For some reason, Sheridan thought that he looked familiar and then he heard a whisper in his mind that sounded exactly like Cami's voice.

Edgar Allen, it said. *You know? The famous horror writer? Mom's sworn off rock stars and now she's into authors.*

23

He blinked and looked at her in surprise, receiving a small nod of acknowledgement and an inscrutable smile.

That's right, Joe, he heard, *we don't just read minds. We can also send thoughts. So from now on, if you've got something private to say, just think it. I'll hear you.*

In the meantime, Star was introducing her houseguest. "Eddie is so *heavy!* You should read some of the stuff that he writes. He even wrote a story about me. He calls it *'The Oval Portrait'. Very* cool stuff."

I don't want to tell her that he's just rehashing old material, Cami thought to Sheridan. *He's been doing that ever since he came out of the coffin. Not that he really needs any new stuff. All the back royalties he was owed made him a multi-billionaire and pissed off a whole shitload of greedy publishers.*

"Pleased to meet you, Mr. Poe," Sheridan said aloud. "I read some of your stories back when I was a kid. I really enjoyed *'The Cask of Amontillado.'* How on earth did you dream that up?"

Poe gave him an odd, half smile. "I didn't. They say 'write about what you know'. The real Fortunato was a right bastard and I made certain that he got exactly what he deserved. Although, I must admit to *some* embellishment in the narrative."

"Uh, okay," Sheridan responded, not quite sure if the vamp was kidding or not. The undead tended to have an odd sense of humor.

By now, Cami had run out of patience. "Hey, great to meet you Eddie. Mom? We're on the clock. I need you to look at this and tell me if you know what it means." She offered her the tear-off stub.

"Fine," Star huffed. "Eddie, you good on your cognac?"

Poe nodded, and as he returned to his seat, she examined the stub. "I've got it," she told them at last.

She became a blur as she moved across the room to a bookshelf, selected a volume and returned in less than half a second. "It's in here," she stated, paging through the tome almost as rapidly.

"Yeah. This is it. See? The corner matches with your ticket stub."

She held up the image and Sheridan saw the match right away. The watermark was part of some kind of magical design, filled with strange characters and odd symbols.

"Okay," Cami asked, "so what am I looking at?"

"It's a *capcană*," Star said. "A *capcană de oameni*. That's Romanian and it means a 'people trap' or a 'people catcher'. Whoever this vampire is, he's old enough to believe in the *Magie de Sânge.*"

"Oh mom," Cami responded dismissively. "Come *on.*"

"Hey! You asked me what it was and I told you," Star retorted.

"I'm sorry Star, but I'm a little lost here," Sheridan admitted. "Can you explain it to me?"

Star flashed him a fanged smile, pleased by his deferential attitude. "The Magie de Sânge is Blood Magic," she stated. "Ancient stuff that only vampires know. The mark on your flyer is part of a sigil, a magical diagram that's supposed to capture a mortal and bring them under a vamp's power. Sort of like a flytrap--but for souls.'

"Whoever this vamp is, he's older than you think, and he believes in magic. He's also probably insane. The Magie de Sânge uses a lot of demonology, pacts with the Devil and human sacrifice. If he has her, your missing girl is in big trouble. Like I said, bad, bad karma, man."

Her features knitted in confusion, and she inspected the stub more closely. "There's also something really weird about this *capcană*. "I'm not sure, but it looks like he might have added something to it."

Consulting her book again, Star nodded to herself. "Yeah, he's made changes. I don't know what they mean, but I'll check some other books. It might be important."

25

"Okay, mom," Cami replied. "If you find out what he did, lemee know. Come on, Joe. We've got some more stops to make."

Star put her book aside. "You're going? Already? Well, at least take some brownies along for the road." She indicated a plate on the living room table. It was piled high with the confections. They were also glowing, and Sheridan knew right away that they were laced with Cosmic Charlie.

So did Cami. "No thanks, mom. Gotta stay straight for the job. Call me if you learn anything else."

***

Once they were back on Laurel Canyon, Cami drove them into the San Fernando Valley. They had just turned onto Ventura Boulevard when she pulled into the center median and made an abrupt U-turn.

Sheridan looked around to see what had inspired their change of direction. "I thought we were going to Tarzana."

Then he spotted the familiar golden fangs of a McBloodie's fast food restaurant. It was built into the side of the area blood bank, and naturally, there was a drive-through.

"In a few," she promised. "I'm hungry. I think all that Cosmic Charlie in the air back at mom's place gave me a contact high. I've got the munchies somthin fierce."

Looking at her, Sheridan noted that her pupils were almost completely dilated. She was as high as a kite, he realized, so he didn't make any objections. If it kept her happy and brought her back down to earth, he was all for it.

Cami pulled in and surveyed her choices. After a moment, the speaker came to life. "Welcome to McBloodie's. May I take your order?"

"Yeah," she said. "A tall hemo, heavy on the clots. Do you have the Midwesterner?"

"Sorry," the voice replied regretfully. "We're all out, but we do have the Southerner. It has a nice chicken-fried flavor."

"Fuck," Cami scowled. "I wanted the Midwesterner. Those corn-fed boys are primo. Okay…one Southerner." She turned to Sheridan "You want anything? My treat."

"I'm on a non-hemo diet," Sheridan said politely.

"Hey, no problemo, "Cami replied with a wink. She spoke to the speaker grill again. "I need something for my partner. Do you have anything for daytimers?"

"Orange juice and cookies—and there's some stale coffee in the back."

"Stale coffee then. Oh, and throw in some donuts if you've got 'em. Make sure they're the ones with the little sprinkles. My partner deserves the *best*."

After they had received their order, Cami parked in a corner of the parking lot where they could observe the traffic on the street and went right to work on her Southerner, sucking down the contents with her oversized straw and sighing contentedly. "Ah, *muuuch* better."

Sheridan had started in on his donut, but was pointedly ignoring his coffee. The clerk hadn't been lying to them about it. One sip had proven that it was not only stale, but also the oldest and foulest cup of java that he had ever offended his lips with.

"So," Cami said, arching her chest provocatively and awarding him with a blood-stained smile. "Do you want to *touch* it?"

Sheridan nearly choked to death on his snack. "W-what?!"

"You've been looking at it ever since we met," she answered. "Do you want to find out what it feels like--in your hand?"

"I—didn't—I—mean—I," he managed to splutter.

This made her laugh. "The gun, you *doofus*. Not my tit! You've been eyeballing my gun all night. You *know* you want to."

27

In fact, he had, but he simply hadn't worked up the nerve to ask. As nice as her breasts were--and they were truly works of art--the gun that she had in her leather shoulder holster had been drawing his gaze like a magnet. There was no point in denying it.

Prior to beginning his assignment as a Liaison Officer, he'd been given one night out on the LANPD range to familiarize him with firearms, and as hateful as it was to admit, he had felt the seduction that the things exerted. Once, they had been the very symbol of Diurnal power.

"Okay," she said with an impish smile, "I'll make this easy." For a moment it seemed as if she was actually going to undo her blouse, but then she grasped the pistol and withdrew it in one fluid motion. He was appalled at the size of the thing. It looked more like a piece of field artillery than a hand weapon.

As he watched, she unloaded it, cupped the bullets in her hand, and handed it over to him. It proved to be even heavier than it looked, and in a strange way, quite sensual.

"It's the most powerful handgun in the world, Joe. A .44 Magnum Model 29 with a six and a half inch barrel," she informed him. Then she lowered her voice, mimicking a male, "You've just got to ask yourself one question: 'Do I feel lucky? Well, do ya, punk?'"

She laughed again, amused by whatever this was a reference to. Without bothering to enlighten him, she opened her hand to show him the ammunition that the thing consumed. "Silver-jacketed with ash wood tips. Totally wrecks a blood cow's day, and it'll put down a vamp long enough to stake him out."

The bullets were as impressive as the weapon itself. He gave it back to her.

"You know, if you live through this, "she said, returning it to its holster, "we'll have to go out to the Department range and let you shoot it. It's--totally orgasmic." More laughter followed.

"Yeah, sure," he replied. "Thanks."

Finishing off the last of her Southerner, she started the car. "All right, let's see what we can find at the copy shops. But first, I think we need some tunes."

Ever since VA day, most radio stations had dedicated themselves to playing Oldies. The definition of what constituted an 'oldie' had changed dramatically however. Selections ran the gamut of the entire history of music, from contemporary classics, to ancient Babylon and Sumeria, and each station had its own audience of loyal vamps. Cami's preference matched her era; disco, and when she switched on the car radio, the strains of *"Disco Inferno"* began to fill the cabin.

"I thought disco was dead," Sheridan remarked, only realizing his mistake as he made it.

Cami's response was immediate and emphatic. She spun around in her seat to face him. Her eyes had transformed into glowing red coals and she bared her fangs.

"No!" she shouted. "Disco is *not* dead! Disco is *undead!*"

"Okay, okay!" Sheridan retorted, shrinking away. "Hey, I *like* disco. I'm sorry. Really."

The hellfire in her eyes faded, then disappeared. "Good. But if you *ever* say anything like that again, I'll make you listen to *Abba* for the whole shift. Got that?"

Sheridan didn't have the foggiest idea what Abba was, but he wasn't interested in finding out. "Sure thing, Cami."

The Sergeant *had* warned him, he thought ruefully.

***

It turned out that the area around their suspect's residence was home to no less than six 24-hour copy shops. They catered to students from Pierce College pulling all-nighters to finish up term papers, insomniac musicians, scriptwriters on a deadline, and of course, vamps.

Most of the clerks they spoke with didn't remember a vamp matching the description of their suspect, but this came as no surprise given the vampiric ability to befuddle Diurnal memories. And they didn't even bother with the rental computers.

The trail seemed to have gone cold. But then fortune turned in their favor. They were leaving the last shop when Cami spotted something in a bin set aside for recycling paper scraps. She stopped in her tracks and went straight back to the clerk.

"I need you to open that recycle bin for me," she instructed him. After the clerk had done so, she slipped on a pair of vinyl gloves and reached inside. She came out with a scrap of blood-red paper. It looked exactly like the stock that had been used to create their tear off stub—and even better, Cami's keen senses detected the ghostly image of a *capcană*.

"Another visit to your mom then?" Sheridan inquired, just as pleased as she was with their find.

Cami stuffed their prize into an evidence bag. "No, we'll send her a scan. She's probably still up. Meantime, this scrap and our stub need to go off to the lab for a positive match. I also think that we should check the traffic cams around here. My bet is that we'll find ourselves a black Lincoln."

Sheridan had never thought of himself as a gambler, but even if he had been, this was not a wager he would have risked any money on. "Okay," he agreed, inclining his jaw towards the eastern horizon. "I'll get on it once we get back to the station. I don't mind staying up for a bit."

Cami looked in the same direction and sighed wistfully. Although there was only the palest suggestion of a glow, dawn was coming, and their shift was nearing its end. She needed to get back to her coffin.

"All right," she conceded. "You handle it. We'll pick this up tomorrow night."

***

In the absence of any coherent pattern, the mind imposes its own order. Rocks become alive with faces, clouds turn into dragons, and the world is populated by the fantastic. Every child discovers this for themselves, and the capacity to imagine stays with them for the rest of their lives.

Rayven was no exception. Lacking a sky to gaze at, or anything else beyond the confines of her cell, her imagination used the canvas of the walls around her to paint its images.

Up near the ceiling, a dimple in the plaster gradually transformed into a bat, frozen in mid-flight. Further down, something that looked like a snake wriggling along, came into being, and below this, the profile of a man eventually emerged. To her eye, he resembled Vlad Drakul, except that his nose was too large and his cap was all wrong.

These shapes, and others, were the constellations of her imprisonment, illusions created from the shadows and the uneven places. Their effect however, was very real. The helped to fill the long hours and provided her a respite from her anxiety, and her doubts.

She was tracing the lines of a crack with her eyes, and considering how closely it resembled a great river seen from space, when she heard the bolt to her door being thrown. The river vanished, along with the bat, the snake and the man. Fear replaced them.

This time though, Athanasius hadn't brought a TV dinner or an IV kit. He had a key and he used it to unlock her handcuff.

"No dinner for you tonight my little peach," he said. "We have too much work to do and too little time to do it in. Come along, now."

With that, he grabbed her by her hair and began to drag her out. Rayven cried out in pain and tried to pry his fingers loose, but he ignored her protests, and hauled her through the house and up the stairs to the second floor.

When she stumbled on the landing, the vamp dealt her a blow that left her ears ringing. "I said, *come along!*" he barked.

Terrified, she did her best to stay on her feet as he dragged her to a door at the end of the hall. As it opened, her nose was assaulted by the combined smells of incense, blood and decay.

"Please forgive the mess," he said with feigned politeness, forcing her across the threshold. "I have been so busy that I simply haven't had the time to straighten up."

At one time, the chamber had been a bedroom, but all the furniture had been removed and replaced. One wall was dominated by a large mirror in an ornate frame. The glass within the frame wasn't mirrored though. Instead, it was black, and covered with strange diagrams that had been painted on its surface with a dark, brownish substance.

A wheeled table, reminiscent of a hospital gurney, was positioned nearby, and it was occupied by the corpse of a young woman. From the gash in her neck and the puddle of gore beneath her, it was hideously obvious that she had been bled to death. Seeing this, Rayven cried out and tried to break free, but Athanasius's grip was like iron. Keeping ahold of her, he dragged her over to the table and casually shoved the corpse onto the floor. It hit with a sodden thump and rolled over onto its side.

"Again, my deepest apologies. I have simply been far too busy to take my meals in the dining room. The demands of my work have required everything of me."

A harsh tug on her scalp compelled her to rise, and she was forced to climb up and take her place on the table. The instant she had done so, the vampire produced thick leather straps and lashed her down.

"Still not begging, eh?" he asked. "You are indeed *different*. Every daytimer that I have ever brought here has pleaded for their life at this juncture—until now. Perhaps there is more to you than just your special blood."

He deliberated this novel concept for a long moment, and then gestured towards the black mirror. "But I see that I have been rude. All this time, you have been contributing to something without any knowledge of what it was. Behold the reason for your continued existence; the eye of fortune itself. A window into the very future! A window that your rare blood opens wide for me like paint on the canvas of a masterpiece. *My* masterpiece."

Despite her dread, she looked, but saw nothing except the dark glass and the weird symbols defacing it. Symbols which had been created with her blood.

What would a vampire want with a mirror? she wondered. It made no sense, and only confirmed what she already understood about her captor. Athanasius was irretrievably insane.

"You stupid blood cow," he hissed. "Your kind simply doesn't have the wit to apprehend such a marvelous thing. It does not matter that I cannot see myself. The visions in the glass are what are important, and they are only meant for the eyes of Immortals, not lowly creatures like you.'

"And what have these visions shown me, you might ask? That we will finally overthrow the weaklings that call themselves our leaders. I have *seen* it! I have seen us rise up against them, and I have witnessed the great festival that we will hold once true vampires have assumed their rightful place in this world. The glass does not lie. This planet will run red with mortal blood and we will feast on all of you."

Eyes alight with madness, Anthasius reached over to another, smaller table, littered with old books and papers. After a moment of rummaging around, he produced an IV kit.

"Have no fear though. I do not plan to kill you. Not tonight at least. Not when I am so close to finding the path that will bring these great visions to fruition."

While he was telling her this, he inserted the needle into her arm and began to fill the collection pouch. When it was full, he attached another, and went to work with the first one, carefully emptying some of its contents into his palm and using his finger to trace fresh designs onto the glass. All the while, he chanted in

33

a strange language that sounded like nothing Rayven had ever heard before.

Eventually, he stopped, and laughed in delight at whatever he thought he was seeing.

***

Sheridan was already hard at work when Cami came in the following evening. He had a stack of printouts waiting for her on his desk.

"Hey", he said, smiling and indicating the papers. "Got some good news for you. I found the Lincoln. It was in the area of that last copy shop a few days before the flyer went up. I've also been doing some research on our guy."

Cami nodded absently and hung her purse on her chair. "Tell me what you've got."

"Well, he's some piece of work," Sheridan began. "Looks like he started out as a priest back in Alexandria. But then he had some serious disagreements with a couple of the Roman emperors and got himself exiled five times. In fact, he kicked up so much dust that he wound up being called '*Athanasius Contra Mundum',* 'Athanasius Against the World.' I guess he couldn't play nice with the other kids."

"Anyhow, once he got Transformed, he completely snapped. The records aren't complete, but he's linked to a string of murders and disappearances in Paris, and some more in Germany. Oh yeah, and he had to run for it both times. Sometime after that, he came to the New World and when the Net became a thing, he started up a web site for some group calling itself 'Vampires First!' I checked it out. It's crazy stuff."

"Yeah, I've heard about them," Cami replied. "A wacko fringie group. They hate the whole idea of what we're doing. They don't think we went far enough when we took over."

"I'll say," Sheridan agreed. "He wrote a couple of blogs about how Diurnals need to be put in camps and milked like cows. Sure sounds to me like someone who wouldn't have a problem snatching up a few daytimer girls."

"No, he probably wouldn't," Cami returned. Something about her mood struck Sheridan as odd. She seemed quieter than the night before, even pensive.

"So, what's up?" he asked her. "I know we haven't been working together very long, but you seem a bit off tonight. Sorry, I don't mean to pry, but…"

She sat down. "Nah, it's okay. I *am* a bit off. After we finished shift last night, I was just gonna go home and curl up with my Undeady bear, but then I remembered Rayven's journal. I wound up spending most of the morning reading it in my coffin." She paused, and Sheridan waited for her to elaborate.

"I had it all wrong, Joe," she admitted. "About her being a 'Bela', I mean. There's some really deep stuff in there, and she convinced me that she might just have what it takes to become a Nocturnal."

Her change of attitude surprised him. "Oh?"

Cami reached into her purse and produced the journal. Several places had been bookmarked with strips of paper.

"Listen to this; '*Daytimers don't know the dark. They see it. They fear it. But they don't know it. Not like I do.'*

"*The dark is safety. The dark is my home, welcoming me into its loving arms. I am a refugee from all the sunlight, the noise and the people.'*"

She paged to another marker, and continued. "'*When I was little, they tried to put me out in the sunlight, and I screamed and cried until they put me back in the shadows. When I was old enough to walk on my own, I would get up in the middle of the night, while everyone else was asleep and run around the house with all the lights turned off, and enjoy the peace. It was safe, and it was quiet. The dark is like that. Sunlight is noisy, but the Dark is quiet.'*

"'*Of course there were ghosts there, and sometimes they frightened me. But not enough to become a daytimer, and*

35

*certainly not enough to make myself stop seeing them. That's
what the daytimers did, and I wasn't a part of their world. I
didn't want to stop seeing the ghosts, or forget the night. It loved
me, and I loved it, and nothing could ever be allowed to stand in
the way of something so perfect. Not even fear.'*

"So, I stayed and told the ghosts to leave me alone. To go
and frighten someone else. This was my world too, and they
would have to get used to me. They listened, and they spent their
time terrifying the daytimers instead.'*

"She also wrote this; *'Have you ever seen the moonlight?
Really seen it? Drank it like wine, or danced in it laughing? I
have. Have you ever swum among the shadows like a diver in the
ocean, and felt them embrace you?'*

"*'Did you know that there are a thousand shades of grey
and blue? Or that things live there? Things which are so fragile
that the slightest sliver of sunlight can tear them apart like the
finest silk? Things that laugh and play under the moon? I do.
I've danced with them.'*

"*'I'm dancing with them now. But you can't see me. I
never wanted you to. Go back to your world of light and pretend
that I'm not real. I'll do the same thing with you.'"*

Sighing deeply, Cami closed the notebook. "Deep stuff,"
she repeated. "And there's more. After I got up, I ran Rayven's
background, and I don't think Athanasius will kill her. Not right
away at least."

Sheridan regarded her quizzically. "My Department
already did that. What did you find that we didn't?" To the best
of his knowledge, both Departments shared the same data-base.

"I checked *our* database, Joe," she answered. "The one we
keep on all Diurnals. Remember back when you filled out your
first tax return?"

He did. Among other things, it had required that he declare
his blood type. Basically standard stuff.

36

"Turns out that she's very special," Cami said, logging into her computer and bringing up the data. He got up and came around her desk to see the screen.

She pointed at the blood type. "H/H," she stated. "*Extremely* rare. Only four people in a million even have it. They're part of what's called the Bombay Group."

"Okay," he nodded. "So?"

"So I called my mom as soon as I found out and told her. She completely freaked out. Can you guess why?"

"Because it has something to do with that Blood Magic she was telling us about?" Sheridan guessed.

"*Exactamento!*" Cami replied. "It's used for very special spells to see into the future. She said that some of the vamps who got into blood magic swore that it gave them visions of what was going to happen.'

"Nutty shit, but when you think about it, it really makes sense—in a totally wigged out and fucked up kind of way. After all, we're immortal. All we have is the future, right? The vamp who can really see it is *way* ahead of the rest of us. So, bottom line, he needs her for his fortune telling. He needs her bad. It's not like another H/H is gonna come boppin down the street anytime soon."

She was right, Sheridan concluded. More importantly, it meant that they had some time on their side.

Cami got up. "I think we have what we need to start closing this case. Let's go talk with Captain Van Helsing."

Sheridan followed her through the maze of desks until they reached the Captain's Office. The legend on the door read, *"Investigative Services. Captain Abraham Van Helsing, Commander"* and beneath this *"Lieutenant Lucy Westenra, Deputy Commander."*

She didn't knock. She didn't need to. The door opened all by itself. Inside, Captain Van Helsing was seated at his desk, and a breathtaking brunette that Sheridan presumed was Lieutenant Westenra was standing next to him.

Van Helsing waved them in "So, tell me all about your kidnapper."

Behind them, the door closed. *Another vamp trick*, Sheridan thought, but a pretty handy one. *If I could do that, I'd never need a remote.*

Van Helsing smiled at him. "I don't." He looked to Cami next. "Okay Cami, amaze me."

She proceeded to share everything that they had discovered so far, including her conclusion that their victim was safe for the moment, and why. While the Captain and the Lieutenant listened, Sheridan eyed the decorations in Van Helsing's office.

One of these was an autographed picture of Bela Lugosi in his famous cape. The caption was, *"To my good friend, Abe. Thank you for all your inspiration and expertise."*

Another item was a realistic sketch showing a pair of men standing in front of a mountain with a castle atop it. The first one was tall and thin with long black hair, sunken cheekbones and dark, intense eyes. He was dressed in an odd costume that seemed like something out of the Middle Ages, and his arm was draped companionably around his partner. This was an elderly fellow attired in an antiquated three-piece suit, and although he was older by many decades, and wore thick glasses, he bore a strong resemblance to the Captain.

Sheridan had no idea who the tall figure in the drawing was, but he assumed that the other one had to be Van Helsing's grandfather, or even his great grandfather. Like the Lugosi photo, the sketch was also signed, but the script was archaic and when he failed to decipher it, his gaze travelled to something else.

This was a polished wooden plaque bearing a stake, plated in gold. The brass plate attached to it proclaimed that it was the *Golden Stake Award for Outstanding Police Work.* It had been awarded to the Captain by something calling itself the Order of the Dragon. Whoever they were.

Cami had finished her narrative by this point, and Van Helsing noticed what Sheridan was looking at. "That's not my grandfather," he said, hooking his thumb at the drawing. "That was me, before Vlad Drakul managed to knock some sense into my thick skull. I'll tell you, I sure as hell don't miss those damned glasses."

Sheridan regarded him with disbelief. If he had had to guess, he wouldn't have placed Van Helsing at any more than 35, and although he had just enough grey at his temples to lend him some distinction, he was nothing at all like the old man in the sketch. Instead, he seemed to be at the very peak of masculine health. Just looking at him made Sheridan feel out of shape.

The Captain and Lieutenant Westenra shared a conspiratorial smile, and then Van Helsing leaned forwards and steepled his fingers. "Okay Cami, you've hooked me--as always. But since our suspect lives out in West Valley's turf, we'll have to reach out to them."

Cami glowered. "Just as long as they don't assign Plogojowitz to the case. That horn dog has been trying to jump my bones for the last forty years."

"I'll bear that in mind when I speak to Captain Ruthaven," Van Helsing reassured her. "We'll also contact LADPD Valley Division and have them do a tag team with West Valley so we can keep eyes on our suspect twenty-four seven."

"Thanks, Captain," she said. "He's our perp. I know it."

Lieutenant Westenra had something to add. "One thing about this bothers me greatly. Our suspect was quite fortunate to capture a girl with H/H blood. The odds are quite long against that. In fact, I would venture to say that it is nigh impossible." She had a soft, English accent that conveyed a sense of great refinement, and a lurking sensuality that sent a shiver up Sheridan's spine.

Van Helsing concurred. "Yeah, Lucy's right. As far as we know, Alexandrías hasn't been hunting in this area for very long, and he hits the jackpot right away.'

"I'm not buying it. I know there are more bones in this graveyard, so I want you to do a little more digging, Cami. Meanwhile, I'll check with RSS downtown and see if they have anything on this guy that we should know about."

In addition to bank robberies, Robbery Special Section also handled extortions, kidnappings and human trafficking cases that required prolonged investigation, or exceeded the resources of a division's detectives. They had city-wide jurisdiction, and often handled the high-profile cases. If there was more to this abduction as Lieutenant Westenra had suggested, Sheridan knew that the chances were good that the RSS would have some useful information to provide.

"Yes, Captain," Cami replied.

"Oh, and nice meeting you, Sheridan," the Captain said. "You've got a great partner here. Just follow her lead and we'll have this perp staked in no time. And Cami—you be nice to him okay? Diurnals break easy."

Cami rewarded him with a crooked smile, and pulled Sheridan out of the office.

Obedient to Captain Van Helsing's orders, as soon as they were back at their desks, she placed a call to her mother.

"Mom? You said there was something weird about that people catcher thingy. Did you ever find out what it was?"

A moment went by as she listened to the reply, and then she beamed. "Yes! That fits! Thank you *sooo* much!"

She cut the connection and looked at Sheridan. "Come on, Joe! Let's go see the Captain again." They returned to Van Helsing straightaway.

"Captain," Cami announced to him. "I just spoke with my expert. She says that the people catcher was personalized. It had some runes on it that added up to our victim's name. Alexandrías *knew* about her! This was a targeted thing."

40

Just then Lieutenant Westenra entered, a cup of hemo in hand. "Has something of importance occurred?" she inquired.

"Yeah," Van Helsing said. "Our guy set his victim up. It's just the 'how' that I'm wondering about. It's almost as if..."

"--as if he were supplied with her information," Westenra ventured. "By someone who was aware of her blood type, and the status of her application. Someone who has access to such records. *Federal* records."

"Uh huh," Van Helsing agreed. "There might be a lot more to this than just one lone wacko on a winning streak. This could even involve the VBI, or the Order. Cami, I gotta hand it to you. You've managed to amaze me twice in one night. Now just don't get too big for your coffin, little girl."

"Not a chance, Captain," Cami grinned. Again, she led Sheridan out of the office. But this time, they were headed out to the parking lot.

"Where are we going?" Sheridan asked.

"Out to sit on this clown's house," she told him.

"Excuse me, but isn't that something that West Valley and my people are supposed to be handling?" Sheridan wondered.

She waved this away. "Only until the Captain can get someone out there to spell us. I don't want this creep spending one more night without some eyes on him. Come on, it'll be fun."

Sheridan had spent plenty of time on stake-outs, and 'fun' wasn't the word he would have chosen to describe it. Despite what they showed on TV and in the movies, real surveillance work was long, boring and uncomfortable. His partner was correct though. They needed someone out there right away.

***

They had just exited the Ventura freeway and were making their way up into the side streets, when Cami received a call. It was from Lt. Westenra. Captain Van Helsing had kept his word and made arrangements with the West Valley detectives and their LADPD counterparts. A Daytimer unit had been sent to watch the house, and then a Nocturnal car had taken over. They were instructed to meet with it a few blocks away from their suspect's home.

When she laid eyes on the unmarked vehicle a few minutes later, Cami wasn't pleased. "Oh, *great!*"she exclaimed with a sour expression.

Whoever they were, she knew the occupants--and didn't care for them one bit. Despite this, she pulled in alongside them, and rolled down her window.

"Hey, beautiful!" the driver said.

"Peter Plogojowitz," she sneered. "What's the matter? Couldn't find any maggots to go on a date with you?"

"You're just saying that because you can't admit that you're madly in love with me," the vamp replied.

Cami didn't rise to his bait, and looked past him to his passenger. "Savanović? Are you two losers still partners?"

"Hi, Cami," the other vamp waved.

She didn't return the greeting and addressed Plogojowitz. "So, anything happen so far?"

"Actually yes," he grinned. "Before they left, the LADPD unit presented us with a little gift. I'll tell you what it is for a kiss, and if you throw in a little tongue, I'll even get it out of the trunk for you."

Cami's eyes began to glow, and Plogojowitz laughed. "All right, I'll settle for your number instead. What I've got back there'll cinch up your case nice and tight...and speaking about tying things up..."

"What is it?" she snarled.

"Number first, gorgeous."

She grimaced, considering her options. From the way she was gripping the steering wheel, it was obvious that one of these involved reaching across the space and tearing Plogojowitz's larynx out with her bare hands.

"Fine," she finally growled. "867-5309. Now, what do you have?"

Plogojowitz smirked and gestured for her to wait as he tapped his EarPhone and spoke the number into it. "Trash," he said, after saving it to his Contacts. "The daytimer boys did a little dumpster diving before we got here, and do you know what they found?"

"I'm *sure* you'll tell me."

"TV dinners--and receipts from an online delivery service," Plogojowitz answered. "Now, what would a vamp want with Salisbury Steak and Fish Sticks, I wonder?"

Despite herself, Cami was very interested. "I want it."

"I know you do," Plogojowitz replied. "But be patient, my love. Business first." He pressed the trunk release.

Flashing him a murderous look, she fished out a pair of vinyl gloves from her glove box and handed them to Sheridan. "Go get it, partner."

"Yeah," Plogojowitz added. "That's a good little blood cow. Do what your mama says."

"Hey!" she snapped. "Go stuff some garlic up your ass." Her eyes had lit up again.

Plogojowitz raised his hands in mock terror. "Whoa! Save the dirty talk for when we're alone, sweetness."

Ignoring Cami's profane reply, Sheridan donned his gloves, and transferred the plastic bag to their car. Exactly as Plogojowitz had advertised, it was filled with empty TV dinner boxes and receipts. Although there was the thin possibility that the food was intended for a daytimer servant and not a kidnaping victim, given everything else, it strongly indicated that their suspect was guilty as hell. He just felt bad for Cami and the price that she had had to pay for it. Plogojowitz was a Class-A scumbag by any standard, Daytimer or Nocturnal.

"It's good stuff," he told her as he got back in.

"What did I tell you, beautiful?" Plogojowitz asked. "I *always* satisfy--as you'll find out." He started his car, and as he began to pull away, he winked suggestively. "Talk to you later."

The moment Plogojowitz and Savanović were gone, Cami's expression completely changed and she burst into laughter.

"What's so funny?" Sheridan asked her.

"That number that I gave him," she said. Struggling to control herself, she tapped her EarPhone and sent him a file. "You'll see. It's *'Jenny'*, from my music folder."

It was only after his earpiece had accepted the incoming file, and he listened to the first minute of the song, that he completely understood--and joined in her laughter. Plogojowitz wouldn't be getting in touch with her any time soon.

"Every girl needs to know a few bogus numbers," she told him. "I would have used the one for a BDSM sex-line, but he would have enjoyed that, and the only other number I know is the Incontinence Helpline. God, I think Plogojowitz gets stupider by the decade."

Still giggling, Cami started the car. "Okay, let's go sit on our house."

She drove to a spot that hid them in the shadows but still afforded a clear line of sight on the front gate. According to the online maps that they'd consulted, it was the only entrance, and although the hedges around the residence were high and obscured most of the house itself, nothing would come in or out of the property without being detected.

While they settled in for their vigil, Cami closed her eyes, and it seemed to Sheridan as if she was trying to sense something. After a few minutes, her eyes reopened and she looked at him.

"She's in there, Joe."

"How do you know that?"

"It's a talent that some vamps have," she explained. "We can reach out and feel for someone that we're looking for, especially if they're close by. She's there. I can hear her thoughts. So is our perp."

Her brows knotted in concern. "Joe, he's getting ready to kill her. He just made up his mind." She was getting out of the car as she said this and jamming a stake into her belt.

"Wait!" Sheridan said. "Aren't we going to call for back-up? This is something that SVAT needs to handle."

Cami considered this and tapped her EarPhone. A moment went by, and her party picked up.

"Captain? This is Cami. Our girl is in the house, and our perp is getting ready to *do* her." She listened to his reply and added. "Sure thing, Cap."

She ended the call and faced Sheridan. "Captain Van Helsing said the same thing that you did, Joe, and he's sending SVAT. But we're not gonna wait. By the time Special Vampires and Tactics gets here, she'll be dead--and I mean *daytimer* dead."

"But--"

Although he knew that it was pure lunacy to go into a situation like this without back-up on scene, he was unbuckling and opening his door. The rules in the LADPD were the same as their Nocturnal counterpart; you never let your partner go it alone. You always backed their play.

She threw him the car keys, drew her pistol and started moving towards the house. "I'll worry about the reprimand later. There's a shotgun in the trunk. Grab it and make yourself useful. It's loaded."

Swearing under his breath, Sheridan opened the trunk and found the weapon. Hefting it, he tried to remember everything that he'd learned on his day at the LANPD range. Fortunately, the shotgun was a simple, no frills model, so its basic operation wasn't an issue.

Just make sure you seat it firmly against your shoulder, the vamp Instructor had advised. *Then point it at whatever you want dead and pull the trigger. It'll do the rest."*

45

He certainly hoped so--and 'Nighttimer dead', or as close as the silver-plated buckshot could manage.

Following Cami down the driveway, he was amazed at how quietly she moved. To his ears, his footsteps sounded loud enough to wake the dead, but she was as silent as the shadows all around them. The only way that he even knew that she was there were the occasional glimpses of her silhouette, and then only for a second. Compared to her, he felt painfully clumsy.

Up ahead of them, the house was dark, nothing more than an outline against the stars and he was just able to make out the side door that Cami had chosen for their entry. She stopped there, and listened.

She's still alive, he heard her think. *He hasn't taken her out yet, but he's working himself up to it.*

What about SVAT?

Back-up's still a few minutes away, she reported. *But we gotta go in now Joe. Ready?*

No, I'm not ready, he replied.

She raised her free hand. *Good. On three. OneTwoThree...*

The fire that he'd seen before in her eyes returned. In response, the door bulged in the middle, snapped in half like a cracker, and flew inwards. It had been blown completely off its hinges.

Why didn't you just kick it in, he asked.

With these boots? she retorted mentally. *Do you know what they cost? Not gonna happen, Joe. Come on, let's go.*

Then she was in motion and he was following. The interior was even darker than the night outside, but somehow, she seemed to know exactly which way to go.

She's straight ahead and down the stairs, she thought. *Can't feel our perp though. He just dropped off the radar. Stay frosty-- he may try to jump us.*

They were in a narrow hallway by this point and headed towards the kitchen. Looking past her, Sheridan spotted the stairway she'd mentioned. The fact that they hadn't made any contact with the kidnapper so far was bothering him, and his instincts began to warn him that something was about to happen.

It did. The wall to his left exploded in a cloud of lathe and plaster, and a dark form slammed into him, knocking him into the opposite wall. At the same time, the shotgun was wrenched from his grip and the vamp rammed the butt end of it into his skull, sending him crashing to the floor and filling his vision with stars.

But he was still able to see Athanasius bring the weapon to bear on Cami, and fire. The buckshot never hit her though. At the last instant, she leapt onto the nearest wall, ran two steps down its length, and sent herself into a flying kick that caught the vamp in the jaw. Athanasius sprawled backwards, letting go of the firearm. It hit the floor, and they came together, snarling and snapping at one another with their fangs.

Sheridan scrambled out of the way, and clawed for the weapon. By the time he had it, the battle had moved down the hall and into the dining room behind him. There was a deafening roar as Cami's pistol discharged, and then he saw it hit the floor and spin in place.

"Joe!" she cried, "I lost my gun. Shoot this freak!"

Sheridan racked another shell and pelted into the room. They were up on the ceiling, and as they fought, he looked for an opportunity to fire, but they were too close together to risk it.

"Cami," he shouted. "Get clear!"

She responded with a backwards somersault that would have been the envy of any Olympic gymnast, and the instant that she was clear, Sheridan pulled the trigger. The recoil made him stagger, but the buckshot hit the vamp squarely between the shoulder blades.

Athanasius screamed in agony and fell, but to Sheridan's astonishment, he spun in mid-air and landed cat-like on his feet, collapsing the dining room table. Then, with a murderous expression, he charged, catching Sheridan in the hips and sending them crashing into a china cabinet. The doors buckled under their combined weight and the sheer violence of the attack. Pieces of antique china, glass, and wood, showered down on them and Sheridan suddenly found himself pinned and using all of his strength to keep the creature's fangs from ripping his throat open.

Cami came to his rescue. She dropped to the floor, snatched up a heavy candelabrum, and slammed the butt end of it into the vamp's head like a medieval battle mace. It hit with a dull thud, and sent him sprawling sideways. Had he been a daytimer, the blow would have been enough to kill him, but since he wasn't, it only managed to stun Athanasius long enough for Sheridan to extricate himself and gain some badly needed distance.

It also gave Cami the chance to recover her pistol and point it at him. "Freeze sucker!"

Athanasius raised his hands in surrender, but he had a savage grin on his face and a dangerous, desperate gleam in his eyes.

He was going to try something. Sheridan was sure of it. He'd seen enough suspects make the decision to go down fighting not to recognize the signs.

Cami saw the same thing, and thumbed the hammer back. "Go ahead," she said to him in a low voice. "Make my day."

The vamp made his move. With a roar, he threw himself at her.

She fired three times in rapid succession. The vamp jerked as the rounds slammed into his chest, and toppled backwards.

Holstering her weapon, Cami leapt on top of him and took the stake from her belt. "You have the right to remain silent," she said, raising it above her head.

Then she brought it down with all her might. "Anything you say can and will be used against you in a court of law." It pierced Athanasius's chest with a wet crunching sound and a spray of dark red blood.

Ignoring the shower of gore, she slammed her fist into the butt end, driving it halfway in. "You have the right to an attorney."

48

Athanasius grunted, and reached out for her in a feeble attempt to ward off the assault, but Cami batted his arms aside and struck again. "If you cannot afford an attorney, one will be appointed for you."

He convulsed as she dealt the stake a fourth and final blow. "Do you understand these rights as I have just explained them to you?" This time, it went all the way through and embedded itself in the floor. The vamp's body went limp.

"With these rights in mind, do you wish to speak to me now?" she finished. *"Hmmm?* I guess not."

Wiping off some of the blood from her face, she looked over at Sheridan. "You okay, partner?"

He nodded. "Is he dead?"

She shook her head and rose. "Nah, just staked. He'll stay there until we're ready to move him." Her eyes flicked to the kitchen and the staircase beyond. "Come on, let's go get our girl."

The reinforced door at the bottom of the stair didn't prove to be much of a challenge. Cami simply pulled on it and the heavy bolt was wrenched out of the wall.

"Rayven?" she said as she entered the young woman's cell, "The cavalry's here. Time to leave."

Another tug separated the handcuffs from the pipe, and then they were hustling Rayven back up into the kitchen. Seeing Athanasius's prostrate form, the girl paused for a moment.

"Don't look," Sheridan urged.

"No," Rayven said. "I want to see him." For a moment, it seemed as if she was going to spit on Athanasius, or visit some other form of humiliation upon him, but then she allowed them to guide her away.

Once outside, they made straight for the car.

"What now?" Sheridan asked as the Camaro came into view. He was certain that at any moment, their LANPD back-up would be arriving to take their suspect into custody.

Cami stopped, and looked back over her shoulder at a woodpile along the side of the house. Rayven followed her gaze. A bright orange chainsaw sat there, propped up against the logs.

"Now we finish things. Right Rayven?"

Rayven went over and picked up the tool. She brought it roaring to life with a single pull of the starter cord.

"What the hell?" Sheridan demanded, starting to move towards her. But Cami stopped him. "Let her go. This needs to be done. She knows that."

Saying nothing, Rayven turned and went back into the house. A few seconds later, they heard the sound of the saw doing its work, accompanied by unearthly shrieks of agony.

"Sweet Jesus!" Sheridan exclaimed, suddenly putting it all together. Smiling through the whole thing, Cami's grip tightened on him like a vice, holding him in place.

At last, the screams died away and Rayven rejoined them. Both she and the chainsaw were drenched in blood. "He's still alive," she informed them hollowly.

"I know," Cami acknowledged. "We'll have somebody come by and burn the pieces." She let go of Sheridan as she said this, and he pushed past them and went back inside.

When he came out again, he was pale, and fighting the urge to vomit. Athanasius was nothing but chunks of bloody meat now. Chunks that somehow, still managed to squirm around on the floor in a futile effort to find one another, and become whole again.

"It had to be done, Sheridan," Cami said calmly. "We have our own laws. If she hadn't done it, I would have. This is how we handle rogue vamps."

As he struggled with this, she walked over to Rayven and took the chainsaw away from her. Tossing it out onto the lawn, Cami looked her in the eye.

"So, what about it?" she challenged. "Do you still love the night like you said you did in your journal? Or did that *fuck* change your mind? 'Cause if you do, I can make it last forever, right here and right now. *Well?* Do you want to leave the daytimers behind, and join us in the moonlight?"

Rayven gazed back at the house for a long moment before she closed her eyes, brushed her hair back, and exposed her neck. "Yes," she whispered. "Do it."

Cami put her arms around her and gathered her in. "Welcome, sister."

To her credit, when she was bitten, Rayven grimaced, but she didn't cry out, and as shocked as he was by everything else that had happened, Sheridan had to admire her grit. She was one tough kid, he decided, and Cami was right. She would make a damn good vamp.

Rayven's knees buckled, and Cami stepped back and lowered her to the grass so that she could sit. "You're gonna feel real bad for a while," she told her softly, "and it's gonna get worse. It's gonna feel like the nastiest fever you've ever had, mixed up with the hangover from Hell. But I'll be there with you through the whole thing, I promise you. You'll never be alone ever again, Rayven. *Ever.*"

She looked up at Sheridan, wiping away the girl's blood from her lips. "So what about you, Joe? I wouldn't mind keeping you around as a partner. I think we make a damn good team. Wanna live forever?"

Sheridan shook his head. "No, Cami. The night life's not for me. I'm a confirmed daytimer. I know that."

Before he realized it, she'd moved, and he felt a small, sharp pain on his scalp. When she was standing still again, she was holding up something for him to see. It was a single piece of hair. Even in the uncertain light, he could tell that it was grey.

"You'll change your mind when you start feeling old, Joe," she said, tucking it into his shirt pocket and giving it a gentle little pat. "When you do, you'll know where to reach me."

The pheromones that she was giving off right then were stronger than ever, and despite himself, Sheridan was as hard as a rock. The primitive, animal part of his brain wanted her and what she was proposing more than anything he had ever desired. Only the fact that he knew what was happening, and why, is what prevented him from accepting her offer.

Off in the distance, he could hear cars coming, and through the trees, he spotted the blue lights of LANPD patrol units entering the drive. At the same time, he detected the soft sound of wings flapping overhead as a vamp air unit arrived and took up station. Backup had finally arrived.

Cami wasn't paying attention to any of this though. She was smiling at him.

They both knew the same thing. For her and for Rayven, the night would last forever. For him, the sun would rise, but he would greet the dawn with that grey hair in his pocket, and a lot to think about.

The Reconquista

To my friends in the valley. Thank you for showing me patience.

The pack had been hunting all night. They were a small band, only three individuals, and their leader stopped when the snarl of a truck, making its way down Arizona 82, pierced the desert air. When he was satisfied that the machine was moving away from them, he started forwards again. His companions followed.

Just an hour earlier, they had bagged a rabbit, but it was hardly enough to fill their bellies. They needed more food.

The leader scanned the landscape, searching for other prey, and also for any sign that humans might be anywhere nearer than the highway. Men were their only real enemy, and the thin strip of pavement that slashed through the parched landscape could mean death if they came too close to it. The huge machines that roamed its surface moved much faster than any wolf could run, and sometimes, the humans riding inside of them carried guns. For the moment at least, they were well away from any such dangers, and the hunt could go on.

The arrival of a newcomer startled them. The ground ahead had been clear just a moment earlier, but as they watched, the air over it shimmered like it did on a hot day, and then a shadowy form materialized. It was blurry and indistinct at first, and they could see right through it to the mountains in the distance. Then it resolved itself, sharpened, and became opaque.

It was another wolf.

The leader laid his ears back and growled a warning at the interloper, trying to lend as much confidence as he could to the sound. She was much larger than any wolf he had ever seen, more than twice his size, with a huge, flat head and glowing amber eyes that were offset by jet black fur. He didn't know it, but he was looking at something that had not called this desert its home in over 10,000 years. She was one of the great dire wolves that his ancestors had descended from. But, he was absolutely sure of one thing; if it came to a fight, it would not go well for him.

The stranger answered his challenge with one of her own. It was an impossibly deep rumble that spoke of tremendous power and an utter refusal to give ground. Then he caught her scent, and a deep, primeval part of his consciousness registered what she was at last.

She was the leader here. Her kind always had been. Without hesitation, he lowered himself to the ground in submission, and when she padded up to him, he rolled over and exposed himself. The dire wolves' gigantic jaws closed lightly on his throat, and once again, she growled, emphasizing her dominance over him and his pack mates.

When she was satisfied that he understood the proper order of things, she released him and backed up a pace. Her body shimmered once again, compressing and elongating into a new shape. Now, what looked outwardly like a human woman stood before them.

She seemed like any of the brown-skinned ones who regularly travelled across the desert from the lands to the south. But her scent told the pack an entirely different story, reassuring them that despite appearances, she was still the great wolf, and their new alpha.

Juana turned her back on her companions and gazed out across the desert to the point where Arizona 82 met with 80. Her eyes narrowed in displeasure at the sight of the US Border Patrol station and its brilliant lights.

The tales that she had heard when she was a young cub came back to her at the sight. Once, The People had roamed freely between the First and Second Worlds, she recalled. They had hunted where they willed, taking any shape that they desired, and when the first human copper-skins had come, they had worshipped The People as Gods.

In return, The People had blessed some of them with their blood, intermarrying, and creating hybrids. Even now, the

54

distant offspring of those primordial unions, the skin-walkers, still lived in the First World, ignorant of their true heritage, and the debt that they owed to The People.

This great, golden age had ended when the white-skins had arrived from the east. Greedy for wealth, they had come with their Churchmen, and their deadly silver. They had driven The People from the First World and forced the copper-skins into submission.

All of that was going to change. In their arrogance, the white-skins had become weak, and after years of enduring shameful exile, The People were returning to take back what had been theirs for millennia. Already, groups of Scouts had been sent through the thin barrier that separated their two dimensions, and what they had reported seemed promising.

Now it was Juana's turn to infiltrate the lands of their usurpers, and she was still confused over her selection for this task. She was no dissembler or spy like the Scouts. She was a warrior, and the only way that she knew was direct action and combat. But as incomprehensible as her assignment was, she could not argue with the Elder's decision; what they willed for the pack, was law.

Carefully, she took a count of the humans that she saw at the station, and liked the results. Thanks to the recent war between the white skins and the yellow ones, the number of patrolmen had been dramatically reduced, and something that the humans called a 'tank' sat there guarding the intersection.

Juana was unconcerned by its presence. She knew that such machines were only as strong as their owners. When the time came, pulling them out of their metal fortress would be like prising a desert tortoise from its shell. Difficult, but hardly impossible.

Putting the war engine out of her mind, she looked further east, to where the town of Tombstone, Arizona lay, and sniffed at the night air. The odor of chemical pollutants was obvious even at this distance. In their tenancy, the white-skins had contaminated the land with their infernal machines.

Her skin also tingled with another by-product of the white-skins. Not strongly, but enough for her to notice. The Scouts had called it 'radiation' and it was the result of the white-skins war. Further north, they said that it had reached lethal levels, and that the prevailing winds had kept it from this region.

Like the 'tank', this mattered little to her. Even if the winds had shifted, The People knew from what their spies had discovered, that their kind was not affected by this invisible poison. Only one thing in the First World was truly lethal to them, and Juana searched for it with her senses. Despite what she had heard, she had to know the truth for herself.

When she failed to locate it, her heart leapt in joy. The silver, the deadly killing silver, was mostly gone. A few faint traces of the toxic substance remained, but they were negligible.

The mines had indeed 'played out'. Tombstone, once the center of silver mining in the region, and the very symbol of all that had prevented The People's return, was nothing but an empty skeleton now, picked clean of its meat by the vultures of time and fortune.

This left her with one final concern. The Churchmen. They had been the ones who had led the white-skins against The People, and they had taught them to use the silver as a weapon. According to the Scouts, the Churchmen still polluted the area with their presence, but their numbers had become small, and few of the humans still listened to them. By all accounts, they and the rest of the white-skins, had forgotten their past. And their crimes.

The land seemed ripe for the taking and the desire for revenge rose in her breast like a white hot flame. Juana was tempted to give into it and make straight for the Border Patrol station to challenge the soldiers.

But she still had her mission to complete. Later, she promised herself, when the time was right, she would go down there with her fellow warriors, and take care of them and their stupid little 'tank'.

She shifted back into her dire-wolf form and began to move towards the town. Her new pack trailed behind her, keeping a respectful distance.

The term that the brown-skins used, came back to her as she loped along. They too had been displaced by the whites, and they had called their bid to recover what had been stolen from them the *Reconquista*. The Reconquest. She liked the sound of it…

…Frank Havner had lived in Tombstone for years, and he'd seen his share of strange things. Like the time he'd spotted a huge hairy figure—a Bigfoot--crossing Orante road in the middle of the night. Or the weird lights that sometimes appeared over the mountains near Bisbee.

Nobody had ever believed him though. They'd called him a drunk, or just another 'Tombstone bum'. That didn't change the fact that he'd seen what he'd seen.

There were wolves prowling around Tombstone now. Not coyotes, or dog-coyote mixes like some suggested, but *real* wolves. And big ones at that. The fact that the Mexican gray wolf hadn't been spotted in the area for decades didn't matter to Frank. They were there, and if people were too stupid to listen to him, then they would get what they deserved. He was going to be prepared.

That was one of the reasons why, when he'd hitched a ride from his cousin into town, he'd brought his gun along. As long as the .357 was in a holster, where it could be seen, it was perfectly legal, and even the Marshal couldn't tell him what to do with it. Frank didn't like anyone telling him what to do. Even the Marshal.

He also wasn't the only one carrying. His cousin had brought his own weapon along, and lately most of the people that Frank knew had taken to doing the same thing—even if they still ignored his stories. None of them had been able to overlook the war with the Chinese, or the infiltrators that had slipped in from the south with the illegals. Frank had seen all of this coming, and long before anyone else.

He'd also predicted that the United States would lose, sold out by the commies in Washington. Thanks to their cowardice and a fleet of submarines that nobody knew the Chinese had built, the entire Pacific Fleet was gone, most of the big cities on the West Coast had been nuked and the East wasn't doing much better.

The only thing that had saved *"The Town Too Tough to Die"* from finally meeting its Maker had been the closure of Fort Huachuca a few years earlier, for budgetary reasons. If the US Army Intelligence Center had still been there, the whole area would have been turned into a lake of radioactive glass. It was the only thing that Washington had ever done right for Arizona, he reflected—even if it hadn't felt that way at the time.

And if all of this wasn't bad enough, something else was getting ready to happen. Frank could feel it in his bones, and smell it on the air, mixed in with the dust and sage. With the Mexican border as close as it was, southeastern Arizona had always been a troubled region, and now it seemed like a new danger was coming their way, gathering itself up like a storm in the mountains. His money was on the Chinese reneging on the treaty that they'd just signed, but even that didn't feel quite right. Deep down in his gut, he knew that whatever it was, was much worse, but his mind couldn't give it any kind of coherent shape.

As he walked away from his cousin's pickup towards the Circle K, he gazed furtively out across the desert in the direction of the border. It was dark out there, and something about that darkness made a shiver run up his spine. Like he was being watched. Patting his pistol to reassure himself that it was still on his hip, he entered the brightly lit convenience store.

The night clerk gave him a smile, and he nodded back, trying to seem cheerful despite the headlines on the newspaper rack. Frank had never learned to read, but this didn't prevent him from knowing what they said. His cousin had read them for him on their last visit.

"President Signs Peace Treaty with China!" they declared, and, *"China Pledges Not to Invade US Soil"*. The fact that the store manager had updated some of the signs with what Frank strongly suspected were Chinese characters, didn't brighten his mood one bit. America had never lost a war before, and now that it had, it made the whole world seem wrong. Broken.

Hoping that some sherbet would banish his gloom, he made his way over to the frozen section. But a sixth sense caused him to stop and look back over his shoulder, out the store windows, and into the night. A woman was walking up the highway, coming towards them.

Or more precisely, a Mexican woman. He could tell just by looking at her that she was an illegal. He'd seen plenty like her in his time. Her tennis shoes were cheap and worn, and the thin jacket that she was wearing was just as shabby. The small backpack that she carried on her shoulder had also seen a lot of miles, and she had a hungry look to her that came from a hard life and the long journey that she had made there on foot.

The only thing that didn't add up were her eyes. These were a strange light amber, and they stood out in stark contrast to her dark skin and blue-black hair. He didn't like the way that they looked. They seemed to see through everything, like some of the vets that he'd known with their weird thousand yard stares.

She entered a moment later, and the night clerk started watching her as well. Frank didn't blame the clerk one bit. If you didn't keep a sharp eye on these illegals, they would steal a place blind.

And this one looked particularly suspicious to him. Just by the way that she began to wander the aisles, he was beginning to think that she was on something, or maybe even a little light in the head...

...Juana was confused by all the brightly colored packages on display. She could smell some of the food inside of them, and every scent was something foreign to her. She was also aware that the humans were watching her, but she didn't care. She had been drawn to the place by its bright lights, and once she had come inside, she had realized that she was ravenously hungry.

Finally, her nose caught something enticingly sweet coming from one of the packages, and she picked it up, inspecting its scent more closely. Then she opened it, and discovered that it was meat, with some kind of substance sweetening it. Something called "Teriyaki"—whatever that was.

Experimentally, she took a bite, finding it drier than she had expected, but not altogether unsatisfying. It was cooked, but it was still good.

She ate some more. In the meantime, the white-skinned male was still observing her, and she suppressed an urge to snarl a warning at him, and took her meal with her instead. She didn't like being looked at while she was eating, and she would finish her food outside, away from his unpleasant gaze. Besides, he smelled bad, even for a human.

She was almost to the door when the female white-skin yelled at her. "Miss? Where are you going? You have to *pay* for that!"

Frank came up and laid a meaty paw on her shoulder. "Hey! You better stay here and--," he started to say. At the same time, a car was pulling up outside, and the illumination from its headlights reflected in Juana's eyes. Just like it would have with any wolf.

Frank went pale. "Jeezus--what the hell is wrong with your eyes, lady?"

Juana spun around, and half shifted into her wolf form. Her amber eyes transformed into hellish yellow coals and fangs sprouted in her mouth like ivory scimitars. She bared them at him in a challenge.

Horrified, Frank tried to let her go, but she had taken hold of his arm and her claws were biting deeply into his flesh. Mewling in desperation and terror, he fumbled for the gun on his hip with his free hand, and finally managed to draw it.

It went off with a roar, and Juana flinched involuntarily. But the round passed through her chest harmlessly, burying itself in a drink dispenser.

The bullet had not been made of silver, she realized. It was nothing but useless lead! Letting out a ferocious roar of triumph, she tightened her grip on Franks' arm and pulled.

Juana had never been terribly strong—not by the standards of The People at least—but she was still strong enough compared to a human. Frank's arm came out of its socket with a wet, tearing sound and a flat 'pop'.

He shrieked in agony, but Juana paid this no attention. The blood fever was upon her and she lunged at him, tearing out his throat with her fangs. As his lifeblood spattered over her in a crimson rain, she bit in deeply, and when she found his spine with her teeth, she snapped it apart with a savage jerk of her head. Frank's body dropped to the linoleum, his head only attached to the rest of him by the few threads of muscle that had managed to remain intact.

Then the clerk's screams registered in Juana's ears; wild ululations of absolute, incoherent terror. Seizing up the severed arm, she jumped over the counter and began to beat her with it.

Finally, the wailing stopped, and so did the woman's breathing. That was when Juana recovered enough of herself to remember what had caused the entire incident. The car that had pulled in was still outside and another one had just joined it. She could hear their engines running.

Dropping her improvised club, Juana strode to the door, grasped it by the handle and wrenched it from its hinges. Throwing it away from her into the night, she was outside in two steps and facing the machines and their occupants, fully intent on killing them all.

The closest vehicle bore the distinctive green stripe of a Border Patrol unit, and the human inside was speaking frantically into something in his hand. Juana assumed her full wolf form and sprang onto the hood, her weight and the sheer force of her jump leaving deep dents in the thin metal. Before the man could react, she shoved her huge muzzle straight through the windshield and seized his head in her jaws. Then she pulled him out through the jagged hole and gave his body a violent shake.

Knowing that he was dead, she tossed the broken corpse away from her. It sailed through the air, smashing through the windows of the store and into a rack of potato chips, scattering their contents everywhere.

But Juana was already wheeling around to face the people in the other car. What she saw, made her hesitate.

Instead of encountering more white-skins, it was a trio of copper ones; a grown male, a woman who she presumed was his mate, and their cub. The female was cowering inside the car with the child, and the man was standing near the back, with the nozzle of the pump lying at his feet.

When their eyes met, he took off his hat and meekly lowered his gaze to the cement. Then he spoke to her, and as was the way of The People, Juana understood him from the shape of the thoughts in his mind.

"We are very sorry, sister wolf," he said in the ancient *O'odham* language, "for trespassing in your hunting grounds. Allow us to leave in peace and we swear that we shall never return."

Juana's eyes widened in astonishment. This copper-skinned human had manners, she realized! Just like the Elders had said they did. He still knew enough to show proper respect to a warrior of The People, and he had even acknowledged The People's rightful claim to the land.

She decided to show him, and his little pack, mercy. But when his mate started to make the sign of the Churchmen on her breast, Juana nearly reversed herself.

62

The female stopped when she saw the direction of Juana's gaze—and demonstrated not only wisdom, but propriety. Had she completed her cross, she would have condemned her family as followers of the Churchmen, and liars. Dead liars.

Willing herself back into her human disguise, Juana regarded the male again and gestured towards the highway. Understanding her meaning, and the reprieve that they had just been granted, the male nodded back to her with a cautious gratitude. Then he got into his car and left, tires squealing.

As she watched the taillights recede into the darkness, Juana had no doubt that he would keep his promise. His shadow, and those of his little pack, would never darken this part of the desert again.

Perhaps there was hope for some of these humans after all, she mused. Perhaps not. Whatever the case proved to be, everything would get sorted out after the *Reconquista*.

In the meantime, there were new lights flashing in the distance, coming from the Border Patrol station. As much as she dearly wanted to remain and give them the battle that they sought, she knew that the time had come for her to leave. She also understood at last why she had been sent on this mission. The Elders, in their wisdom, had known that she would find a reason to fight—in fact, they had counted on it.

Now, because of her actions, they could be absolutely certain that nothing could stand against them. This, she realized, had been the final scouting mission, a reconnaissance by combat. Something that only a warrior could ever have accomplished.

Remembering her hunger, and her debt to her pack, she went back inside to retrieve the severed arm. Then, prize in hand, she made for the desert...

...Frank Havner had been right after all, even if he wasn't alive to enjoy the fact. Two days later, a People's Liberation Army armored infantry column reached Tombstone at three in the morning. They had come in over the border at Nogales, and after a brief firefight with a few poorly organized American units, they had pushed hard for Highway 80.

When they came within range of the Border Patrol station, their commander had his unit deploy into a line of battle, and he surveyed the scene. Just as his reconnaissance units had reported, there was American armor there—or what was left of it. Adjusting his NVG glasses, he saw what they had seen. The tanks had been peeled open like cheap tin cans and there were marks all over their hulls suggesting that something had clawed its way in.

This was impossible of course, and Commander Yeung decided that the real cause had been some kind of new anti-tank weapon, wielded by a renegade faction of the Arizona National Guard. With the Chinese invasion, a lot of local units were defecting, or shooting at each other by mistake.

Whatever the source had been, the tanks were out of action and the road was theirs. That was what mattered.

Yeung radioed to his subordinates to fall back into line and advance. They would move into the small town of Tombstone, where he would establish his headquarters. He also intended to locate his Recon Unit and get an explanation from them for their failure to maintain contact. They had been off the radio for 24 hours. Such a thing was inexcusable, and he wanted to know why they had committed such a serious breach of discipline.

Five minutes later, the town came into view and Yeung was surprised by the sight that greeted him. His advance party and their Type 86 fighting vehicle were parked at a convenience store that called itself the "Circle K". A patrol car, belonging to the local law enforcement agency was also there, and an American in a cowboy hat was standing with his men. They were all waving at the column. There were also civilians with them, and despite the late hour, Yeung saw women and children in the crowd. It was as if the entire town had left their beds to rise and greet their new masters.

Sending another order to spread out and approach with caution, Yeung waved for the column to move forwards. No ambush occurred however, and as his command vehicle came to a halt, the American came forwards, sketching a salute against the brim of his hat with his fingers. A woman had joined him by this point—a Mexican by the look of her, but with strange amber eyes. Both of them smiled up at him, and for some reason Yeung found this disturbing.

"Howdy, Commander," the Marshal said. "Pleased to meet you. Your boys told us a lot about you when they got here. Did you know that Tombstone once had the finest Chinese restaurant west of the Mississippi?"

Commander Yeung shook his head, already tiring of the conversation and eager to speak with his reconnaissance force.

"Well it did. And now that you folks are here, we aim to rectify that problem." As the Marshal said this, the townspeople began to close in around the column. "The People will come from miles around to eat Chinese. You'll see."

That was when Commander Yeung realized several things all at once. The first was that the illumination, cast by a spotlight mounted on one of his armored personnel carriers, had been reflected in the Marshals' eyes. Just like it had with the wolves from his childhood in the remote Heilongjiang Province, on the Russian border.

The second thing was that the Marshal had been speaking to him in perfect, unaccented Mandarin.

And the third was that the townspeople were clambering up onto the vehicles, led by his strange female companion. To the last, they were all smiling, but there was hunger in their yellow eyes. They were also growling, deep in their throats.

These were the last conscious thoughts that he would ever have.

After just a few minutes, it was all over, and The People returned to their new homes to await the rest of their kind. Off in the distance, a storm was gathering over the Dragoons. Soon, it, and The People, would engulf the entire region.

The 13th Hour: A Tale of the Plague

Interviewer: "Thank you for joining us today for this exciting segment of 'Focus on History'. For those who have just joined us, I'm speaking with Ms. Hera n'Lynn, and Dr. Lyysa t'Marnia.'

"Ms. n'Lynn is a direct descendant of Lena Calidrayth, author of the controversial book *'Where the Blue Flowers Grow'*, and Dr. t'Marnia is a member of the University of Thermadon's Pre-Sisterhood Department of Literature, and also the author of *"Famous Books of the Early Sisterhood: An Examination"*. Together, they are here to give us some insight into Calidrayth's life and times, and to share them with us in the author's own words. Hera, did any of your relatives ever talk to you about Lena Calidrayth, or the MARS Plague?"

N'Lynn: "Yes, they did. My great-great-grandmother told them to my great-grandmother and she shared them with my grandmother and my mothers, and they passed them down to me."

Interviewer: "What did they tell you?"

N'Lynn: "One thing was that in Lena's time, Essylt wasn't as big as it is nowadays. The towns back then were a lot smaller, and there were fewer people--and of course, everybody knew each other--or at least that's how the stories went. They also read to me from Lena's diary and when I was old enough, they passed it down to me. It talks about how things happened once the Plague reached her world, day-by-day, and apparently, it was what she used to help her write *'Blue Flowers.'*"

Interviewer: "That's fascinating! I also understand that you have published the diary, under the title: *'The Last Watchwoman: the Diary of Lena Calidrayth.'* Isn't that so?"

N'Lynn: "Yes, with the help of the University of Thermadon Press. They were great. I'm no writer and their editorial staff helped me put it together and get it out there so that other women could read it."

Interviewer: "I know that our audience would love to hear some excerpts. But before we begin, my network's Advocates require me to make a statement on behalf of our Network. May I do so?"

N'Lynn: "Certainly."

Interviewer: "I must warn our viewers that the material that they are about to hear comes before the advent of Motherthought, during a very primitive and unenlightened period in women's history. Some viewers might find portions of it to be offensive.'

"Parents should also be warned that this is not material which is considered suitable for younger viewers, and should they decide to allow their underage daughters to view it, that none of it represents the views of SNN or its affiliates, and that SNN takes no responsibility for its contents, or from any damages that might arise. With all that said, let's get started, shall we?"

N'Lynn: "Yes, let's. And as you just mentioned, the material in the diary is quite backwards, but it's still very worthwhile from a historical point of view. With the help of my friends at the University, I managed to pick out several parts that are worth sharing today. The first one actually dates back to a few days before the Plague. Shall I read that to you?"

Interviewer: "Please. It should be fascinating!"

N'Lynn: "*'14 November, 2445: They had me on patrol over in Talyswood tonight. Very slow--no calls. And it's the end of the shift, so I'm taking the time to catch up on my entries. The Sergeant said that I have a good chance to make Corporal if I do well in my orals. I've studied like crazy, but I'm still pretty nervous...*"

...Lena Calidrayth put down her pen and looked out over the open farmland spreading away from her windshield, and out into the hazy distance. She was parked in her favorite spot, the overlook at McAyvers Peak. This was the highest point in the area, and it commanded a breathtaking view the towns and farms of the Crystalwood and Evenfar districts. Except for a few groves of trees here and there, the occasional farm house or barn, and the crumbling Drow'voi spires at the very edge of the horizon, there was nothing between her and the dawn but long grass and the beautiful blue flowers that were native to the region. It was a lovely spot and she always came there when she needed to reenergize and reorganize herself. This was certainly such a time.

She'd been cramming for her Corporal's exam, putting in hours that should have been spent sleeping, and it still didn't seem like she'd studied enough. Spending time on her personal diary certainly wasn't helping her cause at all, but like coming to this place, it had been something she had done since she was a little girl. With all the stress that she was under, she needed the comfort that writing down her thoughts always gave her.

She reopened the little book and had just managed to finish her last sentence when a call came in over the cruiser's Com. "14-A-6."

"14-A-6, go ahead."

"14-A-6, respond to the spaceport for a report of a hit and run, property damage only, suspect GOA. Meet the woman, parking lot 9, row Baker."

"On my way." Now that sounds like an exciting call, Lena thought sarcastically. There was nothing like a routine accident report to get the blood pumping. Police work, it had turned out, was not what she had imagined it to be when she had joined the force. Despite the fact that Third Shift tended to have the most action of all the shifts, the majority of her time had actually been spent stopping drunks, breaking up fights at the spacer's bars, or running stupid little routine calls just like this one. With a reluctant sigh, she put her diary away, started up the 'lectricar and headed for the port.

When she reached it, the complaining party was easy enough

to find. Lot 9 was almost empty, and by some stroke of incredible bad luck, the woman's car had been hit when it had been sitting all by itself right in the middle of the lot. A trail of glittering plastic clearly showed that whoever had done the damage had driven off. And naturally, the owner was irate and demanding swift and terrible justice.

"Ma'am," Lena told her patiently, "I have already explained this to you: we'll let our units know that someone hit you, and we'll keep an eye out for anyone with new damage to their 'lectri. That's the best we can do. If you want a report for your insurance company, just reference the number that I gave you."

"So, you're not going to check the other lots and see if they're still around?" the woman challenged, incredulous.

"Yes, I will. But I seriously doubt they're still in the area," she answered. She printed out the flimsy for the woman and handed it to her. "You'll need the number on this for your report. Have a better day."

Then she got back in her cruiser and did as she had promised, taking the time to check out a few of the nearby lots. There were a couple of 'lectris that had new damage, but without a witness to tie any of them to the other car, none of the vehicles could be definitively linked to the hit and run.

One of these cars had passengers in it, and she let Dispatch know where she was, and that she was getting out of her vehicle to speak with them. Then she lit the 'lectri up with her red and blues and walked up to a point just behind the driver's window, unsnapping the holster of her lazegun as she did so. By the jumpsuits that they wore, and the patches on their shoulders, she immediately identified the two men as crewmembers of one of the visiting merchant ships. A lot of crews left their 'lectris in the spaceports lots when they went on a voyage.

"Morning," she said to them. "You two been here very long?"

"No Officer," the driver answered. "We just got in on the *Mirabelle* about 20 minutes ago and..." He stopped midsentence, and coughed. It was an evil wet-sounding thing, and she hoped that whatever he had wasn't contagious. Spacers often caught the flu when they came to a new world that their bodies hadn't acclimatized to, but there were also cases where they brought something down with them. A ship's medstaff was supposed to catch that kind of thing, but sometimes 'bugs' got through and everyone downside suffered right along with the new arrivals. Lena earnestly hoped that this wasn't the case here. She didn't need to get sick right before her exam.

She waited until the spacer got himself under control before continuing. "I'm just checking on an accident. Did either of you see anyone hit a car in the next lot?"

"No ma'am," the man replied. More coughing followed this. "Like I said, we just got in. We're on our way to visit our families in Altaria." Then he handed her his identification. His partner did the same, and although he wasn't coughing, to her eye at least, he didn't look very well either.

She swiped the cards through her data pad and when no 'wants' or 'warrants' came back, returned them, privately making a note to herself to liberally wash her hands in some sanitizer the microsecond that the opportunity presented itself.

"Thanks," she said. "You guys have a good day. And maybe see someone about that cough, okay? We have a good hospital just up the highway. Wouldn't do to bring something back to your kids."

The driver nodded in agreement, and she left them. Neither of them knew it, but he would be dead by the end of the day, and his partner by the dawn of the next.

Time had run out for Esyllt.

***

The next week began early for Lena. A half dozen of the male patrolmen on Second Shift had called off sick, and the Watch Commander had begged-slash-pleaded-slash-ordered her to come in and help cover their areas, adding another four hours on top of the eight that she was already expected to work. It was another 'perk' that came not only with police work in general, but for anyone bucking for promotion. Something had been making the rounds in the last week, and a lot of people that she knew seemed to be coming down with it.

'At least *I* haven't gotten sick,' she thought, recalling the two spacers at the port. It didn't take a detective to realize that it had probably arrived with the *Mirabelle*, and she decided that if the great Gods of Dispatch allowed it, she was going to go over to the hospital and share this information with the staff. They probably already knew about it, but she wanted to cover all the bases. And also get a shot of something for herself--if they even had anything for it. The problem was that a lot of bugs didn't have any cure other than rest and chicken soup, and she was afraid that this might prove to be the case with this one.

When she reached the Hospital, she was surprised at how many 'lectris were in the lot, and how busy the ER looked. It took her a few minutes before she was able to speak with Dr. Jannahan, the senior most physician on duty. The woman looked just as tired as Lena herself felt.

"Afternoon doc," she said. "You look busier than we are today. More people coming down with the bug?"

Jannahan brushed a stray lock of hair from her face and smiled raggedly at her. "You could say that. I don't know what it is, but it seems to've hit us hard this time around. We're also short staffed. A lot of the doctors have called off. But those are my problems. What can I do for you, Officer?"

"I just wanted to drop by and let you know that I think that it may have come in with some spacers that landed here last week, from the *CSS Mirabelle*. Both men looked pretty sick. I told them to drop by here and get themselves looked at."

"Both *men*--"the doctor replied, stroking her chin pensively. "Yes, that makes sense. This bug is a lot different than most. It only seems to affect male patients."

72

That was when Lena realized that all the patients in the ER, except for a few 'routine cases' were male, just like the doctor had said. And also, that there were very few, if any, male staff on duty to attend to their needs. A sudden chill went up her spine. She certainly wasn't any doctor like Jannahan, but she knew instinctively that what they were dealing with wasn't 'just another bug.' It was something a lot worse.

"Well, I hope my information helped," she said, masking her anxiety with a calm, relaxed facade. "Let us know if we can do anything for you."

"Will do."

***

There was more bad news waiting for her when she returned to the station to report in for Third Shift Roll Call. The Third Shift Lieutenant and most of the men for Third had all called in, and the Captain had also fallen ill and gone home early. Call-offs had been getting steadily worse over the last few days, but this was a brand new low.

Now there would only be a skeleton crew left to handle everything--a crew that would be composed mainly of the Department's female officers. With the Lieutenant out of action, it also suddenly fell to Sergeant Tarranne Cartwright to conduct the night's pre-patrol briefing. And until she could get the Chief to answer his home phone, she wasn't just in charge of the briefing, or the shift. She was also the highest-ranking officer in the Altaria Police Department.

Cartwright gathered everyone in the squad room. Third wasn't the largest of the shifts, but Lena couldn't help but notice that there were a lot more empty seats around her than normal. Walta Jonson and Corporal Jon Mayfield were there, just as she had expected, but Jonson looked like death warmed over, and Mayfield wasn't exactly what she would have called a poster-boy for perfect physical fitness. Harri Peterson, another Third Shift regular, was missing, and so were a number of others.

73

The Sergeant got down to business right away. "Okay, I know that staffing is on everyone's mind, so I'll get to that first. A few guys agreed to come in to help cover Day Shift, but I had most of them stay home because they sounded too shitty to be much good for anything. And Peterson wanted to come in for his shift tonight, but I told him the same thing. So, that leaves us."

"Calidrayth, you've got Tammerlane and Amberway. And Montrose, you have Goldgrove and Eventide. Jonson, you have Wednesburgh. Mayfield, you have Daynian.'

Both men nodded, and then Mayfield was overtaken by a violent fit of coughing. It was obvious to everyone, including Lena, that he was in no shape to work. "Damn it, Mayfield!" Cartwright exclaimed, "I don't need this shit! Get your sick ass out of my squad room, and get your butt in bed. For fucks sake!"

"No, it's okay Sarge," Mayfield protested between more coughing. "I can do the shift."

"Bullshit! Go home, Mayfield. We'll manage without you." Sheepishly, Mayfield nodded and left the room. This left only the three women and Corporal Jonson.

"Okay," Cartwright said. "Same as before, but Calidrayth you get Tammerlane, Amberway, and Wednesburgh. And Montrose you get Daynian added to your watch. Jonson, you still have what you have, but I want you to help out in Wednesburgh and Daynian."

"Now, if there aren't any *more* interruptions, I need to let you know that after I tried the Chief tonight, I also called the State Police, and asked them if they had some spare bodies they could farm out to us. They said that they'll try to help out, but they're in the same situation that we are. They're short on officers.'

"So, until they get back with us, or some of our own people get over this bug and get back to work, it's just us. You'll have to listen for each other and back each other up. I'll also be roving between your zones. I'm not sure when we'll get relieved, so its coffee for dinner--on me. Aren't I nice?"

74

This managed to elicit some laughter from everyone, but it was short lived. Their Department would be hard pressed to provide the kind of service that their citizens expected, and they all knew it. Cartwright went through a few more important items and then she dismissed them. There was none of the usual chit-chat afterwards, and they all went straight out to their 'lectris and hit the streets.

Mercifully, the watch proved to be quieter than any of them had anticipated. There was very little traffic on the road, and only a few calls came in. The most exciting was a disturbance call in the Talywood area; neighbors had reported a man walking outside their homes screaming that the world was about to end, and hollering something about 'blowing the neighborhood up.'

He'd been drunk, high, and sick with the bug, and they'd been forced to use the stun pistols on him before they were able to pack him in the back of a cruiser. But other than this one nutcase, everyone else seemed to be staying home, even the other bad guys. Either they were too sick to go out and commit crimes, or they were caring for their fellow criminals.

Dawn eventually found the entire shift gathered together in a deserted parking lot that was more or less in the middle of all their patrol zones. It had always served the Third shift as their informal meeting place when they were in the field.

Only Jonson was absent. Too ill to continue, he had been excused by Sergeant Cartwright mid-shift and had gone home. This left the rest of them to cover everything including the first half of the morning shift, but no one said anything about it. There wasn't any point in complaining. This was their job and they had to do it. Instead, they concentrated on wolfing down their meals. Cartwright had kept her word about the coffee and had also brought some sandwiches along with it. It was one of those small, but important touches that made her a good leader, Lena reflected between bites. No matter how bad it got, the Sergeant took care of her people, and she made a note to herself to remember that. When her time came to be in charge--and it would come, she vowed--she wanted to be as good as Cartwright.

The Sergeant let them finish eating their combined breakfast/lunch/dinner before she made an announcement. She did this just as the first rooster began to crow somewhere off in the distance. "Well, you know about Jonson and Mayfield. They're out for the count until further notice. I also heard from the 'Staties'. They aren't going to relieve us. They're spread too thin to do anything. All of their male officers are out sick and their ladies are taking up the slack."

"*All* of them?" Lena couldn't quite believe this news. "What about our Reserve Officers? Can't we call them in? Or ask the Feds for help?"

"I reached out for the Reserves, but so far, I haven't gotten any calls back. Hell, I even left a message with the Police Scouts just so we could have some warm bodies answering the phones. No joy so far.'

"As for the Feds, they told me that the bug has hit everyone, not just us, and they said that we might see Planetary Defense troops coming in. But if they do, they'll only be securing the spaceport and the main highways, so we'll still be on our own."

"This is bad, isn't it?" Sharra Montrose asked. Worry was writ large on her features.

Cartwright nodded somberly. "Yes it is. Sharra, I know that you've got a brother up over in Bed's Harbor. If you want to, once the PD troops show up, I'll try and let you go so you can check up on him. But for right now I need you here."

Sharra nodded, and without having to say it, everyone standing in the dusty lot knew that she had been considering the idea of deserting her zone to check on her relative. She hadn't done it yet, so there was no foul. Not yet, Lena thought worriedly.

"Okay, let's get back out there," Cartwright told them. "I'm going to try the Chief one more time, and if I can't get him, I'll also go check up on the Captain and the Lieutenant. Calidrayth, I need you to drop by the hospital when you get the chance and get me a status report. We need to know how bad this thing is going to be and how much longer we can expect it to go on. Also, let them know about the PD people coming in--they're bound to bring some medical staff with them and I'm sure Dr. Jannahan could use some good news herself right about now."

***

"27 November, 2445: We got word that Walta Jonson and Jon Mayfield checked themselves into the hospital today, and that Kurtis Peterson is so sick that he can't even get out of bed. His wife is taking care of him. There were a dozen more officers who called in--including those that were helping us out on First and Second shift, and they all seem to be just as sick as Jonson and the others. I hope that whatever is going around won't last much longer...'

"29 November, 2445: Nothing but bad, bad news today. We finally heard about the Chief. He got worse and had to be taken to the hospital in an ambulance. Cartwright and I went to see him, but they wouldn't let us in. Even though none of us are sick like the guys are, they didn't want to take the chance. The same went for Jonson and Mayfield.'

"And Kurtis is dead. I still can't believe it; he was the high school track champion, and he had never been sick a day in his life. Then this thing came along. And his doctor didn't say it, but I could tell. Things don't look good for the others.'

"Sharra took the news about Kurtis pretty hard. She never told anyone, but he and she had a thing going last summer and they still felt something for each other. We cried together outside in the parking lot. His funeral is set for this Friday."

"30 November, 2445: More bad news. The Captain is gone and so is the Chief. They both died last night, and so did Walta. Why is this happening to us? And why aren't we getting sick? What is going on? I can't write any more.'

"31 November, 2445: Jonson passed away, and Mayfield too. This is hell..."

...Interviewer: "Excuse me, but it looks like Dr. t'Marnia has something that she'd like to interject at this point."

T'Marnia: "I do."

Interviewer: "Please."

T'Marnia: "I'm sorry for the interruption, Jantildamé, but I wanted to place this section into the proper context for our viewers. The audience should be aware that while Ms. Calidrayth was advanced enough in her thinking to be what the ancients called, a 'lesbian'--a woman who practiced normal sexuality by our standards, she and her fellow women were still under the spell of their heterosexual male masters, and didn't realize the incredible opportunity for liberation that the MARS Plague had offered them. Only Motherthought brought us to see that truth, and sadly, they knew nothing of that philosophy.'

"While we should certainly feel pity for these women, as the passage demands, we should also be aware of what was behind the affections that they felt for the males around them, and the societal pressures that compelled them to act as they did."

N'Lynn: "Absolutely. And may I add that I appreciate the interruption, Professor? My ancestress was a wonderful woman, but she came from a very backwards time. Although I still love her, and cherish her memory, she was definitely unenlightened. One of the editors who helped me once said that reading her work is like reading the writings of a medieval Christian monk in Dark Ages Europe. She called them a window into the times, but not a guide for modern minds."

Interviewer: "Certainly not. And thank you both for illuminating this point. Please Hera, continue."

...The Hospital had become something out of a nightmare. The waiting room was crammed with male patients, and every hallway was filled to capacity with gurneys. A sickly sweet smell permeated the air, overpowering the scent of antiseptics. It was the odor of disease, and its grim companion, death. And as

78

she passed them, Lena knew in her gut that more than a few of the men lying there had already expired, or were near enough that it didn't make much of a difference.

She found Dr. Jannahan in the break room, downing what was probably her 5000th cup of coffee. She looked even worse than Lena remembered.

"You were right," Jannahan said, regarding her with a haunted expression. "About the *Mirabelle*. Whatever it is that we got, it definitely came from their crew. They're all dead by the way."

"Doc? What the fuck is this thing?" Lena asked.

Jannahan laughed bitterly. "Officer, if I knew that, I'd be closer to putting the fire out. All we know for certain is that it's airborne and 100 percent fatal. The only plus, if you can call it that, is that it seems, for the moment at least, to be leaving all our women alone. It just kills men.'

"In case you're wondering, I contacted the Centers for Disease Control on Earth to get their take on this, and they're just as lost as we are. The only thing they could tell me was that this thing is everywhere; they've gotten calls from just about every world in the Federation. There's almost as many theories as they are victims, but the most popular theory is that it came in on merchanters like the *Mirabelle*, and that they probably caught it from some of the smugglers that they sometimes deal with— not that any merchanter captain would admit to such a thing."

"And the smugglers?" Lena asked.

"At a guess--and it's just a guess--the CDC thinks that the smugglers got by trading with the Kaseigians. They also think that the Kaseigians deliberately created it as a bio-weapon, and gave it to our smuggler friends on purpose. The only question is how long ago they did this. Some experts believe that the infection could have occurred as long as a decade ago, back when the civil war had just started, and others are saying that it's a more recent event. But there isn't any real proof one way or the other."

Lena couldn't disagree with the CDC's theories. The Kaseigians *were* the best suspect. Ten years earlier, the Kaseigian Confederation had seceded from the Federation, and since then, they had been at war. For the Kaseigians, the issue was independence, and for the GSF, it was crushing the rebellion and maintaining the integrity of the Federation.

From the start, the rebels had never been a match for the GSF; they lacked the same great fleets and the seemingly endless supply of nova bombs that the GSF could field. From a purely cold, satanic perspective, a bio-weapon was the most logical and inexpensive way for them to match such overwhelming superiority. Given that the vast majority of the GSF's military personnel were male, a bug targeting them would effectively destroy the Federation's ability to fight. Game over.

And if it also killed civilians? Either the Kaseigians didn't care, or they had actually wanted such an outcome; after all, Lena thought, if enough honest tax-paying citizens died right along with their soldiers, the survivors would demand that the Federation seek a peace treaty. That, or face another rebellion right at home. She didn't profess to believe in any deity, she was an atheist, but suddenly she found herself praying. If there were in fact a God, she hoped that He, She, or It, would visit a particularly nasty death on the Kaseigian leadership, and then reserve a special Hell to receive them.

"Can't we do anything about this?" Lena asked.

The doctor shook her head wearily. "No. I won't bullshit you. There's no time for lies and I'm too damned tired to think one up. This situation is what they used to call in medical school 'the 13th hour'. That's the point where we're past being able to save the patient. And that's where we are with this bug; it's here, it's spread itself all over the place, and we can't stop it. All we can do is to try and make our patients as comfortable as we can."

Lena had to sit down, suddenly thinking of the Chief, the Captain, Jonson, Mayfield, Sharra's brother, and all the other men that she knew. One hundred percent fatal is what Jannahan had just said. One *hundred* percent.

"They did give the bug a nice name by the way," Jannahan added with a sardonic laugh, "They're calling it MARS, which if you're interested, is short for 'Male Acute Respiratory Syndrome'. Cute huh? You know, men being from Mars and all?"

Lena didn't laugh with her. She couldn't think of how to react, or what to say.

"Oh, and to top it all off, one other thing; we also had a little surprise yesterday. Did you ever meet Nurse Harris?"

Lena shook her head. She hadn't.

"Well, she died," Jannahan stated flatly. "She was sick, and she didn't tell anyone. She just fell down right in the middle of the ER, and that was that. And we were scared shitless. We thought that the bug had mutated--and was finally coming after women. You know that it can still do that, right?"

Lena shook her head.

"Well, it can. But it turned out that that wasn't the cause, thank Christ."

"What was?"

"It was her, or should I say 'him'? Harris transferred here from a facility on Luna, and before she-him-whatever--became a nurse, she had had her sex changed. She was a transsexual. Records didn't tell us about this because at the time she came here, it wasn't anything important, and then they just forgot." The doctor laughed again, bitterly. "A hell of a clerical error huh? I never would have guessed, that's for sure."

The physician fell silent at this and just looked out into space, staring at nothing. Finally, Lena reached over, and squeezed her hand gently. Jannahan didn't look up, or even respond to her touch, and finally Lena let go and left her alone.

When she reached her cruiser, there was a message waiting for her. It was labeled 'Urgent, Respond on Private Channel Only.' It was from Cartwright, and Lena called her back right away. "The PD arrived," the woman told her. "They've locked down the spaceport and the main roads. We're supposed to support them locally; nothing is allowed to move in or out of our area without a special pass."

Then Lena told her what Jannahan had said about the bug, and how things were at the Hospital. "Don't tell Sharra any of this," Cartwright advised. "She's ragged enough as it is and we need her. We're all we've got."

Lena nodded. "But what about the Lieutenant? And the other guys who are still out?" She already knew the answer, but a part of her had to hear it coming from someone else.

"None of them answered my calls," Cartwright replied. "You can figure out the rest."

They ended their discussion on this grim note, and Lena returned to her patrol zone. There wasn't really anything to patrol however. With the exception of a few military vehicles that passed her, the streets were more deserted than she had ever remembered them being. Even the sky above her was clear of any traffic; all commercial flights in or out of the spaceport had been forbidden. Nothing was taking off, or landing.

In fact, it was so still that she didn't even realize that she had fallen asleep at the wheel until her cruiser started going off the shoulder.

"Shit!" she cried, fighting to keep the 'lectri from sideswiping a line of fencing. She wasn't fast enough to avoid the impact, however. There was the sickening sound of metal and wood scraping along the side of her car before she was able to bring it to a halt. And when she got out, she saw the damage. It wasn't something small enough to avoid reporting, or pass off as anything but sheer stupidity on her part. "Shit!" Furious at herself, she kicked the 'lectris tires.

Then she laughed. 'Here we are,' she thought, 'in something right out of the Middle-Fucking-Ages, and I'm worried about my damned car.' She turned her back on the damage and called Cartwright. She had to report the accident.

"Don't worry," the woman assured her. "It's just a car. At

least you're not lying in it, upside down and on fire. If that'd happened, I would've had to write you up." They shared a moment of laughter. Then, "Tell you what Calidrayth, take a nap. I'll cover things in your area for an hour. Sound good?"

It did sound good. Very good. And Lena took her up on her offer without argument or hesitation. Her nap however, lasted only thirty minutes before Cartwright woke her on the Com.

"We just got a call out on Sannerson Road, shots fired. Sending the address to you now. I'll meet you there." That woke Lena up better than any stimulant might have. "What about Sharra backing me? She's closer than you are."

"She didn't answer the call," Cartwright replied. "I think she finally went over to Bed's Harbor to check on her brother. So, until I hear different, it's down to just you and me now."

"Okay, I'm on my way." 'Fuck', she thought. 'Two officers for all this? Fuck, fuck, fuck!'

They were good and screwed, no doubt about it.

***

Lights on and siren wailing, Lena pushed the 'lectri as fast as the road would allow. She was almost at the intersection of Sannerson and Broada when she nearly had her second accident of the night. Two Planetary Defense vehicles were sitting right in the middle of the roadway, and she had to send her vehicle into a desperate, sideways skid to avoid hitting the troopers standing in front of them. They were dressed in head-to-toe exposure suits, and the instant that her vehicle came to a halt, they ran up.

Their weapons were pointed straight at her.

"Get out of the car!" one of them barked. Her instincts screamed at her to back the vehicle up, or draw her lazegun, but she did neither. Instead, she just rolled down her window.

"I've got a call down the road," she said. "Someone's shooting down there."

83

The trooper flicked off his safety. "Get out of the car! NOW!" Lena had no option other than to obey.

"Okay," she said, surprisingly calm. "I'm out. Now, you can see that I'm a uniformed policewoman, and that this is a patrol car. And I have a call to go on. I need to get down to Sannerson."

"No one's allowed past this checkpoint," the man responded. Then he coughed, and for an instant they stared into each other's eyes and shared a silent realization. Despite his protective suit, he had the bug.

"There are people down there," she insisted. "And they are in danger. And I'm a public official. I'm allowed to go wherever I have to. You know that. Now let me through."

"Jaxx, let her go man," his partner said between coughs of his own "The El-Tee said to keep civilians off the roads, not the cops."

Jaxx considered this for a moment. Then he stepped back and waved to the driver of the nearest armored vehicle. "Fuck it. Let her through."

Lena got back into her car as the other machine started up and backed out of her way. "Thank you. There'll be another unit coming through here in a few minutes." But Jaxx was having another coughing spell, and just waved her by without acknowledging that he'd even heard.

***

Lena turned off her headlights and parked the 'lectri where it wouldn't be seen from the house. As tempted as she was to sneak up to it by herself and check on the occupants, she knew better, and waited behind the engine block with her weapon out and ready. A few minutes later, Cartwright's car glided up. The Sergeant got out and crept over to join her.

"Sorry I'm late. I got delayed by the same troopers that you did. Anything so far?" she asked.

84

"Nothing," Lena replied with a shake of her head.

"All right, let's move in. I'll cover you."

The two women stayed low, moving out from behind their vehicles and over to a line of trees that bordered the property. When they reached this, they stopped, and waited to see if anything was happening in the house. It remained silent however, and as soon as they were certain that it was safe to do so, they moved on until they were alongside the building. There, they listened again.

Stillness greeted their ears, and at a nod from Cartwright, Lena crept over to a side door and tried it. It was unlocked, and from inside, she could hear the sound of a holocast. Cartwright moved up behind her, pointing her weapon at the door, and Lena opened it up all the way, exposing as little of her body as possible.

At another signal, she moved inside, and quickly took up a position to cover the room, and the one beyond that. It was a pantry, and she could see into the kitchen and a little bit of the living room. Cartwright entered right behind her and made herself ready.

"Police Officers!" Lena announced. Her words echoed throughout the house, but there was no challenge, or answer of any kind.

They went in deeper, until they reached the living room itself. This they found, was occupied, but not by anything living.

The body of an elderly woman was sprawled on a large chair, in front of the holojector. The wall behind her was covered in gore, and her face was a ruin of bloody meat. There was also a chemical pistol in her hand, and a note pinned to her chest. It said, *"We lived together and we died together. Forgive me, Jesus."*

"Fucking shit!" Lena whispered, nearly gagging. Cartwright moved past her and removed the weapon from the corpse's hands, and then waved for her to follow. They were on their way upstairs to check out the rest of the house.

85

Both of them knew what they would find when they reached the top, and at the bedroom, their fears were confirmed. A man, about the same age as the woman downstairs, lay in a large bed. He was dead too, but not from any wounds. Various medicines sat on the end tables around him, and there were plates of half-eaten food sitting nearby.

Cartwright holstered her weapon and contacted Dispatch. "We're okay here. We have two confirmed dead; one suicide and the other looks like he got it from the bug."

"Confirmed," the Dispatcher said with no trace of emotion. She was just as tired and as numb as they were. "I don't have anyone to send by to pick them up. And I've also got another call holding. Looks like someone tried running one of the roadblocks at the spaceport and flipped their 'lectri. Sending the location to you."

Cartwright looked to Lena. "Come on," she urged. "There's nothing else we can do here."

Lena gave the corpse in the bed one final look before she followed her partner downstairs to their cars.

***

When they passed the checkpoint, the military vehicles were still there. This time though, no one was standing in the road to challenge them. Lena wasn't certain of it, but as they turned off onto Broada Road, she thought that she saw someone slumped over the wheel of one of the armored vehicles, and something that looked suspiciously like a body dressed in an exposure suit lying in a nearby ditch.

She didn't try to confirm this. Instead she just flipped up her rear view mirror, and drove on.

A few weeks, and many horrors later, she finally found the time to catch up on her diary.

"09 December, 2445; the bug seems to be over now. We haven't gotten any calls about it, and the Hospital isn't getting

any more male patients. But Dr. Jannahan is becoming concerned about other diseases now.'

"She told Cartwright that we need to organize the women into Burn details or we'll see things hitting us that we won't be immune to. I'm on that job, and Cartwright is busy working with other police agencies and their city governments to help coordinate basic services.'

"The Burn detail is hard work. We have to go down each street with a dumper truck following behind us and knock on every door. When there's no answer, we kick it in, and go get the bodies. That's the toughest part, but I learned a trick; you just don't' look at the faces. Instead, you pretend that you're hauling out rubbish or old clothes, or even one of those training mannequins they use for CPR. If you do that, and mask the smell with something like menthol-rub, you can get through it.'

"At first we wanted to bury the bodies, but there were just too many of them. So, we decided to burn them. Once the dumper is full, we take the load out to the edge of town and take care of things there. There are still enough petrochemicals stored around town to do the job, and the girls with Special Weapons and Tactics have some flamethrowers that they got from the PD's. I can't believe that I'm writing this, but I'm actually starting to get used to the smell. I hardly notice it now.'

"As for the rest of the galaxy, who knows? There was a broadcast that came from Mars, but it was garbled and it hasn't come back. All we do know is that a lot of other worlds got hit even worse than we were. There was also some rumor of an invasion out there somewhere, but Cartwright says that this is most likely pure bullshit. I hope she's right. I really do. We don't need anything else."

Three days later, Lena made another entry. *"12 December, 2445: There's been some talk of someone collecting all the names and making a monument, but everyone's too busy and too tired to really think about that right now."*

The job of collecting the dead and disposing of their corpses prevented Lena from continuing her narrative for several more days, but then she wrote;

"18 December, 2445: Things are more or less cleaned up now--and quiet. Very, very quiet. I think everyone is still trying to deal with what happened...and trying to believe it. I know that I am.'

"Some of us are doing better than others. We never did find out what happened to Sharra, but we do know that her brother died, and that she stayed with her mother for a bit before she disappeared. I'd like to think she's all right out there, but a part of me knows better.'

"We've also deputized some of the local women and the Department is more or less back on its feet. Cartwright was made Chief, but I never saw Corporal after all. I went straight to Sergeant. Never thought that would happen! So now it's Sergeant Calidrayth. God help Altaria (haha).'

"Our call volume is way down too, but not enough. There have been a few more suicides. The worst two were Jill Smith and Dr. Jannahan. I guess the bug finally got them both in its own way.'

"Smith had been a mother of two boys, living on the farm that she and her husband had bought. When he'd left her for another woman, she'd stayed on. The bug killed both boys, and Smith ended it by dousing herself and the whole house with petrol, and lighting everything on fire. By the time the Fire Department got out to her, the place was burned down to the foundations.'

"And Jannahan hung herself with some electrical wire. None of us knew it, but she had started to drink heavily, and eventually all the people that she'd lost to the bug was too much for her. A few days went by before anyone realized that she hadn't shown up for work, and she was pretty far gone by the time they found her. I made sure that she got buried up near the Hospital. I didn't want to see her burned. She was a hero and she didn't deserve that."

Then, *"21 December, 2445: Chief Cartwright and I attended our town hall meeting last night. The lights keep going out; the grid is automated, but it still needs someone to repair it. There are only a couple of residents that know how to do this, and they were put in charge of training others. Food is still good, and so is water, but medical supplies are starting to get low. Some of the other towns around us are having the same problems, and it looks like we're going to pool what we have. Dr. Susa Langtree, who became the head of the ER after Jannahan, is in charge of that, and she says that they're working on synthesizing what we need. At least until we get re-supply. But we have no idea when that might happen; Earth hasn't answered us for a while. Nobody has.'*

"There was also more talk about the monument again, and this time, it caused some shouting. Just to shut everyone up, I took it on myself to start collecting the names. We'll probably never get them all. I'm putting Dr. Jannahan's name on the list, and everybody else that's passed on since then. I think that they'd want that."

And later, *"22 December, 2445: The list is done, at least for our area. No telling when or if we'll ever put the monument up. Personally, I have to agree with all the shouters--we need time to deal with all this. It's just too early."*

Then, finally: *"25 December, 2445. Some of the women got together at the church and held a Christmas service. I was invited and I went along for the ride. I'm not a Catholic--or really a 'believer' in anything, but it still felt kind of strange to see Cartwright standing in for old Father McNamara (I didn't even know that the Sarge was Catholic!). I mumbled my way through the service, and added my voice when they all said prayers for the dead. I think the service really helped the others..."*

Lena stopped writing and looked out through the window of her cruiser, thinking about what else to add to the entry. Circumstance decided it for her a minute later. It was Dispatch.

89

"14-A-6"

"14-A-6, go ahead."

"Respond to the spaceport and meet with Chief Cartwright. We have a situation."

'A 'situation'?' she wondered, now feeling irritated. She liked to have more detail than that when she got a call. But then she reminded herself, their Dispatcher was new. The old one had been promoted to oversee the entire Com Center, and her replacement was a new girl. And very, very green.

"14-A-6, Dispatch, can you explain?"

"14-A-6, we have reports of a spacecraft in orbit. They're trying to send down escape pods."

That was a 'situation' all right; and a bad one. The last time that they had heard from Earth, all of the worlds in the Federation were being required to refuse any ship the right to land as some sort of last ditch attempt to contain the MARS bug. They had also been told to shoot down anything, or anyone, that tried to breach the quarantine. Lena turned her engine on, peeled rubber as she reversed from her parking place and then switched on the lights and sirens. "14-A-6 en-route, code three."

"Acknowledged," the Dispatcher replied, sounding even younger and less experienced than ever.

***

The escape pod came down fast, screaming through the atmosphere like a banshee before it popped its chutes and the retro-rockets cut in to slow its descent. It was coming straight for the spaceport, Lena saw. And it would land close to where everyone had parked. It was almost as if the men inside of it *wanted* to end it all fast, instead of hiding out in some wilderness area and dying there, she thought grimly.

She took up a position and drew her side arm. The other women around her were doing the same thing, or breaking out the blaster rifles from the carry racks in their patrol vehicles.

In a way, she could understand why the spacers had abandoned their ship. They knew that they were dead any way it went, and probably just wanted to die on solid ground. If it had been her, she would have done the same thing. And they *would* die; either by starving to death inside their pod, or the minute that they opened the egress hatch and tried to step out. The thought of killing them, of murdering unarmed people under any circumstances, made her feel ill.

But they really weren't unarmed, Lena forcefully reminded herself. They had the bug, and if they were allowed to mingle with the community, everyone would be exposed to whatever strain they carried. And this time, it could get them all.

The men in the pod knew this. She knew this, and Cartwright knew it as well. They couldn't take the chance. Their job was, and always had been, to serve and protect the citizens of Altaria. They were police officers, and their community was in danger. From sick men on their last legs. It was one of the worst situations that she could have ever imagined finding herself in, but it was also undeniable, unavoidable, and floating down out of the sky right towards them.

Then the pod was touching down, and for a moment, each woman looked to her neighbor. They all had the same question on their faces. It asked if they would do what they had to, if any of them could. If what they were doing was even right. And the wordless answer that each woman gave her sister was also the same; they had to, and they would. Lena found some small comfort in that; if it was a sin, it was going to be a shared one.

The egress hatch made a hissing noise, and popped open. Then, with an agonizing slowness, it swung open to reveal a darkened interior. As one, the policewomen tightened their grip on their weapons, and aimed for the gap. From somewhere behind her, Cartwright spoke on her megaphone.

"You have landed in a restricted area," she warned. "Do not leave your escape pod or you will be fired upon!" For a moment, there was no movement inside the pod, and nothing filled the

91

hatchway.

Lena felt a faint surge of hope. Maybe they would stay inside, she thought desperately. Maybe they would just accept their fate and remain there until their rations or their water ran out.

They didn't. One, and then another man appeared, shielding their eyes from the sudden brightness of the sun, and her heart sank as she saw them take their first tentative steps out of the craft.

"STOP! Do not attempt to exit your craft! Remain where you are!" Cartwright's voice had a frantic edge to it that no one could hold against her. The men weren't stopping and she was running out of options. Lena's finger tightened on the trigger of her lazegun as her superior made one final appeal.

"We WILL shoot you! Stop where you are and return to your craft immediately!"

"You have to help us!" one of the men croaked. There was blood all down the front of his jumpsuit. It came from the coughing, Lena knew. She'd seen enough examples in the Hospital firsthand. In some cases, when the Plague reached the lungs, they bled, and men literally drowned in their own blood. But not before their coughing managed to spread the disease everywhere.

The order came. The one that they had all dreaded hearing. It was only a simple word, but it possessed just as much gravity and finality as any other death sentence had ever had; "Fire!"

And before she even realized it, she was firing. So where all the other women. The lazeguns cut the stumbling, pathetic figures down in seconds.

Immediately after this, one of the Special Weapons Team members threw a grenade into the pod. It was an incendiary model, and it hit the lip of the entrance, and bounced around before it disappeared. A dull 'whump!' followed, and the thing went off, instantly transforming the pods interior into a lifeless inferno. Thankfully, no one ran out of it on fire and screaming, like they did in all the holos. That would have been more than Lena could have handled and remained sane.

The fire burned hotly for a few minutes before the women with the Hazmat Crew from the Fire Department could come up to the bodies outside the pod. They were dressed in their weird spacesuit-like exposure gear, and each of them carried a flame-thrower.

Lena made herself turn away right before they turned the devices on and incinerated the two corpses lying on the plasticrete. She would have enough memories to haunt her as it was without adding this horror to her collection. Later, when she returned to her journal, all that she could manage was the briefest of entries.

"29 December, 2445; A few days back, some men tried to land," she wrote. *"We killed them."*

***

A week went by before she was able to bring herself to carry on with her journaling. This time, the passage concerned far more than her tiny little planet and its problems.

"08 January, 2446; we got a call from Mars! Cartwright patched it through the Com so that everyone could hear it. The Galactic Federation is gone! There's a new government now. It's called the United Sisterhood of Suns, or something like that.'

"That's the good (?) news. Now the bad. It's been confirmed; we're at war again. The fight with the Kaseigians is over. The rebellion ended with the bug and some nova bombs that the GSF sent up their asses. Good riddance. Now we're fighting some race calling themselves the Hriss. The 'cast said that the Navy is doing its best, and that the fighting is still very far away from Esyllt. Hopefully, things will stay that way…"

Unless things went from bad to worse, Lena reflected soberly. After all they'd been through on Essylt, this wasn't as hard to imagine as it had once been. Lena and her world had grown up. They knew now that the Universe wasn't always a nice place, and that bad things happened all the time to good people.

Monstrous things. Like the bug. Or having to kill sick, desperate men.

Suddenly, an inspiration came to her to add more to her entry. *"I remember something from the third grade,"* she wrote. *"My teacher shared a quote with us. It went something like this; 'History often makes the ordinary man great. It forces them to act beyond their baser aspirations'. I guess that's what happened here. And I have something to say to whoever came up with that: Fuck you!"*

She almost erased this, but then decided to keep it, just as it was. It was honest, and it was how she really felt. None of them had ever wanted the bug, or what it had forced them to do, and whoever eventually read her little diary needed to understand that.

If anyone was still alive once the present generation on Essylt had died out from old age, or something worse, she thought grimly. For a terrifying instant, Lena wondered if the men that they had cut down at the spaceport had actually been the last men anywhere. MARS had hit the entire human race, and it had spread everywhere. It was just possible, and if it were true, then they were all well and truly doomed. The Human race would become extinct, and the bug would win.

This notion was too terrible to contemplate, and she forced herself to think about something else--about anything else. The view outside of her windshield helped her greatly.

She was up on McAyvers peak again, parked at the overview, and facing east. The valley lay below her, still shrouded here and there by the evening's mists, and as always, dotted with the little blue flowers that she loved so much. It might have even looked peaceful and undisturbed to anyone that didn't know what had really happened down there. And beyond the beflowered valley, gilding the stony tips of the ancient

Drow'voi ruins with its light, was the sun.

Altair was rising, as red as blood, and bringing with it a new day, and the future. Whatever this was going to be, she knew with a certainty that women just like her would have to face it alone, and do the best that they could. They would be great, whether they wanted greatness or not.

Twilight

Anstace stood at the door of the temple of Hecate and looked out through the sacred *temenos* to the path that ran down to the village. The sun was high in the sky, and its harsh light beat down on a trail that was pitilessly clear of travelers.

The priestess sighed in disappointment and went inside to fetch her broom. Eusebia was late and as Anstace swept the temple steps, she began to worry about her. Until today, the old woman had never failed to make her way up the rocky trail to pay her respects to the Lady. Although she had been late a few times, she had never been *this* late. A shiver of apprehension went up the priestesses' spine that she knew was not a Kiss from the Lady, and she bent to her work trying to ignore the growing feeling that something dire had happened.

Eusebia was the last of her kind in the village — the last of the older generation that still paid proper homage to the Gods, and recently, the only visitor that came to the temple. All the rest had either died off, or like the younger generation, turned their backs on the old ways to follow the priests of the new God, and his son.

Even the worshipers of Zeus had been caught up in the craze, and now the people worshipped him in his temple at the foot of Mt. Olympus without any thought for the rest of his siblings. They had declared him to be the supreme and only god. It seemed to Anstace as if the entire world had been caught up in the mad rush to abandon the Gods, for one single deity. Only the names that they called it were different. But the concept was the same. So was the lack of respect that it showed for all the other Gods who had served them so faithfully, and for so long.

And if, as she feared, Eusebia was gone, then the very reason for the temple and for that matter, her own existence, had also ended. Anstace had spent a lifetime in the service of Hecate and she knew nothing else but that service. Now like Eusebia, she had grown old, and the idea of any other life for herself was utterly incomprehensible. What did a priestess do with herself when there were no more worshippers to guide or teach, she wondered? For that matter, what did the Gods themselves do when no one offered them any more prayers, or sacrifices?

These were questions that she had avoided asking herself many times over the years. Now, they would not be ignored, and she had no answers for them. Disquieted, she channeled her growing anxiety into her sweeping. A stubborn patch of dust in one corner of a pillar resisted her, and she was glad for the distraction that it offered.

As she worked, the memory of the woman who had been both her priestess and her initiator into the Mysteries returned to her. Helenka had been a wise teacher, and she had often reminded her that Fate's decree could not be disobeyed. If it was the will of the Fates that misfortune came to pass, even the Gods were in no position to question it.

Finally, she managed to work the last of the dust out of its hiding place, and as she swept it away down the temple steps, something made her look up. A traveler was coming, and for a moment she felt her hopes rise, but then as the waves of heat dancing over the trail cleared, she realized that it was not Eusebia, but Nikolos, the goatherd. As he stopped short of the sacred gate, she saw that his expression was grim. Bad news, she thought.

Anstace put down her broom and walked up to him. Nikolos, she knew, would not cross the threshold to meet her halfway. Christians didn't enter pagan temples.

"Greetings *Hiereia*" he said. Even though he didn't subscribe to her faith, he still made certain to use a respectful form of address. He would never acknowledge her by her true title, *Karuai,* a priestess, of course, but she had long since learned to overlook this small discourtesy. "I have news--ill news, I am afraid."

"It's Eusebia, isn't it?" She did her best not to let her shoulders sag and kept her voice as level as she could.

The man looked down and away from her, as if he was afraid to meet her gaze, and his words came out hesitantly. "Yes, my lady. She is gone. She passed on in the night."

"I know," Anstace replied, ignoring the cross that Nikolos drew over himself as she said this. "Thank you for coming and telling me. I know that despite your differences, you and she were close." In fact, Nikolos had tried many times to convert Eusebia to his belief system, and failed. But despite this, and his fear for her immortal soul, he had always cared for her like a favorite aunt.

There was a long silence between them, and at last Nikolos spoke again. "What now, lady? What will you do? What will happen to this--place?" There was no trace of gloating in his question. Although he strongly disagreed with Anstace's beliefs, his family had been devout followers of Hecate for generations, and he still felt a certain deference for the long tradition that surrounded the temple, pagan though it was.

"I do not know, Nikolos. I must pray to the Lady for an answer." Anstace started to turn back for the temple, but Nikolos was not finished.

"I have more news, Lady, and it will also be hard on your ears."

Anstace fought back a sudden wave of vertigo and waited, dreading what might come next.

"Yesterday, a traveler came through the village. He had news from New Rome. He said that the Emperor Constantine followed the council of his mother. He had the temples of Asclepius and Aphrodite destroyed.'

"The traveler also said that the Emperor has ordered the crucifixion of all magicians, soothsayers and pagan priests as heretics. And he told many tales of mobs sacking the old holy places and killing all those who still served there."

Anstace shook her head wearily. As Christianity had taken hold of the people's hearts, she had heard reports of such things happening, but never to such a degree, or so widespread. Until recently, the old ways and the new had coexisted side-by-side, even if the Emperor himself had converted to the new religion. And both of them knew, without having to say it, that it was only a matter of time before such madness reached even villages as remote as theirs.

"I understand," Anstace said, feeling as if she was speaking her words from somewhere miles away. "If you would, come back tomorrow. I may have need of you."

Nikolos bit his lip, betraying his reluctance, but Anstace had expected as much. "Fear not, Nikolos, what I will ask of you will not betray your Risen God, nor your vows to Him."

Nikalos didn't make any reply. He simply nodded his assent and departed.

Anstace watched the man as he made his way back down to the village and when he was finally out of sight, she crossed the sacred courtyard and went inside the temple. There, she lit the oil lamps, and sat before the image of her goddess.

The statue was old, older than Anstace herself, and it had been fashioned many generations before by some unknown devotee. It was not as fine as some of the other images of the Great Soteira, but it more than made up for this by the simple, ancient power that it expressed.

She had cared for it since her very first days as an acolyte; gently dusting it and making sure that the Goddess it represented received regular devotional offerings, even when she herself had had to do without. And over the years, her ancient Lady had rewarded her for her devotion, bestowing her with peace and wisdom whenever she needed it the most.

Now was just such a desperate time. What would become of this temple, she wondered again. Of the thing that had been the very center of the only life she had ever known?

The Lady answered her with a vision. It was of the temple, but not as it was. It was as it soon would be. Firelight flickered across its once clean walls, and its altar had been overturned. Loud shouts of anger rang out in her ears as she saw the image of her goddess, being grabbed by dirty hands and smashed to pieces on the floor. Fighting back her horror, she took a deep calming breath and prayed to her Patroness.

"Tell me Mother, Great Bringer of Light," she whispered. "Tell me, what must I do to serve you now?" Then she waited in silence. The hours passed, and somewhere in the far reaches of the night, the answer finally came.

***

Nikolos arrived with the dawn, and Anstace greeted him at the gate. "What would you have of me, Lady?" he asked.

"Only to borrow your donkey, "she said. "Nothing more," She held out a handful of coins to him. It wasn't much. In fact, it was all that she had managed to save over the long lean years, but she knew that it would be enough to pay him for the animal.

Nikolos took the money from her. "And so, you are leaving?"

"Yes" she replied soberly. "And with me leaves the Lady. I would not stay here, nor would I leave Her here to be violated by my neighbors. Nor do I think that they would wish to live with such a memory. My way is much better for all, don't you agree?"

Nikolos considered this for a moment. "Yes" he said at last. "It would be best. " There was a sad, knowing look in his eyes as he put the coins away in his waist sack. "Please, send my donkey back when you are done with him."

"I shall," she promised. "Goodbye, Nikalos."

Anstace left the village later that morning, stopping only to visit the local herbalist, and carrying nothing more than a tiny cloth-covered bundle on the donkey. A few villagers saw her

100

leading the beast out of the settlement, and some crossed themselves, or made signs against the evil eye, while others pretended not to see her.

But a few nodded furtively towards her in respect. For all her pagan beliefs, she was still a priestess and some of them, like Nikolos, still respected the past that she embodied. For her part, Anstace made sure to walk as straight and as tall as she was able until the village and its inhabitants were far behind, and out of sight.

Towards sunset, she found the path she had been seeking. It was a faint track in the landscape, barely noticeable for all the growth that had overtaken it in the many years since she had last been there. She urged her beast up the trail and together they made their way up into the hills. When her final destination was in sight at last, she removed the bundle from the donkey and gave the beast a slap on its flank, sending it back down the hill to find its own way home.

Then Anstace began her climb. The cave wasn't far from where the trail ended, but the years and arthritis had taken their toll on her, and she was forced to stop and rest many times during her ascent. It was almost sunset by the time she reached its mouth and its cool breath came as a welcome relief.

After another short pause to catch her breath, she went inside, groping along the rocky walls until she located a cleft in the stone. It opened into an inner chamber, further back in the hillside. A stranger to the place would never have found it, but even though age had dimmed her memory of many things, she still knew the spot from her younger days when she had been brought there by Helenka, to be initiated into the Mysteries. Back then, she had been terrified, but now she knew it as a place of comfort and peace.

The chamber was still as she recalled, although it seemed smaller now, and on the far wall, was the empty niche created by nature itself. With great reverence, Anstace, unwrapped her burden and placed the statue of the Lady on the natural shelf, making a gesture of respect before it. Then she brought out a tiny fire making kit and brewed herself some of the tea that she had bought from the herbalist.

To her surprise, her drink was not bitter, but actually rather pleasing. As a dull numbness began to spread over her, Anstace laid down on the cave floor, and gazed up at the Lady's image. *'What indeed does a priestess do when there are no more worshippers'* she reflected. *'What do the Gods do?'*

But now, she knew the answer; They hide what is sacred and wait patiently until humanity is ready once again to receive Their wisdom.

She closed her eyes, feeling at peace. After a lifetime of service, she had performed the ultimate duty to her Lady--the only duty that had been left to her. Darkness closed in around her. It was not the darkness of the approaching night, but something far more permanent.

Anstace was not afraid though. There was a light in the distance, beckoning to her, and she knew who it was that was waiting there. She went to Her, with a smile on her lips...

...Not long afterwards, a powerful earthquake rocked the land. It toppled the small temple, depriving those who would have vandalized it with their chance for mayhem. It also sealed the cave and made the villagers cry out to their new God, and in some cases, to the old ones as well. All of them understood what had really caused this event, and why.

Only Nikolos did not despair. He knew that the ancient Goddess that Anstace had served was not displeased. Not with him, at least. And he wasn't surprised at all that his home had suffered little damage from the event.

The years passed, and turned into centuries. The village became rubble itself and then nothing but memory, and finally, not even that. It was not until another tremor came, and the entrance to the cave was re-opened that Fate played a hand once again. A goatherd, who had no idea that he was descended from an ancient relative called Nikolos, found the opening, and what he saw inside made him run excitedly to the nearest phone…

…Dr. Andrea Tamerlane had received the report of the ancient find with a healthy amount of skepticism. Fortunately, the goatherd had chosen not to plunder the tomb, and the local police had stationed a guard to make certain that no one else decided to do otherwise. But she knew that the chances were excellent that all they would find would be a few pieces of broken pottery and possibly some old goat bones. The days of Tutankhamun and other fabulous archeological discoveries were long over, and the ancient world had been picked clean. Even so, there was always the hope that something, somewhere, had been overlooked, and this is what had motivated her to drive out in her rental car to the remote location.

When she arrived, the policeman and the mayor of the nearest settlement where expecting her, and after a few pleasantries were exchanged, they led her to the cave. At first, Tamerlane couldn't see much, but as she shined her flashlight beam inside, it caught on a pile of bones.

They were not from a goat.

Then the light played across something in the shadows of a niche in the far wall. Tamerlane gasped, and unconsciously fingered the little golden labrys that hung around her neck. The carved face that regarded her from the darkness was no ancient king wearing a golden mask. Instead, it was a Queen.

Now Tamerlane understood why she had been guided to this place. And she also knew that she had some phone calls to make. This was not something that she could allow to be cataloged and then forgotten in some dusty museum storeroom. The Lady that she had quietly served for years wouldn't want that. She had spent enough time shut away from the memories of men.

Lifer

To Julian. I hope that you will consider the consequences next time.

Day 1

Stillman felt himself getting hard the instant that the woman entered the conference room. She was the classic 'nerdy professor type'. Her hair was done up in a business-like bun, and she even wore a white lab coat. But the sterile looking garment did nothing to hide her figure. Only a dead man would have missed her ample breasts, or the generous curves of her body. And thanks to the agreement that his attorney had convinced him to sign, he wasn't dead, or on death row any more.

It also didn't take much imagination for him to picture what she would look like without anything on, or the image of her dark brown hair, unpinned and falling to her shoulders. Even though he preferred blonds, she was beautiful. All he could think about was shoving her up against the nearest wall and watching as her delicate face distorted in terror as she realized that he was going to kill her. It was too bad that his restraints, and the military policemen in the room, were preventing him from turning his visions into reality.

"Thomas Wade Stillman?" she asked.

The sound of her voice only added fuel to his fantasy. She would sound amazing as she pleaded for her life, he thought, or when she screamed as he stabbed her to death. Christ, she would probably cum with every thrust, he told himself. Women like her loved it when he gave them their final thrill. They were all whores—especially the uptight ones.

"Call me Wade," he said. He made sure to flash her his best 'mad-dog' grin, just to see if he could get a little glimpse of what her fear really looked like. That was how you got to know the truth about people. When they were terrified, it all came out of them. All the bullshit was stripped away and you saw who they *really* were. To his surprise though, she didn't recoil, or even break off eye contact. She just smiled, pleasantly.

"All right, *Wade*," she replied. "My name is Dr. Sodora, and I am the Team Leader for Project *Mindsinger*."

"What's your first name?" he asked. "I like to know a woman's first name." Learning that bit of information was one of the basic keys to getting past their defenses.

Dr. Sodora smiled again. This time it was a knowing expression. "So I've heard," she said. "It's Anne."

Stillman was caught off guard. Usually the women who thought that they 'were somebody' insisted on hiding behind their title. Clearly, Dr. Sodora was something different.

And why the hell was she so relaxed? Most people were nervous around a convicted killer. She looked right at home, and this made him want to hurt her even more.

"Thirty one murders, wasn't it?" she asked. She tapped a key on her laptop and the wall behind her lit up with a group of pictures. They were all young women, between the ages of 16 and 25, all blonds, and Stillman knew each and every one of them. They were his victims.

Except for one. He didn't remember her, and he knew what his score was. It was 30. Not 31.

"Thirty", he said firmly. "I don't know that last bitch."

Doctor Sodora had to be working with the cops, he concluded. They were always trying to 'clear their books' of unsolved cases, and this was probably one that they wanted to pin on him. And right then, he wasn't in the mood to help out. The flight from Delaware to wherever he was now had been a long one, and the only thing keeping him from collapsing from exhaustion was the luscious little professor sitting in front of him. *Damn*, he thought, *she is fine. Centerfold fine.*

"Thirty it is," Dr. Sodora agreed. "I presume that your attorney thoroughly briefed you about the terms of our arrangement?"

"Yeah," he answered. "I play lab rat for your little experiment, and I get my sentence lowered. I become a lifer"

"That is correct, Wade," she replied, giving him another smug little smile. "Life without possibility of parole, but life."

Seeing her expression, Stillman vowed that if he ever got her alone, he would skip the foreplay and go straight to cutting her up. Then that smart-ass look would be wiped off her face for good.

"Tell me, Wade," she asked, "Do you know what Vialabs manufactures?"

Stillman certainly did. He'd heard about the device from some of the other inmates. They said that it was better than a porn holo; you actually got to be there—in your mind at least.

"Yeah. They make those weird-ass *realie* sets," he said. "They're some kind of toy for the rich and famous to jerk off to."

Dr. Sodora nodded. "That would be an accurate description. Crude, but accurate. The realie system works off of the principle that we don't actually experience reality directly. It comes to us as a signal from our sensory organs, as electrical impulses, and our brain interprets those signals. This includes sight, sound, smell, touch, and taste. What we consider 'real' actually occurs in the brain.'

"The Vialabs realie system uses a highly sophisticated computer program to translate these sensory impulses, and then to compile and transmit its own signals to the subject's mind, overwhelming and replacing the originals. The brain doesn't know the difference. It believes that whatever we tell it is real, is real."

"Sounds sexy," Wade remarked. "Do you think that you can put something together that *my* brain would like?'

Another condescending smile. "Anyone's brain can be fooled," she said. "But the realie system is more than just a platform for pornography. Our nation's military believes that it has the potential to help us combat terrorism, and to serve our intelligence agencies."

"Cool," Wade replied. He didn't really care, but he knew that if he played along, *Doctor Sexy* would get to the point.

She did. "The focus of Project *Mindsinger* centers around the ability of the realie to affect human memory. And that's why you're here. We're using our system to extract memories from the human brain, and studying the process of implanting replacements. I am sure that you can appreciate the value that this has when it comes to dealing with our nation's enemies."

"So you fuck with people's heads," Stillman stated.

"In a manner of speaking, yes," Dr. Sodora admitted. "We are learning how to change what the mind thinks that it remembers, and finding ways to make it forget what we don't want it to recall."

"Why do you need me for this?" he asked. "Why not just use some nerd?"

Dr. Sodora laughed softly. "Because we've tried 'nerds', and found out that the mind can sometimes be damaged by the experience. You, Mr. Stillman are expendable. You will help us to surmount the obstacles and refine the process."

"And I get my sentence lowered?" Stillman challenged. "To life?"

The woman nodded. "To life, exactly as promised. Vialabs has an excellent relationship with the United States government. In fact, this location was leased to us by the Central Intelligence Agency. It used to be a secure interview facility. Now, it serves our purposes, and with their full blessings. The Justice Department is also on-board with the entire project. I assure you, we will deliver on our agreement, just as your attorney said."

Stillman grinned. "So, where am I?"

"You are 1000 feet beneath the Groom Lake Testing Facility in Nevada," she said. "But we locals like to call it the Paradise Ranch."

"Catchy," Stillman agreed. This fit in with what he had been able to pick up on his own. Even though he'd been wearing a hood, he'd smelled the desert the moment that he had been taken off the plane. There was no mistaking the distinctive mix of sage and dust.

And it also explained the Military Policemen. He was inside some kind of super-secret government installation.

"So, when do we get started, *Annie?*"

"Right now, *Wade,*" she replied. She signaled to one of the MP's, and the man came over to him with what looked like the head-band from a pair of wireless headphones. It was made of gleaming white plastic, and instead of ear pads, the ends of the object were rounded off like teardrops. From the size and width of the thing, Stillman realized that it wasn't intended for his ears at all, but designed to rest directly against his temples.

"For the duration of this project, you will wear that headset at all times," Dr. Sodora instructed. "If your remove it for any reason, our deal will be nullified, and you will be returned to death row immediately. Is that completely clear, Wade?"

"Even in the shower?" he asked.

"At *all* times. Even when you are sleeping. The system monitors everything that you think, including your dreams."

"You really want to see *my* dreams?" Stillman replied.

"Everything," Dr. Sodora said.

Stillman laughed, and allowed the guard to put it on his head. *Get yourself ready for some really scary shit, Annie,* he thought acidly.

She typed another command into her laptop. Then she produced a digital recorder from her lab coat, and spoke into it. "Case number 13148-A. Subject: Stillman, Thomas Wade, Day One. Initial realie calibration and testing."

At another nod from her, the second guard stepped forwards. He held a bottle of whisky and a shot glass, which he set down on the table in front of Stillman. To his delight, Stillman watched as the MP twisted the cap and opened it, breaking the paper seal with a crisp 'pop'. Then the soldier filled the shot glass to the rim.

"Go ahead, Wade. Drink it," Dr. Sodora invited, gesturing towards the glass.

Stillman chuckled. "Don't mind if I do, Annie." It had been years since he had had anything to drink but jailhouse hooch, and even with the handcuffs restricting his movements, he had no trouble picking up the glass and tossing back its contents in one gulp.

The whisky burned its way down to his gut and a pleasant warmth filled him immediately. As weird as this whole thing was, he was definitely starting to like the deal he'd made. He had Dr. Sexy around for eye-candy, and now he was drinking quality booze. It beat death row by a mile and a half.

"Let's take him to the lab now," Dr. Sodora announced.

Stillman couldn't wait to see what would happen next and he obediently set his glass down. As soon as the guards had him up and on his feet, Dr. Sodora led them out of the room and down a long, antiseptic corridor lined with small doors. From their tiny observation windows, and the sealed slots at waist level, he knew right away what the rooms behind them were for. He'd spent enough time in isolation cells to recognize one when he saw one. But he didn't bother to see if they were occupied or not. Instead, his eyes were riveted on Dr. Sexy's shapely ass.

There was a sealed doorway at the end of the passage. It was equipped with an optical scanner, and two large windows were set in the walls to either side of this portal. As Dr. Sodora put her palm to the scanner, Stillman glanced over at the window to his left.

Inside, he saw rows of computer servers. They were arranged in neat, orderly rows that marched away from him until they disappeared into the shadows. Clearly, Project *Mindsinger* and Dr. Sexy required a *lot* of computing power to do their thing.

Expecting an equally impressive laboratory, he experienced a small pang of disappointment when they went through the sealed doorway and into the space itself. The space turned out to be on the small side, and it was just as sterile as the hallway.

An examination chair that reminded him of something from a dentist's office sat in the center of the room. There was an equipment tray sitting right next to it, and a metal stand for intravenous fluids. Two bags of clear liquid were hanging off of the stand, and the tray held a sterile packet that contained the needles and other supplies for connecting them. Beyond all this was a portable rack of monitoring equipment, and at the far wall, was what looked like the control booth for a recording studio. There was a chair inside the booth, a microphone and several flat screen displays.

While Dr. Sodora entered the booth and took her seat, Stillman was brought over to the exam chair, and handcuffed to it. A moment later, a nurse dressed in plain scrubs walked into the lab. She wasn't as foxy as Dr. Sodora, but she was still pretty in a 'girl next door' kind of way, and more importantly, she was blond. From the way that she held herself, Stillman pegged her as military right away.

He was also keenly aware of the fact that she was terrified of him. She hid it well, but not well enough to fool him. Like any predator, Stillman could sense fear, and she reeked of it. He also knew that she hated him, and he could have cared less.

The corners of her eyes tightened visibly as she approached him, and opened up the IV kit. Then she had Stillman expose the inside of his arm, applied a rubber tourniquet and searched for a vein. It took her a few seconds to find a good one, and when she did, she jabbed the IV needle in with just a little more force than was absolutely necessary. It hurt like hell, but Stillman just

110

grinned at her as if it had been nothing. That made her hate him even more, which is exactly what he had been hoping for.

The nurse retreated with a frown on her face, and Stillman was distracted by the screens behind Dr. Sexy. They had come to life. The largest of them showed a graphic that resembled the waveforms from a sound editing program he had played around with as a kid. There were five separate bands, and when he moved slightly, they all changed in response.

"What's that, Annie?" he asked, inclining his head towards the screen.

"That, Mr. Stillman is your mind-track," Dr. Sodora replied. "Each track shows a different level of brain activity. The topmost band displays all of your sensory input. The one below it, your conscious thoughts. The layer beneath that are your subconscious thoughts, and the fourth represents your memory associations. Collectively, it could be called a chart of your mind, displayed in real time."

"Is that what your realie thing works on?" he inquired.

"Exactly, Wade."

"And what about that one on the bottom?"

Dr. Sodora smiled at his question. "Those are your autonomic functions. That is the part of your brain that governs breathing, heart rate and so on. It is what keeps you alive."

"And you can 're-work' any one of those tracks?"

"Oh yes," she said. "Or erase them and leave nothing at all. A simple mouse-click or two, and everything that you think you are will simply cease to be." She highlighted the lowest band as she told him this, and inwardly, Stillman cringed. He liked breathing, and he wanted to keep right on doing it.

"Well, Annie, then it's a good thing that I'm useful to you," he volunteered. "I'd hate to have all that go into the recycling bin."

"Yes," she agreed, slowly de-selecting the track. "That is a good thing."

"So now what, Annie?" Stillman asked, privately relieved.

"Now we are done for the day," she replied, looking up and meeting his gaze. Suddenly, the room went into a spin. Stillman's vision exploded with bright, painful flashes of light and his stomach lurched. When these sensations finally ended, he realized that he was back in the conference room, sitting in his original chair.

"Did you enjoy that?" Dr. Sodora inquired.

"Enjoy what?" he replied.

"Your first exposure to realies," she returned, inclining her head towards the shot glass on the table. It was empty, and the paper seal on the bottle next to it was intact.

Stillman did a double take.

"You actually arrived here two days ago," Dr. Sodora informed him. "What you just experienced were your own memories, played back to you. By the way Wade, there was no blond nurse in the lab with us. She was entirely a creation of the computers that you saw on your way to the lab. One of the guards actually inserted your IV needle. As I told you, anyone's brain can be fooled."

"Whoa," Stillman exclaimed, deeply impressed. It had all seemed so real! Even the feeling of the needle going into his arm. "So what about my first two days? What happened to them?"

"Erased," Dr. Sodora answered. "There wasn't much to it. You were taken to your cell, you were fed, and then you slept. I saw no reason to retain those memories."

She allowed him a moment to digest this, and added. "That will be all for today, Wade. We will resume our work tomorrow."

"How about the whisky?" he inquired. "Don't you think I deserve a little reward for losing two days of my life?"

"Yes," she agreed. "You definitely deserve a reward of some kind, Wade." As the guard opened the bottle—for real this time—and let him have his drink, she rose and left the room.

There was an odd gleam in her eyes that made Stillman uncomfortable, but he banished his misgivings with the whisky.

"See you tomorrow, Annie."

Day 2

Instead of eating breakfast in his cell as he had expected, Stillman was taken to a small cafeteria-style dining room, and to his pleasant surprise, discovered that his morning meal wasn't going to be the usual prison fare. For the first time in years, he enjoyed a real steak and eggs, topped off with hash browns and good coffee. The guards even let him finish it.

As a result, when he was brought into the laboratory a few minutes later, he was in high spirits. His mood cooled slightly when he saw that Dr. Sodora had someone else sitting in on their first session together. The newcomer was an older man, with snow white hair and a well-tailored three piece suit. He also wore an ID tag, but all it said on its face was "Visitor." No name, and no agency.

Mr. Visitor had to be a senior investigator of some kind, he thought. His suit was just a little too expensive for the salary of a street level detective. *FBI? State Police? Some Big City Department?* he wondered. Since going to prison, he'd met them all at one time or another.

"I've invited Agent Harrison to sit in with us today," Dr. Sodora explained. "Currently, he is attached to a special FBI task force."

Stillman caught the inference immediately. Whoever Harrison *really* worked for, he was only on loan to the FBI.

Homeland Defense? Even the CIA? It was certainly possible. Dr. Sexy had mentioned a whole bowlful of alphabet soup agencies. Everyone was in on her little project.

"We are going to go through a series of memory exercises today," Dr. Sodora continued. "We will begin with your first homicide, and then move on in chronological order. I want you

113

to recall each crime in as much detail as you can, and be prepared to answer any questions that we might have for you."

"Sure thing, Annie," Stillman replied as he was secured to the exam chair. This was exactly what he had been hoping for. Once they got into the juicy details, Dr. Sexy would flinch. He was sure of it.

"Good," she said. "Let's begin."

His first victim had been a woman who had broken down on the highway. He had taken her off onto a side road and done his 'thing' to her there. As he recounted the event, he obliged Dr. Sexy and Mr. Visitor by making certain not to omit a single detail. He even embellished the narrative when he got to the actual rape and murder.

Unfortunately, his tactic didn't work. Dr. Sodora listened to his tale without displaying any emotion whatsoever. And Agent Harrison was just as unfazed, although in his case, Stillman had expected as much. A typical cop, the man kept his features straight and unreadable.

Sighing with regret, Stillman pressed on, describing his second and third murders. Finally, as he was about to recount his fourth homicide, Dr. Sodora interrupted him.

"Tell me something, Wade. Have you always felt this way?" she asked. "Did you always want to kill people?"

Stillman laughed at her question. Dr. Sexy was trying to *understand* him. That meant only one thing; that she didn't, and what he was saying was troubling her. He'd seen this happen before with the prison psychiatrists and councilors. It was an opening that he intended to fully exploit.

"I didn't want to kill *people*, Annie," he answered carefully. "I wanted to kill *women*. There's a difference."

Dr. Sodora didn't rise to his bait. She just considered his words with a little half-smile. "Is there? That's a very interesting perspective, Wade."

"Ain't it though?" he replied. *"Annie?"*

114

"Then let me rephrase my question," she said. "Did you always want to kill *women?*"

"Yeah--even when I was a kid," he returned. "I used to get the other kids in the neighborhood together to play Cowboys and Indians, and I always made sure that the girls got included. It turned me on when they got shot. Later on, when I was a teenager, I spent a lot of time watching slasher flicks and jerking off."

Dr. Sodora didn't even blink at this confession—and it had been one of his best lines. *Damn,* he thought. *She is one icy bitch.*

"And when you finally acted on these feelings?" she inquired. "What was that experience like?"

Stillman laughed again. "Well, I was sure I was going to get caught—and when that didn't happen I finally got the rush I'd been looking for my whole life. It was a better high than booze or pills, Annie. I was good and hooked, and I had to have more."

Dr. Sodora arched an eyebrow. "Did killing get easier for you after that?"

"Much easier." Stillman answered, eyeing her appraisingly. "You know, you're starting to sound to me like someone who knows what I'm talking about. Maybe even someone who's *into it* themselves. You ever killed anyone, Annie? Ever felt the rush?"

"Let's keep the conversation focused on you, Wade," Dr. Sodora responded crisply. "Tell us about your next murder."

Stillman finally felt a sense of accomplishment. His question had rattled her. He could tell. *There is definitely something off about you. Dr. Sexy,* he thought. He couldn't wait to find out what it was.

Day 12

When Stillman was led into the lab, he saw that Agent Harrison had returned, and was deep in a discussion with Dr.

Sexy. There was an open file sitting between them on the equipment tray, and for the first time ever, she seemed upset.

"I simply don't know how I can help you any further," she was saying. Realizing that Stillman and his guards were standing there, she stopped speaking and quickly schooled her features back into their usual, emotionless mask.

Agent Harrison took this as his cue and rose from his place. "We need results of some kind, Doctor. We'll continue this conversation at a later date." With that, he left the lab.

"Problems with the cops?" Stillman asked her.

"No," Dr. Sodora answered just a shade too quickly. "Just a professional disagreement." It was pretty obvious to him that she was lying, but it also wasn't his problem, and he chose to let the matter drop right where it was.

Dr. Sodora went into her booth and started inputting commands. "Before we get started today, I wanted you to see what our sessions have produced so far." A video began to play on the display screen behind her. It depicted a bearded man who seemed to be from somewhere in the Middle East being escorted into the lab.

He wasn't entering quietly though. The MP's had him by his arms and he was screaming something in Arabic and fighting them every step of the way. When they reached the chair, he bucked wildly and did his best to keep them from securing him. But a third, and then a fourth guard rushed in and finally, they managed to strap him down.

When he went limp a second later, Stillman could tell that the realie had begun. After a few seconds had passed, the man began to tremble and cry out. Stillman had seen enough raw terror in his lifetime to realize that whatever Dr. Sexy was putting him through was scaring the living hell out of him. And when it finished, he looked like someone who had just run a marathon straight up the side of Mt. Everest and back down again. Unable to stand on his own, he had to be carried out.

116

"That is your work product, Wade" Dr. Sodora stated. "We subjected him to your visions, and after a few sessions, he told his interviewers everything that they wanted to know."

"What a pussy," Stillman snorted derisively. "Guess he just couldn't handle a little fun."

"Not playing the part of the victim, no," Dr. Sodora replied.

"You can do that?" Stillman asked. The notion hadn't really occurred to him.

"Yes," she said. "We can program the realie so that it can be experienced from any perspective. I assure you, he felt *everything* that the victim went through. His mind simply wasn't ready for that experience."

Stillman whistled in appreciation. "Nice to know I could help my country out, Annie."

He actually meant this. Just because he was a convict didn't mean that he wasn't patriotic. As far as he was concerned, any terrorist that messed with the good old US of A deserved what he got, and he was happy that he had had something to do with it.

"Now Wade, let's work on recalling murder number 17," Dr. Sodora said. "I believe that that was one of your more--*artful* pieces."

It was. He had cut the woman's head off when he had finished with her. But he had something that he wanted from Dr. Sexy before he was ready to comply.

"How about a little taste before we move on, Annie?" he asked her. "You've been working on my little stories for quite a while now, and I think I deserve a reward for helping you break that little rag-head down."

Dr. Sodora considered this for a moment. "Fair enough, Wade," she finally said, typing in a command. The lab disappeared.

Stillman found himself in a hallway. A young woman dressed in nothing but a sheer nighty was running away from him. He remembered this kill vividly; it was murder number 15, and it had taken place in a college dorm.

This is going to be good, he thought excitedly. Just as he recalled, his weeping victim ran into the bathroom, slammed the door and locked it. It wasn't going to do her any good however. The original door had been made of thin wood, and had had a cheap lock. Putting his shoulder to the barrier, Stillman gave it a good shove, and just as he had expected, it surrendered to his attack with very little effort.

Then he was inside, and grabbing her. In the middle of spinning her around, he was hit by a wave of vertigo, and his perspective changed again. He was back in the lab, sitting in his chair.

"Damn it, Annie!" he complained. "I was just getting to the best part!"

Dr. Sodora regarded him with one of her cold, enigmatic smiles. "We are not here to satisfy your lusts, *Wade*. You asked me for a 'taste' and you received it. And I promise you that you will get quite a bit more when we complete our work together. In the meantime, you can sate your desires in your cell, with your hand."

Bitch, he thought. But he refrained from saying this to her. The deal that he had was too important to mess up at this stage. "All right, Annie. I'll wait."

Sullenly, he started in on murder number 17. This time, he kept strictly to the facts and didn't add in anything extra. He was too pissed off at Dr. Sexy to even bother with fluffing it up.

At noon, they paused for lunch, and when they returned to the lab, Dr. Sodora had his guards hand him a file. It was the same one that he had seen her discussing with Agent Harrison. Opening it, Stillman saw that it contained the picture of the woman she had mentioned on his first day. The so-called 31st murder. The one that he hadn't committed.

"What's this, Annie?" he inquired.

"An exercise in creative visualization, Wade," she answered. "I know that you told me that you had nothing to do with this particular crime, but I want you to read the through the file, and as you do so, try to picture yourself in the situation. Don't change any of the details however. Just imagine that you are there, doing what it says."

"Okay", he responded. "But why? I can give you plenty of stories of my own."

"I know that, Wade," she said. "This will allow us to compile something entirely fresh. Something that never actually happened. That file is not about a real event; the murder never actually occurred."

Stillman considered this. "Why not?" he finally shrugged. He spent a few minutes reading it over and then, he looked up at her.

"You sure you're not secretly into all this? Come on, you can tell me. I'd like to think that we've become friends."

Dr. Sodora didn't reply. She merely nodded her head, and turned her attention back to her control panel. Stillman sighed deeply, and continued his reading. The kill that the file described had taken place in some rich woman's home. By his standards, it was a pretty 'vanilla' event; the perpetrator had broken in, snuck into her bedroom, and finished the job there. No sex, no torture, no fun.

Finally, after he had gone through the entire thing, and had repeated certain sections to Dr. Sexy's satisfaction, he was excused for the day and returned to his cell.

Day 13

Stillman awoke with a cramp in his neck. Even though he had been wearing the realie headset for over two weeks, he still hadn't gotten used to it. The damned thing kept his head from moving during the night, and this was the result.

Sitting up and rubbing the ache away, he tried to recall his dreams from the night before. The details were fragmentary, but what little had managed to survive centered around the file that he had read for Dr. Sexy. As more and more pieces came back to him, he smiled to himself.

The dream, and the file, had both been about his last, and best murder. *31 kills before getting caught*, he thought. *Not a bad career at all.*

He heard the guards approaching, and then the slot in his cell door slid open. After years of practice, he knew what to do without being instructed. He stood, went over to the slot, and put his hands through. As soon as the handcuffs had been applied, the door was opened, and the guards put on his leg shackles and attached the chain to his wrist restraints. Then he was taken to eat breakfast, and afterwards, escorted into the lab.

Agent Harrison was back, and this time, Dr. Sexy didn't seem troubled by the man's presence at all. Whatever their disagreement had been about, it had clearly been resolved, he observed. She was her usual professional self, with no hint of emotion on her face except for the mysterious little half-smile that she seemed to reserve exclusively for him, and him alone.

He also saw that the file that he had read for her was back on the equipment tray. Harrison was hovering next to it with an expectant expression on his face.

"Good morning, Mr. Stillman," the man said. "By now, you've probably guessed that my job is to follow up on unsolved cases for the Bureau. I'd like to talk with you about this particular case. "He nodded towards the file.

"What do you want to know?" Stillman inquired.

"Well, for starters, did you do it, Wade? Was this one of yours?"

Once again, the memories came back. The break in to the mansion, hunting the woman down in the bedroom. Killing her. Everything. Just as if it had happened only hours earlier.

"Yeah," he replied. "I did her. She's number 31."

Agent Harrison's eyebrows rose at this, and he turned to regard Dr. Sodora for a long moment. The look that they exchanged between them was pregnant with meaning, but Stillman couldn't puzzle the reason. Finally, Harrison broke off eye contact, and nodded to himself with a resigned expression.

"All right, Mr. Stillman," he said. "Why don't you give me the details? There are a few aspects of the case that I'd like to have clarified."

"Sure thing," Stillman answered. He began with the break-in, and took things from there. As he gave the cop his confession, he realized that it felt good to do so. It was as if a heavy weight was being taken off his chest with every word. If Harrison hadn't been a Fed, he would have even thanked him for the opportunity to unburden himself. But he was, and that didn't happen.

Day 14

"Today is a very special occasion, Wade", Dr. Sodora announced. "We've completed our work together. The project is done."

"Graduation, huh?" Stillman asked her. "Do I get a cap and gown?"

"No," Dr. Sodora responded. "But, as a way of showing my gratitude, I intend to keep a promise that I made you. You once asked me for a 'taste'—a special realie to properly reward you for your efforts. This is it." She typed in a command, and the lab disappeared.

It took Stillman a moment to orient himself. When he did, he realized that he was in a small bathroom. For some reason, it was strangely familiar to him. And outside in the hallway, someone was throwing all of their body weight against the wooden door. There were already cracks appearing across its surface, and he knew that in only a few seconds, the intruder would be through it.

"I wanted to take the opportunity to thank you, Mr. Stillman," a voice said. It was Dr. Sodora.

Stillman spun in place, and saw her. She was standing over in a corner, her arms folded across her chest as she leaned casually against the wall.

"You did a great service to your country," she said. "You gave it more of the tools that it needs to combat terrorism.'

"You also supplied us with all the ingredients we need to create more men like you whenever the need arises. Did you know that we can use your realies to transform perfectly normal people into monsters just like you? Well, we can, and it's amazing what a few horrific murders can do to convince the public to surrender their civil liberties.'

"But perhaps the most important thing that you contributed was the personal favor that you did for me. You were right, you know. I really am 'into this'. You see Wade, you didn't commit the 31st murder. *I did.*"

"W-what?" he stammered. "What the hell are you talking about?"

The door shook again, and this time, the cheap lock began to push through the thin piece of wooden furring that was holding it in place. Stillman rushed over and tried to hold it shut against the intruder.

"What I am telling you Wade is that I killed her," Dr. Sodora said evenly. "She was my older sister, and she stood in the way of a great deal of money. If she hadn't died, I never would have inherited the fortune that I did.'

"As it was, you had just killed your last victim a few days earlier, and when I read the news, the idea occurred to me. That is why I asked you for so many details about your crimes during our sessions, and why I had you visualize the details from the case file. They helped me to put together the new tracks that I needed to rewrite your memory, and once you fully believed that you had committed the crime, you were kind enough to confess.

122

Case closed. Agent Harrison has his culprit, and I am no longer a suspect."

"You're fucking crazy!" Stillman declared.

Dr. Sodora shook her head. "No, I'm not crazy at all. I'm just another predator, like you. And now, our business is finished."

Still holding the door, he tried to strike at her with his free hand, but his fist passed right through her image.

Dr. Sodora ignored his feeble attack." Enjoy the realie, Wade," she said. "Given your history, I think that you'll agree that it's rather appropriate." Flashing him one of her signature half-smiles, she vanished.

That was when Stillman really took in the sight of his fist. It was smaller, and more delicate than it should have been. The fingernails were also longer, and they were painted. Reflexively, he looked down at his body, and gasped. *Holy shit!* he thought *I've got tits!*

His eyes darted feverishly to the bathroom mirror, and what he saw there terrified him. Wade Stillman's image wasn't looking back. Instead, he was gazing into the face of victim number 15, the young woman that he had taken in the college dorm. His features were now blond, pretty, and absolutely vulnerable.

He cried out in panic at the sight, but the sound that came out of his throat was high pitched and feminine. At the same time, he finally realized where he was, and what was about to happen to him.

An instant later, the lock gave way and the door flew open, confirming his worst fears. The grinning, knife-wielding man that filled the doorway was exactly what he should have seen in the mirror. He was looking at himself.

"Stop!" Stillman wailed, putting out a hand to ward the hellish apparition away. The gesture accomplished nothing however. His twin stepped in, and before Stillman could do anything else, he was slammed against the nearest wall, and spun around. As his legs were forced apart with a vicious kick, Stillman tried to resist, but there was nothing he could do to win his way free. The body that he was trapped in was too weak to put up much of a fight and his twin was just as strong as he himself had always been in real life.

"Annie!" he exclaimed. "You made me a promise! We had a *deal*." But Dr. Sodora didn't make a reappearance, or answer him. He was trapped in this illusion. Alone.

Even as his mind processed this, he felt the man entering him and grunted from the pain. Every thrust was pure agony, and finally when he couldn't take it any longer, he began to weep. That, more than the physical sensation, was the most humiliating part of the experience. He was crying just like the little bitch that he had taken in the dorm. And just like him, his twin only became more excited by his misery.

Finally, he felt the man pull out of him, and for a moment, he was left where he was, with nothing but the cold plaster of the wall and his shame to keep him company. Then powerful fingers grasped him by the shoulder and spun him around.

This is it, he thought in horror. *This is where I get it.* That was always the way he had done it himself, when he had been in charge of his reality. When he had been a man.

The blade went into his belly with a sound like a shovel biting into wet earth, and it felt like he'd just gotten a gut-punch from a prizefighter wielding a red-hot poker. The force of the impact knocked the wind out of him, and he folded over. A second later the pain arrived, and it was a thousand times worse than what he had experienced up against the wall. *My god!* Stillman thought. *I've been stabbed! He's killing me. He's really killing me.*

But his double wasn't finished with him quite yet. His tormentor reached down and roughly grabbed him up by his hair, forcing him back up. Then he stabbed him again. And again.

Unable to scream, or even take in a breath of air, Stillman just stood there open-mouthed and took every bit of it.

Somewhere in the middle of his torment, he felt his knees giving way and the edges of his vision going gray. An eternity later, everything faded to black…

…Dr. Sodora ignored the alarm tone from the EKG machine. She already knew that Stillman's heart was beating dangerously fast. This was exactly what she had been hoping for.

For a moment, she considered the fifth band of his mind-track, and she even highlighted it in preparation for deleting it. She stopped herself however. That was too easy, she decided. What Stillman really deserved was the personal touch.

Leaving her control console, she walked over to a locked cupboard set in the wall. There, she took out a pair of fresh syringes, and two bottles. One of these contained Pancuronium and the other, potassium chloride. Carefully, she inserted the needles and drew up the appropriate amounts. Then she went over to Stillman's IV, and injected them into the line. As they took effect, the monitors warned her that his respiration and heart rate had just dropped to zero.

Dr. Sodora silenced them, and consulted her watch. After five minutes had gone by, she reached into her lab coat and brought out her digital recorder.

"Case number 13148-A, Stillman, Thomas Wade," she said. "Subject suffered a terminal myocardial infarction caused by the stress from a full harmony realie session. Time of death clocked at 20:25 hours. No autopsy required. Subject was under continuous medical supervision. End notes."

She looked down at his body, giving it the same mysterious smile she had always given him when he had been alive. "Enjoy your time in hell, Wade. You've certainly earned it."

Der Deib (The Thief)

For Moshe.

The bonds between men can be forged for many reasons. For some, it can be a devotion to a fanatical cause. Or it could be the shared hatred of those that they consider inferior. It can even be as simple as the mutual desire to take a short break before committing the next atrocity.

For *Obersturmbannführer* Karl Schneider, it was all of this, and his addiction to tobacco that had wedded him to his Senior NCO, *Hauptscharführer* Willi Müller. Schneider didn't particularly like Müller, and they had little in common. Schneider was an officer who had been accepted into the SS because of his superior breeding and the influence of his wealthy family. A former SA thug, Müller came from the lower echelons of society. The only reason that he even wore the death's head insignia on his collar was because the Reich needed men who weren't afraid to get a little blood on their hands, and didn't care how it got there.

But they both loved to smoke. Although this went against the Party's official policy against tobacco usage, they had met regularly behind the Commandant's office to indulge in their common vice ever since they had first been posted to the Krwawazłota Concentration Camp.

There, and only for as long as it took them to finish their cigarettes, they were equals of a sort. Even so, they had always been careful to restrict their conversations to neutral subjects, and avoided discussing camp business. There were simply too many things that they had both done in the name of the Fatherland that they didn't want to speak out loud about. Or the shared doubts that they had about the wisdom of their leaders and the outcome of the war. Doubts that would have earned

126

them a date with the firing squad as defeatists if they had been overheard by the wrong ears.

It was the distant sound of Russian artillery, and the fact that the Commandant had disappeared from the camp two days earlier, that had finally forced them to break their silence. Müller was the first to speak.

"So," he said, exhaling a small cloud of smoke, "It looks like the Boss isn't coming back." He was gazing over the barbed wire fencing to the
eastern horizon.

Schneider looked in the same direction and grimaced. He was seeing what Müller was. It wasn't the sky, made hazy from the fires of recent air attacks, but the future, coming towards them on the treads of Lend-Lease tanks. After Operation Barbarossa, and the long, bloody war in the east, 'Ivan' was coming, and he had no mercy for SS men. Least of all those serving with the *Totenkopfverbände* Division.

In addition to the Jews, the Gypsy's and other enemies of the State, the Death's Head units had eliminated Russian prisoners by the thousands, either by outright execution, or through sheer neglect, and now the butcher's bill was coming due. As the Assistant Camp Commandant of Krwawazłota, Schneider knew that he would be one of the first to pay it. And he had no intention of simply waiting around for his bullet, or a rope around his neck. The problem was, that unlike many senior officers who had pulled up stakes and run from the approaching Red hoards, he didn't have a nest egg set aside to aid in his escape.

"No," he finally said. "He isn't coming back." He turned and looked at Müller. "Well? Out with it, Willi. You aren't sweating like the rest of us. You've got to have some kind of angle. You always do."

Müller's eyes narrowed, and he looked around to see if anyone was within earshot. His devious expression reminded

Schneider of a pig. A clever little pig that was always looking for a way to get more slop for himself.

"I heard that one of the Jews in the tailor's shop squirreled some money away before he got sent here," Müller said in a low voice. "A fellow named Eli Katzev."

Schneider snorted doubtfully. "There are always stories like that around here," he said. "Did this Katzev tell you this himself?" If so, then it was a lie. Inmates were always coming up with promises of hidden wealth to buy themselves some more time.

He knew better though. The SS-WVHA had always been thorough when it came to cleaning out the Jewish prisoners. Even the dead ones didn't get to meet their desert god with the gold in their teeth, and he was shocked that Müller, as seasoned as he was, had been taken in by such patent nonsense.

"No," Müller assured him. *"Obergefreiter* Kurtzman told me. He knew the man, before the war, in Poland. Kurtzman's family are all ethnic Germans, and the Jews had their own town just a few kilometers away. Kurtzman said that when it came time to round them up, all of the *untermenschen* gave this Katzev their valuables and he hid it all away somewhere. Our guys never found any of it, but Kurtzman swears it's still out there."

Schneider was still unconvinced. "How is it that Kurtzman is so sure? Is this Jew his friend?" Everyone had heard Reichsführer Himmler's warnings about the dangers of 'the good Jew'. Their kind were masters at winning the trust of their victims, and more than a few SS men had been taken in by their deceit. He however, was not one of these weaklings.

Müller shook his head. "No. They were never friends. Kurtzman only knew him because his family borrowed money from some of the head Jews. He said that this Katzev was their leader. That he was some kind of special rabbi. One of those crackpots that studies their Torah trying to find some magic in all that Hebrew gibberish."

Schneider chuckled dryly. "A mystic then. His magic didn't get him very far did it?"

"No, not very," Müller laughed, and then his expression became serious. "Here's the thing though; Kurtzman also told me that Katsev has family in another camp, a wife and three darling little daughters. He's willing to give us everything he has to save their necks."

Actually following through on such an arrangement was completely out of the question, and they both knew it. Although some SS men were now taking great pains to buy themselves some good will from their prisoners, Schneider and Müller didn't have that option. They had committed too many crimes to think that it would make any difference. For them, it was better that all the eyewitnesses were dead. Dead men after all, said nothing.

"How much are we talking about?" Schneider finally asked, treating himself to another cigarette.

"*Millions* of marks," Müller answered slyly. "In *gold*. Enough to get us clear and keep us warm and comfortable in our old age."

Enough to get to South America with Lisl, Schneider thought hopefully. With allied air raids increasing over the larger cities and towns, he had sent his daughter west, to the tiny village of Schönfeld in northern Germany, to stay with distant relatives.

Then the Americans and the English had landed at Normandy. With sheer numbers and pure brute force, they had broken Fortress Europa wide open, and now, nothing seemed capable of stopping the *Ami's*, or their Russian counterparts. The vice was closing from the east and the west, and Germany was in its jaws.

Although the money that Müller was talking about certainly wouldn't save the Reich, it could be the answer to his own problems, he reflected. With it, he would have the means to get himself and his daughter out of Europe. If the whole thing didn't turn out to be just another Semitic lie.

One way or the other, he intended to find out. His situation was becoming far too desperate to ignore any possibility of salvation.

"Bring this fellow to my office," he said. "We'll see about this treasure." He finished his cigarette and as he crushed the butt under his boot, he added, "One other thing, Müller. Transfer Obergefreiter Kurtzman to another unit. Someplace east, where he can become a hero of the Reich. I'll sign the papers."

Müller grinned maliciously. It was as good as putting a bullet in the man. Except that it would be *Ivan's* bullet, and not one of theirs. Things would be much cleaner that way.

***

To anyone who was not hardened to the reality of existence in a concentration camp, the figure standing before Schneider's desk would have been a pathetic sight. A mere 40 kilograms, the old Jew's filthy prison clothing hung off of his emaciated body as if they had been made for a much larger man.

Which in a sense, they had. When Eli Katsev had first been imprisoned at Krwawazłota, he had weighed over 80 kilos. A combination of poor food and harsh conditions had transformed him into a shadow of his former self, and it was his eyes more than any other feature, that were the most noticeable by-product. They had become dark, haunted windows that looked into a soul that called death and despair its constant companions.

Schneider however, was unimpressed. To him, Katsev's condition was only what he and all his kind deserved. They had betrayed the German people at Versailles, and bled them dry during the Weimar years. In his opinion, all that Katsev had really lost was the fat that he had gained from good living at the expense of others, and by camp standards, he was positively obese.

He also ignored the fresh injury to the man's right eye. From Müller's satisfied expression, it was quite obvious how he had acquired it. Instead of simply fetching the man to his office, the NCO had obviously paused to visit some abuse on him.

Müller was like that though; he was always showing initiative and that was what made him a good subordinate. Schneider also had to admit to himself that the beating would serve a valuable purpose. It would make their 'guest' more receptive to his proposal, especially if it was served up with the patina of kindness.

"Herr Katsev?" he said, gesturing to the empty chair in front of his desk. "Please, sit."

The man hesitated, and his eyes darted nervously to Müller, who grimaced threateningly. Katsev sat.

"May I get you anything? Some coffee perhaps?"

Katsev shook his head, and looked down at the floor. "No, Herr *Kommandant*."

Schneider smiled at this. With the actual Commandant away without leave, he was only acting in that capacity, but it was still pleasant to hear the title being applied to him. And if this Jew was actually telling him the truth, it would only be a temporary responsibility to bear.

"I understand that you have an offer to make us," he began. "You are willing to return the gold that you stole from the honest, hard-working German people in exchange for your freedom and that of your wife and daughters."

"Yes, Herr Kommandant," Katsev replied, keeping his eyes lowered.

"The Hauptscharführer has already told me some of the details, but I would like to hear them directly from you," Schneider said. "How did you get your hands on this gold?"

Katsev hesitated for just a hair too long, and Müller stepped in and boxed him in the ear, knocking him out of the chair and onto the floor. "Answer the Kommandant, you bastard!"

131

"Hauptscharführer Müller," Schneider interposed. "There is no need for that. I am sure that Herr Katsev was only taking a moment to gather his thoughts. Help him back into his seat, will you?"

Müller frowned, and hauled the man to his feet, and then stood back as Katsev righted his chair and re-seated himself. It was all an act of course. He and Schneider had played this game with prisoners before.

"It was just after the war began, Herr Kommandant," Katsev said, wincing as he rubbed at his swollen ear. "Everyone was worried about what would happen to us, and they asked me what they should do. I told them to hide everything until the fighting was over."

"And where did you put it?"

"At a spot in the woods, outside of my village. It is an old cemetery, from the time before our people came and settled there," Katsev replied. "A gentile cemetery. We knew that you would not come looking for Jewish gold in a Christian holy place, Herr Kommandant."

"That was very clever of you," Schneider conceded. "What is the name of this village of yours?"

"Malawoiska, Herr Kommandant."

"How do we find this cemetery?"

Katsev finally met his eyes. "I would have to take you there and show you the way. You can only reach it by going through the woods. The trail is very overgrown and we were the only ones who ever knew the path."

"Of course," Schneider returned amicably. "I expected as much, and before I asked you to come here today, Herr Katsev, I took the liberty of placing a few calls. I have some good news to tell you; I learned that your wife and daughters are still in good health, and I can have them released just as soon as we have successfully transacted our business. Is that agreeable?" In fact, his inquiries had revealed that all of them had been dead for months, but naturally, he had no intention of telling him this.

Katsev's demeanor changed slightly, and Schneider thought that he saw a faint glimmer of hope beginning to shine in his eyes. "Yes, Herr Kommandant. It is agreeable."

"Excellent!" Schneider declared. "Müller? Have someone take this man back to his barracks."

The NCO started to escort their prisoner out himself, and Schneider adopted a harsher tone, "Hauptscharführer, you will remain with me. I need to speak with you about your methods."

Again, this was all part of the act, and Müller played right along, making certain to give Katsev a venomous look before calling the guard who was posted outside. The instant that the prisoner was gone, both of them relaxed.

"So," Müller asked. "Do you believe it now?"

Schneider had risen from his chair, and was scrutinizing a wall map of Poland. "I believe that it merits a short trip," he answered reservedly. "If this isn't a fairy tale, then we'll be set. If it proves to be nonsense, then we can be there and back again before anyone starts to wonder about us. His village isn't very far from here. Half a day perhaps."

He didn't add that Katsev would not be returning with them. That much was a given. "See to it that he is cleaned up and requisition us a truck from the motor pool."

Müller clicked his heels and gave him a crisp military salute. "*Jawohl*, Herr Obersturmbannführer. " He left the office.

Schneider returned to his chair and leaned back in it to gaze at the photograph on his desk. It had been taken just before a Party rally. He was in it, in his somber black dress uniform, and his wife stood next to him wearing her finest dress. Her arm was around their beautiful teenage daughter Lisl, who was in her *Bund Deutscher Mädel* outfit, smiling proudly.

They were the very image of the perfect Aryan family; blond, healthy and utterly devoted to their Führer. But those happy times were gone now. His wife had lost her life in an allied air raid, and Lisl was in the country, waiting for him to come home to her.

Not for very much longer though, he vowed. *I'll come for you and we'll leave this shit-pile behind for a better life.*

With that, he went out to speak with his adjutant. To get where he was going, he would need the proper papers, or at least something that could withstand scrutiny.

***

Several hours passed and then Schneider was summoned to the motor pool. He was impressed with what he saw waiting for him. Müller had truly outdone himself. The man had not only managed to wrangle them a 3.2 ton Opel *Blitz*, but enough cans of gasoline for the entire trip, along with a siphon hose, and a large wooden munitions box to hold the treasure--if it actually existed.

Müller had also gotten his hands on some Wehrmacht uniforms and a license plate from one of their trucks. These, Schneider knew, would be used once they got nearer to their destination, and possibly even save their lives if the Russians caught them up in their net. Wearing SS uniforms was tantamount to a death sentence, and while it wasn't a foolproof measure by any means, it gave them a good chance of survival.

He wasn't certain how Müller had managed all of this, and he pointedly didn't ask. Fuel was precious in any form and their inventory of vehicles was carefully monitored, but he imagined that the Hauptscharführer had employed an artful combination of threats and bribery.

Which also meant that Müller had drawn on personal funds that he hadn't bothered to mention to his new 'partner'. Schneider wasn't surprised or offended however. Like many of the camp's guards, the NCO had had years to extort money from the inmates. The fact that he was now willing to spend some of his riches only served to banish the few lingering doubts that Schneider had been entertaining. Müller really believed that the treasure was out there. All they needed to do was to go and take it.

"Well done, Müller," he said. "Let's be off then." He nodded towards Eli Katzev who was standing off to one side, wearing shackles.

Müller grinned and urged Katzev aboard the truck with the barrel of his submachine gun. When their prisoner was aboard, Schneider joined him on the wooden bench, and Müller took the wheel.

At the main gate, the guards were surprised to see them, but the minute that Schneider made his presence known, and told them that Katzev was being taken for questioning by the Gestapo, they grinned knowingly. Death was what Krwawazłota dealt in, but so did the State Secret Police, and their methods were none too gentle. They were allowed to pass.

As the camps gate receded from view and its motto,"*Arbeit Macht Frei*" became more and more indistinct, Schneider felt a sense of elation, and trepidation come over him. If they succeeded in this little venture, he would be wealthy, but he would also be a traitor and the SS wasn't a very forgiving organization. Once it was all over, he would have to move fast and keep moving.

***

In better times, the trip would have been much faster than it actually proved to be. Because of the Russian advance the highways leading east from Krwawazłota had places where bomb damage had rendered them unusable. Even where they were still functional, the roads were clogged with retreating soldiers and desperate civilian refugees, and the pace was slow. Müller did his best to find them backroads around the mess, but even these had their share of travelers, and they didn't always go in the direction that they wanted, forcing them back onto the paved sections.

These delays were also compounded by allied aircraft. After the Luftwaffe's defeat in the Battle of Britain, the Allies and their communist partners owned the skies and anything caught on the ground during daylight became easy prey. As a result, they were forced to travel at night, and used the waning moon and the feeble light cast by the blackout covers on their headlights to find their way.

They also had to contend with squads of Wehrmacht *Feldgendarmerie* who had set up roadblocks to intercept deserters and control the flow of traffic moving west. But their SS identity papers, and Schneider's claim that they were on important Reich business, got them through every time. That, and the fact that with the entire army in retreat, anyone crazy enough to deliberately travel east was welcome to it. The military police simply didn't have the time or inclination to bother with a pair of SS lunatics bent on suicide and a single Jewish prisoner.

Finally, when there were no more troops in sight and they had left the last roadblock far behind, Müller pulled up to an abandoned farmhouse. There they changed into the Wehrmacht gear, and hid their SS garb and papers under the floorboards. The Opel also received its new plates, and after the old ones had been added to the cache, they resumed their journey.

The roads remained deserted, and after a few hours, they turned off the main highway, and went deeper into the countryside on a winding dirt track. At dawn, they reached their objective.

The war had been cruel to the village of Malawoiska. All of the residents had been rounded up by the SS and sent off to the camps, and with no one to vent their hatred on, the local Poles had taken out their aggression on the buildings themselves. Not a single structure remained untouched. To the last, they were burned out skeletons, and where the walls were still standing, there was graffiti. It was all in Polish, and it demanded that the Jews never return.

This had once been the great National Socialist vision for the entire world and for all of the mongrel races; their forcible removal, and their villages returned to the forest, or plowed under for farmland in the name of *Lebensraum*. Now, that task would remain unfinished, Schneider thought sourly. The Jews would return, and rebuild.

They were just as eternal as Dr. Goebbels had said they were. No matter how hard anyone tried to eradicate them, they always found a way to survive. But not all of them. The SS had seen to that. *He* had seen to that. Personally.

"Which way to the trail?" he asked, not bothering to hide his loathing for the man sitting across from him. They had just entered the woods beyond the ruined village.

"It is just a little ways further," Katsev answered, craning his neck to peer out the back of the truck to get his bearings. "It is near a large tree along the road."

After a few minutes, he spoke again. "We are here, Herr Kommandant. I recognize this place."

Schneider rapped on the back of the driver's cab, "Müller, this is it." The Opel stopped, and he looked through the rear window and down the road to see for himself.

The tree was an ancient thing that looked as if it had stood witness to all the armies of the world's great conflicts. The *Grand Armee* of Napoleon, headed towards their defeat by the Russian winter had certainly been one of them, and then the Tsars troops marching on their way to the trenches of World War One. And after that, the German army to conquer the east. Soon it would see the Russians, coming to ravage western civilization. Schneider only hoped that they too would meet their doom.

Müller interrupted his dark train of thought when he came around the back and lowered the tailgate. "This had better be what you said it is," the NCO warned Katsev, "or you won't like what you get." He had the shovel that the Opel carried as part of its standard equipment.

137

Katsev nodded passively at Müller, and took the tool. Then he led them into the forest.

Thanks to years of neglect and disuse, the trail they followed had almost become as much of a memory as Malawoiska. In some places, it was completely invisible, and in others, only fragmentary. Despite this dismal state, it eventually brought them to a small clearing and the remains of the cemetery. The graveyard was almost completely overgrown, and most of the headstones had fallen over, but a trio still stood upright in the very center.

One in particular stood out. It leaned against its neighbors like a drunk looking for support, and Katsev made straight for it. "Here," he announced. "This is where I buried it."

Schneider felt his excitement rising. *This could be it. This really could be it.*

Müller unlocked the man's shackles. "So, start digging then." Katsev got right to work.

After a few minutes, his shovel bit into something solid, and he got down on his knees and brushed away the soil. It revealed a battered metal box roughly half the size of the coffin that should have been there.

Schneider stepped up and gestured towards the container impatiently. "Well? Open it. Let's see this treasure of yours."

At first, the lid refused to budge as if the ghosts of the place didn't want to part with their riches, but after Katsev had worked at it with the shovel blade, it came free. Despite himself, Schneider gasped at the contents. The box was filled with riches, from antique gold jewelry to solid bars, and enough coins to buy a kingdom with. It was the accumulated wealth of generations.

He reached down and picked up one of the necklaces. It was less elaborate than the others, which was why it had caught his eye. A cylinder half the length of his finger, the object was covered with Hebrew characters and decorative filigree. From the cap on the top, it was also obvious that it contained something, and he didn't hesitate to open it. There were no diamonds or gold dust inside however, just a simple roll of parchment. He upended the thing and shook it out into his hand to inspect it more closely.

The parchment was inscribed with more Hebrew characters, along with another script that he could not identify, and some mysterious designs. *Some of this fellow's so-called Jewish magic*, he decided.

"What is this?" he asked him.

"A charm for protection against evil," Katsev answered. "I made the talisman myself. It is very special; it protects the righteous by destroying the evil-doer." Oddly, he had not addressed him as 'Herr Kommandant', and there was an odd look in his eye.

Schneider shrugged the man's foolishness off, and put the parchment and its case into his breast pocket. The cylinder looked like it was made of solid gold and it would melt down into something useful. It was even remotely possible that the little scroll would fetch something from the right buyer. That was what *really* mattered. Not some ridiculous Jewish superstition. "Take the rest of this to the truck," he told him. "Don't leave a thing."

Katsev set down his shovel and started to gather up the first armload. It took him more than an hour to empty the box and transfer the contents into the munitions crate in the truck. When he had finished, Müller marched him back to the cemetery. They stopped at the open grave.

"You're going to kill me now, aren't you?" he asked them. There was no trace of fear in his voice whatsoever.

A veteran killer, Schneider wasn't caught off guard by Katsev's question or his demeanor. Some people, knowing that they were going to die, panicked. Others fought, and some, like this miserable creature, meekly accepted their fates and went quietly.

That only made his job that much easier. "Yes," he answered, leveling his pistol at him. "I am."

"So they're all dead? My wife? My daughters?"
Schneider nodded.

Katsev let out a long ragged sigh. "I thought as much. I suspected it for a long time, but I became certain when you assured me that they were well."

This piqued Schneider's interest enough to prevent him from squeezing the trigger for a few more seconds. "Why did you help us then?" he asked him. "Why bring us here, and lead us to all this wealth? You could have just kept your mouth shut."

"Because it means nothing," Katsev said, waving dismissively in the general direction of the Opel. "I learned that much in all my studies of the Kabballah. It is only gold, with no soul and no life of its own. It did nothing for us, and I think that in the end that it will do even less for you. Besides which, I have gained something far, far more valuable for myself."

Schneider strongly suspected that he was about to hear another plea from Katsev to preserve his life, and he was willing to listen if it meant getting his hands on more riches. "Oh? What is that?"

"Freedom," Katsev answered. "I wanted to come home and die a free man, breathing free air. That was worth more than all the gold that was in that box. So was making certain that you took my little charm for yourself. You see, it has to be accepted to work properly."

Schneider started to give him a cynical smile, but his expression died stillborn. At that instant, in the uncertain light, Katsev no longer seemed to be the wretch that he had known. Instead, the man stood erect, and rather than pain etching his features, a strange serenity seemed to have come over him.

Katsev smiled mysteriously, and closed his eyes. "Please, finish this," he said. "I am very tired."

Schneider obliged him with a single, precise shot to the heart. Then he walked back to the truck with Müller in the lead. The NCO was whistling a happy tune to himself.

As the Opel came into view, Müller ended his impromptu concert. "So," he asked. "What are you going to do with your share, Karl?" When he looked back for his answer, his eyes widened in horror. He was looking right down the barrel of Schneider's pistol.

Before he could beg for his life, Schneider fired. Müller's head bucked back, spraying blood, and he toppled backwards onto the dirt.

Calmly, Schneider wiped off the bits of gore and brain matter from his cheek with his handkerchief, and then bent down to retrieve Müller's submachine gun. He didn't feel sorry for killing him any more than he did Katsev. Müller had always been a lower class pig, and pigs didn't know what to do with money.

He did, and now, it was all his, and Lisl's. He boarded the Opel and drove off in search of a quiet place to sleep away the daylight. In the evening, when the sun was down and it was safe to travel again, he would begin the long journey back to Germany, and the promising future that would await him and his daughter.

***

On the fifth day of his trip, the clouds had moved in overnight and the morning sky was overcast. It was a condition that the Germans had come to call 'Hitler weather' because it offered a respite from air attacks, and the chance to travel during the daylight. Everyone, military and civilian, was taking advantage of the break, including Schneider. The roads filled up quickly and the going was slow, but he still managed to make progress. By noon, his maps informed him that he was only 20 kilometers away from Schönfeld.

By then though, the weather was beginning to clear, and as he drove along, Schneider kept peering up through the windshield, damming the growing patches of blue sky, and watching nervously for the first sign of enemy aircraft. He became so engrossed in this that he very nearly ran over the soldier who had stepped out onto the roadway.

"*Scheiss! Du Arsch!*" the man shouted, jumping aside. Schneider hit the brakes just in time to avoid another soldier who was waving for him to stop.

The reason for the interruption became immediately apparent. The kübelwagen that the men had been driving had broken down, and it was over on the side of the road with white smoke rising from its engine compartment. Two other soldiers lay on it on stretchers; one was lashed to the hood, and the other had been secured across the back seat, and everyone was wearing bloody bandages. Overall, they were a sorry, sad looking lot.

"We need to commandeer your vehicle," the soldier informed him. "We have to get these men to the field hospital in Wittenhof and rejoin our units." From his shoulder tabs, Schneider could tell that he was a lieutenant. He was also with the Wehrmacht, and therefore no one that an SS man had to listen to.

"*Fick dich ins knie*," Schneider growled. "I'm on important Reich business, and I can't be delayed. Move aside."

The officer frowned. "You son of a bitch! These men will die if you don't help us." His subordinate began to raise his rifle.

Schneider brought the barrel of his submachine gun and trained it on them. One handed, it didn't promise much in the way of accuracy, but it still lent his reply all the authority that he required. "I don't give a shit. Move aside."

Grudgingly, the infantryman lowered his weapon, and the officer retreated with an oath. Schneider laughed at them, released the clutch, and drove away.

He was in the midst of congratulating himself when he spotted the dark, deadly shape of the fighter plane. It was descending rapidly and coming straight towards him. A split second later, the Yakovlev 9D was close enough for him to see the blue-white flash of its 20 mm ShVAK cannon firing. The pavement ahead of the Opel began to shatter, and he reacted instinctively, opening his door and throwing himself out of the cab.

Searing pain lanced through his shoulder as he landed on the unforgiving roadway, but he kept rolling until he came to a stop in a shallow ditch. He flattened himself against the earth, and the Yak 9's gun found the truck. There was a hellish cacophony of metal being pulverized, glass shattering and tires exploding, followed immediately by the fierce roar of the plane as it flew on.

When Schneider finally dared to look up, he already knew what he would see, but the sight still sickened him. The Opel had been completely demolished. The heavy rounds had ripped right through its sheet metal body, and set it ablaze. The driver's cab was a roiling mass of flame, and as the stink of burning rubber and gasoline assaulted his nostrils, he realized that the fire was spreading to the cargo bed and its priceless contents.

Seized by panic, he rose to his feet and ran to the vehicle, heedless of the possibility that the Yak might come back around for another strafing run. All that mattered was rescuing the treasure box.

He reached the tail-gate in seconds, and jumped aboard, and immediately had to shield his face from the intense heat. And when he tugged on the munition boxes' rope handle, the container wouldn't budge. The weight of its contents was simply too great.

Swearing, he wrenched open the lid, and grabbed up what he could, stuffing everything that would fit into his tunic. In the meantime, the canvas tarp above him was burning and the wooden slats at front of the cargo bed were beginning to catch.

He had run out of time. If he didn't abandon the box and get himself clear, he knew that he would be burned alive. Cursing at his misfortune, Schneider hastily backed out and jumped off, swatting at the places on his uniform where the embers had taken hold.

After that, all he could do was watch helplessly as the fire consumed the vehicle, and with it, his only hope of getting the treasure out intact. While he watched, he wept, and howled in anger at the skies that had betrayed him.

It was some time before he was finally able to collect himself and think rationally again. *You've had a bad setback,* he told himself, *but you can't give up now. You still have some of the gold. You need to figure out what to do next. Come up with a plan, Schneider. Think, man. Think.*

He would walk to Lisl's village, he finally decided, or hitch a ride if fortune chose to favor him once again. Once he arrived, they would leave Schönfeld and blend in with the other refugees fleeing from the Allied advance. Fascist Spain seemed like a good destination.

He didn't relish the idea of the two of them hiking across the Pyrenees like a couple of gypsies, and Spain certainly wasn't South America, but what he had in his pockets would still buy them a sanctuary. The old Jew would be proven wrong; despite this misfortune, the gold would still do them *plenty* of good in the end.

He started walking.

An hour passed and then Schneider heard gunfire. Right away, he left the road and made for the tree line. As he moved along it, a vehicle passed by, and he knew right away that the men in the motorcycle weren't Germans. *Scouts,* he thought. *Red scouts.* This meant that the main body of the Russian forces couldn't be very far away.

He moved further away from the road. Eventually, he found an animal trail and he followed it up the hill and over to the other side. There, he walked into the aftermath of a battle. It had been a small thing compared to the great engagements like Kursk or Stalingrad. Only a few men had been involved, some

German and others Russian, but the result had been no less bloody.

From what he could piece out, the two squads had met, and exchanged fire. Their dead littered the forest floor and who had won, or lost, wasn't entirely clear. What was obvious was that he needed to arm himself with something better than his pistol, and get out of the area before anyone else happened along.

Going over to the nearest body, he picked up the man's submachine gun. It was a PPSh-41, a primitive weapon by German standards, and not nearly as fine as Müller's MP-40 had been, but it was still quite lethal. From the weight alone, he could also tell that it had plenty of ammunition left in its drum magazine. Enough to defend himself if it came down to it.

He started off again. Eventually, the trees thinned out enough to see that he was coming up on a small meadow. It wasn't unoccupied however.

There was a squad of Russians there. They were standing around their half-track, and they had five German soldiers at gunpoint. Schneider guessed right away that the Germans were survivors from the firefight that he had just scavenged. He also had a pretty good idea about what was going to happen to them.

A moment later, his suspicions were confirmed. Someone barked out an order in Russian, and the track's gunner opened up with his heavy machinegun, cutting the prisoners down. An officer walked out next and finished them off with his sidearm.

This entire area has to be crawling with Ivans, he thought desperately, *and they aren't giving any quarter.* Quietly, he faded back the way he had come, and returned to the bodies at the skirmish site. There, he undressed one of the Russian corpses and put the man's uniform tunic on over his own, and buttoned it up. It was snug, especially with all the wealth that he had stuffed in his pockets, but it worked. At a distance, and as long as he didn't have to speak with any Russians, he could pass for one of them. Later, when he reached Schönfeld, or when he met up with German forces, he would discard the disguise.

He also knew that he didn't have any more time left to lose. He had to hurry and get to the village before the Russians did. If Lisl had fled to somewhere safe, as he was hoping she had, he would learn where, and go to her. And if his worst fears were true and she hadn't left, he would get them out no matter what he had to do, or whom he had to kill.

Hold on, he thought. *I'm on my way.*

***

"You're all swine!" Lisl Schneider shrieked, "Filthy swine." The soldiers trudging by her ignored this, and all the insults that followed it. All they cared about was getting away from their enemy, and not the ravings of some stupid girl who didn't have enough sense to leave with them.

They have given up, she thought angrily. *They have turned coward instead of holding the line.* "Cowards!" she hollered. "Spineless, gutless cowards! Is this how German men protect their women?"

Just then, a staff car carrying several officers pulled up. One of them opened his door and beckoned to her. "Hey, girl? Don't you know that it's all over? Get in and we'll take you somewhere safe."

Lisl gave him a hard look and spat on the ground. "Not when there is a centimeter of sacred German soil left to defend. Stay and help us. Regain your honor!"

Over the man's shoulder, she spotted Herr Oppermann. The elderly man was still wearing his Volkssturm armband, and he looked away when she tried to make eye contact. All summer long, he had patiently trained the citizens of Schönfeld in the use of what few weapons they had. But now the man who had won an Iron Cross for himself in the First World War, was slinking away like a dog. It was an outrage.

Screaming in inarticulate fury, she picked up a rock and threw it at him. It missed, and earned her a peal of derisive laughter from the officers. Lisl rounded on them.

"Traitors!" she yelled. "You should all be shot!"

"Listen, you little fool," the officer said. "The Russians are coming here by the thousands and we can't stop them. Now get in, or stay here and get yourself raped."

She grabbed another rock, and hefted it threateningly. "No, I'm staying and fighting, and so should you."

"Fine," the officer retorted. "The hell with it. Go and get yourself killed." He patted his driver on the shoulder and the vehicle pulled away.

Lisl watched it go until it turned a corner, and then she dropped the stone and stomped down the street in the opposite direction. The flags which had once flown so proudly there were all gone now, and most of the residents had shuttered their windows, or simply disappeared in the night.

Not at her house though. There, the swastika banner still hung from the window, declaring to everyone that the inhabitants were loyal Germans who counted a member of the valiant SS as one of their own. Not cravens who pretended to be soldiers of the Reich and then left its citizens to fend for themselves.

She was halfway back to her home when she spotted her friend, and fellow BDM member, Maria Daecher. "Didn't you get any of them to stay?" Maria asked.

Lisl shook her head. "No," she replied, ignoring the hot, angry tears that were coursing down her cheeks. "They're leaving. It's up to us now. Come on."

She led them to the edge of town. An MG-42 light machinegun that had seen better days, had been set up along the road by the Volkssturm several weeks earlier, along with an assortment of vintage grenades and the newer *Panzerfaust* anti-tank weapons. She had trained with the '42 like everyone else, but she had never imagined that she would be manning it with just Maria to help her.

But she seemed to have no choice. They would either handle it themselves, or step aside and let the Bolsheviks roll right over them. And after all the sacrifices that her father and his valiant comrades had made cleansing the east of its impure blood, the idea of facing him and having to admit to such an act of weakness was unthinkable. It was better to fight bravely like the true daughter of an SS man.

She put on the helmet that she found in in the dugout and took her place behind the machinegun, waving for Maria to come and serve up her ammunition belts. After that, they waited for the first Russian to appear…

**

Schneider had reached a road that he was fairly certain led straight into Schönfeld. It was still daylight and he kept to the edges of it, ready to bolt for the woods at the first sign of danger.

His caution proved to be well-justified. The motorcycle came around a bend in the road before his ears had the time to warn him, and when the soldier in the sidecar saw him, he shouted something. It sounded like a challenge and Schneider waved at him and smiled, hoping that this would be enough.

It wasn't. The soldier yelled again, and this time, Schneider was able to understand one of the words all-too perfectly, *"Nemetsky!"* "German!"

A chill went up his spine. *God, someone must have gone back to the bodies and found the fellow that I undressed. They know!*

Reflex took over, and he dashed for the trees. Behind him, the light machinegun mounted on the sidecar chattered and the bark on the tree trunks around him exploded. He didn't even try to counterattack. Instead, he just kept running, and firing quick, blind bursts with his weapon back in the general direction of his attackers.

By the time he was approaching the crest of a small hill, another vehicle had arrived, and risking a glance over his shoulder, he saw that it was a truck very like the Opel. But this one was filled with a squad of enemy troops who jumped out and started coming up after him.

Weighed down by the gold and jewelry in his pockets, Schneider's legs felt like they were on fire, and his lungs ached for air, but he forced himself to keep going. When the trees ahead of him suddenly gave way to an open place, he realized that he had reached the fields that surrounded Schönfeld, and the dirt road leading up into the village.

He could also hear the Russians behind him. They were catching up. His only option was to leave the forest and make for the village. Once he had evaded them in the maze of streets and houses, he would slip away and try to find Lisl.

A bullet buzzed by his ear, and he broke cover and ran out onto the road. Then he saw something. There were two people sitting behind a makeshift emplacement at the edge of town. They had to be with the Volkssturm, he decided. One of them even looked a little like his daughter, although he was still too far away to be sure and the shadows cast by her incongruous-looking helmet only added to his uncertainty.

No, he thought as he drew closer, *it is her! It's my Lisl. I have to warn her about the Russians. She has to get out of here before it's too late.* Finding his strength renewed by desperation, he ran faster, and started to cry out her name...

...Lisl Schneider gasped when she saw the Russian running out of the forest. "Look Maria! There's one of them now!"

The man was more than 600 meters away, but well within the range of the machinegun, and she was a good shot. She set her shoulder against the stock just like she'd been taught, centered the sights on the running figure and squeezed the trigger. The '42 went off with a sound like an enormous piece of cloth tearing in half, and brass flew everywhere as it spat out a hail of bullets.

When the dust finally cleared down the road, she could see the body lying there. It wasn't moving, and the 7.92 mm rounds had turned the man's tunic into bloody shreds. Oddly, something glinted in the sun all around the corpse that reminded Lisl of coins or jewelry. She was too excited to wonder about this though.

"I got him!" she said, pointing at her handiwork. "Did you see that Maria? I got the Red bastard."

Maria nodded, looking a little ill, and managed to summon up a wan smile as she brought out a fresh belt of ammunition. "Do you think that's all of them?" she asked hopefully.

"If it's not, then the other Ivan's will be thinking twice about coming here now," Lisl answered confidently. "They know what will happen to them."

Ten more minutes passed before they heard a vehicle clanking towards them. Then the tank came into view. It was flanked by soldiers, and there were more vehicles and men behind it.

Lisl didn't hesitate to fire. The fusillade ripped through the trees and the soldiers ran for cover. At the same time, the tank came to a halt, and for a moment, she thought that the Reds had decided to give up, and turn around.

The loud report and a flash of light from the tank's turret proved her wrong. The next thing that she knew, she was being flung up into the air and then she landed with an impact that knocked all the breath out of her.

For some reason, she couldn't move or even feel her arms and legs, and when she looked for her, Maria was gone. The only thing that she recognized was Maria's shoe. It still contained a foot and a short bloody stub of a bone.

She could also hear voices coming closer and speaking to each other in Russian or something like it. Lisl didn't care though. She had done what her father would have done in the same circumstances, and she knew that wherever he was, that he would be proud of her when he learned about her sacrifice for the Fatherland.

Her only regret was that she hadn't lived long enough to see him come home.

The Curse of Three

Gul'dlax was in serious trouble. The Slipship's transcendence drives had given out completely and the vessel had tumbled back into normal space at the edge of an unexplored star system. According to her charts, system XE801197-333 was still well within the Far Arm, a region that was known for its wildness and savagery. She was thousands of light years from the Galactic Core and any vestige of civilization.

She didn't attempt to make any excuses, or cast the blame elsewhere. The disaster had been entirely her fault.

It had been her Year of Freedom, the last time that she could do as she wished before living out the remainder of her life in the Palace of the Eight Moons. And she had decided to spend it exploring the stars in her own Slipship. Before setting out, the Queen's royal advisors had warned her repeatedly about the dangers of such an adventure, and they had urged her to keep well away from the Von Empire.

She hadn't listened. She had been so eager to make a new discovery, and so blindly certain of herself, that she had flown across the border, and made straight for the most sacred place in the Empire, the Von'daari Nebula. It was where the Von believed that their Gods had fought one another for dominion over the universe, and where legend claimed that the Von themselves had been born, formed from the pools of blood that had been spilled in that primordial battle.

No foreign ships had ever been allowed to enter the region, and the penalty for violating this prohibition was death. A Von warship had caught her trespassing, and only a combination of skillful piloting, and raw luck, had enabled her to survive the encounter.

She had paid dearly for her recklessness though. Her Slipship had been badly damaged; in addition to the transcendence drives, her communications array was burned out, and the energy levels of her in-system engines were beginning to drop sharply. When those failed, she would be completely unable to maneuver, or to prevent her vessel from being pulled into the system's sun.

Somehow, she had to find a place to land. And once she did, she would be marooned until another Slipship happened by, or someone heard her rescue beacon. The wait could be mere days, or it could stretch into years, or even decades.

Or until I die from old age, or misadventure, she thought grimly.

Gul'dlax stopped herself. Self-pity and defeatism were not worthy emotions for a Giposhi Princess of the Blood to entertain. Princesses did not allow adversity to triumph. They took charge, and found a way to overcome the obstacles that were in their way. Which was exactly what she would do, she told herself. She would rise above this crisis, she would be rescued, and she would come out if it all the stronger.

Resolute, she activated the ship's sensors and scanned the star system. As the data appeared, she examined it carefully.

XE801197-333 had nine planets. The three outermost worlds were icy, lifeless places, with poisonous atmospheres of methane, hydrogen and helium.

The next two were deadly gas giants. One was encircled by deceptively beautiful rings that concealed the searing death-trap that lurked within its cloudy depths. Its monstrous neighbor was over twice its size, and looked like the very hazard it was. It even sported a great red eye in its lower hemisphere that made Gul'dlax think of an unblinking predator, waiting for the chance to consume her ship.

This left only the four innermost worlds to consider, and of these, only three were within the habitable range. Like any noble with superior breeding and a higher education, she didn't consider herself to be superstitious, but the common classes all believed the number three to be an unlucky sum. To them, it represented evil and misfortune of all kinds, and the notion was so ingrained in Giposhi culture that the very word for adversity in their language meant 'the curse of three'.

Gul'dlax had no other options however. *Three it is then*, she decided. She immediately requested a more detailed analysis. In a few *millicrons*, the results came back.

The first planet proved to be too hot. The second planet, too cold. But the third planet was just right.

For better or worse, she had found her destination. She set course, and engaged the in-system engines.

***

Three *centicrons* later, her long distance scanners registered another vessel entering the system. It was not a Giposhi ship, nor anything flown by their allies. It was the very same warship that had attacked her in the nebula. The Von had come to finish her off.

Cursing its crew to the Three Hells of Asymmetry and Disorder, Gul'dlax throttled her engines to maximum. She also pointedly disregarded the holographic warnings that were materializing before her pilot's chair. She already knew what they were trying to tell her, and there was nothing she could do about it.

The in-systems would certainly fail, but she had already accepted the fact that her ship was doomed from the instant that it had staggered back into normal space. By sacrificing it now, she had a chance to get herself close enough to the third planet to engage her escape pod, and hopefully, cease to be of any interest to her pursuers.

She checked her heading and distance. The planet's moon was coming up fast, and realizing what she was attempting to do, the Von had increased their speed. In a few more millicrons, they would be close enough to fire their devastator rays.

As she routed additional power to her rear shields, Gul'dlax received another dire message. Already taxed to its limits, the Slipship did not have enough energy in reserve to protect her from more than a few hits. After that, the shields would collapse. It was going to be a close thing.

Another alarm appeared right on its heels. The Von were now within firing range. An instant later, the Slipship shook violently as the first devastator ray slammed into it. Exterior sensors transmitted an image the hull. It was dancing with green lightning as the energy from the blast was redistributed back into space. Simultaneously, power levels dropped, and all of the displays in her control cabin flickered and dimmed.

In the meantime, the Von were powering up their guns for another volley, but her readouts assured her that she had managed to reach the minimum safe ejection distance. Gul'dlax sent the command and the armored walls of the escape pod closed around her chair.

As it dropped away from the ship, the Von fired again. This time, the shields couldn't handle the stress and she watched on the pod's view screen as her Slipship was destroyed. The airless void of space prevented the noise from reaching her, but the event was no less violent for its silence. Once again, green lightning surrounded the hull, brightening until it had reached a near-blinding intensity, and then the ship disintegrated.

Desperately, she searched the world below her for a place to put down. Most of its surface was covered with water, but she spotted a continent that seemed like a good candidate. Although the pod's guidance drives had a limited amount of energy, a quick check assured her that she had enough in reserve to get down safely. This was assuming that the Von were finally done with her.

Unfortunately, they weren't. Another devastator ray lanced out at the pod and it managed to absorb the blast, but not as well as the Slipship had. Everything in the control cabin went offline at once, and Gul'dlax fought to regain power and control.

When the emergency backup systems finally came into play, her instrumentation had more bad news to deliver. Half of her landing thrusters were now inoperative, and worse, two small craft had left the warship and were heading straight for her. The Von captain had dispatched a pair of fighters to ensure that she didn't live long enough to settle into her new home.

Uttering another oath, Gul'dlax increased her rate of descent and launched a cluster of decoys. The landscape immediately below her was densely forested, with coniferous trees covering every square *centa* and she looked for an open space.

There were none. She would have to crash land and hope that the pod was as tough as she had been told. Checking her safety harnesses, she braced herself for a hard impact.

When the pod hit the tree line it proved the quality of its manufacture, turning the ancient conifers into kindling and carving a long, deep gouge in the earth. The instant that it had stopped moving, Gul'dlax released her harnesses and made for the egress hatch.

At first, it refused to open, but when she put all of her strength into the effort, she was able to create a gap that was just wide enough to squeeze through. Grabbing up her survival pack, she clambered out, and ran for the tree line.

A low humming overhead heralded the arrival of the Von fighters. It was followed by the crackling sound of their devastator rays firing, and then a hollow 'whump' as the pod exploded. By this point, Gul'dlax had managed to get herself far enough away that she didn't actually see the blast, but the shock wave still reached her. As the trees around her shuddered and swayed from the explosion, she was slammed to the ground.

She didn't dare to rise until the hum had faded away and the only thing that she heard in her helmet's speakers was the wind and the rain. Then she started moving, trying to gain as much distance as possible from the crash site. She also began searching for some kind of shelter.

It was dusk by the time she found it. It was a cave, halfway up a cliff, and although the face was steep, it only took her a few centicrons to reach it. When she did, she was pleased to find that it was unoccupied. The ceiling within was low, and she had to bend over to enter, but it was dry and deep enough to offer ample protection from the elements.

So this is home--for now, she thought. It was a far cry from the Palace of the Eight Moons, or even her Slipship, and she felt another wave of self-pity trying to take hold, but she refused to give in. She had to stay strong, and get on with the business of survival.

She reached up, unsnapped the catches of her helmet and removed it. It came away with a soft hiss, and as she shook out her long blond hair, she took her first deep breath of the planet's atmosphere. It was pregnant with the moisture from the rain, and smelled of mold, damp earth, and other alien substances, but just as her scans had promised, it was breathable.

And this is what it smells like, she thought. She only hoped that she would not be there long enough to become accustomed to it.

Setting the helmet aside, she went to work unpacking her survival kit. One corner of the cavern proved to be smooth, broad and flat, and she laid out her bedding there. Her purifier, which processed alien food and water sources, was set down next to it, along with a small, but efficient heater. A niche in another wall was transformed into a storage place for her emergency rations and water packs, and once she had triggered it, a palm-sized lantern floated up and took its place near the ceiling, illuminating the space with a cheerful, reassuring glow.

The last item to come out was the emergency com unit, but she didn't switch on the rescue beacon right away. There was still a good chance that the Von were loitering in the system, and the last thing she wanted was to provoke them any further. Instead, she activated its passive long-range scanner and prayed for the best.

When the hologram of the star-system appeared, she relaxed. Content with having stranded her, the Von had departed, and the star system was empty. It was safe to use the beacon.

With a gentle flick of her finger, she initiated device and sat back. It was impossible to estimate how long it would take for the signal to reach a civilized world, but Gul'dlax was confident that someone would hear it, and send help, especially since a Giposhi Princess was in distress. In the meantime, all that she could do was wait, and make the best of her circumstances.

***

On her third day, she encountered her first native. She had been exploring the area around the cave, getting to know the terrain and trying to locate a source of potable water.

Thanks to all the rain, the search had been an easy one. The forest was crisscrossed with small streams created by the runoff, and one of them had turned out to be conveniently close. In addition, her hand scanner reported that the water itself didn't have any parasites or toxic substances that her purifier couldn't easily handle.

Unfortunately, the streambed had also attracted the native. A warning came from the proximity alarms in her scanner, but before she could retreat to a hiding place, the creature had walked into view.

Its very existence surprised her. None of her scans had indicated intelligent life, and she had been in too much of a hurry to look for anything of a lower order. Yet, here it was.

The creature was a living study in evolutionary similarities, and stark differences. Like her, it was a humanoid life form, with the same binocular vision. But where her eyes were golden, slitted, and set between a delicately shaped nose and fine-boned features, the native's were watery blue orbs that seemed to float in a grotesque white sclera. Not a healthy black.

The face that framed these eyes was lumpy and bloated looking, as if it had been half-formed by some inexpert artist who had simply given up on their composition, and walked away. It also had hair, which covered its head and the lower part of its face and jaw, but unlike the metallic sheen that her golden locks possessed, it was dull and lifeless.

Its ears were just as malformed. They were not pointed, but rounded at their edges, and as near as Gul'dlax could tell, they did not seem to be capable of movement. This made her wonder if the poor thing was required to turn its head every time that it needed to focus on a sound, and she concluded from this that its hearing was probably exceptionally poor.

It also lacked the proper number of arms. Instead of four upper limbs like any entity with an evolved nervous system, there were only two. This lent it a crippled, misshapen look. The fact that it was only half as tall as she, and had pale, pink skin rather than a deep blue, only heaped another pair of insults onto its unflattering appearance.

Despite these glaring flaws however, it was also undeniable that the native was at least marginally intelligent. Although they were crudely made, it wore clothing, and it carried a simple pack on its back. It also used a stick to help it maneuver over the uneven ground, proving beyond any question that it was capable of employing simple tools.

The hand that it grasped the staff with particularly fascinated her. There were the normal four fingers and a thumb seen in any advanced being, but oddly, no retractable claws to defend itself with. In addition, the digits themselves were so short and stubby that she was amazed that the thing had any dexterity whatsoever.

While she speculated about the environmental conditions that had given birth to such a weak and stunted entity, the native knelt and brought some of the water up to its lips to drink. A moment later, it stood, and realized that she was there. Its grotesque eyes widened in shock, and it let out a shrill scream and fell backwards, scrabbling away from her in absolute terror.

Trying her best to soothe it, she raised her hands in greeting, splaying her fingers so that it could see that she was unarmed. She even made a point of keeping her claws retracted and refrained from smiling so that it wouldn't perceive her fangs as a threat.

None of this did anything to lessen the creatures panic though. The thing rose to its feet and ran away from her, howling something that sounded very much like words, but in a language that was so harsh and guttural that it was more like the bellow of an animal than anything else.

"Wait!" she cried after it in Giposh'ta, "I mean you no harm." She repeated her message in Tish'vok, and Paaru, the two trade languages that everyone in the Galactic Core knew.

It was useless though. The maddened thing didn't seem to comprehend her at all. It just kept crashing through the underbrush and even collided with several trees in its frantic dash to escape.

Sadly, Gul'dlax watched it go, and then filled her water container. One of her goals had been to make first contact with an alien race, and she had achieved this. Except that like the rest of her voyage, it had turned into a disaster.

Perhaps I was wrong about the number three, she decided. *Maybe it really is just as unlucky as the commoners say.* Listening to the native's screams fading into the distance, it certainly seemed that way.

Back at her cave, she filled the purifier, set it to work, and then thought carefully about the entire encounter. Clearly, the indigenes of this world were xenophobes, which meant that they had the potential to become a serious threat. If her stay on the third planet was going to be an extended one, she needed to find a way forge a peaceful coexistence with them.

But how? she wondered. There simply *had* to be an answer. Other explorers had faced the same challenges, and they had managed to succeed. Surely she, with all of the education that she had received at the Palace, could come up with an equally workable solution.

Small gifts of food and medicine perhaps? Left out where they can be found? One of her royal teachers had once told her that wild animals were tamed that way. Trust was built up in gradual stages until the animal became used to its benefactor. Given the primitive nature of the being that she had observed, the same principle appeared to be valid.

Yes, she thought. *That is how I will turn this disaster into a triumph. I will get the natives to trust me, and when they do, I will become their teacher.*

I will introduce them to naturally occurring chemicals that they can use for fertilizers and insecticides. Their food production will soar, and they will be able to stave off starvation.

After that, I will show them modern medicines! I will teach them how to cure their diseases and increase their lifespans tenfold. Surely after doing all that, they will come to accept me.

There was even the extremely slim chance that they could be taught to read and speak Giposh'ta, or at least, one of the simpler trade languages. After all, the native *had* made sounds that resembled a language, she reminded herself. It had the potential to become civilized, and with the right guidance, its kind might eventually be accepted by the Amethyst Throne as vassals. Their planet could even go on to serve as a Giposhi colony in the Far Arm.

That would show the accursed Von!

She became so excited by all this that she barely noticed that the sun had set, and it was a struggle for her to ignore the heady images that danced in her mind when she finally lay down to sleep. They were the stuff of an amazing ballad; a bright and shining civilization, brought out of its ignorance and darkness by her wisdom and charity. She also saw herself, leading the people of the third planet as the ruler she had been bred to be, adored, and even venerated as a god.

161

It was an accomplishment that would amaze her rescuers and be remembered among the Giposhi for eons. She even had a title in mind for the song that would commemorate this great achievement. Upon her return to the Palace of the Eight Moons, she would insist that the court musicians call it *"The Song of Gul'dlax, Bringer of Peace, Wisdom and Civilization."*

***

Drie Bären had begun its existence as *Tres Ursi,* a Roman settlement. It had been named for a trio of bears that had lived in the area at the time of its founding. Although the bears had long since been driven off, Drie Bären still remembered them, and the Empire that had established the community. Rome might have fallen, but the village continued to fulfil its original role as a local trade hub.

It was a place where farmers could come and sell their wares, drink ale, and buy goods that they could not manufacture for themselves. Drie Bären boasted a blacksmith, a carpenter, an alehouse, and even a small church. Except for the harvest fairs however, it was not a place that was accustomed to much excitement, or brushes with the occult.

As a result, the tale that the disheveled, terrified traveler managed to stammer out alarmed everyone. The village priest was summoned, and by the time Priester Jakob had finished listening, a group of men had already gathered around him, ready to deal with the threat to their community. But to be successful, they all knew that they would need the assistance of an expert.

***

Helmut raised his axe and brought it down on the wood with a sure hand. Years of hard work had made him strong, and his axe was sharp and well made. He split the piece in one stroke, and tossed the halves into the pile next to him before placing another log on the stump. There was already plenty of wood stocked up for the winter, but he enjoyed the work, and the chance that it gave him to be alone, and to think. Generally, his thoughts centered on the business of hunting in the surrounding forest, and the needs of his wife and child.

Today though, he was wondering about the object that had fallen from the sky. It wasn't the first time that anything had ever descended from heaven to strike East Francia. Back when it had still been a part of Charlemagne's empire, his great grandfather had witnessed a rock drop down from the firmament.

Unlike many of his neighbors, his ancestor hadn't regarded it as an ill omen, but a piece of heaven itself. The man had even carved a few bits of it off and had kept them as lucky talismans, calling them his 'heaven stones'. Helmut wore the one that he had inherited from his father on a simple leather thong around his neck.

And just as his great grandfather had believed, the heaven stone *had* bestowed him luck. As an archer, Helmut had managed to survive the bloody civil wars that followed the death of Louis the Pious, cheating death when better men than he had fallen in battle.

After the war, he had returned to the forest, and it had rewarded him by yielding up its bounty to his bow season after season. He had even been blessed with a good wife who was willing to live with him in such a remote location, and she had borne him a healthy son.

The latest object was another matter altogether. Like his great grandfather's rock, it too had dropped out of the sky and cratered the earth. He had not found another iron stone though, but strange bits of metal. They had had the look of things that had been worked by a clever smith, and there were other substances among them that he could not recognize.

Many of the pieces had also been inscribed with letters, and although he could not read, he was a tracker by trade, and had a keen eye for shapes. He knew Latin characters, and the delicate spidery script that had been inscribed on the fragments had been nothing like them. They were from somewhere else, a place beyond his reckoning, and he even entertained the possibility that he had glimpsed the language of the angels themselves.

But then there had been the tracks leading away from the scene. They had looked human enough, but they had been larger than any footprints that he was accustomed to. Following them had yielded nothing but more mysteries however; the rain had erased the trail and whoever had made them had not returned to the site.

For these reasons, he had avoided the place ever since. Such things were beyond the ken of mortal men and better left alone. He also made a point of saying nothing about it when he returned to his wife.

It wasn't that he didn't trust her. He did, with his home and the very life of his young son. Gertrude was a faithful companion and an able homemaker, but like any woman, she was also given to gossip, and this was something that he didn't want his neighbors to hear about.

Overall, the people of Drie Bären were a decent lot, albeit simple at times, and by and large there had never been any animosity between them. Just the same, Helmut preferred his solitude, and he knew that this was viewed by them as peculiar.

The fact that his wife was an expert in plant remedies only added to the oddness that surrounded them both—even if the villagers *did* benefit from her cures. This new event would only magnify all of that, and could even lead to problems.

After all, he thought, no one else in the area wore a piece of the sky around their neck, or had the unusual luck of chancing upon a second object from heaven. People might begin to wonder, and wonder might lead to suspicion, and then, accusation.

Helmut didn't fancy the idea of being banished, or worse. Although the burning of witches had been outlawed by Charlemagne himself, it still occurred. Especially in remote areas where no one would bother to report the death of a lowly forester and his tiny family. It was far better to let the forest keep the mysterious metal fragments, he decided, and live a quiet, scandal-free life.

With the issue resolved, he brought up another log and readied himself for the cut. Before he could split the piece, his dog began barking, and he caught sight of the group of men coming up the path to his cottage.

They were from Drie Bären and led by Priester Jakob himself. To a man, they were all armed. The smith had brought his hammer, several others carried wooden pitchforks or crude cudgels, two had their boar spears with them, and the carpenter held a rusty sword that looked as if it had been taken off of a dead noble during the war. Compared to the men that he had fought alongside with in the war, they were a poor excuse for an army, but no less dangerous for it.

Keeping near his bow, Helmut nodded to the Priester warily. "Ho, Priester. What brings thee so far from the village and armed thus?"

"Devils," the priest replied. "As thou knoweth, a thing fell from the sky not long ago. Then a traveler passing through these woods was set upon by a demon. We have come to hunt the fiend down."

A chill went up Helmut's spine at this, but he still managed to summon up a dry smile and the pretense of calm. "Art thou certain that this 'demon' is not merely the product of too much sun, "he asked him, "or perchance an overindulgence of ale? Methinks the man saw a maddened hermit."

He certainly believed in the existence of the Devil, but he strongly doubted that one of his minions had bothered to come up from Hell just to scare one poor wretch. The civil war had taught him that his fellow men did an excellent job of carrying out Satan's plans, and didn't need the assistance of supernatural entities.

Priester Jakob glowered back. "We are sure of the man's report," he answered firmly. "The very sight of the thing drove him half-mad. Verily, he was so a'frightened that he pissed himself. The foul thing is here in these woods and we have come to beseech thee for thy aid."

"My aid? I am no man of God such as thee."

Jakob's eyes went directly to the stone around Helmut's neck, and narrowed. "No, thou art not, and mayhap thou hast some *special* knowledge of this apparition? Thy family is known hereabouts for its strangeness and its love of wild places."

"By my troth, I am a true Christian, and thou should guard thy tongue with care," Helmut growled. "I knoweth naught of such things, and there is no sin in wanting a life apart from the crowded warren that thou calleth a village."

I can be at my bow in one stride, he thought, *and slay three of them before any man among them could raise their weapon against me.*

But he couldn't kill all of them, and once he had fired his arrows, his pleasant, peaceful life would be over. He and his family would become outlaws and every man's hand would be raised against him.

"Then I challenge thee to prove thy faith," Jakob retorted, "and lend thy skills to thy neighbors as a forester and a bowman. These woods are as well known to thee as our fields are to us, and we would see this business through."

Helmut knew that he had been cornered just as neatly as any game he had ever hunted. He could not refuse the Priester and both of them knew it. To do so would be to admit that he was worthy suspicion, and as a free man, he was honor-bound to come to the aid of his neighbors. Whether he wanted to or not.

He set down his axe and took up his bow and quiver. "So be it," he said.

***

Leading the party into the forest, Helmut came across the unusual tracks once again. In a fresher state, it was clear that they hadn't been made by the cloven hooves of the Evil One, or any of his spawn. Rather, they seemed to have been produced by a large man wearing oddly constructed boots. It was also quite plain that the stranger had had no knowledge of woodcraft whatsoever. They made no effort to conceal their trail, and had often taken routes that wiser, more experienced travelers would have avoided.

City folk? he wondered. That certainly explained the traveler's clumsiness.

Pausing to examine one of the prints more closely, he waved away the Priester's impatience and made a quick estimate. Based upon its size and the length of the stride, he concluded that whoever had walked there was easily over two bow staves tall, and therefore twice his height.

This made the visitor a giant by local standards, but this failed to alarm him. During the war, and the raids that had followed it, he had known men from the far north who had been much larger than himself. He didn't find it inconceivable that there were others, living in more distant lands, who were even taller.

When he shared his thoughts with the Priester, the cleric adamantly refused to accept them. "No man created by the hand of God could attain such a height," Jakob argued. "This thing must be the offspring of a giant, and therefore an unnatural creature."

Helmut knew that it was useless to contradict him, and took the lead again. Several hours passed before the tracks led them to the cliff side, and his seasoned eye spotted the cave right

167

away. He also saw the signs that someone had been making regular trips up and down the rocks. They were subtle clues that only a tracker would have noticed; a clump of grass dislodged from its perch, a rock lying at the base of the cliff, and most telling of all, a tiny piece of silver thread that had become ensnared in the branches of a bush.

The climber had been sloppy, but Helmut still had to award them a sliver of admiration for their choice of a shelter. The cave was too high for any bear or wolf to reach, and most men would have missed it altogether. In his experience, the average man never looked up, or looked around them with much care.

He signaled for the group to halt, and quietly reported his findings to Priester Jakob.

"We must take this monster in its lair," Jakob declared. "Now, before it can terrorize the countryside any further."

"It is still daylight," Helmut replied. "Thou saidest thyself that the traveler reported seeing this apparition by day. Methinks that we should hide ourselves, and catch it when it returns to its cave for the night. I am sure that whatever it is, it is out foraging, and will come back when the light leaves this place."

Jakob shook his head. "Nay, methinks not. We must take it now, before it can employ the darkness to its advantage." With that, he waved for the men to advance.

Sighing tiredly, Helmut began climbing. He knew, without having to ask, that Jakob expected him to be the first one up, and privately, he had to agree. If there actually was anything dangerous in the cave, he was the only one among them who would really know how to handle himself.

At the cave entrance, he stopped, nocked an arrow in his bow and peered in cautiously. The cavity wasn't deep, and he was able to see all the way to the back of it.

Just as he had anticipated, it was vacant, but not empty. Someone had made a camp for themselves inside. He recognized the shape of a bedroll, although it was made of a shiny silver fabric the like of which he had never seen before.

There were also other items inside that totally defied his understanding. Some of them had tiny lamps set in them that glowed and flashed like embers, and a few had small windows that crawled with odd shapes and more of the delicate spidery writing he had seen on the metal fragments. One of these gave off a low pulsing hum that set his teeth on edge.

Whoever they were, the owner was connected with the object that had fallen from the sky, and Helmut began to doubt his original assessment.

Mayhap this stranger is supernatural after all, he thought. *Or a wizard.* It galled him to think that Jakob had been right all along, but he could not ignore the evidence laid out before him. It fairly reeked of witchery.

The Priester and the others joined him a moment later. Seeing the contents, a number of them crossed themselves and Helmut was tempted to join in, but he refrained. He still didn't want to give Jakob the satisfaction.

"Sorcery!" the Priester declared, pointing a long bony finger at the objects. "Tools of the Devil intended to make mischief upon good men. These wicked contrivances must be destroyed forthwith."

Helmut shook his head. "That would be unwise," he advised. "If their owner returns and sees the devastation that we have wrought, they will surely flee and be all the harder to catch. Better that we leave this untouched and secret ourselves nearby."

"The Lord has guided us to its lair," the Priester retorted, "and He will guide us to wherever this damned soul hides itself. Our task must be attended to without delay."

Helmut did not recall being led to the cave by any angel, but by the tracks and his own skills, but again, he chose not to debate the matter. Instead, he kept his tongue and stood aside as the villagers entered the cavern and threw everything down the cliff-side. Even the silver bedroll went over the edge—after someone had slashed it to pieces with their belt knife.

When they were finished, the Priester led the group in prayer and piously announced that the cavern had been cleansed of its corruption. Then they descended back to the forest floor. There, a fire was kindled, and everything was consigned to the flames.

***

The first sign that something had gone terribly wrong was the faint odor of burning plastic carried to her by the breeze. And when the cliff face came into view, Gul'dlax saw the dying fire, and within it, the melted remains of her possessions.

"Oh no!" she wailed, running over and dropping to her knees. "No, no, no!" The heat seared her fingers as she tried to pull out what she could, but she was too grief stricken to care.

There has to be something left, she thought desperately. *Something. Anything.*

It was all gone though. Her purifier, the emergency com beacon, her rations, the medical supplies, and even her bedding, were nothing but cinders and melted slag.

Gul'dlax brought her ash-covered hands to her face, and wept. Without her survival gear, she would never leave the third planet. Instead she would starve, or die from disease.

She was doomed.

***

Three weeks passed and life had returned to normal. There were no further reports of demons, or anything else out of the ordinary. Which was fine as far as Helmut was concerned.

He still came across the unusual tracks now and again, and he continued to wonder about the true nature of their creator, but his concerns about their otherworldly origin had faded.

Whatever was making them was mortal enough, and it was minding its own business and keeping its distance.

So he minded his. As long as the stranger stayed away and didn't attempt to cause any harm to his family, he was content to leave things as they were and focus his attention on other matters.

Today, it was tanning deer hides and preparing furs to sell at the marketplace. That, and eating the porridge that Gertrude was preparing for their midday meal. She had managed to find them some raspberries and currants the day before, and they would transform their simple meal into a veritable feast. Helmut's stomach rumbled in anticipation as he worked the last of the fat from a hide with his blade.

When he heard Gertrude calling him to table, he set down his work, and went into the cottage. She was just adding the berries to the meal as he took his place at the bench. His bowl had received the currants that he preferred, and she was adding the raspberries to hers. Nothing extra had gone into their son's porridge; they had learned from many a tantrum that he was an unusual child. He only favored bland fare---even honey upset him.

"Methinks it tis too hot," she said warningly.

Helmut took an experimental spoonful and winced. Despite blowing on it a few times, he had to admit that she was right. It needed to cool a bit. "Aye, it tis at that, wife."

Intent on returning to his hides, he rose, but Gertrude had other plans. "Husband, before we go to market, I must needs gather more mugwort and houndsbane. Perchance we could search them out together? An extra set of eyes would help greatly."

Helmut wasn't deceived in the least. His mate had a great skill for finding even the rarest of medicinal plants and didn't need his help. But strange events at the cave had unnerved her, and she was still reluctant to venture into the forest alone.

He took up his bow and slung his quiver. "Very well, wife," he agreed "A short stroll and a little more work will only sharpen my appetite."

Patting his thigh, he signaled for their dog to join them. As the beast rose from its place by the fire, stretched, and wagged its tail eagerly, Gertrude smiled gratefully, and began bundling up their son.

***

Gul'dlax watched the native family leave from her hiding place behind a screen of trees. She had learned to recognize the differences in their ages and sexes, and even some of the crude implements that they used for work and hunting.

From the weapons that the male was carrying, and the sling that the female had secured their child in, it was obvious that they were going somewhere. The fact that they were bringing their domesticated animal along suggested that their trip would be an extended one.

She didn't need very much time though. Just enough to enter their dwelling and find herself something to eat.

She knew that she was taking a terrible risk, but there was no choice. The forest had shown itself to be a harsh and desolate place. What animals there were, were wily, and evaded her easily, and the flora was either poisonous, or without any nutritive value whatsoever.

Her worst experience had been with a handful of mushrooms. The scanner had warned her about their toxic peptides, but she had been so desperate for a meal that she had consumed them anyway--and had nearly died in the process.

The local water hadn't been much better. Without the purifier, it had made her ill more often than not, and she knew without consulting the scanner, that parasites and unfriendly bacteria had already lodged themselves in her body. Soon, if she didn't manage to find something safe to eat and drink, she would become too feeble to care for herself. Then the third planet would finally claim her life.

Determined not to allow this to happen, Gul'dlax started forwards. Without realizing it, she had unholstered her necronizer, and when she realized it, she jammed it back into her belt in disgust.

I may be starving, she told herself, *but I am also Giposhi Princess, an heir to a culture of peace and reason.*

Despite what the natives had done to her, she wasn't about to abandon her ideals, or her goal to civilize them. If there was anyone inside the structure, she would try to explain her needs to them, or simply flee. She would not commit murder for a scrap of food. Only Far Arm barbarians, or the Von, did things like that.

She made her way down to the dwelling on unsteady legs. At the entrance, she was forced to pause for a moment, and brace herself against it as a wave of vertigo sent the world into a spin. Spells like this were becoming more and more common, she reflected, and lasting longer each time. But food would change that.

Fighting the tremor in her hands, she gripped her scanner tightly and used it to check the interior for life-forms. Except for a few small rodents however, the structure was empty.

There was no time to lose. She heaved the crude door aside and went in. The cottage had only one room, with a loft set above it serviced by a primitive ladder. A large fireplace occupied the far wall, and a rough-hewn table and benches sat before it, set with three wooden bowls and some eating utensils.

Coming closer, Gul'dlax discovered that they were all filled with boiled vegetable matter. The aroma made her mouth water and she started to reach for the nearest one, but her experience with the mushrooms gave her pause and she consulted her scanner again.

Thanks to the addition of some berries, the first bowl was too acidic for her weakened state to handle. The second, containing a different kind berry, was too alkaline. But the third one, without any additives, was just right.

The third one, she thought sourly. *Of course.*

It was food though, and that was all that really mattered. She seized it up and greedily shoveled the contents into her mouth with her fingers, relishing every bite until the container had been picked clean.

Sated for the first time in weeks, she sat down on the bench and let herself rest. Her limbs felt as if they were made of lead and she had to struggle to keep her eyes from closing. It was as if all of the privations that she had suffered had finally caught up with her and were demanding their due.

I need sleep, she realized. *Real sleep in a place that isn't wet, or cold, or crawling with insects. Someplace like here.*

Again, she understood that she was contemplating something very hazardous, but the thought of getting up and returning to the forest to sleep under some log, or in another damp cave, filled her with loathing. *Just for a few millicrons,* she promised herself. *Then I'll leave. Surely the natives will be gone long enough for me to do that.*

She looked around her for a place to lie down. There were three choices. The first was a large, but serviceable bed which she assumed was intended for the male and his family.

Summoning up what little energy she still had, she went over to it, and lay down, but rose when she realized what a poor location it really was. The bed was facing the door, and far too exposed. If anyone did return, they would spot her immediately.

The second place was a pile of loose straw that had been arranged near the fireplace, and she surmised that it had been set aside for the animal. Gul'dlax didn't even bother with it. It looked hard and uncomfortable, and she was fairly certain that it was infested with vermin.

This left the loft. It was, she saw, just right. She could lie down up there without being seen and still have enough of a warning to escape if she had to.

Only for a few millicrons, she repeated. *No longer.*
Gul'dlax climbed the ladder and settled herself down on an old rush mat that had left in storage there.

The instant that her eyes closed, she was fast asleep.

***

Helmut knew right away that someone had been in their home. Their dog had stopped short of the entrance, and it was snarling.

"A wanderer perchance?" Gertrude asked him, and then her eyes widened in fear. "Or that demon?"

"There is no demon, wife," Helmut said reproachfully. "Methinks a wanderer is more the like. I will check within and make certain that the rascal has departed. If not, then I will send him on his way with a kick in the arse."

He left his bow with her, and pulled his axe free of its stump. If it came down to it, it would serve him better in a close-quarters fight.

Once inside, he saw his son's empty bowl and noticed that his dog's anxiety increased as they came closer to the loft. Then he heard a soft rustling sound coming from that direction and tensed. Whoever it was, was up there.

Gritting his teeth, he climbed the ladder as quietly as he could manage. At the top, he peeked over the lip and gasped when he saw what was lying there.

The Priester had been right after all, and he had been an idiot. It *was* a supernatural being, and one glance at its boot clad feet confirmed that it was also the author of all the strange footprints that he had come across.

It was not a demon though. That much the Priester had gotten wrong. Instead, it was a demoness. And she was wholly unlike anything that he had ever laid eyes upon. Helmut stared at her slumbering form with a mixture of dread and fascination.

175

Her strange coloring, and the extra pair of arms that she bore, terrified him to his very core. But the strange silver garment that clung to her alien body like some kind of exotic hose, did nothing to hide the shapeliness of her form, and only emphasized her lustrous golden hair. It was spread out in thick waves all over the rushes, and even in the poor light, it gleamed like threads of the purest gold imaginable.

He found her to be both lovely and loathsome at once. Then, to his astonishment and shame, he felt himself becoming aroused at the sight of her.

Gott im Himmel, he thought in alarm, *I am being bewitched!* Even asleep, the unearthly creature was casting a spell on him, and tempting him with her seductions. He had to do something before his soul was ensnared and she destroyed his entire family. Summoning up all of his strength, he raised his axe…

…Sensing the danger, Gul'dlax opened her eyes and saw the native standing over her with his weapon. "Wait!" she pleaded, "I only wanted some food."

The axe fell without mercy, and Gul'dlax felt the sting of its heavy blade biting into her neck. Choking on her own blood, she tried to take it away from her attacker, but her fingers refused to obey her command. Inexplicably, they had become numb and clumsy.

The axe descended a second time and suddenly, she couldn't feel her body at all.

On the third blow, her head rolled free. As the native grasped her by her hair and raised her up to meet his eyes, she tried to speak to him again.

Why? she wanted to ask. *I never meant you any harm…*

…Horrified, Helmut realized that the she-devil was still alive. Her eyes were wide and staring directly at him, and her mouth was moving as if she were trying to say something. Certain that it some kind of incantation, he let her drop and plugged his ears with his fingers.

He didn't remove them until the creature's face had gone slack, and the life had drained out of her strange yellow eyes.

Down below, he heard Gertrude coming to the foot of the ladder. Before he could forbid it, she had climbed up, and gave out a small cry as she beheld the grisly scene.

"I-Is it dead, husband?"

"It is, wife," he answered. His gaze was fixed on the rushes where the demon had bled out her lifeblood. It was blue, he observed, not red. That alone was proof positive that the creature had never been anything from the mortal realm.

"Verily, we should summon the Priester," Gertrude urged.

"Nay, wife," Helmut replied sharply. "We should not. This is my task alone."

"Husband, this home must needs be blessed and cleansed of evil," she protested.

Helmut wheeled around and grasped her by the shoulders. "Wife, this demon came to our doorstep seeking shelter, and once that becomes widely known, they will think us to be in league with it. Unless thou wisheth to be burned alongside thy husband and son as a witch, thou shalt keep thy silence until thy very dying day. Dost thou understand me, woman? Now, gather up what sacks and cloth thou canst find and fetch them here. I will have need of them."

Gertrude nodded, and to his relief, moved to obey. When she had returned with what he had asked her for, he sent her outside to wait in the yard and then went to work with his axe.

It took him several hours to drag his burden from the cottage to the place where the object had fallen from the sky. There, he gave thanks to the Holy Trinity for his family's deliverance and buried the sacks in the earth together with the strange bits of metal.

He also added one final item to grave; his great-grandfather's heaven stone. He wanted nothing more to do with anything that came from the sky.

Epilogue

Gertrude did not keep their secret. The burden of what had happened in her home became too much to bear, and three months later, she confided in a friend at the marketplace.

The result was exactly as Helmut had predicted. The villagers came for them, and although he fought them bravely, in the end, he and his family were taken, condemned as witches, and burned at the stake.

Three years passed before a plague came to Drie Bären. Lacking even the rudimentary cures that Gertrude might have offered them, the entire populace perished.

The tale of the Demon of the Golden Locks did not die with them though. It was passed from the lips of travelers to other settlements were it was retold from generation to generation, changing with each new iteration.

Eventually, all of the supernatural trappings disappeared, right along with the memory of Drie Bären itself. The details were blended and changed until the story had been transformed into something entirely different from what had actually occurred. No one ever realized who 'Goldilocks' had really been, or where she had actually come from.

The truth, and the lessons it taught, were not lost on the Giposhi however. Three centuries after Princess Gul'dlax met her untimely end, the Galactic Collective awarded ownership of the system XE801197-333 to the Zeta Reticulans and a Slipship was permitted to visit.

There, the crew found the wreckage of the escape pod and the decapitated remains of its hapless pilot. After a careful analysis of the report filed by the captain of the Von warship, the fate of Princess Gul'dlax became appallingly clear.

Her body was taken back to the Palace of the Eight Moons and interred in the Royal Mausoleum with full honors. The details of her demise not only resolved the long standing mystery surrounding her disappearance, but went on to become a precautionary tale that parents told their children at bed time.

It always ended with the same three admonitions; listen to the advice of your elders, never go where you are not allowed, and most importantly, *"beware the curse of three, for there, death will be."*

Wherever You Are

For the Girl in the Plaza Who Thought That No One Loved Her.

Major William "Bat" Masterson removed his uniform coat, hung it up on a peg, and took his place on the couch. *Why the hell do they all use couches?*

Every shrink he'd been to in the last year had had one, and they had all insisted that he lie down on it for their sessions together. Although he would have vastly preferred sitting up in a chair and talking face to face, he really didn't have the option of arguing about it. There was too much riding on the outcome to quibble over such small details.

Mission Specialist Emma Steichen *did* have a chair however, and the tablet computer that all of the Flight Surgeon's psychologists seemed to prefer. "How are you today, William?" she asked.

"I'm okay," Masterson replied.

Steichen smiled. "Good," she said. "Since we have a limited amount of time together, I wanted to start off our first meeting by talking with you about your daughter."

Masterson frowned and shifted uncomfortably. He'd been warned about the Luxembourgian native. Steichen didn't dither around. She always got straight to the point.

"What do you want to know?"

"Tell me about her," she replied.

"Erika was--"he hesitated, "--an intelligent, and beautiful young woman. She could have become anything that she wanted to be."

But she hadn't. Instead, a year earlier, she had committed suicide. His wife had found her in the garage, sitting in the family car with the engine running.

Erika's death had shattered their world, and it had cast doubt on Masterson's fitness for the Mars Support Missions. NASA simply wasn't comfortable with the idea of using a pilot with potential mental health issues. Not on a mission that was eighteen months long. He'd already missed the first two Mars Support Missions, and if he didn't manage to convince Steichen that he was fit enough for MSM-3, his career in the Manned Mars Space Program was effectively over.

"What do you think drove her to take her own life?"

Again, painfully direct, he thought. *And she already knows the answers. She's got my treatment files right there in her tablet. She's listening for something. What?*

"She became depressed," he said. "We really didn't realize it at first. Teenagers go through mood swings and that's what we thought it was. Just another phase.'

"After that, she started sleeping a lot, and becoming more and more withdrawn. We took her to some therapists, and they diagnosed her with depression, but the sessions didn't really work. She just kept slipping further and further away."

"And you blamed yourselves?"

He nodded and gazed out the window. Steichen's office offered a commanding view of the Kennedy Space Center and the shuttle that would take the next Mars crew up to the International Space Station and the *Orpheus-3*. He wondered again if he would be on it.

"We should have seen it coming," he finally said. "We should have done more for her."

"Guilt is normal in such a catastrophic event," Steichen supplied. "Families and loved ones often blame themselves for mistakes that they didn't really make."

Masterson nodded again. That 'normal' guilt had also eaten away at his marriage. After Erika's death, he and his wife had separated, and even though they were both going through counseling, the prognosis wasn't good. Divorce was almost a given.

"Tell me," she asked. "Have you considered going back to church? Perhaps talking with your old pastor?"

He shook his head. Before Erika had taken her own life, he had believed in God and had attended church regularly. But her loss had changed all that. He had decided that any deity that allowed such a terrible thing to happen wasn't worth his devotion. Or his belief.

Steichen raised an eyebrow, but she made no comment and added another note to his file before pressing on. "The question I have for you today is about closure, William. About being able to move on with your life. Tell me, do you think you are ready to take that step?"

This was another subject that he'd discussed before, and even though he'd always known that the best answer was 'yes', he had never been able to say it. "I'm not sure," he admitted.

She set down her tablet and leaned forwards. "William, you've made a lot of progress. When you first started your counseling sessions, you could barely talk with your caregivers about what happened. I think you've come along ways over the last year."

"But?" *Here it comes,* he thought, already resigning himself to his fate. *I'll be flying a desk.*

"But I need two things from you," she told him. "First, I want you to do something for yourself; to perform an act of closure. And secondly, I need you to agree that if we go on the mission together, our sessions will continue on a regular basis."

Steichen's own seat aboard MSM-3 was already assured. In addition to a degree in Geology, she was a seasoned astronaut with six shuttle missions under her belt, and had spent time aboard the International Space Station. She also held a doctorate in Clinical Psychology and was responsible for monitoring the crew's mental health during the long flight to and from the Red Planet.

"An act of closure?" he asked.

"A ritual, if you will pardon the term," she explained. "Something that says goodbye, but still honors Erika's memory. For most people, that's what a funeral does. It gives the living a chance to offer their farewells, and deal with the loss, but sometimes a little more is needed. Something even more personal."

"Like what?"

"I'll leave that up to you," Steichen said. "Think about it between now and our next session, William."

"I will."

***

Masterson kept his promise and tried to come up with ideas. Unfortunately, everything that he thought of didn't seem to fit the bill, and as the date for their next meeting drew closer, he began to worry that he would have nothing to offer.

The idea however, presented itself.

He was out taking care of errands, and driving in the car that had replaced the one his daughter had died in. *That* change had been the one thing that he and his wife had managed to agree upon. Neither of them had wanted a reminder of the tragedy sitting right where they could see it every day.

The new car was a simple economy model, with no frills and a factory radio that he still hadn't gotten around to replacing. Which meant that whenever he wanted to break up the silence, he was at the mercy of the DJ's and whatever their tastes were. He'd managed to find a station that specialized in 70's and 80's hits though, and between that and one that offered up half-way decent country music, he was more or less content with his lot.

That day, the oldies station was hosting a *Police* marathon. The English band wasn't one of his favorites, but he also wasn't in the mood for country, and let it play. But one song in particular caught his attention. It was their lead single, *Message in a Bottle"*.

As he listened to the words, it hit him right between the eyes. *That's it*, he realized. *That's the ritual that Steichen is looking for.* He was so sure of it that he pulled into a

183

convenience store, bought a bottle that seemed like a good candidate, and dumped the contents out in the parking lot.

And when he saw her, and told her what he had in mind, Steichen agreed wholeheartedly. "Do that and I'll sign off on you," she assured him.

***

Twilight had come to the Atlantic. Although the sun had set, the horizon was bright with the afterglow of the day's memory, and back behind Masterson, the night was starting to draw its comforting shroud across the sky.

This, and early morning, had been Erika's favorite time of day. *What had she called it?* he asked himself. A moment later, it came to him. *The time between the worlds.*

She'd even written a poem about it. Something about it being a special period when the spirits of the dead could cross over into the world of the living if only for a few, short minutes. One line in particular still haunted him, *'Wherever you are, I'll always be with you.'*

At the time, this had seemed a little morbid, but now the memory made his throat tighten. *Maybe,* he thought. *Maybe in some small way, she's here. Right now.*

He stood there for a long moment, letting the cold wind wrap around him, trying to feel her presence. But his only company was a lone gull flying overhead and the waves lapping against the beach.

Wishful thinking, I guess.

He clutched the bottle in his hand a little more tightly, and looked down at the little piece of paper stuffed inside. It was a message. *"My darling Erika,"* it read. *"I hope you are well. I love you always, Daddy."*

"I love you, darling," Masterson whispered. "Wherever you are."

184

He threw the bottle towards the sea, following its flight with his eyes. It arced up into the darkening sky, tumbling end over end, and when it reached its apex at last, it fell.

He didn't see it hit the water though. At the last instant, right when there should have been a small geyser and a splash, there was a brilliant flash of light. It dazzled him, and when the afterimages had cleared, the bottle was gone.

Weird, he thought. *A reflection from the highway? Something on the water?* Nothing offered itself up as the cause.

He stayed there for a few more minutes, trying to spot the bottle bobbing on the waters, but finally, he gave up and walked back to his car.

***

The shuttle for Mars Support Mission 3 lifted off from the Kennedy Space Center fourteen days later at 06:10 hours, 36 seconds. By 1000 hours it had rendezvoused with the International Space Station, and MSM-3's crew traded places with the latest group of ISS researchers heading back to Earth.

Another week of pre-flight inspections followed this aboard the *Orpheus 3*, which was docked with the ISS. Then at 03:24 hours Eastern Time, the interplanetary spaceship released its couplings, engaged its fission-initiated plasma pulse engines, and began its long journey. Aboard it were its pilot, Major William "Bat" Masterson, his co-pilot Lieutenant Sam Stevenson, Mission Specialists Emma Steichen, Xuxiang Mao, Ronaldo Garcia-Vega, and Sergei Mikael Ankudinov.

In six months, and barring a catastrophe, the *Orpheus* would assume orbit over Mars, and use its two landers to ferry down to Armstrong Base, the first permanent research station ever established on another world. In the words of the Senior Mission Controller, MSM-3 was *"playing a vital part in the great cause of advancing human knowledge, and ensuring a future in space for the next generation, and generations to come."*

In less grandiose terms, MSM-3 was a supply and relief run. The *Orpheus 3* was bringing badly needed groceries and important components to the tiny colony. It was also giving the men and women of MSM-2 the chance to return home to blue skies and a landscape with green things growing on it.

It wasn't as significant as the first manned mission, MMM-1, or its follow-up MMM-2, or even the two previous support flights, but Masterson didn't mind the lesser place he would have in history. What counted was that he was going to Mars.

And Erika would be going with him, in spirit at least. He had tucked a small picture of her inside of what little personal gear the mission's weight restrictions allowed. It had been taken on the night of her first junior prom, and before depression had begun to claim her soul. That night had been one of their last happy times together, and for that reason, the image had become one of the most precious possessions that he owned. Steichen knew all about it of course, but she hadn't objected. As long as he stayed focused on his mission, she was content.

***

MSM-3 experienced its first real problems two months into the flight and a little over 20,000,000 miles from Earth. Transmission back and forth between the *Orpheus* and Mission Control began to degrade, and it wasn't long before the engineers back in Houston had pinpointed the problem. The culprit proved to be a bad telemetry unit, and the only fix available was to replace it with a spare that they had on board. And being the pilot on a vessel that wouldn't require his attention for another four months, Masterson was picked for the job.

Not that he objected. He had always enjoyed EVA work and it gave him a chance to get out of the cramped confines of the ship for a short period. A very short period.

Like the other Mars missions before it, MSM-3 had been launched during a period of maximum solar activity, exploiting the fact that the solar wind reduced the amount of deadly cosmic ray particles by pushing them away from the inner planets. It did not remove them entirely though, and the increase in solar radiation posed its own perils to anyone in open space. To minimize the amount of exposure that he would receive, his entire repair job would have to be limited to no more than ten minutes.

Masterson had worked under similar constraints before though, and the replacement unit was designed for a quick swap. Most of his time, he knew, would be eaten up getting to and from the work area which was halfway down the ship. For that reason, when he stepped out of the airlock, he didn't waste time gawking at the billions of stars all around him. Instead, he found the handholds near the lock and worked his way up and around the hull. From there, it only took him a few moments to orient himself, locate the instrument cluster and start working his way towards it.

The moment that he arrived, he clipped himself in and exposed the faulty unit. "Stevenson, I have the ERTM unit in view," he announced. "Preparing to undock and perform the swap."

His co-pilot, who was monitoring the operation from the command station replied right away. "Copy that. You are go for the swap. Total time elapsed 2 minutes, 28 seconds."

"Affirmative," he answered, already undoing the fasteners. "It's coming out. You should see a slight signal drop."

"That's confirmed," his partner replied. "You're at 2 minutes, 45."

In the meantime, the unit had come loose, and Masterson was stuffing it into the bag he'd brought along with him for the occasion. He had just started to reach for its replacement when a brilliant flare of light appeared off to his right.

"Jesus," he exclaimed. "That was bright!"

"What was bright?" Stevenson asked.

"Nothing," he answered. "Just a little something the sun missed."

Like any astronaut, he had had plenty of experience with phosphenes in space before. No one knew the exact mechanism, but researchers believed that they were caused when cosmic rays passed through the vitreous humor of the human eye, hit the optic nerve, or affected the visual center of the brain itself. Whatever the truth was, the result was the same; bright flashes, stars, or streaks of light that were almost universally white in color.

And some people, like him, were especially sensitive to them. He'd even participated in several special studies trying to discover the reason why. They hadn't found anything special.

"Copy that, William. Status on the swap?"

Blinking away what he could, Masterson fished out the new unit and started feeding it into its slot. "I'm installing it now," he answered.

Then another flash obscured his vision. "Damn it," he cursed. "There's another one."

For some reason, he thought about Erika. Even as he was puzzling this out, another thought came to him. Something was going to happen. Something bad. He wasn't sure what it was, or how he knew this, but he was positive that whatever 'it' was, was real.

Fighting back a rising sense of anxiety, he focused on his work. "Sorry, control. The unit should be coming online now. How's your signal?"

"It's back up to full strength," Stevenson informed him. "3 minutes 15." Suddenly feeling very exposed, Masterson was only too glad to close the hatch and return to the airlock.

Two hours later, Houston contacted the *Orpheus* with news.

"MSM-3," the Senior Mission Controller informed them, "we've got a solar weather update for you. SWPC Boulder reports an X9.5 class flare and AFWA concurs. Estimating contact with you in 20 hours. Better batten down the hatches."

Solar flares were rated by their severity, from A through B, C, M and finally X. Numbers assigned to each class were similar to the Richter scale, with ascending levels of intensity. The highest ever recorded had been an X28 (before the sensors monitoring it had malfunctioned), but an X9.5 was a real monster in its own right. Loops of energy ten times the size of Earth were being ejected by the sun into space.

The magnetic field that surrounded the *Orpheus* would protect the crew from most of this, but everyone understood that an X9 would test it to the max, and even though most of the ships vital components were shielded, there were plenty of lesser parts that would be damaged. They were in for a rough ride.

A chill went up Masterson's spine as he listened to this announcement. The 'it' that he had been concerned about was real after all, and it was headed right for them.

How the hell did I know? he wondered.

***

Even though the *Orpheus* was over 560 feet long, four-fifths of its mass was taken up by the engines, storage, landers and instrumentation. This left only a tiny section for the crew to live and work in. Nicknamed the 'can' for its general shape, it was as spacious as NASA could make it, which meant that in actuality, it was cramped and privacy was hard to come by.

The situation was even worse in the portion set aside for the emergency shelter. It was just large enough for everyone to squeeze themselves into, and 18 hours after the warning, the entire crew did just that and sealed themselves in. After that, it

189

was all a matter of waiting out the radioactive storm and hoping that the damage to the *Orpheus* wouldn't be too great.

Steichen didn't let the X9 slow her down though; she used the time to conduct her regular counseling sessions with the crew. The rule, which she had instituted from the beginning of the voyage, was that everyone carried ear-plugs, or buds for their personal entertainment devices, and whenever she brought her clipboard out, whoever wasn't being counseled, popped them in and found something else to pay attention to. It wasn't absolute privacy by any means, but it was the best that could be provided.

When Masterson's turn came, he removed his earplugs as he floated over to join her, moving in perfect time with Sergei Ankudinov, who was going the opposite way, and putting his back on. The two men shared a grin as they passed one another, and Masterson knew exactly what Sergei was thinking. *'Your turn to get your head shrunk, tovarishch.'*

"So?" he asked as he grabbed onto a handhold and spun around to face Steichen, "Thinking about giving me the duct tape treatment yet?" At the very beginning of space exploration, scientists had addressed the problem of a crewmember losing their sanity. Their solution had been simple; to restrain them to their seat for the remainder of the flight with duct tape.

Steichen smiled. "No," she said. "Although I'm keeping a roll handy just in case. How are you holding up, William?"

"Not bad," he answered. "…for someone surrounded by enough radiation to kill me instantly." As it was, they were all getting a year's worth of what they would have received on Earth, mag-field or no.

"I see that you've retained your sense of humor," Steichen remarked. "How about Erika? It's been a while since we talked about her. Has she been on your mind?"

"Not much," he told her, hoping that she wouldn't detect the lie. In fact, he'd been thinking about her a lot. Naturally, his ploy didn't work.

190

"Of course," she said. "You know, William, I can't exactly scrub you from the mission now. You can be frank with me."

He smiled sheepishly at this. "Yeah, I guess I can. I have been thinking about her. I wish she could've seen this. But, she isn't here. I accept that."

Steichen nodded and made a note on her tablet. "Okay," she replied. "Normal enough. Anything else that I should know about?"

For a moment, Masterson considered telling her about his strange premonition and the light flash that had accompanied it. But he quickly changed his mind. It had been a coincidence, and nothing more.

"No," he finally said. "All good. I'm just not looking forwards to cleaning up the mess that this flare's going to leave."

Steichen gave him a look that indicated that she wasn't entirely convinced, but after she made another note, they changed the subject.

***

The damage was as bad as everyone had predicted; although essential components had been spared, a host of secondary sensors and relays had been completely fried. Everyone was forced to put in long hours fixing what they could, and replacing what they couldn't.

Despite this, the engineers at Mission Control finally decreed that MSM-3 was viable and the crew was given the green light to complete their assignment as planned. As long as nothing else occurred, they would land on Mars a little worse for wear, but on time.

Glad for the news, but exhausted from his labors, Masterson climbed into his sleeping bag at the end of his shift, eager for a solid block of sleep.

Space wasn't quite done with him however. He was just drifting off when bright flashes and streaks of light interrupted

191

his slumber. Like malicious pixies, the phosphenes had returned to wreak their mischief on him. When a particularly bright one flared up, he surrendered.

"God damn it," he cursed, pulling off his sleep mask.

Ronaldo Garcia-Vega was floating nearby, completely unaffected by the phenomena and blissfully unconscious. He was even snoring.

What a bastard, Masterson thought, envying him for his lack of sensitivity. As he began to unzip his bag, intent on getting himself some sleep meds, he realized that someone was standing there, watching him.

Standing. In zero-G.

The wave of phosphenes briefly diminished, and the figures' features became clear, making Masterson gasp. It was Erika. She was smiling at him and saying something, but he couldn't hear what it was.

An instant later, he woke up. He was still in his bag, and his mask was over his eyes. When he removed it, Vega was right where he had been in the dream, and fast asleep.

But Erika was gone. All that remained was the eerie feeling that somehow, at least a part of his vision had been real. That, and the fact that after over a year, he hadn't stopped missing her one bit.

***

Three months passed. The phosphenes came and went, but Erika did not revisit his dreams. Gradually, the memory of the vision faded, and Masterson focused himself on the challenges that lay ahead. At least, the day came when the *Orpheus-3* finally assumed orbit over Mars and the shuttles were launched.

Although their descent was greeted with far less acclaim than the first manned mission had received, or the ones which had followed it, the provisions and the personnel that the shuttle brought with it were welcome, and in their own way, no less

192

vital. They allowed the research being conducted at Armstrong Base to continue.

But the instant that his shuttle touched down, Masterson found himself out of a job. The settlement didn't need a pilot, and it wouldn't require one until MSM-4 arrived and it was time to rotate back to Earth. So he did what all the previous Mars pilots had done, and helped out where he could by doing odd jobs that supported the scientists' efforts. One of these, and possibly the least glamorous, was rover repair.

The fact that men were finally on Mars hadn't made these robotic explorers obsolete by any means. With an entire world to explore, the researchers needed all the help that they could get. Their philosophy was, 'the more eyes, the better'—even if some of those eyes were actually imagers and scanners. To keep them up and running, someone had to drive out, find them, and fix whatever problems they had. Many only required a fresh power supply, but others, like the venerable Curiosity rover demanded more attention. Although it had managed to exceed the expectations of the men who had constructed it, time and the physical limitations of its components had caught up, and it had ground to a halt at the verge of the great plain of Elysium Planitia.

But not before generating its fair share of controversy. Mars had always been the focus of wild speculation, misidentification and sometimes, outright fraud. There had been the alleged canals which had never existed, then the 'face' in the Cydonia region that proved to be nothing more than a combination of light and shadow, and after that, a whole host of rocks and geological features that pareidolia had transformed into 'absolute proof' of alien life.

In Curiosity's case, the most famous anomaly had been a bright flash of light, which had been recorded during the second year of its mission. Right away, conspiracy theorists and UFO buffs had declared this to be nothing less than an attempt by extraterrestrials to make contact with humanity. And although

NASA had tried to explain it as nothing more than a shiny rock catching the sun, or a phosphene creating an artifact on the camera, accusations of a cover-up and government conspiracies had refused to die.

Which gave Masterson a secondary job. This was to investigate the hundreds of oddly shaped rocks that the 'nut-cases' back on Earth were calling ancient alien artifacts, and anything else like them, and do his best to help put it all to rest.

Personally, he didn't really believe that his efforts would silence anything. No matter how advanced technology got, mankind would always cling to superstition and fantasy. People wanted to believe in the fantastic; it made the universe seem a little less cold and a bit more hopeful.

Even so, he knew that he had to at least try to enlighten his fellow men. Besides which, it gave him the chance to get out and stretch his legs from time to time. His crawler hadn't been built for comfort, and after hours of grinding along the rocky surface, any excuse to give his joints a break was welcome.

By the time he found Curiosity, the sun had set, and like on Earth, Mars had its own 'time between the worlds'. Twilight was different on the fourth planet though; because of the dust in the upper atmosphere, the fading sunlight created an afterglow that would last for hours. It also made it easy for Masterson to spot the rover. It had stopped less than a kilometer from the location of the last 'alien light' sighting, and sat in a small gully.

"Armstrong, I have arrived at Curiosity," he said. "Initial visuals indicate the rover status to be good. Beginning my EVA."

"Copy that, Repair 5," the tech responded. "Mission parameters call for power source replacement and general maintenance on Curiosity's optical array. Advise if further servicing is required."

"Affirmative," he replied. He got out, retrieved his tool box from the side of the crawler, and started making his way down the gully. He was only a few feet away from Curiosity when something bright flashed on the horizon.

"Wow," he said.

"Wow, what?" the tech asked.

"Nothing Armstrong," he answered. "Just a cosmic ray. Continuing EVA."

Another flash occurred. This time, it was even more brilliant than the first and it had appeared in exactly the same spot. Cosmic rays didn't do that.

"There it is again," Masterson announced, turning towards it. "It seems to be some kind of artifact. I'm not sure what's producing it."

He looked out across the barren landscape trying to locate the source. When the phenomena repeated itself a third time, he was certain that he had found the point of origin. It seemed to be coming from a small rise, covered with loose rock and sand.

"Armstrong base, I'm discontinuing my current EVA track and investigating," he announced, "Show me on heading 270 degrees from my current positon. The objective seems to be approximately 9 meters out."

"Copy that Repair 5," the tech replied. "Let us know what you find."

Probably nothing except another shiny rock, he thought, but he answered, "Yeah, Rodger that."

Nine meters later, Masterson found the source. Back home, on Earth, what he saw there wouldn't have been anything remarkable, but 62 million miles away from the nearest ocean, it was, and he stared down at it, dumbfounded. The object was lying in the sand at his feet, in a place where no human had ever been before, but as hard as he tried, he couldn't deny its reality.

It was a simple glass bottle. The same kind of bottle that he had thrown into the Atlantic. And although it bore a thin coating of red Martian dust, he could still see the small roll of paper inside of it.

This isn't possible, he told himself. *This can't be.*

"Repair 5," a voice in his ear was asking. "Have you reached your objective?"

"Yes," he said at last. "I-I have, Armstrong."

"What do you see?"

He didn't answer. He *couldn't* answer. Half certain that it would vanish like the mirage that it had to be, he knelt down and picked up the bottle. Like a man in a dream, he untwisted the cap and shook the paper out onto his glove.

"Repair 5, what is your status?"

Masterson had stopped listening.

The message had been written in pink ink, in a familiar, feminine hand. It contained only two sentences, but as simple as they were, they managed to destroy all of the doubts that he had harbored, and restored his faith in God.

"Everything's fine, Daddy," it said, *"Wherever you are, I'll always be with you. Love, Erika."*

The tech at Armstrong was becoming frantic now, trying to get an update from him, but Masterson kept staring at the paper, reading it over and over. Finally, he found enough strength to respond.

"Armstrong base," he said. "Repair 5."

"Repair 5, status?"

"I'm fine, Armstrong," he answered. "No--*everything's* fine."

"What happened out there? What did you find?"

He looked down at his hand. It was empty now and the bottle was gone. But not the memory.

"Nothing," he said. "Just a shiny rock."

Then he looked up into the Martian sky and smiled. The afterglow was gone now, and brilliant auroras were beginning to paint the heavens.

There was light. Light everywhere.

A Way Around

For Ray Bradbury

It was 3:45 and Ed was starting to feel anxious. Susan still hadn't arrived. Normally, she was very punctual.

Maybe something happened to her, he thought worriedly. *Car problems? An accident? No, I can't think like that. It's probably just traffic.*

Eager for a distraction, he got up, ordered another cup of coffee from the barista, and returned to his seat. There, he began to scribble down some notes onto his napkin. He was working on his second napkin when Susan called.

"Ed," she said, "I'm so sorry. I got caught up in traffic on my way through Northgate. I should be there in another ten minutes. Is that okay?"

Of course, it was. Ed treasured his meetings with the young woman, and he was more than willing to wait. There wasn't anything romantic involved between them. He was twice her age, and quite satisfied with his bachelorhood and the *scholar's mistress* that occupied his bed. Instead, Susan provided him with something far more precious than sex. She gave him ideas, and kept his mind young by challenging his intellect.

"Sure thing" he told her.

***

Susan McGinnis was actually parked just a block away, and traffic hadn't been the reason for her delay. The real cause was a dark green sedan three cars ahead of her, with two Asian men sitting inside of it. They were watching the *Gamma Grind Bistro*, and Ed.

When her cell phone rang, she answered it. "Go ahead."

"We can confirm. They're from our competitors," the voice on the other end stated.

"Thanks," she replied. Checking her purse, she got out and started walking.

The men in the car noticed her of course. Anyone would have. She was tall, blond, and pretty in a way that suggested a successful young professional with just enough sensuality to make most men imagine what she 'was really like' in the bedroom. The straight ones at least.

From the way that the driver looked at her in his rear view mirror, she could tell that he was already beginning to dream up his own little fantasies. More importantly, he wasn't reacting by doing anything more than nudging his partner.

She closed the distance, looking straight ahead, and moving as if she intended to go right on by them. Neither man got a look at her ass however. The instant that she was parallel to the car, she reached into her purse and pulled the trigger of her weapon.

It didn't make any noise, and there was no visible evidence of it being discharged, but its effect was still conclusive. Both men grimaced, and then slumped over, dead.

Susan loved her microwave gun. It was compact, powerful, and looked enough like a toy that she never had any trouble getting it through airports. The tech people had even made a special edition just for her; all pink with a cute little white kitten on the grips.

She paused just long enough to make another call. It was to the same number. "Clean up on aisle four," she announced cheerfully.

The man listening on the other end didn't laugh. "The cleaners are on their way," he informed her.

Confident that the car and its cargo of dead men would be gone by the time she was ready to leave, she moved on. Like Ed, she was looking forwards to their meeting.

When she entered the coffee house, he smiled, and rose to greet her. "Great to see you, Susan," he said. "I've got some new ideas for the story. I think I found a solution for that engine problem."

"That's great, Ed," she beamed, "I can't wait to see what kind of holes I can poke in it."

"I don't think you'll get me this time," he warned. "I did my homework."

Susan gave him a 'we'll just see about that' expression, and went to get her own cup of coffee.

Six months earlier, Ed had been running a workshop for aspiring science fiction writers, and Susan had been his brightest pupil. Later, after the class had ended, they had continued to meet regularly at the *Gamma Grind*, where Susan played the dual role of Ed's 'idea man' and a devil's advocate, challenging his plot ideas with hard science and a fresh eye. His latest tale centered around a killer asteroid threatening Earth, and Mankind's escape and resettlement on Proxima Centauri 3, a fictional planet orbiting Sol's nearest interstellar neighbor. The concept had originally been Susan's idea, but had quickly become Ed's passion, and the next book that he hoped to publish.

"You were right about the solar sails," he said as she sat. "They wouldn't work."

"Too slow?" she asked, raising a delicate eyebrow. "Even with adequate radiation shielding?"

Ed nodded. "So, I thought about the nuclear thermal angle."

"And found out that it is," she interjected, "'a', dangerous as hell if it fails, and 'b', requires a hazardous fuel supply."

"Yeah," he replied. "I even took a look at the VASMIR engine. The safety concerns were a little less, but they're still there."

"Of course, you also ignored ion propulsion all together," she added. Ion propulsion was nowhere near as fast as Hollywood portrayed it as being. Although it was efficient, it took a long time to build up to any decent speed. One scientist had even compared it to a car driving from Los Angeles to New York that required two weeks to attain its top speed of 60 miles per hour. Set against limited food, air and water supplies, ion engines weren't even a contender for an extended manned mission.

199

"I did," he answered. "I think I found the solution though."

For some reason that Ed couldn't fathom, Susan seemed momentarily distracted. A tow truck was passing by with a green car on its lift and she was watching it intently.

"Yes," she finally said. "I thought you might. What have you got?"

Ed pushed one of his napkins across the table to her. It had only one word written on it, all in caps, and he'd circled it. *"CERN!"*

"Okaaay," she said tentatively. "CERN, as in the CERN project in Switzerland." Based in Mayern and Geneva, the *Conseil Européen pour la Recherche Nucléaire* was on the cutting edge of high-energy physics research.

"I read a post that says that they may have not only discovered gravitonic particles but also how to generate them artificially," Ed said breathlessly. "If it's true, then we have our engine for the *Pegasus*."

"*If* it's true," Susan countered. "So far, the existence of such a particle is purely hypothetical, Ed."

"Not according to the post I read," he said. "They're keeping a tight lid on it, but the official announcement is right around the corner."

"Okay," she conceded. "Let's say it's true. What then?"

Ed grinned like a mischievous child and flipped the napkin over. There was a diagram, depicting a crude rocket surrounded by a bubble, and some kind of emission coming out of the tail that not only propelled it, but also wrapped around it.

"'What then' is a gravitronic engine," he responded. "It generates the grav particles, surrounding the ship and creating its own acceleration shield. At the same time, an opposing gravitational field pushes against the bubble. And *viola!* We have an engine that runs on gravity that can travel through space at unlimited speeds. There are no emissions, no real fuel cost except to generate the field itself, and if we use pulse-based antimatter generators, no issue with antimatter storage."

Susan studied the diagram carefully. "What about stopping when we get there, Ed? Kinda nice to be able to do that, don't you think?"

"Easy," he said. "We reverse the field direction gradually. You can use the same thing to maneuver. You just shift the area of opposition around and you make the thing turn. Honestly, I'm really proud of this. It goes way beyond anything else anyone has thought of so far."

"I have to admit that I'm impressed Ed," she said. "Now all we need are those pesky little gravitons."

"Well, there is that," he agreed, "but I think that the problem will solve itself. You'll see. CERN will make the announcement."

"Maybe," Susan returned, still doubtful. "So what about the food and water? Last I heard, you were thinking about using hydroponics to help filter the ships air and supplement the food supply. Still happy with that? And what about our crews' diet? Do they have to be vegans, or can they have a few cheeseburgers on the way to Proxima?"

"I have a few thoughts on that," Ed began, producing another napkin. In short order, they were involved in a deep debate on air scrubbing technology, and how much food would be involved. By the end of their conversation, the issue of air handling had not been resolved, but Susan was hopeful.

"You'll find a way around," she assured him. "You always do." They parted company on that happy note.

As soon as she was alone again, Susan brought up the internet browser on her smartphone. It only took her a moment to access the remote feed from Ed's home computer and locate the CERN post. He had bookmarked it on his web-browser under "Pegasus Research".

"Damn it," she cursed. A couple of researchers really *had* found gravitons and it looked like they had cobbled some kind of generator together. Ed hadn't been exaggerating after all.

She immediately placed a call and booked a direct flight to Geneva, first class.

So much for getting any sleep tonight, she thought unhappily. She'd never gotten used to doing that on a plane. *But then that's why I get paid the 'big' bucks.*

***

When Susan returned to the United States, it was time for her next appointment with Ed. On the way, she stopped off at the apartment that her team was using for their operation.

The living room was bare except for a large folding table and a bank of computer monitors. The men who sat there greeted her as she entered and re-holstered their pistols.

"The coffee's fresh," one of them informed her.

"No thanks, I don't want any of that pond scum," she replied, walking up and leaning in to inspect the displays. "I'll have plenty of *real* coffee in a few minutes."

One of the monitors showed the interior of Ed's apartment from various angles. Another supplied feeds from the surrounding neighborhood, and the third kept an eye on the coffee shop where one of their compatriots worked as the barista. A fourth screen was reserved for the listening devices that they had in place, and thanks to a friendly doctor, Ed's exact location. He didn't know it, but he had been 'chipped' during a recent outpatient surgery, and was trackable by GPS.

"We had some more of our competitors show up last night," the man announced. "FSB this time. Looks like they may have run out of patience. They were a grab team."

Susan didn't inquire about the fate that the Russians had met. She didn't need to. Her team members knew their jobs. The FSB agents had been 'disappeared' just like the North Koreans that she had taken out.

"Lovely", she grimaced. "The Chinese won't be far behind." Agents from the *Guojia Anquan Bu*, the Ministry for State Security, hadn't made their appearance yet, but their arrival was a foregone conclusion. So was the return of the FSB. The Russians simply didn't understand the idea of 'giving up'.

She looked at her phone. "Well, time to go. I'll pick you guys up a doggie bag while I'm there. Bagels again?"

The agent nodded, and smiled. "Onion, and a tall mocha. Maybe a sandwich too?"

"Don't press your luck," Susan retorted. "You *have* coffee and you'll *get* bagels. And if the Chinese show, maybe they'll pretend to be delivery boys and you can eat take-out. Make sure to save me the dim-sum."

This earned her a laugh.

At the *Gamma Grind*, Ed was in low spirits. "Looks like I was wrong," he said sadly. He turned his phone around so that Susan could see it.

It was a news article about two scientists who had been working at CERN. According to the report, they had been embezzling funds while pretending to search for gravitons.

Now they were gone, their notes were missing, and they were believed to have fled to some third world country to spend their riches. So far, Interpol had failed to uncover any leads on their exact location.

"So the whole thing was a fraud?" she asked. "No gravitons? No grav generator?"

Ed shook his head. "No. They made the whole thing up. Just like that cold fusion scam. *Bastards.*"

At that moment, Susan would have given anything to have been able to tell him that cold fusion had not only worked, but had been adopted by the military for their newest and deadliest toys. She couldn't though. That little bit of information was highly classified. It was one of those, 'I'd tell you, but then I'd have to kill you' things--and she really *did* like him. So instead, she patted his hand sympathetically.

"It's still a good idea, Ed. Maybe someday..."

"Yeah," he agreed disconsolately. "Maybe."

"Look, you still have plasma-pulse drives. Why not use that? I know it's not as safe, but it would still work."

"I can," he said, "but it will take my characters *years* to get there. I'm almost tempted to just make up some futuristic drive to iron things out."

"Ed," she chided, "you know that's a cop out. We agreed that your book has to be as realistic as possible. No *deus ex machina*. Remember?"

"Yes, mother," he frowned. "Plasma it is." Then his expression brightened. "Anyhow, I had some ideas about what they'll find on Proxima."

Susan took a long deep sip of her coffee and inclined her head in invitation. "Fire away. Tell me what this new world of yours will be like." After that, she relaxed and gave herself the luxury of simply listening, and enjoying his company.

Ed didn't know it, but this would be the last time they would ever meet at the *Gamma Grind*. Her confirmation was waiting for her in a text message that she received as she reached her car. It read, *"WR 104: 40.144581,-113.406964."*

She sighed and sent her reply. *"Message received. Will exfil."*

"Rendezvous with transport 2200 hrs, KCIA, Hangar B3. End text," came the response.

Susan wasn't finished though. *"What about Ed?"* she typed. *"He's a loose end."*

"We have already discussed this," the sender replied.

"Requesting confirmation," she insisted.

There was a brief pause before the answer came. *"We'll take care of him. End Text."*

"It's been a pleasure, Ed," she said, gazing back towards the coffee shop. "Sorry that it had to be this way."

She set her phone on the passenger seat and started her car, already planning what she would take with her, and what she would leave behind. She wasn't terribly crazy about Utah, and Dugway was literally the middle of the middle of nowhere, but she had her orders.

I'll sure miss Seattle. Even with the horrible traffic, the outrageous prices, and the smug, entitled attitudes of its citizens, it had been a fun place to live.

At least I won't have to worry about Ed.

***

Sitting alone in the coffee shop, Ed still couldn't believe it. Susan had just sent him an email, saying goodbye.

"I'm moving to New Jersey. My company needs me out there right away. Sorry that I couldn't take the time to tell you about it, but it's a crisis. I'll stay in touch."

Just like that. No advance warning. Nothing.

People could be like that though, he reminded himself. Friends came and went, and they always promised to keep in contact, and never did. He still had his book though, and despite this disappointment, he vowed to keep his promise and thank her in the acknowledgements. Susan deserved that.

With a heavy heart, he bought a fresh cup of coffee, and returned to his notes. He had a planet to create.

Another email reached him the next morning, and it was just as startling as Susan's message. This time, it was from one of the big publishing houses back East. He had sent proposals out to several of them, along with some sample chapters.

Sure that it would be another rejection, he opened it, and when he saw what it said, he had to re-read it several times just to convince himself that it was real.

"An amazing concept," the sender informed him. *"I'll be in Seattle this week and I would love to get together with you and talk about acquiring this property. Please let me know if you will have some free time for us to meet."*

Hands trembling, Ed responded immediately. It didn't take long for an answer to come back. *God,* he thought. *If only Susan was here right now to share this with me.*

***

Although he was excited about his meeting with the publisher's representative, Ed still noticed the dark gray van parked near the *Gamma Grind,* and the men inside of it. Something about the vehicle and the way that they watched him sent a chill up his spine.

He didn't let it deter him though. Resolutely, he crossed the street and began to walk by the vehicle. Suddenly, the sliding door opened, and two additional men jumped out and seized him. He was dragged inside, and before he could protest, or offer them his wallet, he felt a sharp pain in his neck. As everything went gray and then black, he saw the syringe that one of his kidnappers' was holding, and heard him say something to his companions. It sounded like it was in Russian.

Sometime later, he returned to consciousness and realized that he wasn't in the van any longer, but traveling in something that sounded like an aircraft. A bag had been put over his head, and his wrists were bound.

"Who the hell are you" he demanded. "Why are you doing this to me?" He was terrified, but not knowing what was going on, or why, made it even worse.

All his question earned him was a derisive laugh however, and a gruff response, again in Russian. He only recognized a few of the words, but their tone conveyed the speaker's meaning clearly enough. If he didn't behave himself, bad things would happen.

Ed decided to cooperate, at least until he had the chance to speak to someone in charge. It had to be some kind of mistake.

When the plane landed, he was guided into another van. More time passed, and then the vehicle stopped. There was a brief discussion between his captors and afterwards, the side door opened again. Instinctively, Ed knew that he had reached his destination. Wherever it was.

"You know I just listened to you guys as you drove up and your Russian is terrible," a voice said. "Really terrible. Is that what they teach at Sherman Kent these days? *Jeez-o-pete.*"

Ed knew who it was immediately. "Susan?"

"Hi Ed," she answered. "Um, the bag?" His hood came off and Ed looked at her, trying to reconcile what he was seeing with the woman he had known. Or thought he had known.

She was dressed in military-style clothing, and wearing a shoulder holster. There was a gun in it. A *real* gun.

"Welcome to Utah," she said. "Do you want some coffee? It isn't as good as what we had back in Seattle, but it's hot."

Ed didn't know what to say and just stared at her dumbly as his restraints were removed.

"Really, Ed. I think you'll want a cup. We have a lot to talk about."

***

Five years later, Susan stood on the crest of a small hill, listening to the trill of the native insects and the soft snap of an American flag as the warm breeze caressed it. The star spangled banner had been raised especially for this occasion, in honor of all the people that they had been forced to leave behind.

An app on her tablet identified the stars that she was looking for and she turned herself until she was facing them. On Proxima Centauri 3, WR 104 didn't look very impressive. It was just a pair of faint points of light glittering in the darkness.

They were very special though. For the human race, they were the most important things to have ever appeared in the heavens.

Wolf-Rayet 104 had been astronomy's dirty little secret. Part of a binary system 8,000 light years from Sol, it had been on the verge of dying. From the day that the star had been discovered, scientists had debated about when the supernova would occur, and whether or not it would release a gamma ray burst. More powerful than the entire yearly energy output of Earth's sun, such an event had been capable of wiping out all life on the planet.

Despite evidence that suggested that Earth had been bombarded once before by a much smaller GRB in the 8th century, the danger had been deliberately downplayed. Experts had assured the public that such stellar events were rare, and that WR 104 was pointed in the wrong direction to pose any real threat.

207

Ignorant of science in general and unable to confirm the data for themselves, the average citizen had been more than happy to believe this. Mankind had gone about its business, blissfully unware of the time bomb that had been ticking away in the constellation of Sagittarius for millennia.

In reality, WR 104 had been at the perfect angle to strike Earth, and worse, new nanowave detection technology had revealed that the star had finally exploded, centuries before. The radiation had been on its way and Humanity had had less than thirty years to go before it became extinct.

I suppose that what they did was understandable, Susan decided. *The news would have set off a world-wide panic and accomplished nothing. It certainly would have ruined my childhood.* Like everyone else, she had grown up thinking that her planet, and her life on it would always be the same.

Instead, a new space race had begun, an ultra-secret effort by the world's governments to build ships capable of reaching a safe haven on another planet. Competition had been fierce and there had been no prize for coming in second. Whatever nation that succeeded would survive, while the others would perish. It had been a time of hard choices, with harder ones to come.

In the United States, the project had been centered in Utah, at the Dugway Army Proving Grounds, also designated Area 52. But in the same year that she had graduated the CIA training program at The Farm, problems had cropped up. Drive systems and life support designs had proven to be inadequate and the technicians had been stymied.

So another clandestine project had been born. This time it was to tap the minds of the best and brightest for ideas. To consult the writers and the thinkers and discover ways to surmount the technical hurdles without giving away the terrible truth. Men like Ed.

She flashed him a reassuring smile before consulting the chronometer on her tablet. *Any time now.*

A few seconds later, it happened. WR 104 brightened, dimmed and disappeared. Susan's gaze went immediately to another part of the sky. To Sol.

Nothing looked different over there, but she knew better. The side of Earth that was facing the gamma ray burst had just been seared into lifelessness. The other half was being covered by a smog-like layer that would plunge it into what had once been called a nuclear winter.

"They're all gone," she said. "The Russians, the Chinese, the North Koreans and the Jihadi's. All the competition. It's just too bad we weren't able to save everyone that deserved saving."

"It couldn't be helped," her team leader replied, "the *Pegasus* only had so much room. We all knew that."

Susan nodded and saw that Ed was weeping. It was one thing to write about a fictional catastrophe, she reflected, and quite another to witness the real thing.

Vowing to talk with him about it when the moment was right, she watched the death of her home world play out for a few more minutes. When she had seen enough, she left Ed and the others, and headed back down to the base.

Dawn was still several hours away, but they had a lot of work ahead of them when it arrived. A new America was being born on Proxima Centauri, and this time, it wouldn't have any competition to threaten it. And with men like Ed around to help, if problems did come up, she was positive that they would find a way around them.

The Girl Who Could See Everything

For Thomas

The city of Umma' Kaal was a vast collection of delicate, glittering spires, and elegant gardens. Inhabited by a prosperous, well-fed populous, it was the very center of the Empire and an important trade center.

The most lucrative commodity that it traded in could be found in the great slave market of Angataar. Here, males and females of every age or color might be obtained to satisfy any sexual desire. Skilled craftsmen could be procured for a workshop, and captured scholars were on sale to teach the young. There were even seasoned fighters available to do battle in the arenas, or guard the mansions of their owners.

Angataar traded on misfortune; of those who had been captured in war, convicted of crimes, or had simply been sold off by their families out of desperation or greed. And unlike the rest of Umma' Kaal, it was neither gilded, nor perfumed.

Instead, it stank of sweat, of shit, of dust, and most of all, human desperation. Even on the hottest of days, when the twin suns beat down on the earth like the slaver's cudgel, business was brisk. Buyers from all over the Empire, and beyond, crowded the marketplace. And the gold that traded hands there not only enriched the slavers, but the Emperor himself through taxes and bribes.

Today, one of Angataar's most loyal customers was among them. He had visited the slave market on the first day of every month for the last year, and his black palanquin and retinue of guards had become a familiar sight to the slavers, and their human merchandise.

So were his sable-robed form and the strange bronze mask that he always wore. It covered his entire face and was fashioned in the likeness of a man, but with eyes that were forever shut, and lips that were eternally sealed. Despite this, he was still able to see everything around him, and when he spoke, his voice was like something from the depths of the netherworld, cold and commanding.

But these feats surprised no one. Xandarius was after all, the Emperor's Mage, a powerful necromancer, and a master of the darkest of the occult arts. Compared to that, an enchanted mask was a mere trifle. More importantly, he paid in gold, and he paid well. In Angataar, that mattered far more than magic or demons.

Xandarius never tarried, and the present was no exception. The moment that his bearers had set down the palanquin, he was out of it and making straight for the rudest part of the market, where the largest pens were located. This was where slaves with no particular talents could be bought in bulk, and often at a discount.

As he passed them, the sex slaves ceased their lewd gyrations and looked away, the laborers tried to engage other potential buyers, and the fighters simply glared at him. They knew what everyone else did; those whom Xandarius purchased, disappeared. Rumors of demonic sacrifices, and worse, grew ever larger with every visit that the sorcerer made. That, and the sense of relief that they felt when he kept to his routine and walked on. *'Better them than me'* was what they all told themselves.

When he reached his destination at last, Xandarius stopped, brought a pomander up to the slit cut in his mask, and inhaled deeply. It aided him in maintaining his tranquility, and masked the stench of the unwashed bodies huddled in the cages before him. He hated the slave market and would have vastly preferred to have been back in his workroom, surrounded by old books and breathing in rare incense, but the thing that he desired for himself required otherwise.

Seeing him, the slave master hurried over. "I've a wonderful lot for ye ta'day, sor," he told him. "Fit enough fer anything an' cheap s'well."

The slaver was a new man, and clearly didn't know that he was committing a serious transgression by being so familiar. Then the swine compounded his error by having the audacity to actually come closer, and wink impertinently. "N' one or two in thar might even serve ta warm up yer bed, methinks. Got some nice boys and girls in among um, n' all fer one price."

Thankfully, the Mages' bodyguard interceded by backhanding the filthy creature with a mailed gauntlet, sending him sprawling.

"Curb your tongue cur," the guard snarled. "Or I'll cut it outta your maggot-eaten skull and serve it back to ya! Ya speak t' the Mage when he asks ya."

The slave master cowered and spat out a few loose teeth. "Sorry, please f'give me Master Sorcerer."

Xandaruis smiled coldly, but his expression was concealed by the mask. Without replying, he nodded to his guard to begin their transaction. He always preferred to let his underlings handle this part of the business.

"How much for the lot?" the soldier demanded gruffly.

"50 *diyari*," the slaver replied, but when the guard began to draw his sword, he quickly amended himself. "Bu' 35 fer you. Always happy t' please a noble customer such as yerself."

The sword came out of its sheath at this. "*20* you insolent pig!"

The slaver cringed, and nodded. "20. A verra good price."

Xandarius stopped paying any attention to the exchange after that. He was certain that his bodyguard would negotiate an appropriate price—even if it cost the slaver an ear or his nose in the process. He was far more interested in the slaves themselves and he gazed at them for a long moment. Then he decided that as distasteful as the prospect was, he needed to speak with the slave master directly.

"Do they have any talents among them?" he asked the wretch. "Anything of worth?"

212

"None, your worship," the slaver responded. "Aller just a herd a dumb cows, like all ta'rest afore 'em."

Something about one of the slaves struck Xandarius as odd however. She was of northern stock, with long blond hair and pale skin, and just on the cusp of becoming a woman. Most men would have found her handsome, even lovely, but Xandarius was above such sordid considerations. Her heritage was far more interesting to him; northerners were comparatively rare in Angataar. Their kind tended to prefer to die in battle rather than submit to captivity. But it was the way she stared straight ahead, and gripped the fence that separated them that really engaged him.

Curious, he walked over to the pen, and noticed that although the others retreated at his approach, she did not. She wasn't even looking at him, he realized, but somewhere else altogether. And yet, he could tell that she knew that he was there.

Could it be, he wondered. If so, then she was the answer to all of his problems.

"This one, "he said, pointing. "Tell me about her."

"Nuthin ta say, yer worship," the slaver replied. "Jus ta nuther captive from ta wars, n' she's blind she is. Been so since she twas a verra small child, or so I'm told. Fit enough though fer all of it though, as long as ya beat her right."

Xandarius pensively stroked his mask. *"Blind you say? Perfect."*

He reached into his belt pouch, grabbed a few coins, and dropped them on the ground without even bothering to see the amount, or if the slaver had retrieved them. "Have her cleaned up and sent to my home immediately."

The slaver was in disbelief. He had just scooped up enough gold from the muck to pay for the entire group twice over. Then his expression changed to wariness, and Xandarius easily guessed the direction that his thoughts were taking him. The fool was wondering if he had just been cheated out of something of

213

great value. Another unseen smile came to his face as he watched the man's limited intellect fail him.

You could never imagine what her value might be, the sorcerer thought. *Not in all the ages of the earth.*

"What of ta others, yer lordship?" the slaver finally inquired.

"I care not," Xandarius told him. "Sell them, kill them, do as you will. I have what I want."

He strode away, glad to be done with Angaatar. And if the Gods of the Abyss truly favored him as he hoped they did, he would never have to see the accursed place ever again.

***

Unaware that she had just been sold, Thia was hauled from the pen by the slave master himself. Thanks to her, he still had fresh bite marks on him—and all he had done had been to insist on his rights over her as her master!

"Ungrateful lil bitch! Ya still think yer too good fer me, do ya?" he snarled, raising his cudgel. But as much as he wanted to deal her some fresh bruises to accompany her into the afterlife, he checked himself. Xandarius was not a man who tolerated delays, or damage to what was now his property. Unwilling to risk the sorcerer's wrath, the slave master spat on her cringing form instead.

"We'll see how high n'mighty ya are when the Mage is done with ya! Yer goin to to yer death girl, an' the Dark Ones can take ya to da furthest reaches a' hell!"

He signaled to his assistant, who came over and wrenched her to her feet. "Get her scrubbed down, n'dress her in somthin clean. An' as soon as yer done, get this whore outta my sight. I've no time fer dead girls."

Thia was half-dragged, half-walked to a tub of steaming water, where she was stripped naked and scrubbed nearly raw by another slave. Then she was given a fresh garment and ordered to put it on. It wasn't new, but it was reasonably clean and free of lice.

The moment that she had dressed, she was taken to a slave cart, and shoved inside the tiny cage. Watching it pull away, the slave master didn't bother to hurl any more curses in her direction. He just grinned maliciously, spat on the ground, and walked back towards the pens.

***

Xandarius was just as skilled in the Black Arts as everyone imagined. He was more than a mere mystic though. His interests also encompassed the sciences, and when he was not studying ancient spells, or sacrificing victims to the Gods of the Abyss, he spent his time learning about the human body and its limitations when it came to pain.

Although his latest subject had added to his growing store of knowledge, the slave had died far too quickly for his liking, and he wore a frown on his face as he gazed down at the corpse on the work-table. Thanks to all of his bulk purchases, there were many more test-subjects in his pens to draw from, but this didn't mitigate his sense of disappointment.

Human life is so fragile, he mused, tracing the man's wounds with a long, lacquered nail. *But perhaps my newest acquisition will prove more resilient. She certainly seemed healthy enough in the slave market.* Northerners had a reputation for toughness, he reminded himself, and their resilience when it came to injury was near legendary.

This decided him. *Yes! Once she has fulfilled her purpose, I will see how she fares beneath the knife.*

Pleased, he turned to his guard. "Have her brought in."

Then he took his seat at the far end of the room, and waited. The workroom had three tables in it, each one bearing the body of someone that he had been experimenting on, including the latest subject. The sight of this alone was enough to make a sighted person cringe in revulsion.

But he had also seen to it that a trio of thin white cords, equipped with tiny bells, were stretched across the workspace. One was at eye level, another at what would be the waist, and the third, ankle high. More candles had been added to the room as well, making its contents plain to anyone who could see.

If the girl was malingering, and merely pretended blindness, she would give herself away when she entered. And in the process, she would become nothing more than another fresh body for the examination tables.

The next few moments will tell, he thought, caught between the hope that she was genuine, and his desire to vivisect her.

Presently, she was shown in by a servant, and left at the door way. She didn't recoil from the tables however, and just as in the marketplace, her eyes were focused on nothing in particular. But she did seem to be smelling the air, like one of his dogs might have done.

"Girl," he commanded. "Come to me."

She moved forwards, searching the space around her with her hands, and when she found one of the nearer tables, she touched its edge, and then felt along it. Brushing against a cadaver's foot, Xandarius finally heard her give out a small cry.

"Do not tarry," he warned her. "You try my patience."

With noticeable reluctance, she moved forwards, finding the second table, and then colliding with the first string. The bells sounded, startling her.

The Mage was still uncertain though. "I said come, girl!" he snapped. "Do so now, or I will have the guard take your head."

She flinched, found the string with her fingers, and then moved beneath it to take a few more steps. Then she encountered the second string, and when its bells rang, Xandarius was finally satisfied. She was well and truly blind.

"Stop where you are," he instructed. Then, "The slave master said that you have been blind since you were a very young child. Is that so?"

"Yes, lord," the girl responded meekly.

"How did you come by your affliction?" Xandarius inquired.

"In a fall in my second year," she answered. "The healer told me that I did something to the back of my head, and that it caused my sight to flee."

Intrigued, Xandarius took a candle from its stand, walked over to her and tilted her chin up with his finger. When he waved it in front of her eyes, her pupils dilated, but she didn't follow the motion of the flame. Clearly the damage was not to the eyes themselves, he decided, but to something else.

"Lift your hair," he said. "I wish to see the injury." She complied and he took careful note of what he saw, and its location. There was a slight, but noticeable dimple in her scalp near the base of her skull.

Fascinating, he thought, *a well-placed blow here could do everything that a hot iron might otherwise accomplish. Are there other places on the skull that if so struck, could cause similar maladies? Or worse?* It was a matter that would have to be investigated as soon as possible. But not with her. Not yet at least.

"What is your name?" he asked when she had let her hair down again.

"Thia, milord."

A barbarian name, he concluded, but not a disagreeable one. Besides which, he knew that he would not have to worry over what she called herself for terribly long.

"Very well, Thia. You will be taken from the pens and quartered here in the house. I have a series of tests for you to perform. Then, if you pass them, we will discuss an important task I would have you do. Your first test will be now; I thirst, and I would have you fetch me a cup of wine."

"Yes, milord," she replied.

"Here are your instructions. Listen well, girl; you are to leave this room by the door you entered. Turn left and head down the hall. At the third door, enter. A jug of wine and a goblet will be on a table in the very center of the room. Fill the goblet and bring it back to me—and if you spill as much as a single drop, I will have you whipped to death. Is any of this unclear to you?"

"No, milord."

"Then off with you, and do not tarry."

***

Leaving the Mage's presence, Thia was more confused and fearful than ever. The doom that had been predicted for her had not arrived. But Xandarius had proven himself to be just as cruel as she had been told. And now, he had sent her on a task that any one of his servants could have performed—and called it a 'test'.

Having spent most of her life in darkness, she knew that she could have fetched the wine almost as fast as a sighted person—but she kept her pace slow, and moved cautiously. Even though she was aware that she risked the Mage's wrath for delaying, after the cords, it was a certainty that other traps were awaiting her.

But what? There would be no telling until she encountered them, and then she only hoped that she would be able to negotiate her way through in safety.

As her fingers explored the walls, she found the doorways that Xandarius had spoken of at last, and in the process, discovered that she was not alone. There were others in the hall with her. They remained still, and said nothing, but their presence was betrayed by their breathing and the tiny, unconscious movements that everyone made when they stood in one place for too long.

Her unseen companions did not interfere with her however, and soon, she reached the room that contained the wine.

Will there be someone in there, she wondered. *Waiting to trip me, or force me into spilling the goblet?* Concerned, she paused, trying to sense any danger ahead, but the way seemed clear. With no other choice, she entered.

The table containing the wine was six paces in, and as she inspected it with her fingertips, she found the first trap at last. Someone had placed a thin piece of paper beneath the carafe and the goblet. This, she realized, would be checked as soon as she had poured the contents, and if so much as a drop had been spilled onto it, her watchers would know.

Thia had no intention of selling her life so easily however, and she took great care as she filled the cup. Nothing escaped and stained the paper.

Then it was time for her to return. Given how easily her journey had been coming there, she was certain that the worst challenges lay ahead, and she placed her steps with care. At her fifth pace, her intuition, which had always served her as well as her other senses, warned her that something was amiss. She slowed, and felt ahead with her ankles.

Sure enough, they encountered resistance. Another cord had been stretched across the doorway and she stopped. Whoever had placed it was nearby and as she stepped over it, they let out a small breath. From the sound, she determined that it was a man, and possibly the very guard who had attended the Mage.

Certain that he would resort to a shove, or some other tactic to sabotage her, she covered the goblet with her hand and pressed on. But no attack came, and she found herself back in the hall and on her way to the workroom.

Halfway there, a voice suddenly cried out. This time, it was a woman. "Stop!" she said, "How dare you steal the Masters wine! Give it over now!"

Thia was startled, but not enough to spill the precious contents. "I do the master's bidding," she retorted, and then added, "Defy him at your own peril."

"Give it here, I say!" A hard shove was dealt to her shoulder, but Thia managed to stay standing, and pressed past the woman without any of the wine being lost. Her assailant didn't follow, and when she reached the workroom, she discovered that another cord was waiting for her, but she avoided it, and entered.

Xandarius was pleased when she finally handed him the goblet. "Well done, Thia. I shall drink to your success. Rest yourself, for on the morrow, I shall give you an even harder test." He took a sip, sighed with pleasure, and removed his mask.

"You know, since I became a Mage, no one has ever seen my features and lived to tell about it. And yet, here you are, looking right at me, and you cannot see anything at all. Ironic, is it not?"

"Yes, milord," Thia answered carefully.

The Mage laughed, long and heartily.

***

As soon as Xandarius had tired with her, Thia was taken to her quarters by the same servant who had challenged her in the hall. It was a small room just off the kitchen, and its only contents were a mattress packed with straw, and a bucket for her to relieve herself with. She was also provided with a simple, but filling meal of barley soup and bread.

To most of the well-heeled denizens of Umma' Kaal, her lodgings and the fare she had been given would have seemed crude and disheartening. But for the blind slave girl, whose life had been circumscribed by filthy cages and poor rations, it felt as if she was a guest in a palace.

Only one disquieting thing occurred. As the servant left her, she clucked her tongue disparagingly. "The Master has taken a liking to you." the woman said. "You poor, poor thing."

Then she closed the door, and bolted her in for the night.

***

The next day, after Thia had been given breakfast, she was taken back to Xandarius.

"As I warned you, I have another test today," he announced. "Zabrina here will guide you to a set of stairs. You will proceed down them, and when you reach the bottom, you will go into the passage. It will lead to another workroom. There is a book there that I desire to read."

"Yes, lord," Thia answered, already wondering how the Mage would manage to make the task more difficult.

Xandarius enlightened her. "This book is but one among many, and all are alike except that it has a feature which the others lack. You will discover what that difference is, and retrieve it for me." He did not add what might happen if she returned with the wrong volume, and she didn't dare to ask.

At that, Zabrina took ahold of her arm and led her away. After a few minutes, they stopped and there was the rattle of keys, followed by the sound of a heavy door being opened.

"This is the place," Zabrina said. "Many a slave has not returned from this errand. Be vigilant. More I cannot say."

Fighting back her trepidation, Thia reached out and located the doorway, and then her foot found the first stair. It was cold and wet, but she was glad for the fact that she had no shoes. She could feel every bit of its irregular surface, and right away she knew that the first hazard she would face would be where the stone was slick.

Stepping carefully, and feeling along the wall, she began her descent. Partway down, her toes revealed that a portion of the stairs had crumbled away, and what was left was covered with moss and the promise of a fall, possibly to her death. Hugging the wall tightly, and gripping whatever crevices she could find, she made her way to the other side.

Finally, when she was at the very bottom, Thia located the passage Xandarius had mentioned, but as she made to go into it, she realized that it smelled strange. There was the odor of mold and neglect, and more than that, it 'felt' wrong. And venturing in a short ways, she learned why when she encountered the lip of a crevice and a small piece of the stone was dislodged. Nine long breaths passed before she heard it hit water.

Reluctant to make any attempt to maneuver herself around it, she explored the walls more closely. Her inspection revealed two other passages that the Mage had neglected to mention.

The second corridor didn't reek of decay, but again, her intuition warned her that the path it offered was a false one. The slight breeze that came from the third raised her spirits however. It carried with it the faint smell of candlewax—and as she concentrated, she caught a whiff of old paper. She had found her way at last.

The minutes passed, and then she arrived at the workroom. It wasn't difficult to locate the books. They were piled up on an old table and just as Xandarius had stated, they all felt the same to her. The leather was similar, they were all of equal thickness and size, and even their scent was identical. Realizing this, Thia was tempted to give into despair, but she marshalled herself and focused all of her senses on her task.

It was the jewels encrusting the tomes that caught her attention. All of the volumes were decorated with them, and to a stone, they appeared to be perfect duplicates of one another.

Except for one book. Here, instead of the border being adorned with uniformly sized gems, one was slightly larger than the rest. Not by very much, but just enough for Thia to perceive it. It was something that a sighted person might have missed, and she very nearly did so herself. But she had learned to trust what her fingers told her. The difference was there. Pausing only long enough to double-check herself, she gathered up the book and began her long journey back.

When she came before the Mage at last, Thia held her breath and prayed to the gods of her ancestors as she handed him the book. There was a long, agonizing pause as Xandarius took it and made his inspection.

"You did well," he said to her at last. "This is indeed the book that I wanted, and many of those that I have sent for it, failed to notice the one thing that discerned it from the rest. They were put to death."

Thia braced herself.

"Your only failure was in its timely delivery," Xandarius added, "You kept me waiting for far too long, but because I am mostly pleased with you, I will be merciful. Guard, see to it that she is thoroughly beaten, but spare her hands and feet. I will need them to be whole for the task I have in mind for her."

The guard's hand clamped down on her shoulder, and Thia cried out. Xandarius paid this no heed though and began to read his book.

***

Days later and still sore from her beating, Thia was put aboard a wagon along with bundles and boxes of supplies, itself part of a larger caravan that included the Mage, his guards, and most of the household staff. Xandarius had proclaimed that he was going on an expedition and taking her with him. Beyond that, she was told nothing, and tried to make herself as comfortable as the wagon, the road, and her injuries allowed.

Their destination was not far. It proved to be just half a day's ride, in the Shana'toth mountains, at the very edge of the plain of Naakash and still within sight of Umma' Kaal. Tents were quickly pitched, fires started, and the business of the evening's cooking began. All through this, Thia was kept at the wagon and chained to a metal loop normally reserved for tie-down ropes. Certain that she would go hungry that night, or at best, receive a stale crust of bread, she was surprised when Zabrina came and released her from her shackles.

"Xandarius has summoned you to his tent," she said. "You're to be his guest for dinner." Astonished, and certain that the Mage intended something nasty, Thia braced herself for the worst as the woman led her to the pavilion.

"Welcome, Thia," he said as she entered. "Would you care for some wine perhaps?"

This took her aback. "No, my lord," she replied in a small voice. She had never tasted wine, but she had heard that it robbed men of their reason and muddled the mind. Given the uncertain and dangerous nature of her host, she didn't want to be impaired in any way.

"Very well," Xandarius responded, sounding somewhat disappointed. "Please, sit."

Thia complied, amazed at the softness of the cushions, and suddenly feeling very self-conscious of her simple attire. This was a place for a princess, not someone as rough as she was.

"I do hope that you will allow me to share some of my meal with you," the Mage said invitingly. "I am afraid that it's not the kind of fare that you are used to, but I do believe that you will find it passable."

He clapped his hands, and she heard the servants come in, and then her hand was guided to the plate that they had set down for her. The scent of the food beguiled her nostrils and made her mouth water, but she made no move to consume it.

"Come now, girl," he urged. "Eat. Enjoy yourself. And while we dine, we will discuss your quest."

Hesitantly, she took up a handful of what proved to be spiced rice. The taste was so magnificent that she wondered if she would suddenly awaken and find herself back in her cell, or even the pens of the slave market. Such food only existed in dreams.

Yet, she did not wake. It was real. And wonderful.

224

"Is it to your liking then?" Xandarius inquired.

Swallowing quickly, and nearly choking in the process, she nodded. "Yes, milord. Thank you." She had never expected such a kindness, least of all from the likes of him. It made her even more suspicious, and fearful. Surely something terrible was about to happen.

"In a way it is a pity that you have proven yourself to be so valuable to me," Xandarius sighed. "Otherwise, this would have been a marvelous opportunity to test out one of my newer poisons. But…so be it.'

As hungry as she was, Thia stopped eating, and this made the Mage laugh. "Go ahead girl, eat. I shall not poison you, and you will need your strength upon the morrow." Tentatively, she took another handful and resumed her meal.

"I am sending you into a cavern that is not far from here," Xandarius stated. "It goes deep into the heart of the mountain that we are encamped upon. I know all of the passages of the place and their turnings. Given your unique talents, you will have little difficulty finding your way through it.'

"At the center of this labyrinth, there is a great treasure room, and among all the riches there, a pendant which I covet. It is not hard to find this object, for it is suspended from a golden tree adorned with leaves of diamond and lapis. You should be able to pluck it from its branch with ease."

Hearing this, Thia wanted to ask him why he hadn't retrieved this prize himself, and why he valued it so, but she kept her silence.

Xandarius continued. "I know the way to the vault as well as I do because I have sent many slaves in to seize this item for me. Most never returned, and those that did, told me that the labyrinth was infested with evil spirits that tried to beguile them to their deaths.'

"But they were all sighted. You cannot see, and therefore, you cannot be fooled as thoroughly as they were. Your other senses will tell you the truth that they could not perceive. Know

225

this though; when you find it, do not put the pendant on, no matter how tempted you are, for it bears a terrible curse that only I can banish. Instead, put it immediately in this sack and leave by whence you came."

He pressed a small bag into her hand, and added, "If you bring the pendant back to me, I shall reward you generously. You have my word on that as a Mage of the 13th Darkness and an Initiate of the Abyss. You will be freed from your slavery, and given enough riches to have a household and slaves of your own."

Thia wasn't sure that she wanted any of these things, but she knew that refusing him would only earn her another beating, or worse. "Yes, lord," she agreed.

"That's a good girl," he replied, reaching out and patting her head almost affectionately. "Now, there is one other danger that you should be aware of. In addition to the spirits, the maze is said to be inhabited by another denizen. None of my slaves ever encountered this creature, but legends tell of a fearsome dragon that considers it her home, and it allegedly guards the treasure. I am gambling that this is nothing but a tale, but if this beast truly exists, you are small, and it may not take notice of you."

Abruptly, he grabbed her by her hair and wrenched her head back. "And also know *this*; come back without the pendant, or try to steal away with it, and I will make certain that your punishment will be just as great as your reward would have been."

"Y-yes, lord," she stammered through gritted teeth. A moment later he released her. "Guard, take her back to her wagon and chain her there for the night. Zabrina, you are to watch over her until first light. See to it that she does not wander off."

***

At the wagon, she was re-shackled, and Zabrina joined her on the bed. The air had become chill, and when Thia began to shiver, the woman surprised her by producing a blanket. It was thin, and worn through in some places, but the warmth it lent was welcome.

"I know this wizard well," Zabrina whispered as she drew it over her, "If you bring the pendant to him as he asks, he will reward you just as he said. He is cruel, but he is also a man of his word. And he can afford to be magnanimous; compared to the pendant, the things that he promised are mere baubles.'

"But ask yourself; what are true riches? Think on that as you travel beneath the mountain tomorrow, and listen to your heart with every step that you take. I wish you a good night, Thia, and pleasant dreams."

She felt a kiss upon her forehead, and then Zabrina withdrew.

***

The mouth of the labyrinth was cool and almost inviting after the long hike up to it. Thia knew that this was a deception though. Inside, untold dangers awaited her, and the only tool she had was a ball of twine to unwind behind her as she went along, and her own senses.

Xandarius had explained the route in detail to her on the way there, and it was he who unlocked her shackles. "Remember," he said, "If you return with my prize, I will reward you with your freedom, and riches." When she had indicated her understanding, he tied the end of the twine to a thick root that ran down the side of the opening, and stepped back.

"Freedom and riches," he repeated.

Thia felt for the opening and when she found it, started forwards.

The first danger that she encountered was not supernatural at all. Rather it was a simple rock fall that had blocked part of the passage. She found her way around this easily enough, but as she did so, something scuttled across her hand and she froze. Whatever it was, was large, and most likely venomous. As much as she wanted to brush the thing off, she understood that she risked the chance of a bite, and forced herself to endure its presence. After a moment, the thing crawled away and she was able to move her hand again.

Further on, she encountered a branch in the passage, and mindful of the Mage's instruction, she went right. Abruptly, a voice came from nowhere. It sounded very much like her mother. "No Thia," it said. "That is not the way! Go to the left! I am waiting for you there."

Thia knew better though. Her mother had died during the raid that had made her into a slave. She ignored it and continued walking.

Only a few minutes passed before someone else spoke. This time, the spirit pretended to be Xandarius himself.

"Thia! You have done it. This is the place. Look at the riches spread before you and take whatever you wish!" Thia couldn't see the treasure though, and she didn't believe for an instant that the Mage was actually there. Besides which, Xandarius's directions had been explicit, and according to them, she still had a long ways to go. She kept moving.

A hundred steps later, she heard rushing water, and smelled it in the air. Not long after this, she came to a place where her path was bisected by a chasm. The sound had turned into a roar by this point, and she knew that some sort of underground river stood in her way. Taking care on the slippery surface, she explored the area until she discovered that a thin finger of stone seemed to extend out across the gap. Lacking the ability to verify this with her eyes, she had no choice but to lower herself onto it and crawl forwards on her hands and knees.

Eventually, she reached the other side, and for once she was glad for her blindness; had she been able to see the hazard, she wasn't certain that she would have found the courage to have made the crossing. But she had, and another branching in the path lay just ahead.

Her next challenge was awaiting her there. Something growled, and the hair on the back of her neck rose. Only the knowledge that everything she had dealt with so far had been an illusion was what convinced her to keep going. And instead of feeling jaws closing around her, and the agony of teeth tearing into her flesh, there was nothing.

The danger was not past though. Instead, the spirits assumed another form. This time, it was the slave trader from the market. She even thought that she could smell the mixture of sweat and filth that had always accompanied the man.

"Stop where ya are, ya lil cunt, or I'll give ya a thrashin that'll make ya beg me fer death!"

There was no beating though. Not even a restraining hand.

She resumed her journey. A little further on, the spirits of the mountain made one final attempt to stop her. A booming voice filled the corridor, loud enough to make her ears ring and make her worry that the rocks over her head would collapse from its sheer power.

"Stop!" it commanded. "Look into my eyes. No mortal can look at me and resist my will!"

This actually made Thia laugh, and the phantom was confused by her response. "How is this possible?" the thing demanded. "You are gazing right at me, and yet you are not bespelled!"

She didn't provide it with an answer, and left. Behind her, the spirit gibbered and howled in frustration and bewilderment. But it did not give chase, or attempt any further deceptions.

Thia knew when she had finally reached the vault. The corridor widened abruptly, and she heard the tinkling of coins and felt them on her soles as she stepped into the chamber. Exploring the space, she discovered that it was large, and piled high with all kinds of valuables. And at its center, she found the tree, and hanging from it, the pendant itself. Taking it down from its branch, she took a moment to examine it.

Unlike the other riches all around her, it seemed a simple thing. Her touch revealed a plain chain with a functional clasp, and an oval gem encircled by an unadorned band of metal. But as she held it in her hand, it began to throb and grow warm, and although her eyes could not perceive it, an image in her mind that was almost as clear as sight told her that a light was growing in its very heart. Despite the strangeness of this, and the Mage's dire warning, she desperately wanted to put it on, and feel its energy pulsing against her breast.

"Perhaps you should," someone said, startling her. It sounded exactly like Zabrina, and instantly, Thia was certain that she was dealing with another spirit. It had after all, just read her thoughts.

"Not another spirit," the speaker responded. "Not like the ones that you met on the way here at least." It moved as it said this, and she thought she heard what sounded very much like scales rasping against rock. Scales worn by something quite large. There was also an odd scent in the air now; a cross between the cinnamon she had smelled in the Mage's tent, and flint.

Uncertain, Thia took a step back. Whatever this creature was, it was not one of the phantoms. She was sure of that much. And for just an instant, she thought of the dragon that Xandarius had mentioned.

"You have named me," it said. "I am indeed the dragon. You have won the treasure for yourself, Thia. Take what you will of it. There are enough riches here to become a queen if you so wish. You could live in a great palace and own a thousand slaves or more. Nobles would throw themselves at your feet, and you could command great armies to shatter the very world itself."

"I do not wish to own anyone," Thia answered darkly. "And gold makes men cruel."

"It does at that," the dragon agreed. "It also enslaves them just as surely as any chains, except that instead of being owned by a master, they are in bondage to their possessions. That was the trap behind Xandarius's offer; the exchange of one form of captivity for another."

"Then why do you have a treasure hoard?" Thia demanded, surprised at her own boldness.

"To test men's spirits," the dragon replied. "To determine if they are worthy of real wealth. And since you will not have the gold, this leaves us only one thing of value to discuss; the necklace. You can take it back to Xandarius, or you can keep it. You must choose which."

"The Mage said that it is cursed," Thia replied. "Why would I want it?"

The dragon chuckled, a deep bass rumble that Thia felt in her breastbone. "He would tell you that, wouldn't he? It *is* ensorcelled, but not with a curse. Rather, it is imbued with something that is both a curse *and* a blessing, depending on the wearer. Put it on, and see which the case is."

I have a choice, she thought, marveling at the concept. Her destiny was completely hers to command, and hers alone. She could find her way back to the Mage as the dragon said, and give it over to him, or she could go another way. A new way.

Thia knew what the answer was. Hands trembling slightly, she drew the chain over her head. The pulsations increased as she did so, and a wave of vertigo followed this, forcing her to shut her eyes against it. What happened when it passed, and she reopened her eyes, made her gasp in astonishment.

She could see.

For the first time in many years, she beheld the world around her with her own eyes. "H-how is this possible?" she finally managed to ask.

"The pendant's magic," the dragon explained. "This is what Xandarius truly coveted. Not gold, nor silver, but *dragonsight*. With it, we can perceive everything that humans

231

can, and much more besides. As long as you wear the Dragon's Eye, our powers are intertwined and the dragonsight is yours."

Amazed, Thia looked around her, taking in the treasure chamber. Its contents glittered and sparkled, and each piece seemed to beckon to her to gaze upon it and drink in its magnificence. The most mesmerizing object of all was a great golden frame, nestled in among the rest. And within this, she beheld the image of a young woman, dressed very much as she was, and wearing a necklace that was the exact twin of her own.

"Y-you're beautiful!" she declared.

The dragon sighed. "I can see that we have quite a bit of work to do, you and I. You are gazing at your own reflection in a mirror, you silly thing. Look over your shoulder."

Thia did. A woman stood there, smiling back at her. She was older than Thia by a few years, with long auburn hair and bright green eyes.

"Zabrina?"

"Yes," Zabrina said. "The same, although I much prefer Zabrinyya. Over the centuries, I have learned that the best policy is to keep a very close eye on my enemies. In that way, I can learn their intentions, and perhaps, even find those who are worthy of my friendship. Those like yourself. You have proven to be brave and steadfast, and greed and the lust for power have no hold upon you. I can think of no finer companion."

"But aren't you supposed to be—" Thia began.

Zabrinyya's smile widened. "A great beast? I am that too. I can change my form at will. All dragons can. Would you care to see me as I truly am?"

Thia nodded, albeit with a trace if hesitation.

"Then I must warn you, Thia—some find my appearance quite startling. Even terrifying."

Now it was Thia's turn to smile. "Having never seen a dragon before, how do I know if you are startling? Or terrifying for that matter?"

Zabrinyya laughed. "A good point. Very well, you may see me."

With that, her form shimmered and grew. In seconds, her body had morphed into a gigantic creature that nearly filled the cavern. Although Thia did take another step back, she didn't run, or cry out.

In her true aspect, Zabrinyya was easily ten times her size. She possessed great clawed hands, enormous wings and a long, sinuous tail. She was also covered with colorful scales that gleamed more brightly than the treasure around them, and her great slitted eyes glowed with intelligence and power.

She was still beautiful, Thia reflected, but in a very different way. And when Zabrinyya lowered her great head, Thia reached out, and gently touched her nose. To her surprise and pleasure, she found that it was soft, and warm.

"Now, there is still the matter of treasure to discuss," Zabrinyya said. But this time, Thia heard the words in her mind. In the midst of all the other marvels that she had experienced so far, she simply accepted this, and listened.

"I have something to give you that is more wonderful than anything in this chamber, and you will surely accept it when you behold it. First though, we have a troublesome Mage to deal with, and your freedom to secure."

***

Having sent so many slaves into the mountain, Xandarius had adopted a simple routine for himself. If they didn't run out screaming within the first hour or two, he would wait one full day before he assumed they were lost. Then he would depart.

For that reason, he was surprised when just before sunset, word came that Thia had not only returned, but had brought a companion with her.

Gathering his guards, he abandoned the comfort of his tent and rushed up the trail. Halfway to the cavern, he was met by the servant who had been assigned to keep watch.

"The blind girl came out of the cavern, my lord," the man said, "She was accompanied by Zabrina. She does not appear to be addled, and...I think she is wearing...a necklace."

Enraged, Xandarius struck him. "You witless fool! Zabrina must have snuck past you, and now they are conspiring to steal my treasure from me!" He waved for the soldiers to follow him.

When the cavern mouth came into view, he saw that the servant had not lied. The two women were there and Thia was indeed wearing his prize.

"Thief!" he cried, and then to his men, "Seize them both! I want them flayed alive for daring to cheat me!"

Oddly, neither woman pled for mercy and Zabrina had a serene expression on her face. As the guards went to take them, he realized why. In less than a breath, they were facing a dragon.

"Xandarius," she said in his mind. "You have lost. Thia is the rightful owner of the Dragon's Eye, and you will leave us in peace." His men, having heard the same message, faltered, suddenly unsure of themselves.

"No!" he shrieked, "I will not accept defeat. Ten thousand diyari to the man who shoots the girl! Without her, the dragon is masterless!"

Two of the guards raised their bows and fired, and for just an instant, Xandarius was certain that their arrows would find their mark and reverse his fortunes. But Zabrinyya, large as she was, was faster; she extended a wing and pivoted, deflecting the shots away from Thia.

Seeing this, his spearmen lost the last of their courage, dropped their weapons, and ran. The archers however, had not given up and loosed more shots, this time at Zabrinyya herself. The dragon's scales were impervious to them however, and they bounced off harmlessly.

Then she gave out a fearsome roar and charged. There was no time for Xandarius or the others to escape her tail as it swept around and caught them all. To a man, they were knocked off their feet and sent flying into the air. When they landed, a few were able to pick themselves up and flee.

Xandarius was not one of them however. He had come down on a large rock, and lay there motionless.

As Zabrinyya regained her human form and walked up to him with Thia, he came to. His mask had been knocked free, and for the first time, his features were plainly visible. They were contorted in horror.

"Help me!" he cried. "I cannot feel my arms or my legs! And by the gods of the Nether Hells--I am blinded! I cannot see!" The blood staining the rock, just behind the back of his head, told the story of what had happened.

The dragonsight had also revealed everything about him. Thia could see his childhood and the terrible abuses that he had suffered at the hands of his cruel father. She witnessed the lovers who had betrayed him, and all the other hurts that had combined to twist his soul into what it was now. They were as plain as his face.

And Thia almost felt sorry for him. Almost. In the end, she realized, that they had both been scarred by life, but he had made the choice to become what he was.

"We must leave this place," Zabrinyya interjected. "Xandarius is well-favored by the Emperor and His Majesty will not take kindly to this." Ignoring the sorcerer's pleas for help, they left him where he was and returned to the center of the field.

There, Zabrinyya became a dragon again. "Climb up onto my back. I will fly us far away from here."

Although she was frightened at the prospect, Thia obeyed, and a soon as she was astride, Zabrinyya leapt into the air. In just a few beats of her great wings, they were high above the mountain and leaving it, and Xandarius far behind.

At first, Thia clenched Zabrinyya's neck tightly and closed her eyes, but as they flew on, she gradually became accustomed to her situation, and looked down at the land below her. They were soaring over a huge forest and Thia spotted something through the trees. It was a collection of objects and her mind quickly sorted the vision out; cups, jewelry, coins, elaborately worked swords and more, all buried deep beneath the ground in a great cache.

"Why would anyone put those there?" she asked her companion.

"Those are the treasures of men," Zabrinyya informed her. "Hidden from other men, and then forgotten in the passage of the years. How else did you think that we dragons amassed our great treasures? We can see them all, and now, so can you. That is another reason why Xandarius wanted to enslave me. I would have made him wealthy beyond reckoning. Even the Emperor would have seemed a beggar by comparison."

Sobered, Thia said nothing.

Shortly after this, she spied something else. It too was hidden under the soil. But this time, she realized that it was a skeleton, with a rusted knife sunk deep into its breast. She was horrified.

"The evil deeds of men" Zabrinyya said. "Concealed from the eyes of their brothers, but not from us. We can see these as well, and it is why we hide ourselves in our lairs. We know what terrible things humans are capable of."

"Then the dragonsight is a curse, just as you warned." Thia observed.

"It can be," the dragon admitted. "But also a blessing. Come, the treasure that I promised you is not far from here."

The great beast changed course, and they headed away from the forest and all of its dark secrets. Up ahead, the clouds were tinged with copper, and in their midst was the sun, turned blood red by the lateness of the hour. The sight bedazzled the girl.

"This is the treasure that I spoke of," the dragon said. "Something that men cannot bury, or even possess no matter how much they might wish it otherwise. They call it the sunset. Is it not magnificent?"

It was. Just as Zabrinyya had promised, it was the most beautiful thing that Thia had ever beheld. And as they flew into it, tears came to her eyes.

Eyes that could now see everything.

BONUS MATERIAL

Shijak

by

Thomas Trujillo

The crowd in the bleachers erupted in a deafening wave of cheers as I watched three figures standing in the center of the taped-off arena. Two of them were dressed in the white uniforms and protective gear of those who practiced Taekwondo.

The third was wearing an orange suit, white tennis shoes, and a blue badge with yellow lettering. It read *'ISMAL 2165-2195'*.

This marked him as a referee of the Interstellar Martial Arts League, or ISMAL. As for the two contestants, they were differentiated from one another by the colors of their chest protectors; one red, and the other blue.

The scoring judges sat nearby, on makeshift chairs in the northeastern and southwestern sections of the arena. And at the northernmost end, was a table where three more judges watched everything intently. Their somber gray business suits made them easy to spot.

But I was watching the man wearing the blue chest protector, and I scratched my bearded chin in anxiety.

"You are nervous, *Monsieur* Simon?" a French-accented voice to my right asked.

It belonged to Master Emile Moreau. Originally from Haiti, the 45-year-old was the head of the Taekwondo School that I, and the man with the blue chest protector, both attended. Looking at Moreau, I nodded sheepishly.

"I know that you and your brother have been through much," he reminded me, "but remember, Jerrod is Earth's best hope for a gold medal at the next Galactic Olympics."

"That doesn't make this any easier, sir," I replied with trepidation.

Before Moreau could offer up any words of reassurance, our conversation was cut short by a commanding, "Joon Bi!" from the referee.

We immediately focused our attention on my brother and his opponent. As they bounced on their toes and raised their fists into defensive stances, I sized the challenger up.

I'd seen the man in the red chest protector in action before. Adrian Brusseau was Rick Stewart's top student and he was one of the *very* best. But for some reason I found his angry glare particularly disturbing today.

As I pondered why, the ref's left foot slid back and his right hand extended, blocking the two participants. A moment later, he slid back into a cat stance, bringing his palms to his chest and cried, "Shijak!"

My brother let fly with a quick roundhouse kick. Brusseau slid out of the way, and then came back with one of his own. Jerrod was faster though, and v-stepped out of the way. Now that they had tested one another, both men circled, looking for openings.

Careful little brother, I thought.

Then Brusseau tried a fake. But Jerrod didn't act on it, so Brusseau went with a push kick.

Jerrod side-stepped this and launched a side kick that caught Brusseau right on his chest protector. The man lost his balance and tumbled backwards before landing on his pride. Master Emile and I cheered along with the crowd.

"Keuman!" the ref declared, bringing a halt to the match.

He began counting. By the time the ref had reached eight, Brusseau was back on his feet and looking more agitated. This seemed odd to me; I knew Brusseau was temperamental, but his green eyes blazed with a rage that was threatening to explode out of control.

The ref moved back as he said, "Kesok!"

The men circled one another again. Finally, Brusseau tried a roundhouse kick which my brother dodged, and received a hard side kick that sent him staggering several steps back. Then suddenly, he launched a jump 360 hook kick at Jerrod's head.

"*Jerrod*!" I warned.

Somehow, at the last possible second, Jerrod slid away from the kick and the crowd gasped in astonishment and applauded. Right away, he moved back in and caught Brusseau in the head with a front hook kick. Without his protective helmet, the blow would have shattered the man's skull. Instead, it sent him spinning to the ground where he landed face first, before he rolled into a sitting position. His eyes were blazing with anger and his nose was streaming blood. Without warning, he leapt to his feet with a feral growl.

The referee saw the look of murder in Brusseau's eyes. "Mr. Adrian!" he warned.

But the man ignored him, let out a bellowing roar and charged Jerrod. My brother tried to dodge the attack but ended up receiving a hard knee to his chest.

"Hey, that's illegal!" I protested.

Right away, the ref called the match. "Keuman!" He pointed to Brusseau, "Gam-Jeom!"

Brusseau was incredulous. "*Deduction*!?"

The referee didn't flinch however, and glared at him warningly. *"Mr. Adrian!"*

"Outta' my way you little piece of-!" Brusseau screamed, and to everyone's disbelief he grabbed the ref and threw the man aside before rushing at Jerrod.

"Jerrod, sir!" Master Emile warned.

"*Hell*, not good!" I cried, moving to intercept the man. I wasn't' alone either; several other referees were doing the same thing.

Jerrod managed to somersault out of the way as the refs and I tackled Brusseau…and then promptly found ourselves being thrown off as if we were rag dolls! I landed on my back, but I recovered enough to get to my feet.

In the meantime, Adrian Brusseau had grabbed a support for the tape fence. Tearing it off, he began swinging it around him like a weapon, with a glazed, savage look in his green eyes. I knew that look all too well, having taken a number of seminars on identifying his condition.

Desperately, I searched my immediate area and saw two people rush into the auditorium. One was a human female with dark blonde hair and cold gray eyes. The other was a reptilian with a long tail, clawed hands and feet, and scaly blue skin. They were both wearing the red and gray uniform of the Galaxy Rangers, the law enforcement/military of the Galactic Worlds Alliance. And both of them were carrying X-60 shock sticks on their magnetic belts—a ranger's best friend when things got hairy. This situation definitely qualified, and I didn't hesitate. I made a dash for the female officer, and pulled the stick from her belt by its handle.

"Uh, excuse me, need to borrow this. I promise I'll bring it back!" I said over my shoulder as I ran back towards Brusseau.

Leaving the two stunned rangers behind me, I saw that the battle to control the crazed man was *not* going well; the group of referees had been joined by a couple of security guards, and Brusseau was throwing them all off of him. And by the unnatural angle that he held it in, and the pain on his face, it was clear that one of the guards had gotten his arm broken in the process.

I moved in.

Seeing me coming, Brusseau tried to land a side kick, but I swatted it aside with a middle block. Then I switched the shock stick on and pressed it to the man's ribs. Not even Brusseau's protective gear was a match for the jolt of several thousand volts the stick transmitted. He let out a scream of agony and collapsed to the ground, convulsing.

"Hold him!" I called, shutting the stick off.

As the refs and the guards grabbed Brusseau, I looked into his eyes and confirmed my suspicions. "Get a stretcher and strap him down," I declared. "It looks like this guy's a slammer!"

While the men secured the crazed man I moved away from them and walked over to my brother. He was being helped to his feet by Master Emile.

"Jerrod, are you all right?"

He grimaced at me. "My ribs are a little sore, but nothing's broken" Then he glared at Adrian Brusseau. "What the hell's with that guy?"

"Adrian Brusseau is a *slammer*," I stated.

"Pardonez moi?" Master Emile inquired, slipping into his native French.

"A slammer, sir, as in someone hooked on slam," I explained. When both men rewarded me with puzzled expressions, I elaborated. "It's a highly addictive steroid cocktail, designed to increase strength, speed, agility, and endurance...but it also has a nasty little side effect."

"Let me guess," Jerrod quipped. "It sends a person's aggressiveness quotient through the roof."

I nodded. "Yeah. ISMAL and all the major sports organizations banned it in the mid 70's. It takes a physical and emotional toll on anyone who uses it."

By this point, Brusseau was being taken out through the crowd on the stretcher. Then I noticed Rick Stewart, dressed in his school's uniform, with an angry look on his face. I also saw the scowl that had crossed Master Emile's features. Rick Stewart and Emile Moreau had been, and still *were* bitter rivals.

But right now, I wasn't interested in their mutual enmity. Instead, I turned to my brother, "Jerrod, just to be safe, have the medics take a look at those ribs." He tried to protest, but I cut him off. "Please do as your assistant coach says. Master Emile, if you'll excuse me."

Reluctantly, my brother indicated his compliance, and once again Master Emile's eyebrows furrowed in bewilderment. "Where are you going, Monsieur Simon?"

"To have a talk with Master Stewart and then do a little snooping," I told him.

Before either of them could say anything, I left and went straight over to Stewart. The 45-year-old Texan was cussing and swearing up a storm. "Excuse me, Master Stewart?"

The man gave me a hostile glare. "What the hell do you want? Come to gloat over what happened?"

I shook my head. "I assure you, sir, nothing of the sort. I'm speaking in my capacity as an ISMAL official. How long has he been acting this aggressive?"

Stewart nodded grudgingly. Then he answered me. "That's just it. Adrian was behaving normally when he arrived. Hell, he was excited about going up against your brother and kicking his ass. But he wasn't this ornery until..."

He stroked his thick handle-bar moustache as he thought over the events prior to the match. A second later, his face paled. "...until a half-hour after he put that derma-patch on his right arm. The guy who gave it to him said that it was a way to prevent any muscles from getting pulled. At the time, I didn't think anything of it."

"And what exactly did this vendor look like?"

Master Stewart shrugged. "Sixties to early seventies, white hair, pencil thin mustache, and wearing a dark blue vendor uniform." Then he added, "Oh yeah...and there was a patch on the left pocket of the uniform that read 'Travers' I think...yeah 'Travers'."

I closed my eyes and nodded as I mentally processed this information. Having a photographic memory, the facts were burned into my brain for all time. "I see. Thanks for the information, Master Stewart, I'll take it from here."

I turned to leave, but he wasn't done with me yet. "Mr. Wendell?"

He took a long deep breath before continuing. "Make no mistake; I don't like your Master, and we'll never be friends. But I can tell you that I have a zero tolerance policy for that doping crap! Access the information on my school's drug policy and you'll see."

"I believe you, sir," I assured him. "I honestly do."

While an ISMAL official walked over to the stands and calmed a confused and muttering audience, I looked around the room, and saw no sign of the galaxy rangers I'd appropriated the shock stick from. But I did see a man in a blue vendor uniform who looked *exactly* like the one that Master Stewart had mentioned.

He was talking to another Taekwondo student and pulling a small package from a blue box. Determined to speak with him, I made my way through the crowd. "Excuse me, sir..." I began.

At first, the man didn't hear me, and picking up my pace, I called out to him again. When he finally heard me he turned in my direction. The look on his face was like the proverbial fox caught in the hen house. He bolted for the entrance.

I ran after him. "Hey! Wait just a second!"

In desperation, the mysterious figure flung the box away and went out into the hallway of the Portland Convention Center. I was sure that in another few seconds, I would catch up with him.

But just before I closed the distance, he pressed something on his wrist and vanished. Right away, I knew what had just happened. The object on the man's wrist had been a light bouncer field, or as some called it, an invisibility device. Swearing volubly, I had no choice but to stop, and go back the way I'd come.

That was when I noticed a gold-colored card on the floor. Picking it up, I saw that it was blank except for some black lettering, which read *'Recording 1457542'*. Making a mental note of this, I put it in my pocket and searched for the blue box. It was lying open only a few feet away, and its contents were scattered all over the carpet.

They were ordinary derma-patches, and nothing worth running for. *Unless there's something in those patches*, I thought. *Something illegal.*

Gathering them up and stuffing them back into their container, I looked around me to see if the man had left anything else behind that would provide me with clues. In the meantime, the two Galaxy Rangers were walking towards me.

The human female had a look on her face that not only made it clear that she was angry (and I couldn't really blame her. I had after all, taken her shock baton), but also conveyed that she didn't think very much of me in general. I was immediately reminded of a medieval noblewoman eyeing a peasant. Her partner, the reptilian, had a grim, beleaguered air about him, and I got the sense that the Raptorian did not like the woman any more than she liked me.

Putting on the most pleasant smile I could, I extended the deactivated shock stick to the woman, handle first. "There you are. Thanks for letting me use that shock stick. It saved…"

I never got the chance to finish what I was saying. She swiped it out of my grasp. "Next time leave the situation to *me*!" she snapped.

I put up my hands. "Hey, easy! I was just helping out. And anyway my little brother was in danger. Surely you wouldn't expect me to…"

"Shut up! I don't care what you were doing," she retorted. "*I* was about to take control of the situation when *you* interfered! I'm tempted to arrest you for obstructing justice." Then, before I could stop her, she took the blue box away from me. "And I want *those* too!"

"Hey what are you…?"

"That's none of your business. I'll let you off with a warning this time, *sir*. Interfere in my investigation and I *will* arrest you!"

The sullen Rapturian interrupted her. "Sergeant, with all due respect do you know who you're addressing? This is Simon Wendell. He's one of the best referees in ISMAL. His connections could be of use to us."

The woman rolled her eyes. "Oh forgive me, oh great and mighty Simon Wendell…"

Then she turned and scowled at her partner. "And pardon me if I don't give a flying crap what you think! This is *my* investigation Sssuldarth. And *I* will handle it in *my* way! Now come on, we have a suspect to rattle a confession out of!"

I didn't like the sound of that. "What's that supposed to mean?"

"It means that Mr. Adrian Brusseau will soon confess that *he* is a slammer *and dealer*-as if it's any of your business," the woman sneered.

My eyes blazed with outrage. "Now wait just a minute! I grant you he does have slam in his system but there's more going on than you…"

"*There is not*!" she rejoined. "The man had slam in his system and that's all that matters. Good day!"

"Mischa, your tone is most…" Sssuldarth began.

"Sssuldarth, not another word out of you. Move!" The Rapturian growled and followed her off in the direction that Brusseau's stretcher had gone.

"You're welcome, *bitch*!" I said under my voice.

Someone behind me chuckled and said, "She is that isn't she?"

I faced the speaker, and was nearly floored by the sight of a slender and attractive woman. She was in her late twenties or early thirties, and dressed in a dust brown short sleeved shirt, black pants, and slip-on walking shoes. But what really stood out was her short cropped mane of metallic blue hair which fell over her left eye. I nodded to her and mumbled sourly, "And now I'm back to square one!"

"Maybe not," the woman offered. She pulled a dark blue derma-patch packet from her blouse pocket.

My eyes widened in disbelief. "How...?"

"You missed one," she said, "and I figured Mischa Anderson would do this."

"You know that woman?" I asked, even more surprised.

She grimaced. "She and I have had some run-ins. Anyway, I think you might want to get on the ball with finding the *real* culprit, or culprits, behind this."

I gave her a skeptical look. "Why are you helping me?" I asked. "I don't even know you."

She gave me a wry smirk. "Call me, Rachel. Let's just say I'm a fan of the martial arts and a strong believer in the law of the Galactic Worlds Alliance." With that, she handed me the packet.

"Gee thanks," I graciously told her.

"Oh, and some advice, "Rachel added, "If you want to check that derma-patch for slam, go over to the Wu-Shu tournament. There's an ISMAL referee who works for the Galaxy Rangers' Crime Lab there. And he just so happens to have a mobile lab with him that you'd find useful. Ask for Alexander Baxter and tell him Rachel sent you."

"I appreciate the help, Rachel." I took her hand and shook it. "By the way I'm..."

"Simon Wendell," she finished, "one of the best Taekwondo referees in ISMAL. I know your reputation."

I nodded and released her hand. Then I headed for the doors.

247

Making my way down the hallways of the Portland Convention Center, I passed a sign that read, *'The Portland Convention Center welcomes the Semi-Annual Galactic Friendship Martial Arts Tournament of 2198'*, and then another that directed me to the Wu-Shu tournament.

I grinned at this, because I knew an ISMAL official in Wu-Shu who was a good friend of mine.

The moment that I entered the place, my ears were filled with the sounds of cheering fans and families watching the competitors. I also noted there were an unusually large number of security guards posted around the auditorium. The entrance-way itself had a line of competitors and there were several officials looking them over.

One of them noticed me and approached. "Uh, excuse me, sir, but no audience members beyond this point. Only competitors and officials are allowed."

For just an instant, I was a little taken aback. Then I remembered that I was in sweats and chuckled self-consciously. "Oh, sorry I'm out of uniform."

I pulled my wallet from my pocket and brought up the ISMAL I.D. in its memory. "I'm Simon Wendell, a referee for ISMAL, registration number 45x-78449."

The official took it and checked it with a scanner rod before nodding in satisfaction and returning it to me. "Sorry about that, Mr. Wendell, we can't be too careful," he explained. "So what's someone from the Taekwondo Division doing here?"

"I was wondering, is Hiromi Nagashura about?" I asked politely.

The man nodded. "Hiromi? Yeah, he's here and he just finished a match. Hold on I'll get him for you."

A couple of minutes later, the official returned. He was accompanied by a Japanese man in his mid-thirties, dressed in a referee suit. It was Hiromi Nagashura.

"Simon *'Grizzly Adams'* Wendell," he said with a grin. "*Konnichiwa* my friend. It's been a while."

I clasped his hands, equally glad to see him, "It has. I only wish it were under better circumstances."

Hiromi's rugged features darkened. "Oh, is there trouble?"

I nodded. "Someone gave slam to a sparring competitor..." I showed him the packet as I continued. "I need to have this analyzed. Can you help me find Alexander Baxter?"

"Yeah, I can," he answered. "He's finishing up with a match right now. I'll show you to him."

The two of us walked over to an elderly man sitting in a mobile hover chair. He noticed our approach right away. "Somethin' I can help ya' with, Hiromi?" he asked.

"Not him," I said, "Me. I'm Simon Wendell, a referee from the Taekwondo division of ISMAL. I need your help on a case I'm working on."

I winced the moment I said this, realizing that I sounded like a cop from an old TV show, but I pressed on and handed him the packet. "I have reason to believe this derma-patch may have been laced with slam. Someone deliberately gave one just like it to one of our sparring competitors. Rachel told me that you could help."

"You'll have to be a little more specific than that. I know quite a few women named Rachel," he answered wryly.

All it took was my description of her emerald green eyes and the man chuckled. "I should've known that that little pixie of mine would be somewhere around here."

"You know her, Alex?" Hiromi asked.

A fond smile crossed the older man's face. "I'd better. Technically she's my niece, but she and her younger brother have been as much my kids as my biological ones since she was 10 years old. Come on, we can talk while we head over to my mobile lab."

As we followed him, I felt that I had to ask him a question about his niece. "Sir, I noticed Rachel has metallic blue hair. I take it that she's...?"

Baxter stopped the chair and nodded. "Yep, she's one of the survivors of the Abrams Virus on Mischar-12." I shivered involuntarily as I remembered what the melanin eating virus had almost done to my brother.

"She and her younger brother were among the first lucky ones to receive the Vasquez vaccine," he added. "We were a little freaked when the side effect was discovered."

"Where you..?"

The man looked at his chair and waived it off dismissively. "No. This isn't from Abrams. It's congenital. I'm going in for spinal regeneration surgery next month. Amazing how a piece of a person's skin holds the key to replacing a heart, or fixing up a spine. Modern medicine's a wonder I tell ya'!"

By this point, we had entered a small conference room. It was deserted and the only piece of furniture that it contained was a folding table with a metallic brief case sitting on it. Baxter went straight over, and pressed a button on the side of the case. When it opened, a *molecuscope*, a computer terminal, and a screen unfolded while the 'scopes lenses automatically lowered themselves until they were at the man's eye-level.

"Okay, Mr. Wendell" he said, "let's have a look at that derma-patch."

I handed it over, and he opened it and carefully removed the patch with a set of tweezers, placing it in the molecuscope's tray. Then he looked into the lenses and turned a dial. "Let me adjust the power and settings…"

What he saw a moment later made him whistle in amazement. "You were right to be concerned, Mr. Wendell."

"So I was correct?" I asked.

"And then some…" He looked away from the 'scope long enough to bring an image up on his computer screen. It showed various strings of protein molecules. "Tell me, how long did it take for the slam to take effect?"

"I talked to the competitor's instructor and he said it took half an hour," I replied.

Baxter stroked his chin, considering this. "Half an hour. That's unusually fast for slam. Usually it takes twice as long…unless…"

He looked into the lenses of the 'scope again and adjusted the dial some more. Several seconds later, he nodded to himself. "Ah-ha, here's why it took half an hour! Someone introduced dimethylsulfoxide into this new type of slam."

One of my personal areas of interest was pre-spaceflight era martial arts, and I knew right away what he was talking about.

"DMSO, huh?" I inquired. "That stuff's as old as Hershey bars and Harley Davidsons. Well, I have to give this dealer his due. He certainly knows his history—and his chemistry."

"Yes, he does, "Baxter agreed.

Hiromi looked at both of us in puzzlement. "What do you mean?" he asked.

"DMSO is a chemical that athletes used to use back in the 20th and 21st centuries—before we came up with better things," I explained.

"It's really kind of interesting how the stuff worked," Baxter volunteered. "You see, in oxygen breathing creatures there are little sacks in the lungs called alveoli. They carry oxygen to the bloodstream from the lungs which allows the muscles of the body to function. DMSO promotes circulation by opening up the blood vessels of the body. And in sports, the more oxygen the muscles get the better they're able to function."

Hiromi's eyes brightened in comprehension. "And by promoting the circulation of blood it prevented and eased pulled muscles. Interesting indeed."

I nodded. "Now if DMSO were mixed with this new slam…"

Hiromi's features became grave. "…it would allow the slam to take effect that much quicker," he finished.

"Exactly, now it's all the more important that I find this guy," I answered. "But first, Mr. Baxter, a question; what's with the heavy security?"

Hiromi and Baxter's faces flushed and my mental alarms went off. "Let me guess, one of your competitors in sparring suddenly went berserk?"

"Not just one, but two!" Baxter stated. "They were near ready to tear each other apart. It took every judge *and* ref just to incapacitate them."

I gave them a sympathetic smile. "I understand. Are either of the competitors' trainers around?"

Hiromi thought about this for a moment, then, "Yes, Master Jay York is still here. Should I bring him?"

"Yes."

Hiromi left and when he returned he was accompanied by Master York. The man bowed to me and I returned it.

"What can I do for ya?" York asked, his voice thick with a Brooklyn accent.

"I'm Simon Wendell," I said. "I understand one of your students was involved in an altercation earlier. I'm asking because there was a similar incident in the Taekwondo division and I believe they're related. Tell me, did anything happen say, half an hour before the incident that seemed odd?"

York took a moment to ponder this and then he answered, "Yeah, now that I think of it. This old guy was like eh…givin' derma-patches to my student. Said it was to prevent any muscles from being strained. Next thing I know, he gives my student's competitor the same thing. That was say…29 t'30 minutes before they went nuthouse!"

"And this old guy had a full head of white hair, a pencil thin mustache, and was dressed in a dark blue vendor uniform?" I asked.

York nodded emphatically. "Yeah, yeah that's him!"

"Thank you for your time, sir," I replied. "Good luck in the tournament."

With that, the Wu-Shu master left us and I checked my watch. Seeing that it was 10:54 AM, a cold chill went down my spine. My brother's next match began in a half-hour.

"I gotta' go folks! Mr. Baxter, call up the Convention Center Head of Security and tell him to meet me in the Taekwondo auditorium, and then get ahold of the Galaxy Rangers. Hiromi, pass the word along to all the refs and judges in all the divisions about what's happened."

As they hurried away, I headed out of the auditorium, pressing my com watch to contact Master Emile. When the Haitian's face materialized, he looked relieved.

"Simon, where have you been?"

"Looking into Mr. Brusseau's psychosis," I told him, "and I've made some disturbing discoveries. Someone's been giving athletes derma-patches laced with a new type of slam. The situation's worse than I thought."

"That's an understatement sir!" Master Emile replied. "While you've been gone two more sparring competitors, and several

252

others in the other divisions have suffered Brusseau's symptoms." The concern etched on his face mirrored my own.

So our slam dealer is still around, I thought angrily. He was jeopardizing the health and well-being of athletes. But why?

"Sir, I think you'd better meet up with me," I said, "Until this is solved, it would be best if we went around in groups of two for better protection."

"I agree, Monsieur Simon," he returned. Then he pressed something out of sight and added. "I have your location I shall meet you, as you would say, halfway."

"Will do." I shut off my com watch and kept moving.

I was so deep in thought, that as I came around a corner, I didn't notice that I had been followed until I felt a pair of metallic laser pistol barrels pushed against my back. Chiding myself for not paying better attention, I hazarded a glance over my shoulder and saw a pair of large muscular men in business attire and sunglasses.

"Oh goody it's the goon squad how positively...*cliché*!" I said in an annoyed tone.

"Not a word," one of them warned, "*walk*!"

Trying to look nonchalant I shrugged and did as told. I was certainly scared, but I'd been in this type of situation before and I knew that I had to bide my time until the moment was right.

A few seconds later, we turned down another hallway and came to a restroom. "Stop here," one of my captors growled.

"Gee, aren't we *'Mr. Conversationalist'*" I said, sarcasm dripping in every word.

I felt one of the pistols push up against my back and tried hard not to grimace. "That's a real smart mouth you got there, wise ass!" the second goon snarled.

"Let me make this clear to you, Mr. Wendell. We know you've been bothering a client of our boss," the first one said menacingly, "The experiments on the test subjects *will* continue. No questions, *no* interference!"

Is that all you see these athletes as? I thought, outraged. But I kept my tone cheerful. "The problem is that as an ISMAL official, I swore to protect the health and well-being of these competitors."

I felt the pressure of the laser pistol in my back again. "That wasn't a request!" the thug barked.

"Pardon me if I don't beg for mercy," I retorted, "but I've fought Haitian street gangs who were ten times scarier than *you*! And even if I hadn't, my moral stance ain't changing! So you can go tell your boss that he can blow it out his ass!"

One of them deactivated the safety on his gun. "Why I oughta…!"

"Monsieur Simon, is everything all--?" Master Emile asked from behind us.

He never finished his sentence. As the two men turned and began to level their pistols at him, I twisted around, catching one man in his left knee with a low side kick even as I grabbed the other one's arm. Before he could do anything, I pulled it to my right shoulder…and was rewarded with the satisfying snap of his elbow breaking.

Simultaneously, the man whose knee I'd kicked got another surprise. There was a blur of motion and he found himself on the receiving end of a flying back kick to the face from Master Emile. At the same time, I slammed an elbow into my opponent's ribs and then kneed him in his face.

This was why I didn't spar. I'm a dirty fighter.

The two men went down in groaning heaps of pain and Emile looked at me with a wry smirk "Your mouth landed you in more trouble?"

I rubbed my long black hair and gave him a sheepish grin. "Uh…yes sir."

Master Emile shook his head and sighed. "Here is another reason you should have me close by. That mouth of yours may get you killed someday."

I chuckled. "Duly noted, sir. Meantime, we need to call security."

"No need!" a gravelly voice said. A group of men were approaching us, dressed in the gray uniforms of convention center security. Leading them was a tall granite jawed man who looked to be in his early fifties.

"Bruce Stryker," he said. "Head of Security. Mr. Baxter let me know what was going on."

Master Emile and I shook his hand. Then I explained what I knew so far. Mr. Stryker thought about it for a long moment, and then said, "A drug peddler, huh? Well no stinking pusher's gonna' continue operating on my watch!"

Then he regarded the two goons, and a look of recognition came over his features. "Well, I'll be--."

"You know these people?" I asked.

He nodded as he removed halo badges from their coat pockets, "Yeah I've seen these guys on the Galaxy's Most Wanted. They're galactic mob enforcers."

"What are mafia goons doing at a martial arts tournament?" Master Emile asked. "And how did they get security clearance?"

A thought suddenly crossed my mind. "Wait a second..." I said. "Sergeant Mischa Anderson seemed awful eager to make Adrian Brusseau confess to being a drug dealer. And what's even more puzzling is how she got ahold of his name, since ISMAL only gives out athlete information during an emergency. Gentlemen, methinks we have more than one wolf in the fold. Mr. Stryker I need your help..."

I pulled the gold card from my left pants pocket, "Can you I.D. this?"

I handed it to him and he looked it over carefully. Then he nodded. "Yep, just as I thought. This here's a PT-60 holographic recording card. A bit on the old side technology-wise but still useful. Why?"

"Just a hunch," I replied. "Now, if you and your men could come with me?"

The man inclined his head in agreement and had a couple of his men drag the prone goons away. "So where to? And what's going on?"

"I would like to know the same thing, Simon." Master Emile said.

"If I'm correct, then we're about to get to the heart of this mystery," I told them.

We headed back to the auditorium where the Taekwondo tournament was being held. Sure enough, it was quieter than when I had left it and there was a definite aura of tension in the air. As we walked in, my brother approached us.

"Big brother, you are a sight for sore eyes," Jerrod smiled. "You'll never believe what happened while you were away."

My own face was a mask of grave concern. "I know, Jerrod. Master Emile told me everything."

He shook his head. "That's not the only thing. While you were away, some old guy offered me some derma-patches. He said I would need them to help avoid pulling any muscles."

Oh hell, I thought, the blood draining from my face faster than a laser gun firing. "Did you use any of them?" Everyone tensed.

But my brother gave me a reassuring smile and shook his head. "Hell no, something about that old guy gave me the creeps. So I turned him down. I didn't even *touch* those things."

I let out my breath and so did my companions. "Smart move, Jerrod. Those patches were laced with slam."

"Oh shit!" he spat.

I snorted and said, "Understatement of the year! Anyhow, I need your help. You got your holographic card player somewhere?"

"I'll get it," he said. Then he jogged away.

A few minutes later, he returned with a small rectangular device with multicolored buttons and a small lens protruding from it.

I led everyone over to a spot under the bleachers that offered us some privacy and Jerrod handed me the player. With my brother supplying the instructions, I activated the hologram mechanism so we could all see the contents of the card. When I pressed the red play button, I was rewarded with a three dimensional image of the underground parking lot beneath the convention center, and a group of people.

Two were dressed in Galaxy Ranger uniforms, and I recognized one of them as Mischa Anderson. Her partner, a brunette male in his mid-forties was also someone I knew. From the news.

"No way..." I said aloud.

"What is it?" Stryker asked.

"That's Captain Eric Hudson, the C.O. of Galaxy Ranger operations here in Portland," I answered. "And that woman is Sergeant Mischa Anderson, I ran into her earlier."

A nasally voice spoke from beyond the view of the hologram, "Everything is in place. I can begin the experiments with the new slam immediately."

"And what of our delivery boy Travers," Hudson asked. "He might decide to spill the beans on this little operation."

I could almost imagine the unknown speaker's dismissive look as he said, "Pssh, don't worry about him. He's been permanently *disposed* of!"

Hearing that, my blood ran cold.

Then Captain Hudson looked at Sergeant Anderson. "Does Sssuldarth suspect anything?"

An arrogant smile crossed the woman's face. "He doesn't and as long as I'm watching him he *won't*!"

The Captain smiled confidently and regarded the hidden speaker. "The galactic mafia and I have invested heavily in this experiment. This new form of slam you've invented had better be everything you've promised. I've already had to take several pay cuts to throw Internal Affairs off my trail, Dr. Bryant!"

We all gasped as I pressed pause.

"I'm having an attack of *déjà-vu*, here," Stryker said. "I know that name from my Grandpa's fighting days."

"As are we all," I replied. "Dr. David Bryant is the grandson of Dr. Alex Bryant, the inventor of slam,--and one of the old Terran Empire's chief butchers!"

"So it is the grandson of a known war criminal who invented this new slam." Master Emile observed soberly.

"Cha-ching, jackpot!" a familiar female voice chimed.

We all turned with a start to see Rachel's familiar figure coming towards us. "Rachel?" I asked quizzically.

I felt someone nudge me and saw the wolfish grin on my brother's face. "Wow, big brother, your Grizzly Adams look finally landed you a total babe!"

I glared at him. "Oh, shut up!"

To my surprise, the Chief of Security smiled and said, "Ah Sergeant, I thought you'd be somewhere around with everything that's happened."

I just barely kept myself from falling over in disbelief. Then I glared at Rachel, "Excuse me, would you care to explain?"

She gave me a sly smile. "Allow me to fully introduce myself; Sergeant Rachel Beck of the Galaxy Rangers. I've been working *civdigs* with Internal Affairs and Horatio Stark investigating corruption in the Portland precinct."

My face furrowed. "Okay, ya' lost me. Who's Horatio Stark and what does 'civdigs' mean?"

Master Emile explained it to me. "Horatio Stark is a kind of super cop. He and Internal Affairs cleaned out a corrupt Galaxy Ranger force that was operating back in Haiti. Civdigs is Galaxy Ranger talk for civilian clothes."

Rachel came up to me. "I really have to thank you, Mr. Wendell. Because of you, we have all the information that we need to break up Hudson's operation, and arrest him *and* that witch Anderson."

Looking down at the 5'6 woman I could see the appreciative look on her face and the eager sparkle in her aqua blue eyes. "Glad to help. If you need anything else just ask." I said.

"Noted!" she nodded.

By now, my curiosity was getting the better of me. "So, let's see what else is on this recording." I pressed play and the recording resumed.

Hudson was speaking. "Have we a contingency plan if the slam doesn't work or things go better than expected?"

"I've already picked a target," the unseen speaker replied. "The chump's name is Adrian Brusseau. I put enough slam in his athletic bag and enough information to ensure that people see *him* as the slam distributor."

"And if his instructor Rick Stewart gets suspicious?" Mischa asked.

"Well I am a first rate mechanic as well as a chemist. *Accidents* happen."

The three of them chuckled nastily and I felt like I wanted to vomit or tear something apart with my bare hands. "That's enough!" I said in a hoarse whisper as I shut off the holographic recorder.

Rachel gently took the device out of my hands and I turned to Stryker.

"Mr. Stryker, I want to help catch these sons of bitches. These three have just crossed a *very* dangerous line with me!"

"By all means," the man agreed. "Just leave something for the Rangers, okay?"

At that, our group moved out from behind the stands. Then I caught sight of the old man I'd been after since this whole thing began. My vision went red and from somewhere behind me, I heard someone, perhaps Rachel, point him out as I closed the distance between us.

He still hadn't seen me. He was too busy trying to convince an athlete to buy his derma-patches. I was almost on top of him when I called out, "*Hey, Doc!*"

Startled, the old man turned, and then ran like a mouse who had just sighted a cat. I broke into a run, and he ducked under the tape and ran into the arena area, interrupting a match.

"*Stop that vendor!*" I yelled.

The competitors, the referee, and several officials tried their best to tackle him, but the man proved slippery for his age, and evaded them, heading straight for the exit. Seeing where he was going, I raced over to the judge's table and leapt onto it. As he drew close, I tackled him.

Our struggle lasted only for a half a minute before I had a hold of the hand that was trying to activate his invisibility device. My other arm was around his throat.

"Don't make a move, asshole!" I hissed. "You've hurt a lot of innocent athletes and I'm a hair's length away from snapping your neck!"

Wisely, he complied, and I felt someone put a hand on my right shoulder. It was Rachel. "It's all right, Simon, we'll take it from here."

I released my grasp as Rachel cuffed him and removed the light bouncer from his wrist. "David Bryant," she told him, "you're under arrest for conspiracy, distribution of a controlled substance, illegal experimentation on a sentient race, *and* murder!" Then she handed him to one of the guards, and read him his rights.

"But where are Mischa Anderson and Captain Hudson?" I asked.

An angry female voice interjected. *"What the hell's going on here!?"*

Mischa Anderson and Captain Hudson were storming into the auditorium, with an angry Sssuldarth in tow.

I growled as I faced them. But then I felt a strong hand restraining me. "Easy son, easy!" Chief Stryker said.

Taking his advice, and a deep breath, I approached the two conspirators.

Captain Hudson saw me coming, but he addressed Stryker. "What's the idea detaining our chief informant? If it hadn't been for him we'd have never discovered that Adrian Brusseau was the man behind this slam in--"

"Bullshit!" I shouted.

Sergeant Anderson's lips curled into an angry frown. *"You,* I should've known you were the one behind this. Just for that I hereby…"

"You'll do nothing, Mischa!" Rachel snapped. Hudson and Anderson's faces went slack in astonishment and Sssuldarth stared in stunned shock. She smiled at the trio, but it was a nasty expression. "What's the matter, surprised to see me?"

Hudson pointed an accusatory finger at her. "What are you doing here? I ordered you transferred to the Mars settlement!"

"And it *almost* went through," Rachel replied. "Captain Horatio Stark intercepted it and had me transferred to his *new* command as C.O. for all Portland operations."

My anger couldn't stay contained any longer. "It's bad enough you use athletes here as guinea pigs! But when you plant evidence, frame an athlete, and plot his teacher's murder, *that* really ticks me off!"

My outburst surprised them and Anderson finally noticed me. "What are you talking about?" he demanded.

Rachel produced the holographic player. "Mr. Wendell means *this*!"

She pressed play and every audience member and referee in the room was treated to the same recording that we had watched. When it ended, the room was deathly silent.

I broke the spell. "I guess the Doc didn't trust you two, or the galactic mafia. Not that I blame him."

"It's over, you two," Rachel told them. "Your little operation has been exposed. Come along quietly."

A deadly smile crossed my face and I cracked my knuckles. "Please. Resist."

As one, they both tried to activate the light bouncers they were wearing on their left arms. Before they could reach them though, Rachel and Master Emile stepped in and dealt them right hooks to their jaws. They crumpled to the ground, stunned.

"Perhaps that will teach you not to mess with martial artists!" Master Emile snapped.

***

Shortly afterwards, a group of Galaxy Rangers arrived and took the two officers and Dr. Bryant away. Chief Stryker went with them.

Watching them go, Master Emile winked at me. "Well, I imagine that you and Miss Beck have much to speak of. *Est-ce pas alors?* So, I will see you in a few minutes."

I actually blushed. "I'll be there shortly sir." He and Jerrod departed together.

Ssuldarth, who had been standing by the entire time, took my hands in his, and shook them. "I cannot thank you enough Mr. Wendell, for exposing that vile woman," he said "I always suspected there was something rotten about her, but couldn't prove it."

Just then, Rachel rejoined us. "Sssuldarth, Captain Stark wanted me to inform you that you're being reassigned as my partner from now on."

The Rapturian male sighed in relief. "Just like our academy days. I look forward to work on Monday."

But Rachel wasn't quite done yet. "Simon, I have a personal favor to ask of you."

"And that is?"

"Would you care to join Sssuldarth and I for a few rounds at *O' Hare's*?"

Her invitation caught me completely off guard. "Isn't that the famous historical bar and grill in Northwest Portland?"

"*And...*" the Rapturian volunteered, "the favorite watering hole of every off-duty Galaxy Ranger in the Portland area."

"It'll have to be after the tournament," I agreed, "but yeah okay."

Rachel rewarded me with a dazzling smile. "Excellent."

After giving her my address and com watch number, she and the Raptorian headed out to join the other Rangers.

As for me, I made my way over to Master Emile and Jerrod. I had a spring in my step.

Excerpt from "Blackbird: A Warrior of the No-When"

PROLOGUE

When I was very young, the Bookmen were an abstraction; they fulfilled the role of cautionary monsters that my parents employed to ensure my best behavior. *'Behave'* they would warn me, *'or the Bookmen will come and take you away.'*

Much later, two events occurred that taught me that the Bookmen were not mere bogeymen, but quite real, and worthy of both my fear and defiance. They also indelibly changed the course that my life would have otherwise taken.

The first occurred when I was but 12 years of age. I had just begun to change into a woman and my mother had taken me shopping for garments that were more appropriate to my new station in life. I was quite proud of my elevated status and feeling happy, and because of this, I did not notice the man running for his life until he was almost upon us.

I can still recall the stark terror on his face, and the look of utter hopelessness in his eyes as he tried to outrun the *oculon* that was flying after him. There was also a group of uniformed men following the fist-sized metal sphere. Two of them wore the severe black garments of the Bookmen, and the other three were red-coated soldiers equipped with immaculate white pith helmets and rifles fixed with gleaming bayonets.

I can also remember the terrible sound that the fugitive's body made when he tripped on a cobblestone and fell to the ground. And also the cry that came from my own throat when one of the gleaming silver *mechanica* stationed in the square suddenly came to life, and seized him up by the collar of his coat.

Of course, my mother, having far more sense than I, did the right thing and clapped a hand over my mouth as the Bookmen caught up with their quarry. But she did not turn my eyes away from what occurred next, and thinking back, I believe that she may have harbored some hidden sympathies for the Free Radicals, and wanted me to see what kind of justice the Masters dealt out to those who defied their will.

As I watched in horrified fascination, the oculon settled into a hover, apparently to record the event, and in a voice loud enough for everyone to hear, the senior-most Bookman declared the man to be a traitor to the Laws of the Masters. Then he drew his pistol from its holster.

It seemed to be a gigantic thing to my young eyes, and it terrified me, but it was as if I was under some kind of a spell and could not look away as he placed it against the prisoner's temple. Then there was the awful, sharp report as he fired and I felt my knees grow weak as the poor fellow's brains splattered against the stones. Were it not for my mother catching me, I am certain that I would have collapsed.

But before she could whisk me away from the gruesome scene, I witnessed one more thing. It was what the poor wretch had died for. As his hands went limp with death, it rolled from his grasp before being seized up by the nearest Bookman.

It was a simple hand-torch, operated by batteries—a common enough bit of contraband in my world--but no less damning for that. Even at my tender age, it made me to understand more firmly than ever, that to defy the Masters, no matter how small the infraction, meant death.

To soothe my shattered nerves, my mother took me to a sherbet shop that was well away from the place, and did her best to focus my mind on happier things. Nonetheless, the damage had been done, and it had left its indelible mark upon my soul.

The second occasion was far less horrific in nature, but just as drastic in its effect.

This time, I was in school, and our teacher, a wise and gentle woman named Mrs. Welch, called us to attention and pulled down a map of the world. It showed the full extent of the English Commonwealth, and I was both amazed and impressed by the extent of its influence, particularly in North America.

The flag of the United Kingdom waved from shore to shore, overshadowing the paltry achievements of the Spanish in Mexico, and keeping the Russians at bay in the cold dark forests of Canada. And seeing this, I reflected on how mighty my nation was, and how proud I was to be an Englishwoman at such a momentous period in history.

A moment later, Mrs. Welch destroyed all of my self-assurance and sense of superiority with one simple statement. "This is our world," she informed us, glancing briefly at the oculon sitting in its polished brass cradle in a corner of the room.

"It has been completely mapped. Not a single centimeter of our planet remains unexplored, nor unexplained. There are no new frontiers for your generation to explore, and no great causes to embrace.'

"When you come of age, your task will be to take your place in a well-ordered world where your future has already been determined for you by the Masters. And your only calling will be to render obedience to the Crown, and beyond it, to the Masters themselves."

I was utterly shattered by the horrible, grey conformity of this pronouncement. I had never thought of myself as any kind of explorer or adventurer, but to be told that any possibility of a greater life had been stolen away from me before I might have even dared dream of it, sounded like the worst sentence ever passed by any judge, in any court. At that instant I decided that I would become a rebel, and prove both my teacher and society wrong.

I did not realize it at the time, but in all probability, kindly Mrs. Welch was far wiser than my childish mind could comprehend, and like my mother, most likely a Free Radical herself. By telling me that I had no choice, and no future, she had slyly set me on the course of independence, and I think, saved me from a life of mediocre conformity.

Today, in the 406th year of the Ascension, the Masters still rule over us, and the Bookmen continue to carry out their wishes with ruthless efficiency. But like many others, I fight them. And every day brings me closer to seeing them consigned to the oblivion that they richly deserve.

We think of ourselves as more than mere rebels though. We are greater than that. We are scientists, and by studying the technology that the Second Book forbids, we risk the same death sentence that that poor fellow in the square suffered.

But what choice do we really have? Peace? At what cost, and is it worth it? As a proud member of the Free Radicals, I prefer to brave the perils, and help my species to find its way to freedom. That is far preferable to chains, no matter how gilded they might be, nor how predestined we are to wear them.

--Personal Diary of Penelope Victoria Steele.

Chapter 1: A Light in the Darkness

In 1492 AD, Christopher Columbus sailed from Europe to find a passage to China. Instead, he discovered not only the New World, but much more. Landing on the shores of what is now Florida, his party encountered the remains of a long vanished civilization, and a sealed tomb. Greedy for gold, he ordered the sepulcher opened.

When it was penetrated, Columbus found several figures that appeared to be dead. In reality, they were in a state of suspended animation, and after several minutes of exposure to the fresh air, they awoke.

These were the Masters, who had been slumbering for over 20,000 years. After killing Columbus and his entire party, the Masters stepped out into the sunlight and began their conquest of the entire world.

Since that glorious day, and thanks to the great knowledge that the Masters have shared with us through the Laws of the

Book, humanity has enjoyed an unparalleled period of wisdom and peace.

May the Masters and their servants, the Bookmen, bless us, and may they reign forever over all the nations of the earth.

--from *"A Child's Primer of Human History; The Ascension of the Masters"*, *Official Version* (as approved by the Men of the First Book and the Northwestin-Cascadia Unified School District).

A low hum coming from the street outside heralded the arrival of the Bookman's car. Peering out of the parlor window, I made out its sleek black form just as it pulled up to the curb. Most citizens, whether guilty or innocent, would have been unnerved by the sight of the machine, but I was not. And with good reason; its occupant was a daily visitor to our home, however unwelcome I considered him to be.

A moment later, the bell over the door rang, and one of the servants scurried to open it. When I came out into the hall and saw the maid taking his half-cape and leather shako cap, I had to fight the strong desire to grimace in distaste. Instead, I adopted a polite smile.

Bookman Pierce commanded such a performance, for he was far more than a mere street Bookman. He was in fact, the senior most of his kind in our city, although to have looked at him for the first time, one would never have guessed it. Like his fellows, he wore the same severe black uniform, and the only sign of his profession were a pair of winged hourglasses mounted on his high collar, with the dire motto of the Bookmen inscribed on a ribbon beneath them; *"Tempus Fugit"*

Most of the Bookmen, whether they were men or women, were just like him, solemn and silent things, but Pierce was even more taciturn and serious than the whole of them combined. The man never smiled, and no emotion had ever colored his speech in all the years I had known him. The fact that his skin was also as pale as a corpse, made even more so by his heavy black mutton-chops, did nothing to lend him any cheer whatsoever. Taken in his entirety, the man had always reminded me of a great black beetle, with all of the compassion and humanity of such a creature. He made my skin crawl, but because he was my father's guest, I was left with no choice but to greet him and show him into our breakfasting room.

"Bookman Pierce," I said, giving him the Zerodian greeting. "May Nothing be with you."

"And may Nothing be with you, Miss Steele," he replied flatly. I pointedly ignored the heavy cavalry pistol hanging from his great belt, and the efficient looking sabre on the other side. No Bookman ever went unarmed, anywhere, and Pierce was definitely no exception. I had even heard rumors that he favored the sabre for his grim work. He was, like all Bookmen, a servant of the Masters, and therefore an executioner.

I gave no voice to this rumor though, nor to my true opinion of him. Disrespect of a Bookman was disrespect of the Masters themselves, and they dispensed death with little hesitation or provocation.

"My father is still at table," I informed him. "We were just beginning to break our fast."

"Good," he returned. "I have important business to transact with him." His eyes met mine as he said this, and I made certain to keep my gaze steady. More than any other thing, these had always been his most intimidating feature. They seemed to see right through a person to the very heart of any secret that they had locked away.

And I had many secrets to keep. Secrets which would have earned me a quick death if they were ever revealed to men like him. I was, after all a scientist. In our world, those who defied the edicts of the Book, and studied forbidden technologies as I did, risked their very lives. But I was also young, with all the intrepid carelessness of youth, and willing to take the risk without any true perception of the terrible cost that I might someday be required to pay.

No accusations came from his lips on this occasion though. As always, he merely nodded, and followed me into the breakfasting room. Now, looking back at those innocent days, I realize what a pathetic little fool I had truly been, and how much he had really known.

That is for a later point in my tale however. I was still 18, young, and according to some of my admirers, quite beautiful. The future seemed to be limitless and filled with wonderful possibilities, and for all the fear and loathing that he inspired in me, Bookman Pierce and the Masters he served, appeared to have been deceived by my amateurish tactics. Rather than go on about this, I think it best to leave things at that for the moment and return to my narrative.

When we entered, my father rose, and greeted Pierce warmly. Unlike me, he actually liked the man, and beckoned for him to take his customary place at his right hand.

"So, Bookman, how fares the land?" my father asked as they seated themselves. It was the same question that he always put to Pierce when he visited.

"We arrested the members of a Free Radical cell last night," Pierce informed him, taking a preliminary sip of his tea. "When they were apprehended, they had half a dozen electric torches, the beginnings of a megaphone, and a printing press that they were using to distribute their lies.'

"We believe that they were planning on using the megaphone to make speeches at the Public Market and then distribute the tracts to the crowd."

"The bounders!" my father declared, his monocle popping. "When will these reprobates learn not to defy the Masters and simply live their lives as decent, law abiding citizens? Tell me sir, what do you intend to do with them?"

Pierce drank a little more of his tea as my father replaced his lens. "We plan on a public hanging in the Market, two days hence. That should send a different kind of message to the populace than the one that these criminals intended."

"That is the only right and proper way to handle it," Father agreed. "These Free Radicals are becoming far too bold of late, and they need to be taught a firm lesson."

As the Provincial Governor of Northwestin-Cascadia, it was his job to see to it that our land obeyed the laws of the English Crown and the Masters, and to support the Bookmen.

But to hear a man that I loved so dearly, vehemently agreeing with such terrible measures, and unknowingly cursing his own offspring in the process, made me ill. Had there been such a thing as a God, I would have prayed to Him to inspire my father to see the light as I had, and join me in my rebellion. This was impossible of course, for there was no God, and no gentle road for those who chose to fight oppression such as I.

Distressed, and wanting nothing less than to leave the Bookman's presence, I pretended to suffer a mild attack of the vapors and asked to take my leave. Neither man objected, and they stood for me as I left the room.

I made directly for the study, but once there, I did not avail myself of the couch. Instead, I remained standing and sought to compose my roiling emotions.

Yet even there, I could not escape Pierce, nor his sinister occupation. A reminder of it, and of him, hung in a place of honor over the fireplace. It was a reproduction of the famous Flammarion Print, and part of Camille Flammarion's *"L'atmosphère: météorologie populaire."* Pierce had gifted it to my father on the occasion of his 50th birthday.

For those who are unacquainted with this unsettling piece of art, it depicts a robed man crawling through the very edge of the sky as if it were a solid thing, and discovering on the other side what the author called the Empyrean. This is fantastical realm, filled with strange gears, glowing orbs and odd bands of clouds that challenge the starry, well ordered world that the figure is leaving behind. It had always troubled me, not only because of who the giver had been, but for its subject content, and the inference it made; that the incredible and the incomprehensible was separated from our world by less than a hair's breadth.

Unwilling to linger in its presence, I departed the study and finally found the refuge that I craved in the solarium. There, I took up my sewing bag, and practiced my needlework until I heard the front door closing and the sound of Pierce's car pulling away. As soon as I was certain that he was gone, I set down my project and returned to the breakfasting room.

"My dear," Father asked, "are you quite recovered?"

"I am," I answered. "And I must apologize for my abrupt departure, but the subject matter upset me greatly."

"No need, no need," he replied, waving the matter into irrelevance. "A man's business is oftentimes grim work, and we tend to forget to accommodate more delicate sensibilities."

I gave him my best smile, although I was still pained by how easily he had agreed with the Bookman. "I am afraid that I must depart again," I told him. "It is nearly eight and Elizabeth will be coming for me."

He glanced up at the clock, and nodded. "So it is indeed! Mustn't be late for your lecture! Off with you then."

I gave him a peck on the cheek and left him to finish his meal and the rest of his newspaper. As he had said, I had a lecture to attend at the Maddenhill Academy of the Arts and Sciences for Women, and precious little time to make my appointment.

Grabbing my cloak and hat, I stopped only long enough to pin it in place and inspect myself in the hall mirror, before rushing outside.

Elizabeth Brookes was already there, awaiting me in her family's carriage. She beckoned to me with a broad smile that immediately dispelled all of the gloom that Pierce had ushered into our home.

"Come along, Penny!" she called. "We're late!"

Answering with an expression that was just as bright, I hastened to the carriage, and as soon as I was aboard, we were off.

"I saw Bookman Pierce leaving in his car as I arrived," Elizabeth commented. "Was it his usual morning visitation, or something more important?" She was also an enemy of the Masters, and a clandestine seeker of knowledge.

I immediately related the details of Pierce's visit to her, and his dire news of the arrests and public hangings. Seeing my dark mood return, and ever the one to fight off the shadows with good cheer, she comforted me by placing her hand upon mine. This accomplished more than merely easing my mind though, and she was well aware of it, for she and I shared more than just our dislike of the Masters.

We were in fact, lovers, and had been since coming into our teenage years. Although our society did not consider Sapphism to be as serious an offense as homosexual relations, it was something that we kept to ourselves out of concern for the damage that it might have otherwise done to our reputations.

However, in the privacy of her carriage, we had no such concerns, and I placed my other hand atop hers without reservation, gazing deeply into her beautiful blue eyes. Wanton that she was, Elizabeth leaned in and kissed me passionately, banishing the last of my unhappiness in a wave of ecstasy that left me breathless. Had we not been expected for classes, and making such a short trip, I must confess that I would have taken things much further with her than this. This was not to be however, and I had to satisfy myself with a solemn promise to repay her for her wickedness with a full measure of my own, later, and only when time allowed it.

A few minutes later, our carriage pulled up in front of Maddenhill and I spied the latest addition to this sacred institution, and once again found a reason to frown. Thanks to the rise in rebellious acts perpetrated by the Free Radicals, the twin lions which had once graced the entrance had been banished at the orders of the Bookmen. In their place, and standing on the very pedestals that these beloved statues had once occupied, were two mechanica, just as motionless as the lions had been, but a hundred times more intimidating.

An obscene cross between a medieval knight and an insect, these gleaming silver machines served as a warning to obey the Masters without question and it took all of my resolve not to display my true feelings in their presence. Instead, I did as all students were expected to and nodded towards them with a respect that I did not truly feel.

Naturally, a female Bookman was also on duty there, and watching us closely as we observed this little ritual. She was a hard looking creature, and eyed us coldly from under the brim of her black shako as we mounted the steps. I was unconcerned though, and even made a point of acknowledging her with a slight inclination of my head. After all, Elizabeth and I had done nothing that she could find fault with, at least not where any of the Bookmen might have witnessed it. Needless to say, she did not return the courtesy.

Inside, the halls were their usual bedlam. They were filled with other young women, who like ourselves, were rushing to their classes. Rather than join this mad dash however, I took a moment to make my obeisance at the portrait of Maddenhill's patroness. It was set in a niche near the main stairs, beneath a smaller cavity which served as the roosting place for the oculon that patrolled our institution.

The painting depicted the great Hypatia of Alexandria herself. She was portrayed in all of her beauty and youth, garbed in a shining white robe and wreathed in clouds and sunlight. One graceful hand raised the Torch of Knowledge, while the other cradled a book. Officially, this was the Book of the Masters, but for me, it had always symbolized the hallowed legacy of Mankind's forbidden wisdom.

On its pages was a quote that scholars had attributed to her. *"Life is an unfoldment,"* it said, *"and the further we travel, the more truth we can comprehend. To understand the things that are at our door is the best preparation for understanding those that lie beyond."*

All of this was in homage to a woman who had sacrificed her life for the greatest treasure of all, knowledge itself. It was her death, at the hands of a religionist mob that had inflamed the world, and caused the Roman Emperors to ban all false beliefs in favor of the Zerodian creed. From that time onwards, mankind had resisted the urge to believe in imaginary deities, and had embraced the true Nothingness that actually rules the universe.

As was my custom, and out of respect for this great legacy, I took a second to recite Hypatia's words to myself, and deposited the flower that I had brought for the occasion. Then I allowed Elizabeth to pull me away, and we proceeded to Professor Merriweather's classroom as fast as our legs could convey us.

I must pause my narrative again to take a moment to pay proper homage to another pair of figures in my life who are no less deserving than Hypatia of my admiration. The reader must understand that I have always considered myself to have had not one, but two fathers. The first was the great gentleman that sired me, my natural father, and whom I shall always cherish.

The second holds no lesser place in my heart. He was the man who begat my intellect. I had known Professor Merriweather since my 16th year, when I formally entered the Maddenhill Academy. And from my very first day in that hallowed institution, it was he, with all of his wisdom, insight and patience, that was the driving force behind my wish to become a scientist, and pursue knowledge above all else--even life itself. To me, he embodied the very essence of Hypatia's spirit.

I must also admit to having a certain infatuation with him because of his influence, and were it not for my own sexual proclivities, and the great difference in our ages, I would have gladly pursued him as a lover. But alas, the cruel circumscriptions of life forced us into our respective roles, and I had always had to make do with what affections our respective stations and social propriety allowed. Nonetheless, this did not diminish the love and adoration that I held for him. But I think that I have revealed enough of my secret heart, and shall return to the story of my life.

We arrived at our classroom just in time for the reading from the First Book of the Masters. This ceremony was observed in every class in any institution of higher learning anywhere in the British Empire, and no instruction could commence without it.

That day, it was to be performed for us by Bookman Blackwell, a sour-looking woman who resembled Pierce closely enough to have been mistaken for his twin sister. She had the same cadaverous complexion and dark looks, and like him, utterly lacked any vestige of human warmth. As always, she had usurped the Professor's podium, and looked down from it to survey the room and make eye contact with each and every one of us. It was only after we had all gone silent, and she was absolutely certain of our complete attention, that she opened the Book and began her litany.

"Know the First Law of the Masters," she intoned, *"the word of the Masters is the highest law. To disobey the Masters means death.'*

"Know the Second Law; your fate, and that of the bee, shall be intertwined. You are like unto it; part of a hive, and tasked with serving the greater good. You have no other purpose in this life.'

"Know the Third Law: you will be satisfied with your ignorance and content with what we wish you to know. You will curb your curiosity, and sublimate your intelligence to serve our designs. To seek knowledge without our blessing is to earn our wrath.'

"Know the Fourth Law: to see our will fulfilled, we shall appoint men among you. They will be your teachers, and you will heed their council. They shall be the men of the Book.'

"These men will know what we love and what we hate, what is allowed, and what is forbidden. They will enforce our laws and speak for us in all things. Listen closely, and obey their decrees without question."

With that, she clapped the book shut. "I declare this lesson to be in full compliance with the Laws. You may proceed, Professor." Then, much to our collective relief, she stepped down and let the Professor take his place.

His discourse centered on a subject that interested me greatly, and in short order, I was able to put Bookman Blackwell and her grim recitation completely out of mind. It concerned the latest innovations for high-performance steam engines, and the image that he pulled down to cover the blackboard was that of a monoplane.

At this point, I feel compelled to apologize for yet another digression in order to educate my readers. Steam-plane racing was one of the few sports where women were allowed to participate without censure. In fact, the Bookmen, who normally adhered to the strictest of standards when it came to the behavior of the sexes, actively encouraged young women to take part in this thrilling pastime.

And when the newspapers extolled the skill and bravery of our aviatrixes—even to the point of disparaging their male counterparts, the Bookmen did not censor them. Here, they seemed to desire the fairer sex to excel, and although this had always puzzled me, I had never seen fit to ponder the matter. It was enough that this freedom existed.

Both Elizabeth and I, coming as we did from families that had the means to support our interests, were avid air-racers, and each of us had a staff on retainer to maintain our respective monoplanes. So, we, along with many of the other women seated there, greeted this otherwise dry and technical discussion with an enthusiasm that would otherwise seemed out of place and proportion to its content.

I must also confess that Elizabeth and I had two additional reasons for our interest in the Professor's lecture; the first being that an important race was only a month away and we were keen to apprehend any small improvement that would increase our chances of victory. The second was that Professor Merriweather had sent a message to us by way of a junior assistant. In it, he informed us that he wished to speak with us in private concerning a matter of some great importance.

The very instant that the class was concluded, we went straight to his offices. There, his secretary, and senior aide, Jennie Baldwin, admitted us and then went outside, locking the door behind her. We were not alarmed by this measure in the least; we had met with the Professor before and under similar circumstances, for he was far more than just a font of wisdom. He was also committed to the rebellion against the Masters, and a senior member of the local Free Radical organization. Given his position, such precautions were simply necessary.

I immediately informed him about the men who had been caught by the Bookmen, and Pierce's intention to see them executed. As he listened to my news, his brows furrowed in concern.

"This is most serious indeed," he agreed. "And we certainly cannot allow these fellows to go to the gallows without attempting to liberate them. I shall make contact with my associates and marshal our resources to mount a rescue operation straightaway. Tell me Penny, did Pierce share any details about the execution? What time perhaps? Or where the prisoners are being held?"

I shook my head ruefully, suddenly regretting my hasty departure from the breakfasting table. Had I not succumbed to my emotions, and played the spy instead, I would have had more to offer him.

"Well," he replied, "no matter. A few careful inquiries will ferret out what we need to know."

Then his features brightened. "In the meantime, I do have some news of my own which I think you will find rather exciting. I daresay that you will both want to take your seats to hear it."

We obliged him, and sat, waiting breathlessly.

"As you are already aware, Professor James Maxwell was able to show through his calculations that electromagnetic waves could propagate through free space," he began, "and that Dr. Heinrich Hertz, conclusively proved Maxwell's theory of electromagnetism."

We were, and equally clear about the dangerous nature of this conversation. Although the Bookmen allowed us to use the telegraph as a means for communication over long distances, anything concerning wireless transmissions was strictly forbidden. Even a discussion of its theoretical principles, like the very one that we were now engaged in, would have earned us a swift and terrible punishment.

"You should also know that another great scientist, a Professor Crookes, took this concept further and posited the idea of a thing he called 'wireless telegraphy', based upon these Hertzian waves. The idea made the rounds and it seems that several bright chaps ran with it. They became involved in attempts to develop components that would be capable of making such technology a reality."

He paused momentarily to light his pipe, and after taking a puff, went on. "One of them, a brilliant Italian gentleman by the name of Guglielmo Marconi, actually managed to succeed. Reportedly, his wireless device was fully capable of transmitting intelligible signals. After that success, he went on to refine his creation, and several other researchers added their own improvements. I have received a copy of the diagrams for the latest version of this amazing invention, and it seems to be quite workable."

My heart skipped at beat at this and my mind was suddenly flooded by the possibilities. With such a powerful tool at our command, we Free Radicals would be able to communicate with one another right under the very noses of the Bookmen themselves. Ideas would flow freely across the planet, and stoke the fires of a world-wide revolution. The yoke of our oppressors would be lifted from our shoulders at last.

Impassioned, I stood, my breast heaving with excitement. "We must construct this marvelous device immediately!"

Elizabeth rose as well, and clasped my hand. "There can be no nobler endeavor for us to embark upon," she declared ardently.

A worldly and well-educated man, Professor Merriweather had long since guessed at the actual nature of our relationship and was not affected in the least by Elizabeth's intimate gesture. Rather, he was pleased with the both of us and smiled like a proud parent who had seen his children realize all of the hopes and dreams that he had ever had for them.

"Yes, ladies," he agreed. "I had the very same reaction to this news myself."

He reached into his desk and produced a leather folio, which he opened and set out for our review. Still holding hands, we came over and looked down in awe at the schematic.

Marconi's invention proved to be rather complex, although thanks to the Professor's private tutelage, some of its components were immediately familiar. Others however, were entirely foreign.

The device consisted of a number of batteries, linked by wire to a telegraph key, and something that had been labeled as a 'Ruhmkorff coil'. Merriweather explained that the purpose of this coil (which we would be required to fabricate ourselves) was to produce high-voltage pulses from the low-voltage supplied to it by our batteries.

In turn, the Ruhmkorff coil was attached by more wire to the component that would actually produce the radio electromagnetic waves. This was called the 'spark gap', and consisted of a pair of metal armatures with a small space between them that allowed for the generation of an electrical spark.

In addition, the wires were connected to a Morse paper tape recorder that was quite conventional in every sense, except for the addition of a rather curious glass tube. This we learned, was fitted with electrodes and filled with fine metal filings. It was known of as the 'coherer' and Merriweather informed us that it allowed for the reception of incoming signals from another Marconi device through the action of the filings, which clumped together (or *cohered*) in the presence of Hertzian waves. A small metal clapper acted to 'de-cohere' or loosen the filings in order to prepare them for the next impulse.

Two Leyden jars (which we already had on hand thanks to several previous experiments with electricity) completed the system, along with another apparatus, that Merriweather referred to as a 'tuning coil'. It was constructed of tightly wound wire and would be used to adjust the sensitivity of our device. Two additional wires were attached to this coil and served as an aerial receiver and to provide grounding.

In addition to the labor involved in creating the Ruhmkorff coil, the spark gap device and the tuning mechanism, several additional problems immediately presented themselves. While the Morse devices were not prohibited, they were also not equipment normally owned by the average citizen. The Professor was not concerned however, as he had a number of colleagues who were experts in electric telegraphy that would lend us what we needed without making any inquiries.

The coherer was a bit more difficult. It was beyond our means to manufacture and would have to be purchased through a trustworthy middle man from a skilled glassmaker. And once the aerial wire was ready to be deployed, it would need to be mounted somewhere high, and without attracting unwanted attention in the process. Fortunately, the Professor had already retained the services of a professional roofer who was also a

Free Radical supporter, and had reached out to other contacts that could be relied upon to provide us with the coherer.

Despite our ability to overcome all of these obstacles, Elizabeth and I were not spared from suffering one small disappointment. This was the effective range of the device. While our apparatus was more advanced than any technology our society was currently acquainted with, Merriweather informed us that it lacked the power I had so hoped for. According to our mentor, its maximum range was limited to but a few kilometers, making my dream of speaking across continents nothing more than a young woman's fantasy.

Nonetheless, he managed to assuage us with the fact that other Free Radical cells operating in our region were also working to create their own wireless telegraphy machines. Our device would link us to them, and by extension, to an even greater network that in turn, spanned the whole of British North America.

Thus mollified, we turned our attention to designing a scheme that could explain away the time that we would be required to spend working on this project in the Professor's laboratory. Being well-bred young women, we could not simply venture out at night without good cause. Therefore, it was imperative that our ruse would deter anyone from asking questions that would either tarnish our reputations, or worse, reveal the true nature of our endeavor.

In the end, we decided to form a group called the Ladies' Sewing Circle, which would meet at Elizabeth's home on the nights that the Professor required our assistance. Her residence was sited much more closely to his than mine, and only separated by two alleyways, making it a short, and very private journey.

Naturally, the issue of her servants came up, but Elizabeth assured us that they were often given the night off, and would not find it unusual to leave us to our own devices once they had seen us settled in. She also suggested enlisting the assistance of several other young women from Maddenhill that she had become acquainted with.

Although they all came from the best of families, she explained that each of them required a similar situation for themselves, albeit for far less honorable reasons. Largely, this consisted of clandestine assignations with their paramours, away from prying eyes. Additionally, she revealed that one of Maddenhill's younger teachers, who was a widow, might be persuaded to play the role of chaperone for our little farce. According to Elizabeth, she too had a lover, who was imprisoned in an unhappy marriage, and would be eager to assist us.

Naturally, I was scandalized by this, but the value of my lover's plan was immediately apparent. The addition of these other women would lend legitimacy to our ersatz gathering, and as co-conspirators they would be bound to us, thus assuring our secrecy.

There really was no choice except to agree to her plan, although privately I marveled at Elizabeth's deviousness. Just the same, I had no cause for censure, nor any inclination to give it; our cause was a gallant one, and in this instance, her guile was an asset, even if I did find it to be a trifle unsettling.

With our plans finalized, we bid the Professor a good day, and departed his company in high spirits. And by the end of the afternoon, Elizabeth had made contact with the women that she had mentioned. To the last, they were all willing to take part in our plot, and fully convinced that our intentions were just as amorous as their own.

We had what we required to move forwards. All that remained was for me to make my own arrangements. I did so that very night, at dinner.

When I revealed my intention to attend the Ladies Sewing Circle, my father's eyebrows rose slightly, just as I had anticipated. But the mere mention of our companions, coupled with their families' reputations, set the old fellow at ease almost immediately. He gave me his blessings over dessert, and only added the admonition that the entire affair not exceed a decent hour.

Now, our clandestine work could begin in earnest...

Excerpt from *"Sisterhood of Suns: Andromeda"*

Parvulus, Weema System, Pa'lla Space, 1051.08|05|03:43:77

"That's weird," Bel Lissa said.

"What's weird?" Maya asked, looking up from her navigational display.

"I thought that Mercurio told you that the Leptons had cities here," the veteran moonrunner replied. "I'm not picking up anything. This planet doesn't have a trace of energy readings. Are you sure this is the right world?"

"Yes," Maya answered a little testily. 'The coords that Mercurio gave us were clear, and I doubled checked with *heesh* before we left. Maybe the Leptons are using something to run their towns that we don't know about."

"That, or the power levels are so low that we just can't pick them up this far out," Bel Lissa suggested. "Guess we just have to go down and find out. Taking the helm and setting an approach course."

"So, who's going to be the first human they've ever seen?" Zara asked. "Jeena? You up for first contact?"

Taur Kaut'sha shook his head. "Nah, I did the last one, remember? They just got confused when I got to the whole gender thing. How about you?"

"Nope," Zara replied. "Got a few things I need to do to the *JUDI*, and I never liked making history. Inish? You look like a brave pioneer."

The Captain waved the suggestion off. "Not a chance. I think it's Maya's turn." Everyone turned expectantly to her.

"All right, fine," Maya agreed. "I'll do it. Just don't get on me if I give them the wrong ideas."

"Just don't start a war, and make sure that we get paid," Bel Lissa retorted. "The rest is just small talk and gossip anyhow."

The atmosphere of Parvulus proved to be an inhospitable cocktail of various caustic acids, topped off with a chaser of hydrogen cyanide. This meant that when the *JUDI* touched down, Maya was compelled to suit up, and she was glad that she had agreed to let Mercurio strip her of her aversion to EVA gear. She had no idea how long the whole affair would take, and before the treatment, even a few minutes would have been unbearable.

In addition to being encumbered by the suit, Maya also had to negotiate the *JUDI's* tiny airlock. It wasn't used very often; the *JUDI* tended to do business on worlds where the air wasn't lethal to human life, but the value of their cargo mandated that certain inconveniences had to be endured. She sealed herself up, cycled the lock, and as soon as the light went from red to green, opened the outer hatch.

Aside from the magenta colored sky and fluorescent blue clouds, the landscape itself was unremarkable. It was mostly flat, with a few low hills, and covered with fine pebbles and small rocks. But there was nothing that looked like a city, or even a building of any kind.

"I'm not seeing anybody," Maya reported. She was starting to wonder if all of this was some sort of alien prank.

But Mercurio had been adamant about the Leptons, and their hunger for the compound, and that, coupled with the hefty cut that heesh stood to make, argued against this. She decided to make her way over to a nearby hill, and see if she could see anything from its summit.

She was nearly halfway there when she stepped on something. It wasn't a pebble though. Instead, it crunched wetly under her boot like an insect. And to the best of her knowledge, there weren't supposed to be any bugs on this planet.

"What the fek?" she swore, raising her foot and trying to see what was on the bottom. Sure enough, something nasty was splattered all over the sole.

"What's going on Maya?" Bel Lissa asked.

"Uh—nothing," Maya replied, hastily scraping the flat of her boot on the gravel to erase the evidence. Then, inexplicably, she heard what sounded like cries of some kind. They were faint, almost beyond the range of her suit mikes, but she was certain of it.

She also saw that the ground she was walking on seemed to have regular patterns. They were almost like roads, and there were little things that suggested buildings. Even smaller shapes were coming out of these structures, and gathering around her feet. They seemed to be alive.

No, she thought. *It couldn't be.*

"Maya!" Bel Lissa suddenly exclaimed. "Don't move! Mercurio just called. Heesh forgot to tell us something important about the Leptons. They're extremely small life forms. You're standing right in the middle of their capitol city."

"Oh shess," Maya growled. "Inish, promise me you won't get mad?"

"For *what* Maya?" From her tone, the woman was already getting upset, and Maya hadn't even confessed yet. Sometimes, Bel Lissa was just too touchy for her own good.

"Well, I'm real, real sorry, but I think I might have, well…stepped on one of them."

Bel Lissa cursed under her breath. Then, in a slightly calmer voice, she said, "Okay, I'll call Mercurio back and see if heesh can fix this. Stand by."

"No problem, "Maya returned. "I'm not budging." She wasn't even letting herself breathe heavily. She'd fekked up enough already.

As she waited, the Leptons continued to gather around her, and their cheering (which is what she hoped it was, and not shouts for her head) was only getting louder. Finally, Bel Lissa came back on the com.

"Maya," she said, her tone now decidedly upbeat. "You're a hero! Mercurio contacted the Leptons. That thing that you squashed was some kind of giant robot."

"Um--I don't think so," Maya replied uncertainly. "It wasn't that big."

"Not to *you*," Bel Lissa corrected. "But the Leptons are only 1/16th of a centimeter tall. To them it was gigantic. Apparently, they created it for defense, but it got out of control and it's been terrorizing them for years. They were so happy that we got rid of it that they've actually agreed to pay us double. And they're even willing to forgive you for destroying half of their downtown historical district."

"That's great," Maya replied. "Now, how do I get out of here without wrecking the other half?"

"I'm working on it," Bel Lissa told her. "I'll get right back with you. Oh yeah, and something else; they wanted to know your name. It looks like the next generation of Leptons will be naming their kids after you. Nice work!"

"What can I say? " Maya quipped. "I'm good luck."

About the Authors

Martin Schiller

Martin Schiller is the author of the *"Sisterhood of Suns"* science-fiction series. He has also been an associate author with Talaria Press and contributed his short stories to several of their anthologies including, *"Dark Hearts, Darker Deeds"*, *"And I Feel Fine"* and *"Snicker Snack: Monster Stories to Cower By."*

Currently, he is working on the fourth installment of the Sisterhood series, *"Sisterhood of Suns: Andromeda"* and also *"Blackbird: A Warrior of the No-When."*

When he is not busy envisioning the future or exploring strange new worlds, he spends his time with his cat, Jessica who considers all of his time at the keyboard to be a colossal waste of time. Especially when he should be focused on the more important task of paying attention to her.

Thomas Trujillo

Thomas Trujillo was born in Washington D.C. but has spent the majority of his life in Portland, Oregon. He has been an avid science fiction and fantasy fan since childhood, and is also heavily into anime, and computer role-playing games. He has been doing taekwondo since college. *"Shijak"* was actually inspired by his own experiences with taekwondo, of which he is a black belt.

A very opinionated person he often posts on Facebook, and occasionally on YouTube, and Minds.com. He is also legally blind and has a mild form of Asperger's syndrome.

Other Books from Pantari Press and Martin Schiller

Sisterhood of Suns: Pallas Athena (Book 1)

Mankind's time ended in 2445. Womankind's was just beginning… Humanity not only made it to the stars, but by the year 2445, our species had colonized hundreds of worlds. What nobody expected was the MARS plague. No one knew its origin, but within a decade, the gender-specific virus had killed every human male. Only females survived, saved by advanced genetic engineering. And in the wake of the plague, the warlike Hriss invaded and the First Widows War began. Womankind ultimately won the conflict and the United Sisterhood of Suns was born.

Now, a thousand years later, the Sisterhood enjoys the most advanced technology and the highest standard of life in the Far Arm. But an uneasy peace exists between Womankind and its neighbors. It is up to officers like Commander Lilith bin Jeni and her ship the Pallas Athena, to enforce maritime law and defend the frontier against aggressors. Inside the Sisterhood, intrigues brew, and rumors abound. The strangest concerns the Neomen, and the possibility that they might actually serve in combat roles.

As any sensible woman knows, this is pure nonsense; men are too emotionally unstable to handle the rigors of combat. History has proven this conclusively.

Sisterhood of Suns: Widow's War (Book 2)

The dramatic sequel to "Sisterhood of Suns: Pallas Athena" After placing The School under quarantine, the Sisterhood receives a shocking surprise: the society that the tiny settlement is a part of desperately needs their help. Rather than risk another disastrous war with Womankind, Hriss Clans have shifted their aggression to the Esteral Terrana Rapabla. And the ETR is losing the fight. Now the Sisterhood grapples with whether they should help their newly rediscovered neighbors, and what the effect will be on both societies if they do.

Sisterhood of Suns: Daughters of Eve (Book 3)
The conclusion of the Sisterhood of Suns series. Occupied by the Sisterhood, the ETR is on the verge of civil war. In the Sisterhood itself, terrorism is on the rise, and a sinister conspiracy at the highest levels of society threatens to overthrow the government and ignite an interstellar war. Peace, and the balance of power in the Far Arm depends on an unlikely group of heroines and a mysterious artifact thousands of years old.

Available in hard copy and Kindle formats...

www.ingramcontent.com/pod-product-compliance
Lightning Source LLC
Chambersburg PA
CBHW062132170626
46813CB00002B/664